We Must Be Brave

Frances Liardet

We Must Be Brave

G. P. Putnam's Sons

New York

PUTNAM

G. P. Putnam's Sons
Publishers Since 1838
An imprint of Penguin Random House LLC
penguinrandomhouse.com

Library of Congress Cataloging-in-Publication Data

Names: Liardet, Frances, author.
Title: We must be brave / Frances Liardet.
Description: New York : G. P. Putnam's Sons, 2019.
Identifiers: LCCN 2018041587 | ISBN 9780735218864 (hardcover)
| ISBN 9780735218888 (epub)
Classification: LCC PR6062.I137 W4 2018 | DDC 823/.914—dc23
LC record available at https://lccn.loc.gov/2018041587
p.   cm.

Printed in the United States of America
1   3   5   7   9   10   8   6   4   2

Book design by Francesca Belanger

For Betty, Brendan, Bill, and Joan

...and Juliet

One

Ellen

December 1940

1

SHE WAS FAST ASLEEP on the backseat of the bus. Curled up, thumb in mouth. Four, maybe five years old.

I turned round. The last few passengers were shuffling away from me down the aisle to the doors. "Whose is this child?" I called.

Nobody looked back. Perhaps the bombing had deafened them. Or maybe they simply didn't want to hear.

"Please. Someone's left a child!"

But they were gone, making their way down the steps and joining the line of people straggling toward the village hall.

It was lucky I was there, checking every bus. Otherwise this small girl might have gone all the way back to Southampton. Everybody knew the city was still on fire. We'd seen the smoke from Beacon Hill.

She hadn't stirred in spite of my calling. She lay senseless, a gossamer net of light brown hair clinging to her forehead. Her puff-sleeved dress was a dusty mid-blue, the color of the endpapers in the board books of my childhood. No coat or cardigan, despite it being the first day of December. Just a grimy white blanket tangled round her legs, the kind mothers wrapped their babies in, a special knit honeycombed with little holes.

I shook her small round shoulder. "Wake up, little one. Wake up."

Her thumb fell out of her mouth, but she didn't open her eyes. I stroked back her hair. Her skin was warm and slightly damp. Her tongue was ticking against the roof of her mouth. Thumb or no thumb, she was still sucking.

Suppose she started crying when I woke her? I had no great experience with tearful children. Perhaps I should simply carry her into the village hall, and never mind if she was asleep. I took off my new brooch, a silver bar with a pearl, and put it in my pocket. I didn't want it to scrape the child's face.

I slid my hands against her hot sides, into her hotter armpits, and pulled her toward me. She was amazingly solid, made of denser stuff than the rest of the world. I got one arm round her back and the other under her bottom, and hoisted her up. Her head rocked back as far as it could go, forward again to bump against my collarbone. Then her whole body gave a series of jerks, as if a faulty electrical current was running through her. Perhaps she'd been hit on the head during the air raid. I should get her to the doctor.

The dirty blanket fell down over my feet and I kicked it away and walked with a strange swinging tread down the aisle of the bus. You had to walk this way, I realized, with a child in your arms. There was a powerful odor of Jeyes Fluid in the bus but she smelled warm, salty, of new-baked bread.

Deirdre Harper came out of the village hall, forearms red to the elbow and dripping suds.

"Deirdre, is anyone missing a girl?"

She wiped her hands on her apron and delved in the pocket to produce a single wrinkled cigarette. "You're having me on, Mrs. Parr. Now I've seen it all. They can't even remember their own kiddies."

"I'm sure it's not like that. Everyone's in shock . . ."

Deirdre lit up and exhaled smoke with a wide, down-curving smile of contempt. "In a funk, more like. Funk is all this is, you know. Look at them, scarpering on the buses instead of staying put in their shelters."

I didn't point out that not everyone in Southampton had shelters. Deirdre had lost her son at the beginning of the war, in the sea off the coast of Norway; she no longer cared what she said, and nobody took her to task.

"They've got tea, anyway," I said.

"Yes, the stockpile we were saving for the Christmas Carols." She regarded the child sourly. "Your Mr. Parr will find that mother of hers. Trained for this, isn't he. Billeting officer and all."

"Yes. I should go in, Deirdre."

Just then she sighed, and suddenly her eyes filled. "Christ, poor bloody Southampton. Fifteen mile away, and such a glow off the clouds last night, it damn near lit me home."

I made my way into the village hall, carrying the child through the crowd of bedraggled, bewildered, noisy people, edging past over-turned chairs and youngsters sliding through puddles of spilled tea. "Whose is this little girl?" I called out. "Has anyone seen her mother?" Nobody replied. I pushed onward past a squirming terrier, a camp of sleeping babies wedged among baskets and coats, a gang of disheveled old men making free with a hip flask. "Is anyone looking for this child?" I called, louder this time.

"Where are we, doll?" said one of the old men.

"Upton," I told him. "The village of Upton. Do you know this little girl?"

He shook his head. An odd smell was coming off his coat, a reek of something burned. I moved away but the smell remained in my nostrils. I glanced up at the high windows of the hall and saw that the light was fading fast. We didn't have long until blackout.

Halfway down the hall I found Mrs. Daventry and Miss Legg. Two pillars of our little community, they were standing by a table and picking hopelessly at the knot on a bale of blankets. I hitched my burden higher with one hand—astonishingly, she had not stirred—and with the other I grasped one loop of the knotted rope and pried it loose.

"Ellen has such strong fingers," Mrs. Daventry said to Miss Legg.

"She's so practical," Miss Legg said to Mrs. Daventry.

"I simply know where to pull," I told them.

They looked at me silently.

"Have you seen a woman—" I began, but just then the wind rattled the tin roof. A small boy in the corner screamed, cowering like a hen when the hawk goes over. Other children joined him, and then everyone broke out into wordless wails and cries of fright. "I must find Mr. Parr," I told the ladies, and made my way toward the back of the hall. I could hear Selwyn speaking, his true tenor that carried through the hubbub. Such a good singer my husband was, a merry singer. I followed his voice until the crowd parted at last to reveal him bending over a middle-aged couple huddled on their chairs. "Are you hurt?" he was asking them.

"Selwyn!" I felt breathless, as if I had run a long way.

"Ellen, darling." He straightened up with a smile. "Where are you taking this young person?"

I twisted my neck away from the child's hot face. "She was asleep in the back of the bus, all alone. I can't find her mother."

His eyes widened. "She was left on the bus?"

"Yes." I stared around the room. "Selwyn, what are we going to do with all these people? Another busload and we'll run out of tea, and then it'll be pandemonium. And what about the blackout?"

"It will not be pandemonium." He chuckled. "The Scouts are coming to put up the blackout curtains. And we've got blankets for the men. The women and children we'll take into the village. Colonel Daventry's bringing his cart." He scratched his head, disordering his fine sandy hair. "They'll be on the floors, but it's the best we can do. I can't find an empty bed in Upton."

"I smelled something awful," I said. "Something charred. I don't know what it was." To my dismay, tears started to sting my eyes.

"Come now, sweetheart." Selwyn squeezed my arm. "Chin up. Try that lady over there on the camp bed. She's completely collapsed." He pointed with his pen. "I heard her saying, 'Daphne, Daphne.'"

I stared up at him.

"This child may be she." His voice was patient. "Daphne."

The woman lay rigid, her eyes flicking like a metronome from side to side. "Daphne," she declared.

I kneeled down beside her, cradling the child on my lap to let the woman see her face. "Madam, is this Daphne? Is this your daughter?"

Her eyes flicked to and fro. They seemed to glance at the girl. "Daphne."

"That ain't Daphne," said a voice behind me. "Daphne's her Siamese cat. This lady's Mrs. Irene Cartledge and she was right as rain when we got off the bus. We're waiting for your doctor to come and have a look at her."

I turned to the speaker. She was sitting on the floor like me, her huge, pallid bare knees pressed together, one of her eyes half-closed under a swelling purple bruise. "I'm Mrs. Berrow, Phyl Berrow."

"My name's Ellen Parr. Do you need a compress for that poor eye, Mrs. Berrow? I'm sure we can rustle something up."

"No, dear. Shock or what, it don't hurt. Parr," she repeated. "Your dad's got a hell of a job to billet us all."

I managed to smile. "Mr. Parr's my husband." I thought of my pearl brooch, and felt a little swell of pride. "It's our first wedding anniversary today."

"Oh, lor. What a way to spend it." She looked me up and down. "Ain't he the lucky one."

"Actually, Mrs. Berrow, I count *myself* extremely lucky."

A friendly glint came to her eye. "Right you are, dear." She shuffled closer. "Let's have a look at the kiddy."

Once again I smoothed back the light hair from the child's face. She was rosy, disdainful in sleep, eyebrows raised and lips turned down. The piped seam of the bus seat had made a darker pink crease in the pink of her cheek.

"Wake her up, dear."

"She won't wake. And she went very jerky earlier. I'm frightened she might have damage to her brain."

"Bless you." Mrs. Berrow revealed five sound teeth in a slot of black. "They all do that. Sleep through the Second Coming at this age. Give her here."

She stood the child on her feet, blew into her face, and let go. My own arms leaped out but Mrs. Berrow got there first and held her fast, blew again, let go once more. The blowing ruffled the child's eyelashes and she squeezed her eyelids shut. Then she wobbled, righted herself, and sniffed in a sharp breath.

"Here, lovey." Mrs. Berrow grasped the small chubby arms. "Come, open those peepers."

The little girl did so, suddenly, wide open and startled. Her eyes were clear hazel, almost the same color as her hair.

"What's your name, dear?"

"Daphne," said the woman on the camp bed.

"Pack it in, Irene." Mrs. Berrow fixed the child with her one good eye. "Let me see. Might you be called Mavis Davis?"

The child gave a slow blink. Still waking.

"Or Sally O'Malley?"

She shook her head.

"Or Nancy Fancy? Help me, dearie, I'm running out of names," said Mrs. Berrow, and the little girl spoke.

"I'm not Nancy Fancy! I'm Pamela! Where's Mummy?"

Her voice was clear, piping, like a twig peeled of its bark. She was well-spoken.

"Pamela." Mrs. Berrow patted her cheek. "Ain't that a pretty name."

"Where's my mummy?" Pamela spun around. "Mummy? Where's Mummy?" Her voice wavered. She pulled away from Mrs. Berrow. "I can't see Mummy."

Ten seconds had passed, a small time but enough for her mouth to quiver and large tears to spill down her cheeks. "Pamela." I clasped her hand. "We think Mummy got off the bus and left you there by mistake, so we need to find her. What does Mummy look like?"

"Beautiful." She scrubbed at her face. "But she wasn't on my bus, she was on the one before."

"Her ma got on a different bus?" Mrs. Berrow started to heave herself to her feet. "How the hell did she manage that?"

"The ladies said!" Pamela stood on tiptoes to peer into the crowd—so futile, in a person barely a yard high. "They said I should get on the bus with them and then I'd find her."

I gasped. "What ladies?"

"The ladies," she said impatiently, as if it were obvious. "They saw me. The bus came." Her face crumpled. "They said if I got on, we'd find Mummy." Her lungs began to pump out sobs and her arms went up and down, striking her sides. I gathered her to me once again and lifted her up. She wept and thrashed in my arms as I took her over to one side of the hall, set her down on a huge unlit radiator. "What's your other name, Pamela?"

"Jane," she sobbed.

"No, your family name." But she was crying too hard. I stood up straight. "Does anyone know this little girl?" I called out. "Her name's Pamela. Pamela Jane." Heads turned and shook, and I saw women gathering their children together, and a bustle in the doorway—people from the village, arriving to take them away. The tide was running out. "Pamela Jane! Did anyone travel with this child?"

At last. A woman was emerging from the throng, incongruously elegant in a fur coat and maroon toque, making her way to us. "I was with this little one," she said when she arrived at my side. "I helped her on board the bus."

"Didn't you hear me call earlier?" I spoke flatly out of exasperation. If she thought I was rude, she made no sign.

"I might have been in the lavs, dear." She pointed to another, large woman. "That lady said the little girl's mother was on the bus before ours. So we took her on the next one, with us." The large woman was already approaching, buttoning her cardigan over her bust. "Isn't that right?" asked the lady wearing the toque. "You saw her ma on the first bus?"

"That's what the little one said." The second woman's voice was a creaky whisper. "Pardon me. Smoke's got my throat."

Pamela gasped. "You said Mummy was on the other bus. But she wasn't!"

"No, *you* was saying it, sweetheart," the woman croaked, her eyes full of alarm.

"No!" Pamela was frantic. "I just *thought* she was!"

"So *I* said, we'll catch up with Mummy, sweetie, and I took her on board." The large woman put her hands to her cheeks. "Now I think about it, how could any woman get on a blooming bus without her little daughter? But the little one was insistent!"

"I *wasn't* 'sistent!" Pamela continued her choleric weeping. "I saw her head but I didn't know it was her head! *You* said!"

The elegant woman put her hand to her toque. "And we just got off the bus leaving her there." She turned to me. "I'm so sorry. We was bombed, dear. I can't find any other excuse."

Now they were both crying. I heard Selwyn calling. "Ladies— ladies, please come and join this group."

"You both need to leave," I said. "I'll find you if I have to."

Just then Pamela vomited onto the floor. The height of the radiator she was standing on increased the radius greatly, and we sprang back.

Pamela clutched at her head. "My forehead hurts, I banged it against the bus stop." She burst into a wail.

I lifted her down. "Where is the doctor?" I called. "Dr. Bell? You're needed here!" The women, I noticed, were obeying Selwyn and making for the door. Through the ebbing crowd, the doctor hastened toward us. His fur-collared overcoat gave him an oddly cosseted air. Neither Selwyn nor I had taken the time to dress warmly before hurrying out to the village hall.

"Doctor, please could you look at this little girl? I must get a bucket."

When I got back from the kitchen, Pamela was lying on the floor while the doctor shone a small narrow light into each of her eyes. "A mild concussion," he announced, as I started cleaning the mess. "There's a bump under her hairline. She may be very sleepy. But I'm not uneasy."

I took the bucket outside. Selwyn was seeing off a group bound for the village houses. "We'll be sheltering seven souls," he told me. "And I've washed up the cups."

I couldn't help smiling at the expectation of praise latent in this last statement. "Well done." I emptied the bucket into the drain. "But it's eight, not seven. The little girl. Her mother wasn't on the bus."

"How on earth—"

"I'll tell you later."

In a knot in the corner, our group waited, set-faced, to be led to our house. With the exception of a couple of tall, tear-stained girls of about seventeen, they were all women on the elderly side. Mrs. Berrow, I saw, was among them. Her injured eye looked viciously dark now, and she was hanging her head in fatigue. I lifted Pamela up, and Selwyn took off his jacket and folded it around her.

"Shall I take her?" he asked.

"No. She doesn't seem so heavy now. I don't know why."

I followed Selwyn out of the hall, and behind me our people fell into step. Pamela leaned her head against my shoulder. I could hear the tiny chirp as she sucked her thumb.

Then she took her thumb out. "The ladies said they'd find Mummy. They said. So I think they will." She put the thumb back in and shut her eyes.

2

I CARRIED PAMELA down the lane. The sun was sinking into the bare hedgerows and the air was sharper. Our people moved as a single clumsy mass behind us.

"She got on the bus by accident," I told Selwyn. "Two women took her on board, thinking her mother was on the previous bus. But it now seems the mother wasn't on any bus at all. She must be still in Southampton. Distraught."

"Where were these women?"

"In the village hall, of course."

"No, I mean, where in Southampton?"

"I didn't ask."

He glanced back at our followers. "They're not with us, are they?"

"No. They left with that last big group." I wasn't even sure of that, now. "How silly of me."

His hand brushed my arm. "It doesn't matter. There's nothing we can do about it today."

We heard a soft clopping on the road behind us, a rumble and a rattle. Colonel Daventry was coming up with a cart full of slumped figures, women and some small children. The Colonel walked beside the head of his horse, Beeston, a peaceful bay with feathered fetlocks, and the cart was followed by a handful of silent men.

"Mr. and Mrs. Parr, we're on our way to The Place." He named his large house in the middle of Upton. "We can take a few up to your turning."

Selwyn said, "Go on, Ellen." I scrambled up and he passed me Pamela. Mrs. Berrow and our other ladies climbed aboard. The occupants shuffled to make room for us—all, that is, save one woman who sat motionless, shawled in a length of sacking, her face half-covered in brick dust while the baby on her lap kicked its bare foot in the frosty air. We were about to move on when an old man standing by the tailgate of the cart took off his tweed cap in preparation, it transpired, to speak.

"My father worked here, at the big house. Upton Hall. For Sir Michael Brock's father," he told us. "Put the locks into the front and back doors, and the coach house and all the outhouses. This was before the Great War." His eyes began to spill tears, which caught the low sun as they fell, but he spoke on in a steady voice. "We made ourselves busy in the stable block, me and some boys from the farm. Filling haynets. Scampering back and forth."

Then he put his cap back on, wiped his eyes, and turned to take up his journey. The Colonel clucked at Beeston, who leaned into his harness, and the cart moved off. We swayed in our seats. The woman pied by brick dust clutched her baby's foot in her filthy hand.

Colonel Daventry let us down at our turning. We began to walk along the embanked track that ran between two low fields to our mill. It was dusk and the people couldn't see the mill—they hesitated, wondering if they were heading on a long trek out into the countryside. I encouraged them onward, and soon the mill was in sight.

Elizabeth opened the door. "Oh, Mrs. Parr. What a thing. Oh, look at that little mite." She glanced behind me at the crowd with an anxious housekeeper's eye. "I've got all the rugs and cushions out. I hope they'll be all right."

"Well done, Elizabeth." I stepped inside and set Pamela down on the hall chair. "Mr. Parr's following." Pamela drooped sideways against the wooden arm, eyes tightly shut. "This little one's mislaid her mother," I told Elizabeth in a low voice. "We'll put her upstairs, with us."

The women filed past us in a draft of icy air with gasps of relief. When they reached the sitting room, the pair of girls lay down immediately, straight onto the floor, refusing offers of tea. One slipped off a single shoe, covered her face with her hands, and lay still. Now they were in an enclosed space I could smell the charred stink again, coming off their coats. I still couldn't identify it. Perhaps it was something that wasn't usually burned.

Elizabeth and I brought tea and cut a loaf of bread thickly to make dry toast. Those women still awake devoured it. "There's a bit of dripping, but not enough for all of them," Elizabeth whispered.

"Keep the dripping for the little girl. We've got bread, that's the main thing."

When they'd finished their tea and toast, we helped our guests arrange the sitting room to their liking. The young women drowsily accepted a blanket. Then I went upstairs to see the boys.

We had three evacuees from Southampton, two young brothers and their older cousin. They'd been with us a year and a quarter, since the beginning of the war. Very obedient at first, more unsettled since the September raid that had destroyed the Spitfire factory a few hundred yards away from their homes.

"It was a big un last night, wasn't it, Mrs. Parr," said Donald, the youngest boy.

They'd all slept through the bombing, but playground gossip had done its work, and his pudgy little face was pale. I wished, for the dozenth time, that his father hadn't promised to telephone after each raid. I opened my arms and he shuffled over and sat close at my side—too grown-up, at seven, to clamber onto my lap.

"Yes, Donald." I squeezed his shoulders. "I'm sure everyone's quite well, but the telephone lines are down. Daddy might not get through until tomorrow or the next day. Now, tonight's going to be a bit of an adventure." I addressed them all. "We've got visitors. I'm going to put three of them up here, in your bedroom, and you can make a bivouac on the landing, like Scouts do. How does that sound? And you'll have to eat your tea very quietly in the kitchen—go in through the hall door. Whatever you do, don't go into the sitting room."

"Why?" asked Hawley, the cousin. "Are they spies?"

"No." I smiled. "They just need peace and quiet."

Under my direction the boys pitched camp, laying out some old bedding rolls and unused velvet curtains.

"Pooh, this stinks," said Donald and threw the curtain across the floor.

"It may be a little musty," I said. "It's been kept in a chest—"

"Put it back on the mattress, Donald, you twit," said his older brother.

"Shut your gob, Jack."

The two boys fell into a frenzy of pulling, kicking, and thumping, comical because wordless. Hawley folded his arms. "Oy. Lads. Do you want to sleep in the hen house?"

They went still. I looked at Hawley gratefully.

"They need a tight rein, Mrs. Parr," he said.

They came down for their supper, stopping short at Pamela, who was still enthroned, dozing, on the hall chair. It was an ancient chair, with a low seat and a tall back, designed for kneeling on and praying: Pamela, pale, with her eyes somberly downcast, could have been a child of the Middle Ages. I put my finger to my lips and the boys passed by silently into the kitchen. I went into the sitting room and invited three ladies upstairs to spend the night on the boys' beds. "Mrs. Berrow, I insist you come. I will find you a damp flannel for your eye."

Obediently Mrs. Berrow followed me, along with two others, up to the boys' bedroom. I brought the flannel, told them where the bathroom was, and left them to sleep. None of them spoke. They were hungry, I knew, but their tiredness was of a kind to conquer hunger. They rolled onto the beds and lay like deadweights.

I spread a slice of bread with the dripping and took it to Pamela.

"Pamela?"

She opened her eyes and regarded me, blinking. She took the slice of bread, dropped it on the floor. I kneeled in front of her and retrieved it and tore off a dusty piece. She chewed without haste, her jaw moving roundly like a small calf. "Excuse me," she said through her mouthful. "Are we in a village?"

"Yes. A village called Upton."

"So is this village bread?"

I smiled. "I made it, and I'm a villager. So I suppose it is. It's a little stale, darling, that's all. My fresh bread is much softer."

She continued chewing, eyes steadily on me, not the least reassured. The front door opened and Selwyn came in. He took his coat off and smiled at me. "You look like a supplicant, and she your princess. It's the high-backed chair, I suppose. What is there to eat?"

"Bread, and a sausage. About three ounces of tea. Plenty of oats."

Pamela had been looking from one of us to the other. Now she stopped chewing. "Horses eat oats."

"Yes, they do." Selwyn bent over her. "Are you warm enough?" She nodded. He patted her on the head, absently, as if she were his good dog. "Now I think about it, I haven't got much of an appetite. I'll sleep on the little bed in the dressing room. You put her with you, in our bed."

The buttons on the back of Pamela's dirty little dress were tiny. One of them was broken, a shard that slipped under my nail and stabbed me.

I pulled the puffed sleeves down off her shoulders. Her arms were as cold as china.

"Didn't Mummy give you a coat, Pamela?"

"It was so hot in the hotel, she said, 'Let's take our coats and cardigans off.' So we did that."

"What hotel?"

She turned her head to look up at me. "The hotel that we were inside," she said patiently. "I want to keep my knickers on."

She went to the lavatory. I found an old camisole and put it on her. It fell almost to her ankles, the shoulder straps drooping, the low neck leaving her chest bare. I knotted the straps to bring the neckline higher.

"This is a funny nightie."

"Isn't it."

Our bolster made her head jut forward, so I fetched a flat cushion from my sewing seat. The bed creaked in the dressing room: Selwyn was retiring. I went in and found him sitting there in his pajamas. He needed a good diet to keep his weight up, did my husband, and now he was beginning to remind me of my brother Edward. They both went lean in hard times, weathered and springy like the spars of a ship. Selwyn was naturally slighter than Edward, sandier, his blue eyes paler. A cleverer, more far-seeing man.

"She says that she was in a hotel," I told him. "She doesn't know which one."

He nodded slowly. "We'll think about it in the morning." He looked up at me. "Where's your pearl brooch?"

With a jolt I remembered the bus, my first grasp of Pamela's body. "Don't worry. It's in my jacket pocket, for safekeeping."

Selwyn had pinned the brooch on this morning, deftly, and kissed my lips. It seemed like a week ago now. I went and sat on the bed next to him. My eye fell on a small flat brown-paper parcel. "You haven't opened your present."

Exclaiming, he reached for it. "Shame on me. My first gift of this kind too." He pulled the knot in the string and removed the paper from a copy of Edward Thomas's *The South Country*. "Ellen, sweetheart. This is so thoughtful."

"I found it in Bradwell's. Now you really have the complete works."

He gave a single laugh and put down the book. "I promise you one thing, Ellen. Not all our wedding anniversaries will be like this one."

I put my arm across his back and pressed my face against his shoulder. He embraced me in turn so that we were encircled by each other's arms. "I shall complain, next year," I said, with my eyes shut. "If you don't supply at least one busload of refugees."

The brooch was there, in my jacket pocket. I put it into my jewelry box and hung the jacket in the wardrobe. Closing the door I saw the child's image flash into the mirror, a pale face with large, grave light brown eyes. I undressed and put my nightgown on, all the while feeling those eyes upon me.

She'd moved toward the middle of the bed. When I got in, one small hard foot scraped against my calf. "Shift over, Pamela."

"But I was just on the way to my side."

"Oh. I didn't realize you had a side."

"This is my side. The other is Mummy's."

What about Daddy? I didn't say that. It was a question for tomorrow.

We arranged ourselves to her liking. She occupied her little space with self-possession, lying neatly on her back with feet together. I remembered sharing the coldest nights in one bed with Mother. Mother, and in the beginning with my brother Edward too. They had both been bigger than me. I'd never lain down beside such a small person.

"My name's Ellen."

"I know." Her head remained still; only her eyes darted toward me. "But you haven't said if I may call you it."

I smiled. "You may."

How old was she? Her nose was still snubbed, a perfect curve, her cheeks round. I couldn't ask her about her surname again, not now.

"Will we find Mummy tomorrow?"

"I'm sure we will."

I was woken by a rising siren of wails, as sharp and sudden as if rehearsed. I slid out of bed and went out onto the landing. The boys were asleep—two had rolled off the mattresses and were lying legs tangled in the curtains, leaving the third uncovered. I picked my way among them and went down to the sitting room.

The women had pulled the blackout curtain away from the side of the window. They were all crowded around the slit they had made, crying out and clinging together as if they were in a lifeboat on a high sea. "How can they, how *can* they, the devils." "Bloody fucking bastards." "It's vicious. It ain't human."

They'd left the lamp on. The light was shining out through the naked glass.

"Replace that curtain." I spoke in a voice of steel.

One of them sobbed at me, "You should see it, dear, before we do."

Darting to the table, I turned out the lamp. "You've broken the blackout. And you may also have broken the fastenings." I shouldered my way in among them and started lashing the blackout tapes back onto the hooks in the window frame. There it was again, the same rumbling fleshy stain on the undersides of the clouds, punctuated by white flashes, that I'd seen last night rising over Beacon Hill. I tried to avert my face, but with each flash I felt sicker.

"Those are the flares," said one of the girls behind me. "They make it like daylight. So you can see the bomb doors, you see, you can see them opening up."

The other girl burst out into noisy weeping, and several others joined her.

"Please don't wake our evacuees." My voice and fingers were shaking as I worked. "I can't have them seeing this raid. Their families are in the city." The curtain secured, I fumbled for the lamp and lit it again, and saw Mrs. Berrow in the doorway.

"Mrs. Parr's right," she said. "And that light would have carried twenty mile in the blackout. You want their leftovers dumped on us?" She folded her strong arms. "Now pipe down, and no more of that language, thank you very much."

Chastened, the women began to settle themselves down, sighing and murmuring. Mrs. Berrow and I left the room. Just as we reached the stairs, Mrs. Berrow spoke again. "Any whisper of that little girl's mam?"

Her face was benign, expectant, in the shaft of dull light from the sitting room.

"No," I said. "Not yet."

At three o'clock I was startled by a sturdy punch in the back and a long, grinding grizzle.

"Mummy. Mummeee."

She sat up, eyes half-open, arms outstretched. She wasn't awake. I pulled her to me and her arms went tight round my neck, her hot cheek pressed against mine. Very small breaths she took, just puffs of air. Then I laid her down onto her small pillow.

I rose at six. Selwyn's bed was empty. He had already gone up to the sluice gate. Our mill workers would be in at seven.

In the hall I met Elizabeth carrying a bucket of water to the lavatory, her face tight. "I know they've been bombed out, but a cistern still has to fill up before you can flush again, Mrs. Parr, no matter who's pulling the chain."

The women were stirring in the sitting room. I knocked on the door and when I was admitted found them pulling off blankets, shrugging on cardigans in the lamplight. "We're so grateful, madam," somebody said. "But we'll get off home as soon as we can."

As if they'd been banished by a burst pipe, or an overly bold family of rats. "Well, if you're sure . . ."

"Of course we are. You can't feed us, dear."

At least they realized.

I brought two full teapots, each with one spoonful of tea in it. They would simply have to make do with that. They took the teacups with both hands and passed them in a ritual silence. I untied the blackout curtains and drew them. One of the young women said, "We're very sorry about last night, Mrs. Parr." She had fresh lipstick on, defiantly at odds with the graze that slanted across her high pasty forehead.

"It's all right. You were frightened, and with good reason."

There was a silence, broken eventually by Mrs. Berrow. She was sitting in the largest armchair. "There wasn't any thinking," she told me. "We just covered our heads, and as soon as we could find a bus we cleared off without a backward look. We lost our nerve, dear, is all." She gulped the tea. "This is pure nectar. Where's that little girl of yours?"

"Upstairs . . . What happened to your friend, the lady who could only say Daphne?"

"Oh, yes. Somebody did a whopper of a sneeze right by her head and she snapped right out of it. Never saw the like. If you brought the little girl down, we could have a chat. Now that we're in our right minds, or nearly."

"I expect she's still sleeping, Mrs. Berrow."

I hesitated. There were thumps on the stairs.

"That'll be your lads." Mrs. Berrow chuckled. "Not very likely, is it?"

They slept through the Second Coming, little children. That was what she'd told me. I almost pointed it out to her.

"I'll fetch Pamela."

· · · · ·

"So we went into the hotel because Mummy said we had to get some candles for my cake. And then we were going to bed there. Gosh, your eye is like a thunderstorm, isn't it."

Pamela, in blanket, knickers, and knee-length camisole, was standing in front of Mrs. Berrow who, seated as she was, had acquired a faintly inquisitorial air.

"Some candles," I repeated. "For your cake."

"Because I'm going to be six." She gave me a passing glance. I was much less important than Mrs. Berrow. "My cake's going to be pink."

"Could it have been the Crown?" somebody said. "The buses stop right outside."

"It was mayhem there." Mrs. Berrow nodded, remembering. "That's where I live, see, opposite the Crown. So when you and Mummy came out, what happened next?"

A blended howl of outrage and mirth rose from the kitchen next door, along with a crash of cutlery and a thin cry of exasperation from Elizabeth. Pamela peered through the gap in the door. "What naughty boys you've got," she said to me.

Mrs. Berrow sighed. "So when you and Mummy came out—"

"Mummy was coming." Pamela sat down on the floor. "But she was so slow. She was talking to the cake candle man. So I went out first." She crossed her legs and encircled her big toe with thumb and fingers. "This is how you comfort your toes, especially when they're cold. And then I banged my head on the bus stop pole, and after that I looked for Mummy. But all I could see was the top of her head in a bus window. Then the bald lady asked me if that was my mummy, and I said it was, but that bus was going. Then the other lady, the fat one, came, and they took me on their bus. And the bald lady laid me down under a blanket with a lot of tiny holes in, because I was screaming."

"The bald lady?"

"Yes, the one with the special hat. She wouldn't wear that unless she was bald."

Her face contorted and she let loose a single, keening tearless sob. I kneeled down and grasped her. She leaned against my chest and sucked her thumb industriously.

"There were two women," I murmured to Mrs. Berrow. "Between them they got the idea that Pamela's mother was already aboard one of the buses. They didn't stop to wonder how she could have got on without Pamela. They just took Pamela with them on the next bus. I was stupid, I didn't ask them which hotel they were outside."

Mrs. Berrow patted my hand. "Nobody was very clever yesterday, dear."

Pamela stopped sobbing as suddenly as she'd begun. She broke away from me and clasped her feet again. "Your toes you can hold all at once in one hand, look." Involuntarily she rolled onto her back, where she rocked like an egg. We all laughed a little.

"Them knickers need a change." Mrs. Berrow's voice was gentle. "That much dust and dirt, I'm surprised you remember what color they are. Come here, lovey." Pamela obeyed her instantly and Mrs. Berrow pulled down the knickers. She frowned. "There's something crackling in here."

I put out my hand. "I'll take them to wash."

"Wait." Her old nails dug along the waistband. "Something's been sewn in the seam, look."

"Yes, they are crackly." Pamela nodded. "Mummy said it's because they're new. I can do handstands in them."

My hand was still reaching out toward Mrs. Berrow. "I'll take them upstairs. I've got sewing scissors in my bedroom."

Pa . . . P . . . Plymouth
Small hasty handwriting, in pencil on a piece of greaseproof paper, mostly smudged away. I folded it in my hand and looked out of the

window, at a loss. Downstairs the telephone started ringing. I heard Selwyn answering.

Then I remembered the dress. It was nowhere to be seen. I searched under the bed, then turned down the sheet and blankets and found it, crumpled into a grubby ball. Just under the little collar was a square of fraying cotton tacked roughly onto the yoke. I pulled the tacking out and freed the label. The ink was bleeding into the fabric, but the words were legible. *Pamela Pickering, 34 Newton Road, Plymouth.*

Selwyn had finished his call. He was coming up the stairs. "Ellen?"

"In the bedroom, darling."

The door opened. "That was Colonel Daventry. Another bus has arrived." Selwyn went into the dressing room. "Where's my scarf? The fog's vile out there, raw."

"Darling, I found these."

He reappeared, his scarf in one hand. "What?"

I held out my hand. He clasped it so that the pieces of greaseproof and cotton were crushed in my fingers. His hands were thin, cool and dry. Had he been a heavier man, a man whose palms were even just occasionally damp, I could never have married him. He pulled his hand away and I let the labels slip from my grasp.

He uncrumpled them, studied them. "Thank goodness. We've got something to go on, now." He put the scraps down on the bed. "Listen, I'm off to the village hall. There's a chance her mother's come to Upton. She might have found out that Pamela was taken away on the bus." He knotted his scarf with a series of brisk tugs. "Imagine it. Dashing out of your hotel, frantically looking for your child, and somebody says, 'I saw a little girl, madam. Two women took her away on the bus to Upton.' Good God."

"I don't think we can imagine it." I turned to face him. "The ladies downstairs think she might have left from the bus stops outside the Crown Hotel."

"You need to find those two women who put her on the bus. Why

don't you go up to see Lady Brock? She took a great crowd. Didn't you
say they were in the last group? I'm almost sure they're at Upton Hall,
with Lady Brock." He spoke hurriedly, crossing the landing ahead of
me. "We'll try to ring the police. Though the Colonel tells me you can't
get through to Southampton for love nor money."

"We could ring Waltham." Our nearest country town, it had a big
telephone exchange. "I'll take Pamela with me to Lady Brock. Elizabeth's got far too much to do."

"If you want." He gave me a careful, wide smile. "Clever of you to
find those little clues," he said and led the way downstairs.

Pamela was sitting on the lavatory with Elizabeth in attendance. "And
after church they gave us a biscuit," she was saying, "with icing on it,
and I bit mine so I could see the biscuit and then the icing on top like
a layer of snow. *Snow*," she repeated, rounding her eyes.

Elizabeth turned to me. "They're saying they're off home." She
jerked her head toward the sitting room. "And there's not even any
water in the taps."

"But we only got one biscuit," Pamela went on. "I kept a piece in
my pocket for a long time but then it crumbled up. Can you wipe my
bottom? My arms are still too short, Mummy says."

A slap resounded behind the sitting room door, followed by a girl-
ish cry of pain and fury, "That's for ladderin my stockings, you little
cow," said an older, husky voice. "I should put you over my knee, never
mind how big you are."

"The poor devils." Elizabeth sighed. "But I shan't mind if they
clear off."

"Ellen, can you wipe my bottom?"

"You see the ladies out, Mrs. Parr." Elizabeth was firm. "I'm used to
bottoms, with my nieces."

I stood aside as the file of women came out of the sitting room, the
older ladies scrupulously combed and buttoned, the young women's

hair slicked penitently against their scalps. As they passed, they thanked me one by one. Phyllis Berrow was the last to leave. She peered over my shoulder at Pamela, who was coming out of the lavatory. "Any the wiser, dear?"

"You were right. There was a piece of greaseproof. I couldn't read it, but the label in the collar of her dress says Pickering. Of Newton Road, Plymouth."

She mused. "Plymouth, indeed. Plymouth." She scrutinized me. "Lucky about that other label."

I nodded. "Mrs. Pickering was taking no chances."

"Would you, with a little sugar plum like that?"

"I wouldn't have let go of her hand."

She smiled. "Sometimes you has to. Even if just for a minute. And you shouldn't be punished for it. Take care, dear."

"Good luck, Mrs. Berrow. Please come again." Which was absurd, as if she was an afternoon tea visitor.

"Yes," said Pamela. "Please come again."

3

OUR BOYS TOOK a good look at Pamela, who held my hand tightly under their scrutiny. The two brothers, Jack and Donald, gave her an especially thorough once-over from beneath their fringes. Hawley, being older, was more discreet.

"Why's she still here?" Donald asked me.

"I'm waiting for Mummy," Pamela told him.

Hawley, sharp as a tack, held my gaze.

"Take your cousins to school, Hawley, please."

I washed Pamela's knickers and dress and hung them over the range. She watched me while I rummaged in the chest in the attic. I pulled out a smock my old friend Lucy Horne had given me when I was waiting for the evacuees, before I knew they were all to be boys. The smock was beautifully made by old Mrs. Horne, Lucy's grandmother: I could easily picture Lucy in it, a small, pale, dark-eyed child. I would have liked to take Pamela to the Hornes' cottage, show them the beneficiary of the smock, but this was unlikely to happen. For reasons I had yet to discover, Lucy hadn't spoken to me for almost a year.

I sighed. There was nothing I could do about Lucy, especially today. I started to pull the smock over Pamela's head.

"This is brushed cotton, Pamela. It'll keep the warmth next to your body."

Pamela shut her eyes, and when she opened them again she was a small shepherdess, robed to the ankles. I gave her long socks and my smallest pair of drawers.

"These are giant's knickers!"

I pulled the elastic through a gap in the waistband and knotted it at her waist, or rather, the completely circular middle of her little body. "They're like breeches for you."

She beamed. "Mummy will laugh."

"Yes, she will. But we might not see her today. Mr. Parr's going to find out where she is. But we might have to wait another day or so."

The smile vanished. "That's not what the bus ladies said." Her eyes glistened. "I don't know why she doesn't come."

I kneeled down and took her hands in mine.

"Those ladies," I said, "are good ladies. They thought it would be an excellent idea for you to get on the bus, because it's safe here for children. Very safe. Mummy's safe too." My eyelids fluttered, I couldn't help it.

She gave a small cry and stepped from foot to foot but she didn't pull away from me. I let my thumbs stroke the soft backs of her hands. Her knuckles were dimples. "They were naughty." She sniffed. "They shouldn't have said, we'll find Mummy, because they haven't. Mummy was shouting at the candle man all night, you know."

Shouting at the candle man.

"Did you stay in the hotel just one night, darling?"

"That's what you do in hotels." She explained it to me. "You stay all night. They give you soft pillows. We took the pillows to the cellar when the raid started. I was comfy in the cellar but Mummy wasn't."

Her voice was so clear.

"You don't know what the hotel was called?"

"No. But Mummy can tell you when she comes."

I leaned back on my heels. "I thought we'd go and visit those bus ladies. They're staying in an interesting house called Upton Hall. They have an enormous vegetable plot."

Pamela looked unconvinced.

"And a suit of armor. Like knights wear."

That was more like it.

She had no coat, so I got a clean flour sack and pulled holes in the seams for head and arms. It did very well. I lifted her onto the bicycle rack and she clung to the saddle, face set.

"Is it all right, Pamela?"

"The bicycle is digging my bottom."

I lifted her down again, glancing somewhat shamefully at the rack. No one could sit on those black bars. I went and got my old sheepskin from where it lay, somewhat yellowed, on the bedroom floor by my dressing table. Rolled up and tied tightly, it was perfect padding. Pamela screamed with delight as I pushed down hard on the pedal and we sailed off.

"Ow, ow! You're sitting on my fingers!"

"Hold my waist, like I said. Arms round my middle."

Selwyn's fog had cleared and the sky was a pale, uncertain blue marked across with high, motionless bars of pearl-gray cloud. I heard a tinny rattle. "Take your feet away from the wheels, Pamela Pickering."

"How did you know my name?"

"Mummy wrote it in your clothes."

"Well I never." She gave a breathless, adult little laugh.

We crossed the main road. The lane wound on, ruttier now. She was lighter than a quarter of grain, if a little more mobile. The hedges grew higher: nobody had cut them, and soon they'd be as tall as they had been when I was a child, and walked these lanes alone with one wet foot, my left foot.

"I had a hole in my shoe when I was young, you know."

"Didn't your mummy mend it?"

"She didn't know how."

We came to the Absaloms. A row of cottages sunk into the damp of the lane. Mother and I had lived at Number One. It was derelict now, and should have no power to hurt me, but I never came by here if I could help it. Only today, with the child, because it was the quickest route to the Hall. "See those walls? They're called the Absaloms. They were cottages once. I used to live in the end one."

"It's got no roof!"

"It did have. The others didn't. They were already ruins."

"Can we play in those ruins?" Pamela said.

"Not today."

I dismounted at the beginning of the drive to the Hall. The potholes were now deadly. It was hard skirting them with Pamela on the back of the bicycle. I whistled under the trees to keep our spirits up, and eventually we reached the old dairy, which was alive with the chip of metal on stone.

"Hello, young un," said a familiar sunburned face of forty or thereabouts, quizzing us through a rough new gap in the bricks. It was William Kennet, who gardened for Lady Brock. When he wasn't turning over the grounds to food crops he was busy with Home Guard duties—in this case, fitting the old dairy out with gunsights. So many things, these days, had to be seen to be believed.

"Morning, Ellen," he said. "Who've you got there?"

"Morning, Mr. Kennet. Sergeant Kennet, I beg your pardon. This is a little girl from Southampton." I spoke meaningfully, and he gave a slow nod. "Say hello, Pamela!" I used my brightest tone.

Pamela waved from her perch but said nothing. Her face was pinched. I was hungry, so I knew she must be too.

"What are you doing?" she asked William.

"Giving this old wall a few holes," he told her. "To make a nice breeze in the dairy."

"It must be awfully difficult with that bad hand."

"Oh, Pamela, that's not polite."

William smiled, held out the hand to her. "Look, it holds a chisel right well. So I can hammer away with my hammer." He made a claw, to show her. His thumb and finger were huge beside hers, calloused and bent from overuse. Behind the finger was a single nub of a third finger, and then nothing. What remained of the palm and back of the hand was bound by scar tissue now silvered and braided. It was a creation of a shell, during the Great War, at the Battle of Messines. He was a copper beater before that shell screeched over, a high craftsman, but I never knew him as such. To me he was a gardener, with a potting shed that was a refuge throughout my later childhood, a charcoal stove that was the only warm thing in my life.

Pamela, awed, was mimicking him, trying to make her own claw, her small perfect little forefinger sliding off the soft top of her thumb. "Mummy's still in Southampton," she confided to him. "But she's coming to fetch me this afternoon. Do you know, we saw a house with no roof!"

"Did you now?" He raised his eyebrows at her. "That's not a lot of use, is it? A house with no roof. Now, Upton Hall certainly has a roof, and a tower too. Wait till you see it." He glanced at the bicycle. "I'm glad you found a use for that old sheepskin."

"It's not old. It's lovely. I used to sleep on it when I was tiny."

"I know." He gave me his square grin. "It was me that gave it you, when you were new born."

"Oh William, how very kind!" I was astonished. "I never knew! I would have thanked you for it long since!"

He shrugged, still smiling. "It was a cold winter, and I had it to spare. And your ma and pa thanked me on your behalf, very civilly."

"I keep forgetting that you worked for my father."

"You were too young to remember. And I wouldn't call it work. More like a day here and there." Mr. Kennet tipped his hat with the remains of his right hand. "Now, I can't linger, my dear. Come and have a cuppa when you get time."

"I'll try," I said, wondering when I would ever get time.

Lady Brock opened her front door, boots spattered and mackintosh hemmed with mud.

"Good morning, Ellen. How do you like our defenses? Have a care, William Kennet will soon be asking you for the password of the day." She came down the steps. "I saw you, skirting the quagmires. Sometimes I'm glad Michael's no longer with us, you know. He wouldn't have minded the plowing . . ." She indicated, with a wide sweep of her arm, the great pathwayed allotment of ragged nutritious brassicas and rich black potato furrows that had replaced her lawns and rose garden. "But he'd have loathed the drive. We only needed a few ruts for him to say it looked like bloody St. Eloi." She turned to Pamela. "I do beg your pardon, dear, for my foul language."

After the Great War, Lady Brock's husband, Sir Michael, had been an ambulant if rather wheezy hero; over the next twenty years the gas had reduced him by increments to a gurgling wraith in a bath chair before killing him in September 1939, ten days into the present war. Lady Brock as usual had a gorgeous rich red on her wide, rather fish-like mouth. The lipstick, plus a feathered hat and a shy, rarely seen beast of a fur coat, constituted all she had of glamour. On the day of Sir Michael's death, which had been by internal drowning, she had donned them all, to serve as her breastplate, sword, and buckler.

Pamela gave her a guarded look. Lady Brock laughed.

"We've come to speak to two of the women who were on the bus," I said.

"Ah. I know the ones you mean. I'm afraid they've all gone. They departed *en masse* at first light, desperate to get home. Like a shoal of salmon. There was nothing I could do to stop them." She saw my shoulders sag. "Buck up, dear. All is not lost." She crouched down in front of Pamela. "So you came by bicycle!"

Pamela nodded.

"Was it your first time?"

Pamela nodded again.

"That deserves an egg, at the very least," said Lady Brock, "if not some mashed potato."

She cooked without removing her mackintosh, flinging cold mashed potato into the sputtering frying pan along with the egg, stabbing unhandily at the mixture with the tip of a long iron spoon. "I shan't disturb Mrs. Hicks. She went to see her sister in Cosham and got stuck on a train all night. Caught her absolute death." When Pamela was served, she picked up a pan containing the remains of a burned breakfast of porridge. "The girls scorched this specially. Come with me, Ellen, while I feed Nipper."

We stepped outside into the flagstoned yard. Lady Brock scraped the porridge pan into a tin bowl and the dog, a rangy collie with one blue eye, loped out from the empty stables. Upton Hall currently housed Nipper, Mrs. Hicks, William Kennet, six land girls, and Lady Brock herself. The herds were dispatched, the fields turned to wheat and turnips. "I had two hunters in those stables, and now that dog's the only resident," she remarked now, quite cheerfully. "I don't know. What a bloody comedown."

She knew what had happened to Pamela. The two women on the bus had told her.

"Yes," I said. "Anyway, Pamela doesn't know which hotel it was. My guests thought it might have been the Crown. The family's from Plymouth, so they'd have stayed in a hotel."

Lady Brock banged the spoon in the pan to release the last scraps of porridge and the dog snapped at them as they fell. "It *was* the Crown Hotel. The ladies told me."

"Ah. Well." I ran my toe along the gap between two flagstones. There was something comforting about the worn edges. "I'll telephone the Crown, then, and the police if need be. And Mrs. Pickering, who couldn't be bothered to mind her own child, will come with tears of joy to us."

Lady Brock surveyed me, a gentle pike.

"That was uncharitable of me." I felt the blush heat my cheeks. "My people were noisy last night."

"I didn't hear mine. I put them in the drawing room and took a spoon of Michael's mixture." Lady Brock's eyes glinted. "Don't breathe a word to Dr. Bell but I've got some left over. It's absolutely topping. One doesn't move a *muscle* all night. Now, let's go. Pamela's scraping the pattern off that plate."

Pamela and I followed Lady Brock past the ballroom. The chandeliers hung sheeted in canvas from the dim ceiling; the alabaster lions were corralled in some hidden basement, the carpets rolled up and gone. Instead there were a half-dozen rows of trestles bearing camouflage netting for the antiaircraft batteries. Many of us in Upton came here to weave strips of drab fabric in and out through the mesh of tarred ropes. Our first efforts were returned as "insufficiently garnished" or, as William put it when he saw them, "like a pack of dogs with mange. Jerry will see right through 'em and let fly." So now we worked until the sides of our hands were rough and sore. Today the room was empty, the half-finished nets hanging forlorn.

"Aren't those holey tents," Pamela said.

"Yes. They need mending."

We mounted the stairs. The suit of armor glimmered in the darkness of the upper corridor next to the door of Sir Michael Brock's bedroom, the gloom now permanent with the blackout. In former days it stood in the hall, lit around with candles so that its reflection hung, an inverted ghost in the depths of the polished oak floorboards. Candles but no candle man, no candle men here. Lady Brock had been faithful. What kind of a woman comported herself in that way, shouting at a man all night with her child in the room? Too busy to notice when her curious little girl crept off outside? The floorboards were dried out and dusty now, the armor tarnished. "Mrs. Hicks wants to get up here and apply elbow grease," said Lady Brock. "But I'm not having it. We both need to conserve our strength. Who knows how long this is going to last?"

I helped Pamela onto a stool. She lifted the visor and replaced it, transfixed by the grille, the blackness behind, the small creak as it settled into position. "Peep-bo," she said softly. "Peep-bo."

"I've always felt guilty about you, Ellen." Lady Brock's voice, unused to speaking low, was husky. "I felt we didn't do enough."

Creak. Peep-bo. I remembered the grate at the Absaloms, black with past coal but no coal in it to burn, the cold looming from the walls.

"It was very difficult to do anything for my mother," I managed to say at last. "She wouldn't be helped."

We left Lady Brock at her front door and went down the steps. "Perhaps my boys could buff up these floorboards for you," I said as I helped Pamela onto the bicycle. "They're always on the lookout for a job." I was exaggerating the case somewhat, but they were helpful boys on the whole, not overly given to skulking.

She stared out over my head, at the turned earth of the potato beds and the mud of her drive. "I'll be down there with William, you know," she said. "In the old dairy. With my rabbit gun."

"And I hope that William would send you straight back again, Lady Brock. We need you."

"Not before I pot one for Michael." She narrowed her eyes. "I promised him, you see."

. . . . .

We went home, pushing the bicycle through the kitchen garden and out through the back gate. The sky was the same light blue. I let Pamela chatter on, about the bicycle spokes, the brick wall, the crows in their high nests.

Selwyn opened the front door as we came up the path. "Give Pamela to Elizabeth," he murmured. "Let her go in."

"What news? Selwyn? Have you found Mrs. Pickering?"

Pamela slipped past him into the house. Perhaps Mrs. Pickering had come to the village hall. Perhaps she was even now indoors. Yes. Selwyn had let her in for Pamela to find, as a surprise. My heart battered my chest.

"In a manner of speaking." He ran his hand over his eyes. "The Crown was bombed last night."

4

"WE CAN'T BE EXPECTED to behave as if we're made of Derbyshire peakstone." Selwyn wielded his handkerchief. "That poor little child."

The woman's face was untouched, he told me. Her ration book was in her handbag, in the name of one Amelia Pickering, residing at the same Plymouth address she had sewn into her child's clothes. "I called Waltham police station after you left," he went on. "Sit down, darling."

I did so, and so did he. We faced each other in our sitting room's comfortable armchairs. The lower part of my face, my cheeks, felt strange—the skin numb, tingling.

"They managed to get through to Southampton. Then Southampton called them back about an hour ago." He blew his nose. "Mrs. Pickering contacted them when Pamela disappeared, but they couldn't get to the hotel until this morning. By which time it had been hit." A hollow, wooden rumble came from the kitchen, followed by a scream of pleasure. "What on earth is that?"

I cocked my head. "I think it's Lord Plumer."

Lord Plumer was an ancient croquet ball, legendarily unbeatable, named by Selwyn's uncle after the general who, in turning the course of the Battle of Messines, had, in his estimation, spared the life of his nephew. Old Mr. Parr, bereaved of both his sons at the Somme, had been grateful for small mercies. When he gave up croquet he had planed a flat underside onto Lord Plumer, fastened a lead plate thereto, and used it as a doorstop for the pantry. No one else was allowed to win a game with Lord Plumer.

The rumble returned. "That's the way!" we heard Elizabeth say, in a high, breaking voice. "Off it goes."

"You've told Elizabeth, then."

"Yes. She's taking it badly." He spread his hands, clasped them as if washing. "Apparently Mrs. Pickering called the police and then ran out to look for Pamela, only coming back at nightfall. And then, along with a dozen other unfortunates, she placed too much faith in the cellar. The ceiling came down on them all."

I pictured her returning tear-stained in the evening to her certain death. For even while she was running in the streets, shrieking *Pamela, Pamela,* the bomb for the Crown was being loaded into its bay.

"God damn them." I swallowed the stone in my throat. "I wish them eternal perdition."

Selwyn breathed in. "That attitude helps no one, darling."

"It helps me." I swallowed again. "The police will come now, won't they? And take her away?"

"They will. Eventually." He took out his spectacles and started cleaning them. He was going to read the Bible: he always gave the lenses fastidious attention before doing so. "They're looking for her father, obviously, and other relatives. They'll be in touch soon."

I pushed away a lock of hair. The bicycle ride had made it messy. "You could try the book of Job," I told Selwyn. "We need his God now. One who can shut the sea with doors. Unload granaries of hail."

Pamela was sitting on the kitchen floor, wrapping the croquet ball in a tea towel. Elizabeth was putting onions in a baking dish.

"Baked onions," I said. "They take me back. Do you know how lucky we are, to have got all that precious onion seed from Upton Hall? Most people's mouths are watering for onions. They haven't seen one in months and months." I babbled on, in the same bright tone.

"Months and months." Elizabeth's eyes were brimming. I made to embrace her, my hands on her shoulders, but she shrugged me away.

"No, Mrs. Parr," she murmured. "It'll only start me again."

"Dolly needs a headscarf." Pamela held up her swaddled ball. "Otherwise she might get earache in the wind. Do you know what happens then? Somebody irons your ear."

"No!" I feigned amazement while Elizabeth dashed her tears away. "With a hot iron?"

Pamela sucked her teeth. "They put a towel over your ear first. And then they put the iron on the towel, and it's so lovely and warm. Mummy's being very slow."

"Yes, Pamela. She must be very busy."

Elizabeth put the dish in the oven. "Perhaps she's gone to see your auntie. Have you got any aunties?"

Pamela's face puckered. "Why would she go and see Aunt Margie without me?"

"You're right," I said. "Of course she wouldn't do that."

"Aunt Margie's a long way away. She's in Cape Town. They have grapes there and lots of flowers. I haven't been there but Mummy went before I was born. She says it's wizard. She wouldn't go and visit Aunt Margie without me." She hummed a little and unwrapped the ball to fold the tea towel into an uneven triangle. "Bad headscarf."

"Let me." I took the tea towel and made a neater job of it, and knotted it as best I could under Lord Plumer's flat chin. Pamela cradled the ball experimentally, in each elbow, and then set it on the floor to take bobbing steps. "Pamela, we're going shopping. Oh, *do* come on, darling. *Do* hurry up. *Honestly,* it's like wading through *treacle.*"

I set three places at the kitchen table. Selwyn didn't have lunch. Elizabeth started the last loaf, cutting it fine. We listened to the voice of a dead woman piped through Pamela's mouth, Mrs. Pickering exhorting her small child, and prepared the meal.

In the afternoon I found an old bed jacket that my mother used to wear when she sat up against the pillows to drink her tea. It was a flouncy woolen affair with a flapping collar and silky straps, and it hung down almost to Pamela's knees. When I drew it off her shoulders she clutched at the swathes of wool. "No. No, it's too cozy. Let me keep it."

"You shall have it back when I've taken off these silly straps. We need buttons, nice big ones . . ."

I had no buttons large enough. After a long search we found, in a wooden box in the dressing room, the toggles from an old duffel coat belonging to my brother, Edward. That coat had been so torn and stained that Mother and I had cut it into strips and burned it on the fire. I refused to worry about Edward because he'd told me, the day he left to go to sea, that I should never worry, that worry brought bad luck and he would always need luck. He'd been fourteen, I eleven, and since then we had spent a total of nineteen precious days together. His last letter, dated a month ago and headed *Singapore*, said *I'll take my chances here, drst Ell. The company is doing terrifically, what with soldiery everywhere. I've been in a few jams before now and know my way around. Place like a fortress—indeed, it is a fortress and always has been. I've been contemplating calling myself Senhor de Souza and speaking entirely in pidgin. But like as not will end up doing my bit.*

At least doing his bit wouldn't put his life in danger, not in Singapore. I was glad he was far away from all this.

Pamela was delighted with the toggles. They were of such smooth, dark polished wood. I took her to the mill, where she sat on the office floor while I tidied my desk. My eyes lit upon an advisory leaflet on the turnip gall weevil, which for some reason had come my way and which I was going to pass to Lady Brock, with her great root crop. It seemed now that this message, arriving as it did before the bombing, belonged to another world. Pamela sat leaning against the wall, sucking her thumb, putting two fingers over her eyelids to pin them closed. That seemed to comfort her, as did the battering of my typewriter keys when I began my letters. "Do more," she said, whenever I paused.

"Keep going *bangbang.*" It was a noisy behemoth of a machine. We went back to the house an hour before dusk and saw a policeman ahead of us, wheeling his bicycle up the path.

He turned to face us. The strap of his helmet ran beneath a chin now blue with the bristle that accumulated by the evening.

"Mrs. Parr," he said, by way of greeting. "I'm Constable Flack. Suky Fitch's brother."

"Suky's brother!" Astonishing, how such a bulky individual could spring from the same stock as our diminutive mill forewoman.

The constable's flinty fifty-year-old eyes warmed. "We had different mams."

He removed his helmet. For a sickening moment I thought he was about to announce Mrs. Pickering's death. But instead he said gravely to Pamela, "Would you be so kind, miss, and take this hat for me? I've got a great bag of papers to carry."

He and Pamela went into the sitting room. Elizabeth was shutting up the hens, so I made tea the color of washing water and took it through. "That's my number," he was saying to Pamela. "And that there, GR, what do you think that means?"

"It means you're fierce. *Grrr.* So have you been to see Mummy?"

He lifted his bewildered face to me. I heard Elizabeth open the back door. "Pamela, I need to speak to the constable. Elizabeth's got some milk for you."

She burst out with a loud bellow. "Why won't anyone bring me my mummy!" I embraced her but she growled and with surprising strength pushed me away. "Don't keep hugging me! You're not my mummy!" She stamped her foot. "Where's my mummy!" Her face crimson, she threw herself on the floor, roaring, "Mummy! Mummy! Oh, my mummy!"

Elizabeth came in. We gave each other blank, drained stares. The constable shifted in his chair. "I've got to get back before dark," he said through the din.

"Come into the kitchen, Constable."

We left Elizabeth kneeling beside the screaming child. As the door closed I saw her place the flat of one gentle hand on Pamela's stomach. Her face, Elizabeth's face, was a mask of sorrow.

In the kitchen Constable Flack handed me a child's ration book. "This was found in her mother's handbag," he told me. "You must make sure it goes with her."

I gasped. "When will she leave?"

"Sit down, Mrs. Parr."

I did so. We listened to the screams in the sitting room. If she didn't stop, I'd have to go back in there. But just then Pamela gave a choking sigh, and Elizabeth's voice came to us, muffled. "There, there," she was saying. "There, there."

Constable Flack cleared his throat. "We don't know what's become of *Mister* Pickering. He scarpered long before the war, it seems. Nobody in Plymouth has ever seen hide or hair of hubby."

"Pamela hasn't mentioned him . . ." My breath fluttered out through my nostrils. "What were they doing in Southampton?"

He shrugged. "We've got no way of knowing. She said nothing to the hotel staff."

I picked up the ration book, stared at it in a sort of stupor.

"You'll get a pint of milk for the little one. And please obtain a child's respirator. Hers couldn't be found. Register her at your shops here in Upton. However short her stay."

A pint of milk for Pamela. "She mentioned an aunt in South Africa."

"Oh, yes." The constable nodded. "A Mrs. Marjorie Lord of Cape Town. The Plymouth officers found some letters, none more recent than ten year ago. Seems the sisters weren't corresponding at the time of Mrs. Pickering's death."

"She certainly talked about her sister to Pamela."

The constable rubbed his chin. "The Plymouth boys have it in hand, but it'll be a good while before we hear from Mrs. Lord. Any rate, you're stuck with the little girl until Southampton sorts itself out. Telegraph, electricity, telephones, all properly snarled up. Plus there's the stragglers from the raid. One lot were out in a field, in a storm drain. A storm drain." He stood up. "Don't worry unduly, Mrs. Parr. We'll find her somewhere suitable. A nice family who'd take her on. Pack her in like another little sardine."

"We'll have to tell her soon. It's worse not to."

"I expect so."

I stared up at him, and then rose to my feet.

"Constable Flack, we're not unsuitable ourselves, you know. We've got three boys from Southampton already. We'd be happy to pack her in, as you say."

In the silence that followed I heard the front door open, and then Selwyn's light voice. "Hello?" I could tell from his expectant tone that he'd seen the constable's bicycle.

I raised my voice. "We're in the kitchen."

"Ah." Selwyn came in. "Good afternoon, Constable. Have you unearthed any family?"

"This is Constable Flack, darling. Suky's half brother." I gripped the back of the chair. "I was just telling him we're perfectly prepared to take Pamela under our wing for a while."

"Just until we manage to place her, sir." Constable Flack fitted his helmet onto his head.

"She's got an aunt in South Africa," I told Selwyn. "Her father's long gone. There's no one else."

"I was informing Mrs. Parr that we'll do our best to find her a berth"—Constable Flack delved in his tunic pocket and produced bicycle clips—"while we try to get a hold of the aunt. Or, if we're lucky, this darned elusive Mr. Pickering."

"Pickering. Pimpernel. Very good." Selwyn grinned, twitching the buttons out of the buttonholes of his coat with a brisk thumb and forefinger. Most people used both hands to unbutton their coats, but he didn't.

"Quite a job it'll be, with half the men overseas." Constable Flack was somber. "And these blokes who scarper, they're generally a bad lot. No responsibility or fatherly feeling." He dwelled for a second or two on these feckless men. "If they had an ounce of decency," he concluded, "they wouldn't have gone in the first place."

"Some sort of fostering arrangement, then. That would be a capital solution." Selwyn sighed. "Poor little mite." He and the constable left the room, and I heard the front door open once more. Selwyn murmured something, and there was a scrape of boots on the path. Then a loud ticking as Constable Flack freewheeled down to the gate. Only then did I make for the door. I brushed past Selwyn in the hall.

"What the dickens—"

"Just something about the ration book," I stammered. "I forgot to ask him."

I dashed down the path to see the constable's bicycle gathering speed. "Constable." I started running. "Constable Flack!" He slowed and I caught up with him.

"Everything all right, Mrs. Parr?"

"Do remember that *we* could have Pamela. That's what I was saying. We're suitable."

"It's not for me to decide. Mr. Parr seemed very agreeable to the idea of a family taking her." He squinted at me. I was standing against the declining sun.

"Mr. Parr hasn't had two seconds to consider the matter."

The constable gave a couple of slow nods. "Telephone Waltham police in the morning. Ask for Sergeant Moore. He deals with these matters." He ran his finger under his chinstrap. "I must get on."

"Thank you, Constable."

"Sergeant Moore," he repeated, and pedaled away down the lane.

· · · · ·

The boys came home late. They'd been playing football on the Green. I told them that if they went to Upton Hall and gave the oaken floorboards the most brilliant shine, they would then be allowed to polish the suit of armor. They nodded solemnly, awed not by the task but by the sight of Pamela. "She's still here, then." Donald folded his arms against the newcomer.

Jack smirked. "Her clothes are funny."

"Never mind them," Hawley told her. "Do you like rissoles? They're fried-up veg rolls with gravy."

Pamela shook her head, her chin trembling.

I took her hand. "Boys, why don't you play cards in your bedroom? In a little while you can help Elizabeth with the vegetables." The two younger ones tramped up the stairs, Hawley lagging on the bottom step.

"Hawley, try not to worry—" I began, because I knew that no one had telephoned from Southampton.

"Mr. Parr told us the lines are still down." He smiled at me. "It's all right." He turned to climb the stairs.

I gave Pamela some bread and milk. She ate slowly, pausing to say, "I like this food," and then, "But I don't like you."

"I'm not surprised. It must seem strange being in our house. *I* must seem strange."

"No." Her eyes glowed with anger. "You seem nasty. Why are you making me a coat? I've got one already. It's in the hotel." Then the anguish rose again, too large for her body, needing to be expelled in gusts of crying. "I don't think Mummy's coming. I think she won't ever come to get me."

No, she won't. Pamela darling, you must be very brave. I was about to say those words because this seemed the greater cruelty, to let so small a child venture unaccompanied into the truth. But then Pamela spoke.

"She said she'd do it. 'One more naughty thing, Pamela, and I'll go off with the candle man.' And now she has." She began to growl with grief. "Horrid Mummee."

I embraced her. This time she allowed it, her arms hanging by her sides.

I heated two pans of water and poured them into a tin tub in the kitchen to spare her the glacial bathroom upstairs. I kneeled down and unlaced her shoes. Looking up I found her face in front of mine, watchful, dreaming. A world in those large light brown eyes, clear as a peat brook, flecked with the same dark gray as pebbles in a stream. She lifted her arms for me to pull her top clothes off, obediently stepped from foot to foot so I could remove the knickers and long socks. Everything I did must remind her of her mother, and yet she said nothing. She was so small.

She sat gingerly down in the water. "Is it too hot?" I asked, anxious. She shook her head. I should wash her hair, probably. But not tonight. Instead I washed her grubby hands, her grubby knees and neck with my own bath soap, and scooped water over her shoulders and back. Her skin was uniformly pale, dense, creamy. Perhaps I was wrong, and this bathtime was so new and peculiar that nothing about it recalled her mother.

She knew about the candle man long before she'd seen him. She used to hear him come whistling up the path, just after she'd been put to bed with her library books. He had a whistle like a blackbird. He always came on library day. Then one night she went downstairs for a drink of water. And her mother had said, *This is Eric. He's going to get some candles for your cake.* "And he did this with his eye at me." Pamela gurned, trying and failing to close one eye without the other following suit. "And the next day we all went to Southampton. We put everything into a special kind of suitcase called a *vast* suitcase," she said. "When you go away for a long time that's what you need. A *vast* one."

"'Vast' means extremely big, Pamela."

The bathwater lapped around her knees. She floated the face flannel on the water's surface, poking it with a finger until it sank down. She wasn't a fat child but she still had her baby's chubbiness around the wrists. "Vast," she said again.

She didn't know why they had to go to Southampton, why Eric couldn't bring the candles to their house. But Mummy said they needed an adventure. They took a train, then a bus. Then they walked. Mummy was frightened of bombs, but the candle man said the bombers had already got everything they wanted from Southampton. "So we went to the hotel and took off our coats and cardigans. Mummy put me on a chair outside our room while she shouted at the candle man inside. We all went to bed in the cellar. And then in the morning I had to sit on the chair again. That's why I went outside to watch the people rushing around. I was bored."

I dipped my hand in the warm water and scooped it over her pale, round shoulders. "Promise me that if you're bored here, you will stay where you're put. Pamela . . ." I tried to sound careless, conversational. "This candle man. Eric. I suppose he wasn't a bit like your daddy, was he?"

She gave me a blank gaze. "Oh, I don't have a daddy."

"Really? I thought everyone did . . ."

"No. You can be excused from it, you know. Mummy told me. He decided not to be a daddy, and so he isn't. He went off just after I came out. Do you know that babies come out of people, out of a wincy little hole that stretches?"

"Goodness, Pamela!" I had a sudden sharp image of a woman perched at a dressing table, throwing out the facts of life to her little child while lipsticking her mouth. "Yes, I do know that."

"Are you having a baby, Ellen?"

I gave a wavering laugh as the heat flooded my face. "I certainly am not. And it's not a question you ask grown-ups, dear."

"You might be." She was unabashed, round-eyed. "They're teeny when they start growing, like a little nut. So you could have one inside you and not know about it till you start being sick as a dog."

"That's not a nice expression." I smoothed my hands over the pinafore I'd put on to bathe her. "I haven't got time for babies, Pamela. Not with all you children to look after. Now let's forget about all this silliness."

I ran through phrases in my mind. *Pamela, darling, your mother. Mummy. Pamela, sweetheart.* I couldn't get any further. It would have to be done tomorrow. Tomorrow or the next day.

Quite suddenly she started to grizzle, baring small square milk teeth. Her tears fell into the cooling bath. Elizabeth came in with the vegetables for supper, filled the sink with cold water, cast a somber eye on Pamela, and left the room again saying, "Hens."

I told Pamela she'd see the hens tomorrow, that she could feed them with Elizabeth if she wanted, but she shook her head, because hens were no good to her. I dried her and took her upstairs to dress, and met Hawley coming down to peel parsnips. The others were too darn comfortable to move, he said. "They're the lazy branch of the family. No, truly they are. My dad says so."

After supper I put Pamela back in my bed and told her a tale about a swan, one who kept her babies in the soft white feathers on her back between her wings as she glided along a shining dark green summer river. They went for long, long adventures until she grew drowsy.

5

PAMELA KEPT ME AWAKE for a large part of the night, a sleeper in almost perpetual motion. At six o'clock I was in the kitchen starting some bread when the telephone rang in the hall, the bell immediately drowned by thundering feet on the landing and Elizabeth's hopeless cry, "Donald, you're a plain old-fashioned disgrace!" I heard Selwyn say, "Children, stop this bawling," but they took no notice and crowded noisily into the kitchen, Elizabeth following.

"Donald refuses to have his hair cut," she announced.

I was pouring warm water into my flour. I looked up to see the older two were freshly shorn, the black-haired Hawley monklike under his pudding-basin crop. For the first time I noticed the faintest dark down on his upper lip. "Hawley, you look very dapper," I said. "Donald, don't you want to be as smart as your cousin?"

Jack, the elder of the two brothers and a russet boy, spoke for Donald. "He says we look like girls."

Donald scuffed his feet by the range, his fringe in his eyes. Shorter, stockier, and redder than Jack, he was a wayward Highland calf.

"Really, Donald, dear. What sort of girl would have such a plain style?"

"Mrs. Parr, save your strength." Elizabeth scooped oats into a pan, her face creased with exasperation. "Donald won't be told."

The older boys sat down, their necks wet, the snipped hems of their hair still bearing the furrows of the comb. When I was fourteen,

Elizabeth had cut *my* hair. She'd worked for Mr. and Miss Dawes then, who looked after the children of the Parish poor. I was older than these boys but I was nonetheless a Parish child. So Elizabeth had clipped me and deloused me with gentle kindness.

I looked up, met her eyes.

"I've never told Mr. Parr, you know," I said quietly. "About my short crop."

"Of course not." She began to smile. "He doesn't have to know everything."

My corn goddess, Selwyn had said, when he unpinned my hair for the first time. *So easy to worship you.* He knew that Mother and I had fetched up in the Absaloms, but I had painted this era in broad brushstrokes, very broad strokes indeed. What corn goddess in her right mind would regale a suitor with stories of long-ago lice.

Just then Selwyn came into the kitchen. "Good morning, boys. I've been speaking to cousin Hawley's father. They're all fit and well, although there's no water and an awful lot of smoke."

They were too proud to shed tears of relief, but Hawley's shoulders settled and Jack blinked rapidly. Donald gave a series of blowing breaths, a small bullock on a misty morning.

"Donald won't have his hair cut," I told Selwyn.

"I know. The fearful row you made quite impinged on my telephone conversation. Donald," Selwyn commanded, "submit to a trim this evening and at Christmas I'll take all you boys to Suggs' in Waltham for a proper chap's back-and-sides." He wagged a finger. "This is a gentleman's offer, conditional upon meticulous obedience to Elizabeth. Is that understood?"

If the vocabulary was a little high, the gist was clear. Donald said, "Yes, Mr. Parr," and the boys seated themselves with an awful scraping of wooden chair legs on earthenware tiles, and Selwyn sat down too. Elizabeth served the porridge while I kneaded my dough, rolling it and slapping it on the board. "My spoon's jumping up and down on the table," said Jack. "Look. Bang the dough again, Mrs. Parr. There!"

"Pick your spoon up and start eating," Elizabeth directed him through set teeth.

The telephone rang again. Selwyn said, "Damn," and left the room once more.

"Hawley's only eight years younger than you, Mrs. Parr." Jack started to inhale his porridge, speaking between and during mouthfuls. "Don't you find that 'strordinary? That he's already thirteen and you're only twenty-one, but you're completely grown up?"

"She isn't. She scrapes her porridge bowl like we do. Mr. Parr, now he's properly grown up. He's *forty*."

"Donald, I shall tell Mr. Parr how rude you've been about Mrs. Parr."

"Really, Elizabeth." I rolled up my dough and put it back in the bowl. "It's no more than the truth. I'm always starving. And Mr. Parr is forty-one, to be exact."

"Yes, Mrs. Parr. But Donald's *manner*."

Selwyn returned, unsmiling. The boys, seeing it, were quiet.

"Who rang, dear?"

"Sharp's." He sat down again at the table. "The fire hoses did for the grain, nearly all of it, but there's some dry wheat left. They're sending for people to fetch it away and grind it."

"Oh lord," said Elizabeth. "They got Sharp's."

I rubbed dough from my fingers, awed at the knowledge that in hitting the Southampton docks, the bombers had laid waste to the largest flour mill in the south.

I followed Selwyn out to the yard where the lorry was garaged. I tried to match my stride to his; we were both tall, but he was eager to be on his way. "Darling, when I dashed after the constable yesterday, I did mention that we'd be happy to hang on to Pamela for a while."

"We haven't got much choice, have we, in the short term." He spoke absently, fumbling for his keys. We were approaching the garage.

"What I mean is, she wouldn't necessarily have to be with a family. People are so hard pressed now. She might do better with us and the boys . . ."

Selwyn unlocked the door and snapped the padlock shut. "Sweetheart, these past few days we've all been through a great deal. You've been absolutely marvelous—"

"I really haven't. I simply did what had to be done—"

"But I think the experience has left us, perhaps, not quite in our right minds."

The doors gave a rusty scream as Selwyn pulled them open. I followed him into the garage. "What do you mean, 'in our right minds'? Selwyn?"

"Darling, can we talk about this later?" He was opening the cab door, swinging himself up into the driving seat. "It's hardly the most apposite moment."

"Well, I'm taking her to Barker's in Waltham this morning. For clothes. So I won't get to the office till after lunch." My voice was rising. "But she needs some things. I can get her things, can't I? While she's here?"

"Of course you can. Ellen, what's the matter?" He leaned down toward me.

"Nothing. I'm perfectly all right." I shut my eyes. "And I'm certainly in my *right mind*."

"I do beg your pardon. That was a stupid thing to say." He smiled deliberately down into my hot eyes. "Take Pamela shopping and don't worry about the office. Suky and I can dash off a couple of bills between us. I must go."

"Of course you must."

He drove off, to Southampton, and Sharp's, and the undamaged grain.

· · · · ·

I went back inside. Stared at the slowly rising bread dough. Ate my helping of porridge, half-cold, from the pan. Then I went out to the hall and lifted the telephone receiver.

"Waltham police station, please," I told the operator.

Pamela appeared at the top of the stairs. "Miss Ell, Missis Ell!"

"Quiet, sweetheart. I'm telephoning."

She thumped her way down, hopping from stair to stair. Six steps from the bottom her foot slipped.

"Pamela!"

She pitched forward and so did I, catching her as she fell against my chest and knocked me to my knees. Behind me the telephone receiver cracked against the wall.

"Be careful!" I yelped the words as pain shot through my knee. Pamela, unhurt, threw herself on the floor and began to wail.

"Good grief, Mrs. Parr!" Elizabeth was standing in the doorway.

"We're all right." I levered myself upright. "My dear, take her into the kitchen. I must telephone."

Sergeant Moore excused himself for eating his breakfast. His thin voice worked its way through crumbs. "I daresay you'd be unopposed in this scheme, madam."

"I'd hardly call it a scheme. Just a wish. Of course I *have* thought it over. Let's say, a carefully considered wish . . ."

Loud screams issued from the kitchen. "No! No! Not porridge!"

"Do you have other children, Mrs. Parr?"

"None of my own, but we've got three evacuees." I pressed the receiver against my ear. "We're used to looking after young children. We could be—"

The kitchen door opened. "I! Am! Not! Eating! Nasty! Porridge!" Pamela screamed, and thundered up the stairs.

"—like a family to her!" I shouted.

"Just so," said the thin voice, with a little clearing of the throat as Pamela thundered down again, giving a long, roaring bellow, as far as I could see for the simple pleasure of doing so.

When I went into the kitchen she was sitting on a chair with her knees up and the singlet pulled over them. Elizabeth was stirring a pan on the range. "I'm just making some more porridge, Mrs. Parr."

"I gathered." We both smiled. "I'm taking Pamela with me to Waltham to get some clothes."

"Look, I'm in a bag. I'm a bag girl."

"Yes, Pamela. Elizabeth, dear, can you knock back the bread dough later?"

Elizabeth nodded. "I can. But you'll have to hurry if you're to get the bus."

"Let's go upstairs, Pamela, and get dressed." I made my way to the door but she remained on the chair, pulling the singlet over her toes. "You're stretching the fabric. Now, get up."

"Bag girl, bag girl. I want porridge."

"Oh. Now you want porridge. Well, you will have porridge, but you need to get dressed first."

"No, porridge now."

"It's not ready. You must dress while it's cooking. Do you want to go shopping?"

"Yes, but after porridge."

Elizabeth was laughing. She lifted the pan from the heat. "You do what Mrs. Parr tells you, young lady, or I'll feed this to the hens."

Pamela got off the chair.

Upstairs she raced into the dressing room and out again, squeezed herself under our bed. Her laugh was rattling, hysterical. I persuaded her out after three minutes or so. I brushed her hair and she seized the brush from me, tried to brush the back of her hair with the back of the brush, refused to surrender it. I pulled her nightwear off her and she lay on the floor bicycling her legs until I caught one hard little foot and then the other and forced them into the leg holes of her clean dry knickers.

Now we had a bare ten minutes to get to the bus. And now she didn't want to go shopping. I sat her on the kitchen stool, she jumped down. I pulled her back up onto the stool with my hands under her armpits and she went slack as if boneless, flopping sideways.

"Pamela, we'll miss the bus!"

A spoon of porridge went in, and then I pulled the flour-sack shift over her head. "I don't want to go shopping," she growled, her face pasty with anger.

"I will carry you if I have to," I vowed.

I did have to carry her. She dragged her feet, stumbled to her knees, squatted down, all the while yanking at my hand, until I was forced to hoist her into my arms. Just as I broke into a clumsy trot, my shopping basket bouncing against my hip, the bus to Waltham passed by the end of the lane on its way to the stop. I called out, "Wait! Wait!" without the remotest chance of being heard. Perhaps a passenger was alighting: we might still make it. But the bus roared on, flashing through the gaps in the hedge, and I hurried the last few paces to the junction only to see it vanishing heedless into the dip at the bend of the road. I set Pamela on the ground, absolutely winded.

"There," I said. "Look what you've done. We've missed the bus."

"I know." Her eyes were dancing and a delicious bloom had spread over her face.

My own eyes stung with frustrated tears. I watched the bus emerge from the dip and rush on up the hill, through the bare trees and away to Waltham.

"I was going to get you warm clothes and new knickers, Pamela, but I can't now. You'll just have to sit naked while I wash your old ones. Uncomfortable, and cold."

In response she started her nasty, rattling giggle.

"Stop it!" I shouted, but the giggling sharpened, accompanied now by a knowing leer.

I shoved my hands deep in my pockets and breathed right to the bottom of my lungs. "Pamela. *Please.*"

Her face crumpled and she started crying, high and strident as a lamb. I crouched down and put my arms around her.

"Mummy's not coming. Mummy's not ever coming again."

"No. Darling, Mummy won't come back."

"Never come back."

"No."

"Mummy's gone."

"Yes."

She pulled away from me, her wet eyes clear hazel, almost round.

"She didn't go with the candle man, did she. And she didn't go to Aunt Margie where the grapes are either. Those are just tellings."

"That's right, sweetheart."

She leaned back into me, her breath whiffling through her nose. Then she spoke again, her lips moving against my neck. "I bet you're going to say she's gone to Heaven."

I held her tight but without clinging. More to stop her falling. "Yes, Pamela, I am going to say that. Mummy's gone to Heaven."

Smack, her small palm hit me squarely on the cheek. She sprang backward out of my arms. "Nasty lady!" she cried, and ran off down the road toward the blind bend. There was something coming the other way. The thunder of a big engine was filling the air.

"Pamela!" I dashed after her. "Pamela!" I shouted again, as a tractor rounded the corner, pulling a huge spined harrow that seemed to fill the road. I ran harder, flung my arm out, and grasped hold of the flour sack, tugging her onto the verge at the very instant the tractor roared past us, the harrow bouncing after it, missing us by a foot. Pamela and

I both fell down, she under me, screaming like a child in a collapsing building. She flailed at me but I grabbed her hands. She screamed higher: her palms were grazed.

I heard a shout, turned my head. The tractor had slowed down and was pulling into the wide field gateway opposite the bus stop. Then the driver jumped down and ran back toward us. A small woman galumphing in Wellingtons. As diminutive, sallow-faced, black-eyed as ever, and the black eyes just now furious.

"Ellen Parr, what the bloody hell are you up to?" bellowed Lucy Horne. "I nearly crushed that child!"

6

"WHAT DOES IT look like?" I clung hard to Pamela, who was thrashing like a landed fish. "I'm trying to take care of her!"

"You're makin a bloody awful job of it!"

"I'm aware of that!" I cried.

She glared back, panting, her almost permanent wheeze audible after the mad dash and the telling off. Then I let go of Pamela and put my face in my hands.

"I'm sorry," I said. "We missed the bus."

My cares came, mounting one upon the other. It was the bus, and Pamela's naughtiness, and her dead mother. It was the white flares over Southampton, and the smell of bombing in the people's coats. And it was Lucy herself. I had no idea of the reason for her muteness, her ostentatiously blank stares, her turning of the shoulder at church or in the village hall. She'd been my bridesmaid, for goodness' sake.

Well, she was certainly speaking to me now.

I took my hands away from my face. She was holding a dumbstruck Pamela by one hand, alternately frowning at me and squinting up the road toward the tractor. Then she gave an explosive sigh. "Bloody hell, Ellen."

"Yes." I got slowly to my feet and took Pamela's other hand. The child, ash-pale, allowed it. "I won't keep you, Lucy," I said. "I need to take Pamela home and get her warm."

Lucy gave a short chuckle. "Darned if that's not my old smock, under that flour sack."

"Yes."

"Glad it came in handy."

Another pause, which Lucy filled with a long, ruminative sniff. Then she released Pamela. "I'll just run that harrow into the field. I'm goin home for my dinner anyway, so you might as well have a warm-up at my house. Harry Parker won't know if I take a couple on the back." She gave me a dark glance. "If you was inclined to come, of course."

We rumbled into the village, perched on the back of the tractor seat. Pamela gazed dully at the receding road. I pointed out the milk churns on the high stand at the end of the main street, and she blinked slowly in response but didn't turn her head to look. What did she care for churns, motherless as she was.

Motherless, and in the charge, furthermore, of an incompetent, childless woman. Who would give a child to me? Perhaps she should go to a family after all. At least that way she wouldn't end up under the wheels of a tractor. I twisted round in my seat, saw Lucy's shoulders, hunched high and stiff. She'd been on the tractor six months now, and her dainty little hands were skillful on the wheel. She'd been a kennel maid before the war, and I knew she missed the hounds now that the hunt was closed. She would be a kennel maid again, she hoped, when the world dropped back in kilter. I knew about these feelings and hopes of hers because George Horne, her father, had told Selwyn of them, in the course of general conversation, and Selwyn had told me. That was how I learned Lucy's news these days. I wondered, now that the ice had been broken in such a spectacular fashion, what this invitation would lead to.

She parked neatly on the triangle of grass at the end of the street. I clambered off the machine and jumped Pamela down. She stumbled against me as she landed. We walked the hundred yards up to the Hornes' cottage.

"We took three of 'em," Lucy said as we went up the street, and I knew she meant refugees from Southampton.

"Wherever did you put them?"

"On the parlor floor." In the old days she'd have said, *Yes, Ellen, ain't it amazin. Being that our house is no more than a bloomin hovel.* But I felt more sharply rebuked by this measured, adult response.

Pamela tugged at my hand. "I want to do a wee-wee." We hurried the last few yards. Lucy's cottage was set high above the road, up a flight of steps, and the privy was at the end of the garden.

"Why do we have to go in this box?"

Lucy suddenly smiled. "It's the lav, dear."

"Look, it's got a heart in the door." It did, a heart-shaped hole cut out of two planks. They had cut half a heart out of each plank and then matched them. I'd known this privy for ten years and never noticed before how exactly the two halves fitted. Lucy went indoors and I led Pamela into the lavatory.

"Do I just wee-wee into the hole?"

I found myself laughing. "Yes."

Her face darkened. "Mummy hasn't gone to Heaven anyway. She said, 'Pamela, I'll always tell you where I'm going.' And she didn't say anything about that." Her eyes wandered upward, caught in the shaft of light from the cut-out heart, looking for a solution. "Anyway," she said, "even if she has gone to Heaven, she won't be long. That's the other thing she always says. 'Won't be long, Pammie.'"

She shut her eyes and pressed her lips together.

I washed my hands and Pamela's at the kitchen sink. Lucy handed Pamela a slice of bread and butter. The food stemmed her tears but they began to flow again the moment she swallowed the last bite. Soundless this time. "Come, Pamela." I opened my arms. "Sit on my lap."

But she didn't move. Instead she addressed Lucy, jerking her head at me. "She's a horrible lady."

"We won't mind her," Lucy said steadily, looking all the while at Pamela. "Now, do you know what a tortoise is?" Pamela nodded, tears dripping from her chin. "There's one in the shed. He's in a hay box. We can go and take a peek if you like, but we can't disturb him. It's not a normal sleep, you see."

They went out into the garden. I remained sitting, suddenly too tired to move. Lucy came back in. "She's havin a bit of a scramble on the apple tree. Not a tear. They turn on and off like a tap, that age."

How did people know these things.

"How come you've still got her?" Lucy went on. "Where's her mam?"

"Dead." I took a deep breath. "Dead in the Crown Hotel." I told Lucy about the stampede for escape, the well-meaning women. "Her mother never made it to Upton. I've only just told her."

Lucy whistled. "Blimey." She went again to the back door, and I stirred myself and followed her. We both peered out at Pamela. She was jumping, quite unperturbed, onto and off the apple tree's ancient trunk, which bowed like a camel almost to the ground.

"I don't think she believes it yet," I said.

"Oh, the poor mite. Oh, lord." Lucy gave a sad little chuckle. "Explains why she don't like you. I didn't much take to the woman who told me *my* ma was dead. Old boiler of a night nurse." She pursed her lips into an "O." "'I have some very grave noos for yoo, Miss Horne.'"

The hooting tone made me laugh in spite of myself. "She didn't talk like that!"

"She did." We went back to the kitchen and Lucy cut us some bread. She laid the slices on a familiar plate, the edge decorated with pansies that years of scrubbing had worn half away to leave the odd faded wind-blown petal and glint of gilt on the stems. Years ago I had eaten a pie off that plate, and even now it was the most delicious thing I had ever tasted.

We ate now, Lucy breathing noisily, her eyes fixed on the table. No remark, no smile came my way. Finally I took my courage in my hands.

"What's wrong, Lucy? What have I done? Please tell me."

Outside in the garden Pamela chirped like a blackbird in spring. A child used to her own company.

"You've been forgetful," she said at last. "Forgetful of your friends."

My mouth fell open. "When did I forget you? You were my bridesmaid!"

"Yep, and you dropped me straight afterward. Didn't call by, didn't chat. Months and months. So I assumed"—she leaned on the word, using my voice to do so—"I *assumed* that it was my payoff, the brides-maid job, and Mrs. Parr didn't want anything more to do with poor little Miss Horne and her chest"—she coughed theatrically—"and her teeth and all."

Lucy was missing six teeth, many at the front. The teeth were long gone and her gaps were familiar to her friends but all the same she pulled her top lip down to smile, to speak to strangers. And she had coughed every day of her life.

"I invited you to our garden party. You didn't reply."

"Oh, yes. Your garden party."

She spoke softly, as if to a silly child. I studied my clasped hands in sadness and shame. The invitation had been written on a card, *Mr. and Mrs. Selwyn Parr, At Home.* I hadn't even popped my head round her door to ask her in person. Merely summoned her to mill about on my lawn with tea and cake, as if she were any one of my acquaintances instead of my oldest friend.

"Mrs. Parr was happy," I said after a while. "She wasn't used to that. It made her clumsy." I looked up at her. "Lucy, please come and see us. We can bake you a potato, and you can share our parsnip stew. It won't be as nice as yours, because I can't cook like your nan. But we'll spare no effort."

She licked her finger and dabbed at the crumbs on the plate, gathering them up. I did the same thing at home after the children had finished. When she spoke, her voice was gruff.

"They do say you must forgive newlyweds. Their minds run on one thing. Though in your case it was Greek poems like as not."

"Yes, it was. *The Iliad*. He was teaching me Greek."

She burst into a cackle. "You pair!"

I laughed too. "It was fun. We've got no time for lessons now, of course."

"How's it been, Ellen? What you expected?"

A *mariage blanc,* Lady Brock had said. *Have you heard the expression, my dear?*

The sheets of our marriage bed unfurled, heavy white linen. *Is it the French for white wedding, Lady Brock?*

No, my dear, it is not.

Lucy was gazing at me. How dark her eyes were. In the gloom of the kitchen I could hardly distinguish iris from pupil.

"It's been exactly as I expected," I said after a moment. "And I've honestly never been more content, Lucy."

Pamela was still on the apple tree. The bark was fissured and slippery with moss but she was sure-footed, turning on her toe at the end of each pass. As she walked she raised a scolding finger. "No, no, you're naughty donkeys." Her voice carried in the still air. So clear. She would sing well. Selwyn could teach her. She saw me and jumped down immediately, ran to me with her arms open, collided with my midriff. I clung to her and she to me, her arms bound around my waist, her head pillowed on my belly, all her animosity gone.

The door creaked and Lucy appeared on the step, her face sallow in the low light. Pamela continued to cling. "Ellen," she said. "Ell."

"Did the tortoise wake up?" Lucy called. Pamela buried her face in my skirt.

"Pamela, answer Lucy."

Pamela turned her head. "No, he didn't, Lucy-Lou." She broke away from me and took Lucy's hand. "Come on, Lou and Ell. Come and see my donkeys. They're all tied up by the tree trunk." Together we went to the apple tree, Lucy and I, with Pamela between us. We pretended to admire the donkeys. There were a great many of them, all with complicated, mutable names. Pamela became lost, happily, in her naming.

"Here's some news," Lucy said. "Dan's home for Christmas."

"Oh, how splendid!"

Daniel Corey was a friend from our childhood at Upton School. We hadn't seen him since the summer when he came home on leave after Dunkirk. Then he was sent away into the east of England, there to transform the flat shoreline into a bulwark against enemy landings. "Think of all those concrete blocks," I said now. "Like giant sugar lumps, all along the beaches. They'll stop a tank dead."

"That's what Dan says."

"It's true. Anyway, the Germans can't bring an army across. Colonel Daventry says they haven't got the boats."

"Let's hope he's right." Lucy stared for a moment into the middle distance. Then she sniffed. "Tell you one thing. If those buggers come up the high street, there'll be trouble if they shoot *me* dead. I'm the only one who can start that bloomin tractor."

I couldn't help smiling. "How is it on the farm?"

"Cold. The dogs, they worked up a good fug."

The first proper grin of the old days.

"I was thinking of that pie, earlier," I found myself saying. "The first one I had from your nan. I've never forgotten it."

"Oh, yes. Nan's flaky pastry." Her face softened. "You was so perishin hungry." She released Pamela's hand, patting the back of it. "I've got to get back to that harrow. Stay and play with those donkeys awhile, unless you want a lift back to the turnin?"

"No, we'll walk."

"I'll say ta-ta, then, Pamela." She went off toward the steps. "Shut the gate," she called back, "or Mary Wiley's dog'll come and have a go at Maurice."

"Who's Maurice?"

"The tortoise," Pamela said. "Ta-ta, Lou."

Pamela and I made our way home, unprovisioned. We'd all have an early tea of potato pie if there was some lard. I hoped there was some lard. Beacon Hill was caught in pale sunlight. I wanted to take Pamela there and lie on the top as I had with my brother Edward when we were young. She hung on my hand, whining, dragging her feet. "That bread didn't touch the sides, did it."

"Touch the sides of what?"

"The sides of your tummy." But she didn't really understand. I drew her onward down the winter lane to home and found four loaves on a rack on the kitchen table. Quickly I put them away before she caught sight of them. Then I took her upstairs to get warm under the bedcovers. She stared at me as I moved around the room, so small and huddled in the bed. I was already cold and the sight of her, snug against the pillows, made me feel even colder.

"I'll get in with you, Pamela. Five minutes can't hurt."

She rolled away from me and started to breathe hard, in and out. I wondered for a moment if she was starting to sob, but I soon realized she was simply puffing and blowing for the enjoyment of it, like a small engine at rest. The rhythm soothed me and I fell headlong into a deep sleep.

The slam of the front door woke me. The last boy into the house walloped it shut. Pamela was now crying quietly.

She elbowed me away. "No. I want to be on my own."

I made some pastry while the boys, subdued and orderly, peeled the potatoes. "Pamela's lost her mother," I told them. "She died in the bombing." I hated saying this, but they had to know. "Only speak about this if *she* does. Be as kind as you possibly can."

Pamela came downstairs, and the boys fell into a deathly unnatural quiet until Hawley lifted her onto a kitchen stool and gave her a slice of carrot. She ate it and started to groan with hunger. I didn't offer her any bread because it would immediately mean four slices off the first loaf, since the boys wouldn't stand for being left out. When suppertime came, she beat the boys to an empty plate, and Donald, used to being the youngest and hungriest, was aggrieved. "She's as greedy as a dog, Mrs. Parr!"

"Donald, that is *not* kind. Pamela's hungry."

"She's going to eat all our food. Munch and gobble up the meat and everything nice."

"She's got her own coupons. For that teasing, Donald, you stack the dishes. Hawley, please take them to the sink so Jack can start the washing up. Pamela, darling, please don't cry. There, there, darling. Oh, Donald, don't start too, for heaven's sake." The uproar drew Elizabeth from the vegetable garden. She clasped Pamela to her and stood viewing me in the midst of my domestic straits. No help, no calming shushes came my way. Instead, unaccountably, in the face of the sobbing of the two younger children, the clattering of plates, the strewing of scraps of potato peel on the floor, the bullock-like jostling of the two older boys at the sink—in the face of this, Elizabeth succumbed to helpless laughter.

The boys took Pamela upstairs for a game of snap. Elizabeth, Selwyn, and I tackled the remains of the potato pie. The dish was wholesome, with a dried sprig of mint snipped small and mixed with the potatoes. Elizabeth and I ate with relish but Selwyn left a slab of pastry on his plate.

"I'm sorry we missed the bus, darling. I'd have made a better job of supper, if we'd been shopping."

"I wasn't blaming you." He pushed away the pastry with his fork, politely, to show he had finished. "You were saddled with Pamela. By the way—was she playing with the telephone today?"

"The telephone?"

"There's a crack in the receiver."

I remembered the bang it had made as it hit the wall. I hadn't noticed any damage when I'd made my own telephone call. But then I'd been so flustered.

"She shouldn't, you know," he said steadily. "It's not a toy."

"I realize that. No, it wasn't Pamela."

"Did you dash it to the ground in rage?" He gave me a tired smile. "I wouldn't blame you, if you were speaking to the Ministry. We'll have to do another letter. It's getting ridiculous."

The Ministry. Of course. We needed to replace the metal screen that stopped the flotsam of the channel from getting into the mill turbine. The screen was rusting, much patched with wire. The next split would be irreparable. But we couldn't obtain a new screen without an order from the Ministry.

"I haven't yet. I'm so sorry." I picked up my own plate and clinked the cutlery onto it. "I must have replaced the receiver clumsily." I stood up and took his plate. "I wasn't *saddled* with Pamela, actually. We just set out too late. It won't happen again."

Elizabeth and I carried the plates to the kitchen. When I returned alone, he was sitting with his head in one hand. I sat down beside him without speaking. After a moment he lifted his head and stared at the curtained window.

"I passed a house today," he said. "With its face torn away, only the gable remaining." His eyes wandered toward mine. "It reminded me of someone I met in the hospital gardens. Nothing left below the brow line, yet somehow the man was alive. Bandaged, of course. With a tube for breathing."

Where had Selwyn been treated after the Great War? Somewhere in the north, I thought, a stately house of gray stone, viridian lawns, a cedar casting black shadow. He'd told me about it when we met, but the details had since escaped me. We were in peacetime back then. Why should I remember?

"I didn't realize there were any . . . I thought your hospital was only for nerve patients."

"It was."

The horror reigned inside me for a long moment. Then I opened my palm and put my hand over his and formed my lips for speaking. "Next time," I said, "*I* will go to Southampton. You know how much I like driving the lorry."

His own lips moved. "It's no picnic. Slag heaps of rubble. And smoke."

"You'd better give me some tips, then."

"Practical girl."

Elizabeth came in from the kitchen bearing toast cut into fingers and sprinkled with a few grains of sugar. "Pudding," she announced.

I put Pamela to bed without opposition. I said that it was her turn to tell *me* a story, and so she did, one about her imaginary donkeys.

"Did you know, Mummy was killed in the bombs?" she suddenly said, on the edge of sleep. "That's what Donald said when we were doing snap with the cards."

I sat back down on the bed and clasped her shoulders. "I was going to tell you, darling, but I thought I would wait until you asked. You must forgive Donald. He doesn't think before he speaks—"

"All the boys said it." Her eyes were limpid, tearless. "They also said you can't come back from Heaven. You can look down, though. Hawley's grandpa's looking down, he says. He went up there from drinking drinks, though, not from the bombs." She rolled away and put her thumb in her mouth.

7

PAMELA DIDN'T BREAK my night this time. And when I woke early she was still asleep, motionless on her stomach, issuing soft snores, her arm flung over a pillow. I'd do better today. Get her some proper warm clothes—a coat, a nightdress, stockings. We'd have plenty of time if I went to the office early. Got the most important letters done before breakfast.

As I watched, she rolled without waking onto her side and drew up her knees, giving the pillow a hearty kick.

"Silly nonsense," she declared, and I almost laughed. Somewhere in her sleeping mind she'd found a place without grief and knowledge, huddled into it like a mouse into the bole of a tree. I encircled her with my arms for five minutes or so, and she smelled of warm dry brushed cotton, and something else, that somewhat salty aroma of newly baked bread I had noticed when I lifted her off the seat of the bus. What was it? Her heated skin, her hair at the nape of her neck? I didn't know.

Stealthily I got up and dressed, and went to the mill before dawn broke. I climbed the stairs to the office, my feet finding their way in the gloom. The stairs were wooden, with two worn dips in each tread. We were to install a fine iron stair, fit for a century to come, but the war began and there was no metal for such vanities.

I lit the gas lamp and typed in my coat. I no longer had my book from the loft at the Absaloms, coated with dust and mildew and the frass of woodworm. *Typewriting. A Practical Manual Based Upon the Principles of Rhythm and Touch. By W. R. Sedley.* The back had been eaten half off but there had been a keyboard, a cardboard keyboard that folded out, and I used to batter this keyboard with my fingers according to the principles of rhythm and touch. I had no idea, half the time, whether I was right or wrong.

"Darling, what are you doooing," came the worn cooing from the bedroom, and I would reply, "Homework, Mother. Just thinking out my arithmetic."

I found my shorthand pad and wrote now to the Ministry, Selwyn's voice in my ears and in the rhythms of my fingers. *If the screen is regularly put out of action, our stoppages will mount until we are unable to fulfill our orders. There is a certain truth, Mr. Gresham, in the saying "spoiling the ship for a ha'p'orth of tar."* I considered this saying, and substituted another, more apt in my opinion. *For want of a nail the shoe was lost.* And I added: *I am sure, sir, you are familiar with the final lines of this rhyme.* Perhaps this was going too far. But the prevarications of Mr. Gresham were wasting our paper, ink, typewriter ribbon, postage, not to mention the time and attention of our women. Perhaps I should add something about morale. *Our own manager, a capable woman, reports that the constant repairs to broken machinery sap her morale—*

As if by telepathy, Suky Fitch stuck her head round the door. "I'm closing the sluice gate, Mrs. Parr."

"Suky. How do you feel, when the screen needs mending?"

She stared.

"I'm writing to the Ministry. Would you say it sapped your morale?"

"Oh. Yes." She grinned. The most unsappable woman one could hope to meet. "And that of my workforce."

... and that of her workforce. "Thanks. Why isn't Mr. Parr doing the sluice?"

Suky raised her shoulders. In someone less delicate it would be a shrug. "I don't know. He asked me. Oh—I saw you with the little girl. Yesterday on my day off. You were running for the bus. I was on it, but

I couldn't make that old sourpuss of a driver stop. Oh, I felt for you."
She was smiling down at me, warmth in her bright blue eyes.

"Oh, yes. We missed it by a mile. Children." I shook my head as if
knowingly. Where was Selwyn?

"I expect you'll be glad to get her settled," Suky said. "The Henstrows are respectable people, very clean. Mrs. Henstrow I've always
found very . . . practical."

I let my fingers drop onto the keyboard. A handful of keys rose into
the air, the limbs of a struggling metal insect.

"The Henstrows?"

"That farm up at Speeds Hill, yes. You sound like you're getting a
throat, Mrs. Parr. Be sure and tie your scarf high. Peter told me last
night. Peter Flack, Constable Flack, you know he's my half brother.
Oh, Mrs. Parr, are you off, then?"

I fled out, coat unbuttoned. The cold air in my throat like pewter. I
reached the house, skating on the damp flagstones of the path. I went
into the hall. "Selwyn!"

His voice came, muffled, from our bedroom. I ran upstairs.

He was sitting on the floor with Pamela. Between them was a
wavering rank of toy soldiers and a cushion.

"The Henstrows," I said. "Suky told me."

"Yes." He levered himself to his feet, tugging the bags out of the
knees of his trousers. "I arranged it yesterday. We got them in the nick
of time. They were about to take a boy from Portsmouth. I've just been
explaining it all to Pamela. I thought it was important that we had a
proper talk about it as soon as she woke up."

Pamela toured a toy soldier over the plumped cushion. "I'm going
to be with a family, you know, Ellen." She spoke without turning her
head, her face a small pale full moon in the wardrobe mirror.

"You telephoned." I looked at Selwyn. "Yesterday afternoon, while
we were out."

I sank down onto the bed. He came to sit beside me, leaning forward with his elbows on his knees. His wrists were thin, the veins stark, his cuffs frayed. His large, spare hands were beautiful. "Darling—"

"Why didn't you tell me yesterday?"

"I should have. I know."

In the mirror I saw Pamela's face close. It was almost nothing, a barely perceptible tightening of the corners of her mouth. Many people wouldn't have noticed, but I knew her face already.

Selwyn spoke. "We were thinking about packing, Pamela and I."

I got up and left the room. On the landing I paused. In front of me was a picture, a Victorian oil of a family of bucolics desporting themselves in a tree-shrouded lane entirely free of mud and animal dung. Young and old alike were rosy-cheeked, clad in clean white smocks. I felt a blunt stab of pain, as if from a bone needle.

Selwyn followed me out, laid a hand on my shoulder, withdrew it again when I didn't turn round.

"Selwyn, did you know I hate this picture beyond measure?"

He gave a small puff of soundless laughter, agonized. "I love you so much."

"What?" The word broke out of me in a stunned gasp. "What's that got to do with anything?"

Pamela opened the door. "Why are you whooshing?" she asked.

"Pamela," I said, "why don't you make a battlefield? You can show the boys when you've finished."

We went downstairs. The boys were chattering in the kitchen and Elizabeth was hanging the children's smalls on a clotheshorse in front of the sitting room fire. We slipped outside and sat on a bench in the garden. For a minute, sitting straight-backed in the sharp frost and the low morning sun, I felt that we were both young, with everything before us. A great shiver convulsed me.

He began speaking immediately. "I can't have a child in this house. It's too dangerous."

I gaped. "What are you talking about? The house is full of children. They're here because it's safe."

"It won't be, in an invasion."

"My God." The nerves leaped in my belly. "Have you heard something? Has there been a warning?" I clutched his arm. "Selwyn—"

"No. Nothing like that. I'm simply looking to the future. If they invade, the children will all have to be moved." He squinted up at the mill. "You know our building's strategic. I told you, Ellen. William Kennet and his party will be up there tomorrow with their chisels."

"He didn't say anything about that when I saw him."

"Discretion is the watchword. He probably didn't know then."

Above me, the mill rose quiet in the sunlight. Such a fine place it was, well-founded and built for peace, the only damage two centuries of weathering by frost and sun. I could not picture it pierced by gunsights, even less wreathed in smoke. The idea was sickening. I wrapped my arms around my body. If no one would comfort me, I would do it myself.

"Why just Pamela?" I spoke mutinously. "Why aren't the boys going?"

"Their families will take them when the moment comes."

"*If* it comes."

"If it comes. But with Pamela it's different. Her life's been shattered. We can't risk her taking root here, and then having to be moved again. It wouldn't be fair. Constable Flack suggested we find her a family, and that's what I've done. On a farm, far from the roads, as safe as can be, for the duration of the war. That's no more than our duty, in my view."

The sun was lifting into the bare branches of the rowan tree. There was a rowan outside my house at the Absaloms, and an owl that used to perch in it. The tree and the sun were tainted now with a dreadful bitterness. If only Selwyn hadn't driven down to fetch the grain. If only he hadn't seen the city after the air raid.

"I should have gone to Southampton," I said.

He laughed, it was an unpleasant sound. "Yes, you should," he said, "You'd have seen the children then, with tears running through the soot on their cheeks. It'll be worse, of course, after the actual invasion." He turned to look at me. "You really should have seen France in the last war, Ellen. Children standing alone in shelled houses, too stunned to cry, surrounded by the bodies of their families." He nodded slowly. "Yes, France," he said. "You'd know, then, what could happen to Pamela."

A long moment passed. Selwyn's eyes were slitted against the early morning light, his face worn, crumpled.

"I don't understand," I said in the end. "I thought you agreed with Colonel Daventry. He doesn't think it's remotely—"

"Daventry's making petrol bombs."

The sun was rising higher into the tree. A branch had split it across.

"People make a better job of things," I heard Selwyn say, "if they're not utterly terrified. That's what we find. So we encourage a certain superstition, in the Home Guard. That the more thorough our preparations, the less likely it is that they will be needed." He stood up slowly, pushing his hands against his knees. "Now. Pamela needs to get ready."

She raised her arms obediently as I pulled the singlet over her head. I could believe that children were born out of the buds of giant flowers, little gods and goddesses, so perfect was her body. Those extraordinary clear peat-brook eyes, wide-set in a round face. This hair the color of the darkest honey. Those neat, plump little toes. I wondered if Mrs. Henstrow would look on her and marvel.

"Can I come and take you for walks?" The tears bathed my eyes.

Her eyebrows kinked. "Just me, will you take? Or all the

Henstrows? There's five, Mr. Parr said so. A boy and a boy and a boy and a girl and a girl, and that last girl is ten. The boy at the top is a farmer, he's so big. So he would be too busy to come, I expect."

I buttoned her dress. Reached the broken top button. "Let me snip off this button and sew on a new one. Hold still." I opened my sewing drawer. My scissors lay beside Mrs. Pickering's slips of greaseproof paper and cotton.

"I might stay with the Henstrows forever, or Aunt Margie might come and get me after the end of the war. But we don't know when that'll be. Why are you sniffling? Do my button."

If she was in South Africa, I'd find her. I would find her on all points of the earth. "Say please."

"Do my button please. Please may you do my button."

"We don't say please *may* you." I cut the button fragment off and tore out the broken threads.

"Yes, we do. It's polite."

"No, we only say, please may *I*." I licked the end of the thread and inserted it into the needle, holding my eyes wide so that the tiny shining oval hole should not blur. "We say please *can* you, or *could* you. Put your head forward."

She bent her neck. I pushed her hair aside. Her nape was covered in fine golden down. How could anyone refuse this glory. I kneeled behind her and put the needle's point through the loop of a small pearl button.

As Pamela ate her porridge I took hold of her free hand and rubbed my thumb across her dimples of knuckles. The hand small enough still for the fingers to radiate, like a starfish. A crease at her wrist, the babyish plumpness. Her whole forearm I could take in my spread hand.

"If Mummy comes here, will you tell her I'm at the Henstrows' house?" she said suddenly. "I do know she's gone. But just in case."

Blessed art thou.

"Yes. Of course I will. Would you like some more?"

"Is there any sugar?"

"No."

"Then no more."

Selwyn stood in the doorway in his hat and coat, his thin jaw cuddled by his scarf. "Hurry, Pamela, or the kitchen pig will come and snuffle you away."

"What kitchen pig?"

"This one." He made an absurd snort, and she giggled like bubbles coming up through a stream, and for that astonishing glimpse of fatherliness, now that it was too late, I wanted to strike him.

The motor car coughed and struggled into life. "How much fuel have we got?" I asked Selwyn.

"About a teacupful."

There would be no more until after Christmas. We ought to walk, but she was so small and it was cold. And this way it was over quicker. Pamela got in with a practiced air, her face set. She was carrying a bag holding the smock and singlet and the bed jacket I had given her to wear. "When I was small, I did ballet." She peered out of the car at me, as if it was of great moment, and I had to be told this instant. "We used to go together. Mummy and me and Mr. Dexter. It was Mr. Dexter's Humber car. Or it might have been Mr. Watts's. I can't remember. This isn't a Humber car, though, is it?"

I didn't know what to do. Whether to sit by Selwyn and try to persuade him against giving her away, or beside Pamela, to drink in the last drops of her.

Selwyn opened the passenger door for me and paused. "Darling, would you prefer to stay here? It might be easier."

"I'll come." I got into the back beside Pamela, and held her close to me.

She struggled out of my grasp. "That's not comfy."

"Sit on my lap, then."

"No." She composed herself, and looked out of the window intently, as if at an unfolding panorama instead of the dank stretch of winter hedgerow.

I raised my voice so Selwyn could hear me. "Nobody has asked her what *she* wants."

"What?" He didn't turn his head. His hat brim bent the tops of his ears down. I leaned forward.

"We haven't asked her where she wants to be. Who she wants to stay with."

"I did, actually." He threw the words over his shoulder. "She says she wants to be with the children. The children and the pigs, she said."

"And the donkeys," said Pamela.

"But you've got donkeys, remember?" I scratched in my mind for their names. "Floriday, and the others?"

She was contemptuous. "They're not real."

We drove out of the village and up the lane shrouded in bare trees. The line of the hill traveled upward along with us. I knew Speeds Farm of old, when I walked up there and Mr. Speed drove the sheep down. After he died, his daughter took the farm, and then she married a Henstrow. She had five children and now, with Pamela, she was to have another. *To those that have, it shall be given.* There were tussocks all the way up to the brow of the hill above Speeds Farm, where they'd chopped the trees down and left the stumps and the turf had grown over. When my mother and father were alive, Edward and I used to take bread-and-butter picnics up there, and we'd sit down on the tussocks and look over at Beacon Hill across the valley. But that was long ago, ten years after the Great War, when nobody believed there could be another.

When the gate was in sight Selwyn drew the car to a halt. "Here we are."

"Why don't you go on up into the yard?"

"I don't like the look of those ruts."

Pamela and I got out of the car. Selwyn's face was hollowed, slightly shiny behind the windscreen.

Pamela and I walked the remaining distance to the frosty, deserted yard. A collie loped toward us. Pamela put out her hand. "Good dog, good dog." The dog gave a long, ripping growl and she snatched her hand back again.

"Not all dogs are good, Pamela."

Mrs. Henstrow appeared at the door. Her red hair was scraped into a round bun on the top of her head and her legs were bandaged, the crossovers running as neat as ears of wheat up the fronts of her calves. "My veins." She pointed at the bandages. "This is the best thing for them. My niece does it for me, she's on her nurse training. Oh my lord, what a little one. I thought she'd be eight or nine. Let's hope she's not a gusher. I can't abide a gusher. Keep clear of Tig, dear, he'll give you a nasty nip. He don't mean nothing by it, it's his job."

Pamela wound her hands into the front of her skirt, her face pale, round, uncertain.

"Mrs. Henstrow." I spoke in as low and as steady a voice as I could muster. "Have you been told what happened to Pamela?"

"Oh yes." Mrs. Henstrow rolled her eyes. "Her ma copped it in Southampton, down in the cellar of the Crown. That's it, dearie, in you go. There were a fancy man, weren't there. Oh, I've got my spies. Just because I spend all my days up here turning the collars on shirts and feeding stock don't mean I'm ignorant. He copped it too, the fancy man, didn't he, so there is some justice. Have you got the coupons, dear?"

Her kitchen was dark, clean, and full of male people. They all rose to their feet with many scrapes of boots as Mrs. Henstrow said, "There's John, Archie, and Newton, they're my three boys, and them two old lads are the Lusty brothers, the farriers. They don't talk much.

Come up for the Shires today. The girls are out in the hayloft doing lord knows what. Gossiping I expect. I must say, I thought she'd be nine or ten."

The young boys were different shades of their mother's rusty red. Two elderly men, both with mouths that pushed forward and turned down like coal scuttles, nodded. Pamela squeezed my fingers.

"The coupons," repeated Mrs. Henstrow, with extra clarity, as if English were not my mother tongue.

The kettle began to whistle. "I need to speak to my husband," I said above the thin wail. "He's parked down in the lane."

"Didn't fancy it, did he?" Mrs. Henstrow said, spooning tea into a pot. "Little ones can bawl so, can't they, when things don't go their way."

"Please, no tea—"

"Don't worry, madam, it's not for you. I was going to get out some rose-hip syrup, dear," she said to Pamela, who was standing dumb beside me and didn't so much as nod. "Hmm. Another one with no manners. No syrup for those with no manners. Oh no. We'll have to do something about that."

I took Pamela by the hand and we left Mrs. Henstrow considering what precisely she would do about Pamela's manners. We made our way across the yard. She called after us, "You can leave her here, my dear, while you fetch her things," but I didn't turn my head. Pamela skidded on an icy puddle and I tugged her upright before she fell, my legs shaking so much that I too almost lost my footing.

Selwyn was waiting, huddled deep into his scarf with his hat tipped forward.

"I'm not leaving her there, Selwyn."

He sat up, peered out at Pamela.

"I don't like that dog. But I like dogs. But that one is a dog, and I don't like him. Even so, I do like dogs." She stood, trying to reconcile it, run through by deep shivers.

Selwyn looked from Pamela to me. Then he got out of the car. "Get in and keep warm," he said.

We waited four or five minutes. I showed Pamela the game with the folded fingers. "Here's the church and here's the steeple. Open it up and here's the people." She laced her soft little fingers at the knuckles and turned her joined hands over, and laughed to see a wiggling row of pink fingertips. Here were the people, praying on their knees. Here were the church bells, tolling for the invasion. They'd been silent since the beginning of the war, but when the time came they'd ring out over our streets and fields. At first we'd simply not believe it, and then we'd begin to believe it, and we'd start running, and shouting. We'd hold out our hands to each other, and start to speak urgently about the children. I fastened my arms round this child, though it squashed her a little, and then I too laced my fingers together to keep her in my embrace.

Selwyn was making his way back to us. He got into the car without speaking and started the engine. As we jolted down the track, he made a sort of flapping gesture to me with one hand. I interpreted it as best I could.

"Pamela, you won't be staying there. The dog was too nasty."

After a few minutes we ran out of fuel. The engine died and we coasted the rest of the way down the hill. The tires tore quietly over the tarmac. At the bottom Selwyn stopped the car and went to fetch the boys from the house. Pamela began to cry. "Will I go somewhere else now, or can I go to bed?"

"Sweetheart, you won't go anywhere before morning."

Selwyn returned with Hawley and Jack. They pushed the car while Pamela and I steered. She sat on my lap holding the wheel, turning it and straightening again with me until the car was back at the mill and safely inside the garage. For five or ten minutes we were absorbed in this task like a happy family. Elizabeth appeared and silently put out her hand to Pamela. The boys swarmed past her into the house. Soon Selwyn and I were alone in the hall.

"Just because I couldn't leave her with that vile woman—"

"Doesn't mean you won't find someone else," I said. "A more kindly farmer's wife. I know. You've already made yourself clear."

He shook his head. We stood in the dim light of the hall. He touched my face with his fingertips. Something I usually adored, but today my skin felt numb. I had to find something of him, grab some scrap of the man I loved, out of this wasteland.

"Please play the piano, Selwyn."

"I haven't the heart."

"For Pamela, then, if not for me. Please."

Pamela wanted "Jingle Bells." It was only a few days to Christmas. Selwyn played it for her roughly three dozen times. It was getting dark, but not yet time for supper. Pamela and I cut out some newspaper dolls, some with skirts, some with trousers, and the boys joined us to sit cross-legged and snipping, and Pamela spread them out on the floor.

Elizabeth came in and sat on the arm of the sofa. Selwyn asked her what song she would like to hear.

"I've always been fond of 'Sally Gardens.' I'm making a macaroni cheese." She and I sang together and Pamela dragged the lopsided dolls across the carpet. Selwyn's fingers pranced over the keys, his eyes hidden behind his glasses. Pamela went into the kitchen and Elizabeth followed her. His fingers stilled immediately.

We ate the macaroni cheese. It was delicious, all that baked hot milk and flour and those shavings of cheese. I had taught Elizabeth to make the body of the dish with milk only, and as much salt as was tasty, and to reserve the cheese slivers for the top. Selwyn quarantined the mixture in his mouth before manfully swallowing but the rest of us ate it up with gusto. We put the house in order and went to bed, all of us, at eight o'clock in the evening.

. . . . .

I put Pamela on the small bed in the dressing room and admitted Selwyn back into our double. Selwyn lay on his back, hair tufted against the pillow. Our first night together we'd read poetry, Edward Thomas, lounging on the pillows. We still did this from time to time but I sensed it wouldn't happen again for a long while. So little time it took, for a small girl to bring me to this. The least likely thing to happen, as astonishing as an imago in a chrysalis. I let my gaze become absorbed into the gloom of the curtains, their heavy, somewhat threadbare blue velvet a powdery gray in the lamplight.

"You would never have let her stay," I said. "Even if there had been no war."

"If there had been no war, she would never have been here."

That was unanswerable.

"Somebody will come for her, Ellen."

"No. She's got no one. Her aunt hasn't been in touch for ten years. Her father's probably forgotten she existed."

He made a sound somewhere between a sigh and a groan. "If this child is taken away from you, and you suffer, I don't know how I'll forgive myself. You say you don't want children, but—"

"I *don't* want children."

"You want Pamela."

I stroked my hand over the linen sheet. The sheets didn't smell of lavender now, since Elizabeth and I hadn't found the time or the spirit, last summer, to make up new lavender bags. I was eighteen the first time I saw this bed. It was so beautiful. The headboard of polished wood the color of toffee, and the sheets heavy, crisp, and scented. They had reminded me of my earliest childhood, before our ruin. I pulled myself away from his reaching arms and got off the bed. I started tearing my clothes off, tossing my woolens onto the floor, stripping my legs of their stockings. I trampled my way out of my skirt and stood barefoot in my slip, tugging pins out of my hair.

"Darling, do put on your dressing gown. You'll catch cold."

"You think this room is chilly?" I laughed without pleasure. "When I was a girl I woke with frost on the carpet. The carpet that we put on our bed, Mother and I. It stank of mice, even in the frost, but we couldn't get to sleep without it."

He got out of bed and came to me. His pajama-clad body was warm against mine and this time I let him put his arms around me. "I'd be the last person to make light of your hard years." He pressed his cheek against the top of my head. "But—forgive me, I can't see what bearing they have."

I released myself from his embrace, stood so that he could see my face. "What bearing?" I shook my head in wonderment. "Seriously, you can't see it?"

He gave me a baffled, unhappy stare. "You told me how you and your mother suffered. How you had to scrimp and save—"

"Scrimp and save." I laughed again. "Do you know why I'm not frightened of the cold? Because I know about it. How you can let it sink right into your bones, and it won't damage you at all. I know how to suck on a pebble to keep hunger pangs away. You have to do that, you know, if you've just given a child your own food. The pain's excruciating otherwise. And I can carry her, farther than anyone. I can walk twenty miles with nothing inside me but the skin of a baked potato. You say I've got no idea about war, and shelling. Well, you've got no idea what I can endure for her sake."

He stood in front of me, a mild man, a clever man. Pajama'd, be-spectacled. So beloved. Pushed beyond his bounds. He'd tried to push me too. But he'd simply forced me down onto my bedrock.

"I don't care what happens after the war," I told him. "That's not the point. You can put her where you want, but I'll go with her. She needs me now. Me. Do you see? We're the same, Pamela and I. I was a child like her. A child who lost everything in the world."

Ellen

1932–1935

8

I WAS ELEVEN when things started disappearing.

First it was my rocking horse, a beautiful thing with a blood-red bridle of suede. I was really too big for her now but all the same I loved her. When I asked Connie and Miss Fane, and they both said, "She's gone to be repaired," using those exact words, I knew they'd been taught a lie. Three weeks later I saw Miss Fane in the hall, planting her foot on the lid of her trunk and bending to tug the strap tight. Then she too was gone.

I ran outside, found my brother Edward in the orchard, swinging a stick. The orchard was the jewel of our house, which was known as the Stour House after Godfrey Stour, who had sold it to my father, and the generations of Stours before him who had planted and grafted and filled the apple press with cider jars. Edward looked up as I came running, crying. He put his arms around me and chose words a little too young for me, perhaps to soften the blow or perhaps just because he too, at fourteen, was confounded.

"Daddy's made a mistake with the money."

My mother and father didn't shout: instead they went to the study and spoke in a level tone, each word separate as if etched into the air.

"It's simply gossip, Susan."

"People are gossiping because they haven't been paid. And they haven't been paid because you've ruined us."

"I'm an investor. There are always ups and downs—"

"You're a gambler."

On the word "gambler," my mother's voice tightened to a whisper and the acid bit deep.

On the following morning, Daddy came to my bedroom resplendent in waistcoat and watchchain, his mustaches groomed, his round blue eyes full of glory. He kissed me on the side of the head roughly, said "Kitten," and went downstairs. I heard the front door slam, his footsteps on the gravel, the gorgeous cough and chug of the engine of his car. He changed gear once, twice, as he tore away down the drive. He was awfully skillful at driving.

In the hall I found his goggles, gloves, and driving coat slung across the hall table.

I asked Edward if he shouldn't be back at school, and he gave a bark of a laugh. "What do you think has happened to our father, Ellen?"

We were loitering on the stairs where Mother couldn't hear us. On a post at the top of the banister sat a small wide-eyed oaken owl looking at us, his feathers in neat carved rows.

"We don't know exactly," I said patiently. "Mother said he's away, trying to salvage what he can." The word "salvage" made me form a picture of Daddy, a great figure in oilskins, seawater sluicing off his sou'wester, pulling treasure from a wreck in the pounding surf.

"He won't be coming back. He's absconded. Do you know what that means?"

"Of course I do," I said. "And it's utter nonsense. He's on his own, he hasn't absconded anyone."

Edward let loose a groan of fury. "That's *abduct*, Ellen!" He clattered away down the stairs. "To abscond is to escape on pain of *arrest*!" And he left the house, slamming the front door after him.

I started to brush the dust from between the owl's ranks of feathers.

. . . . . .

Connie, our maid, stayed for a while longer, and then I did Mother's hair on my own, and it was just me, Edward, Cook, and Jennie, to look after everything. Edward made the fires and I folded the sheets with Jennie. She wouldn't look at me as she took the sheet from my fingers, nipping the edges together neatly; she turned her head away. She'd been eating onions, she said, she didn't trust her breath.

Mother couldn't stay downstairs for long. "I'm finding our circumstances extremely trying," she would say. "I need my rest."

She couldn't salvage her friends. Lady Brock was far too busy with the shoot, Mrs. Daventry preparing to travel to India. "You have no idea what has to be done, children, when one shuts up a house like The Place," Mother told us, glassy-eyed. "It was silly of me to expect her to linger chatting in the street."

My friends too were beyond rescue. I no longer went to dance Scottish reels with Esme and Lucinda Drake in their drawing room with its delightful carpet the color and texture of moss. I didn't sit cross-legged anymore in Clara Mayhew's bedroom where Palgrave's *Golden Treasury* and Malory's *Morte d'Arthur* were kept in cupboards of black oak. Anyway, how would I get to their houses? The car, with its leather seats redolent of luxury and nausea as he swung me around the lanes, was gone, of course, along with Daddy.

Edward sold the pig. Cook's brother took it away to be butchered and came back with a warm newspaper parcel. "You give that to Irene, my love, it's some nice hocks and trotters." That was how I learned Cook's Christian name. But soon afterward Cook and Jennie went, and we were alone. And then Mr. Dawes from the Parish was at the gate, grimacing under his mustaches, because what expression is suitable when you're turning the Captain's family out of their home; and there was a cart outside, and I wore my plaid coat and carried a small case containing my first workbook when Daddy's hand had cupped mine as I wrote *Ellen Beatrice Calvert* on the first page. That great thumb I remembered, and the ring with the claws holding a garnet. It was astounding how quickly we'd fallen. The apple trees had been in blossom when my rocking horse disappeared, and now the early desserts were cropping in the orchard. The time of the rocking horse and Miss Fane seemed like the dimmest age of the ancients.

I remembered, as the dirt came, how white everything had been at the Stour House. A tongue of milk spooling into a jug, and the jug itself, white china with a white beaded cloth on top against the flies. And the apple blossoms, of course, and my petticoats and drawers, and the tablecloths that Mother embroidered out on the porch in full sun, white silk thread on white linen, and *why are we doing this?* I would ask.

And Mother's secret smile. "It's a present for you."

"But I don't want a tablecloth."

Smiling more secretly. "You will."

I kept my plainest drawers and the cotton underskirts. Miss Dawes, the sister of the Parish man, sold the embroidered linens discreetly for us. They fetched a good price. We put our furniture—two beds, an armchair, two chests, three kitchen chairs, and a table—on the cart. A firescreen decorated with Arcadian scenes, a fluting shepherd and a lolling goatherd, so that Mother could sit facing the fire and forget that the house was gone, the dining room, the sunroom, the sleepy sunlit bedrooms with their wrinkled quilts of eiderdown. Mr. Dawes and Mr. Blunden, who mowed the graveyard, lashed everything together with stiff ropes. "Heave ho," said Mr. Blunden, bearing down on the rope and guffawing as if our belongings were a pile of bric-a-brac for the Whitsun Fair.

We left the Stour House, that stood out on its own beyond Beacon Hill, aloof from the hamlet of Barrow End and the village of Upton. We left owing money in Barrow End, Upton, and Waltham, and no doubt in Southampton and London too. And if anyone were to come and dun us, whether it be for the price of a buttonhook or a hundred railway shares, we had nothing to give them but the charity shown us by the Parish, and if they took that, they might as well take our bones for bonemeal too, because we'd surely die.

The cottage was on the edge of Upton, the first of five dwellings clustered at the top of a dead-end lane that petered into a wasteland of ruined shacks, nettles, and broken fencing. The other cottages were empty, too dilapidated to live in. Mary Absalom, who had given them over to the Parish, had been dead a hundred years but people still called the place after her, a fact I learned on my first day at Upton School when a sallow-faced girl said, "You're the one that's come to the Absaloms, then."

From this girl I also learned that the last occupant of our house had been one Vic Small, who when drunk fired a crossbow into the front door, which accounted for the splits.

"I prefer not to know about Mr. Small," I told this girl, whose name was Lucy and who cackled, "Only being friendly, dear."

Edward couldn't come to this school because the pupils left at fourteen. I refused at first to go without him, but it was cold in the cottage and Mother said that I'd be warm there. "You don't have to speak to anyone, darling. I'm sure Miss Yarnold will be kind." Her voice wavered: she was sure of no such thing. "And don't bend your head too close to another child's. Something may leap from their hair."

I'm sure it won't be for long, she said. *Something will come up.*

We stood by our desks and recited the Lord's Prayer. We would do it every morning thereafter, so that, for me, the words remained saturated with the body odor of those children. *Amen,* we said, and stank, because when I got home I did too, and we didn't know it but soon I would on my own account, and our smell was unnoticeable save to people who washed.

Miss Yarnold took the register. My mother had always greeted her when we met in the haberdasher's in Waltham. "How nice you look, Miss Yarnold, so fresh," my mother usually said, or something like it, and I'd nod and smile as well, tilting my head the way my mother did. Now I felt the heat envelop me as she reached my name: "Ellen Calvert," she called, and my "Present" came out as a choking cry that made one boy crow like a cock in imitation. I looked her straight in the eye then, because she'd said my name a shade too loud and sharp, almost trippingly.

"Daniel Corey," she said next, with a guileless gaze and a tweak of a smile.

On that first day she announced the national competition. Each of us was to write two essays, one about a bird, the other about a tree. We would observe our birds and trees over the course of the autumn.

We set to work. I sat at a double desk with the girl Lucy. I chose the waxwing and the rowan, being that there was a rowan tree outside our house at the Absaloms. I hoped to save myself labor since the waxwing was a migrant and fed off the rowan. I might whip it all into one text and have done, since surely by winter I wouldn't be in this school. Daddy would have come back and rescued us by then. He'd come bounding into the schoolroom, tall and mustached, and gather me out of my seat. *Come, my kitten, not a minute more.* My fingers squeezed my pen.

"I'm so sorry, Ellen." Miss Yarnold smiled over our desk. "But the rules are specific. It must be a native bird. And do choose an unrelated tree, since otherwise there would be too much repetition. And now, Lucy. There's nothing on your page. What is it to be?"

"The linnet, miss."

"And why?"

Lucy shrugged.

"And your tree?"

Another shrug.

Miss Yarnold smiled more brightly. "Dear Lucy. Always so slow."

By mid-morning Lucy had written "linnet," which I had spelled for her, and "prity," which I hadn't. There followed a break during which I stood at the edge of the yard and watched the boy Daniel Corey, whose name came after mine in the register, try and fail to push an other boy over a log. This second, stronger boy was called John Blunden. It was his father who had helped us lash down our cart of shame. As they broke from their wrestling, John stepped back and glanced at me, and frowned a hot embarrassed frown.

At midday the classroom emptied at the first strike of Miss Yarnold's little handbell—emptied, that is, apart from me and two small twin girls. "We stop at school," one said, and the other added, "Our dinnertime's not till night. Is your dinner at night too?"

"Yes."

There was a silence. They were pale and long-haired, the hair dark and lankly curling.

"What are your names?"

"I'm Amy and she's Airey."

"I'm Airey and she's Amy." They'd spoken in unison. I smiled and pointed at the left-hand twin. "Amy?" When she smiled back I saw the distinguishing mark, the tiniest chip on her front tooth. Then they placed their folded hands on their desks and laid their heads down. I sat still as their breathing fell into a single rhythm.

"I must say, Ellen, you're bearing up awfully well."

A month of this life had passed. Edward and I were returning to the cottage from the copse on the other side of the lane, pulling behind us a bundle of dry dead branches lashed together with Edward's belt.

"It's not so bad." I copied his tone, stout, cheerful, and schoolboyish. I knew it was worse for him. He'd been to petition Mr. Dawes over and over again for work, anything, clearing field drains, beating for the shoot. But all jobs were taken, it seemed.

"We shall keep warm, I'm sure," I went on, "if we throw ourselves into our tasks."

We stacked the branches and set to cleaning the windows. There was vinegar in the cupboard, and newspaper in the kitchen drawers, left, we assumed, by Vic Small. The windows were so crusted that we used all the newspaper on four panes, creating four clear bright holes ringed by a fuzz of grime. Edward went inside and I tried scrubbing with a hard brush, but it had been left outside in the weather and only made the glass dirtier.

"More paper, look." Edward reappeared with a bold, red-lipped smile and handed me a sheaf of illustrated pages. I glimpsed a corseted female torso, a suspendered leg cocked upon a stool, and dropped the pages in the mud. Edward broke into a baying laugh. "You can't afford to be so nice. Not anymore!"

I heard tapping and looked up to see Mother's fingers against the glass. "She wants tea." My eyes were stinging. "I'll go."

The police came one afternoon late in October, all the way from Southampton in a black car whose headlights illuminated billowing tents of rain as it drew up outside the cottage. The car disgorged two men, a constable in a cape with skirts shining in the wet, and a detective sergeant doffing a trilby whose brim shed a short stream of water onto the floor. And then Miss Dawes, a surprising, straggling third.

The detective introduced himself and his junior. "I'm here to inform you, Mrs. Calvert," he continued, "that we've found your husband."

"What do you mean, you've *found* him?" Mother stared. "He's not lost. He's simply absent for the moment, retrieving our finances. He's a capable, resourceful man. A very good provider." She waved an airy hand. "I expect he was fairly cross when you *found* him. Busy as he must be. He does get so involved in his enterprises."

For a moment nobody moved or spoke. Then Miss Dawes turned to me and Edward. "Let us put the kettle on."

"We've got no fuel in the range," I told her. The wood we did have was wet, and I wasn't burning our coal for Miss Dawes.

"We'll pop into the kitchen, dears, all the same."

Edward folded his arms. "I'm staying with Mother."

I stood with Miss Dawes in the yellow shaft thrown from the open kitchen door into the dim room. The detective began to speak but his words were soon drowned.

Edward went with the policemen to identify Daddy. It was a formality. A formality, I learned, was a senseless cruelty whose sole purpose was to inflict a lasting wound on a boy most innocent and undeserving. I would have gone too, but Miss Dawes told me to stay with Mother.

I learned the truth the following day, in the course of a halting catechism given by Mr. Dawes. Daddy had died by his own hand, three days previous, in Southampton. Daddy had felt terrible shame at ruining us. Although he'd made a dreadful blunder in suicide, Daddy couldn't be blamed because the balance of his mind was disturbed. Daddy was now at peace, we should know; he loved us, and we should remember that his heart was in the right place.

Edward told me later that Daddy had put a gun to his own chest. His blue eyes looked black as he spoke. "Ha. Ha. Daddy's heart certainly isn't in the right place now."

I screamed in his arms as he begged forgiveness for saying such a thing.

In school Miss Yarnold sat me nearest the fire with Amy and Airey for company. It transpired that they had also lost their father. "Dad fell from a roof and broke up his leg," Amy said.

"His leg and his back," added Airey.

"And they wouldn't mend so he expired," said Amy. "We do pity you, Ellen dear, but you'll get over it. We got over it didn't we, Airs?"

As if the loss were a high fence on a bleak upland field.

No one else spoke to me—no one, that is, except the girl Lucy, who instructed me to accept her condolences and take them to my mother and brother. "On my behalf and on behalf of my dad and nan. That's Lucy Horne, George Horne, and old Mrs. Horne. There ain't no young Mrs. Horne because my ma passed on."

I cast around for words, and then put out my hand. "I'm very sorry to hear it, Lucy."

We shook hands. Her palm was warm and the hand itself small and dainty. She said, "Long time ago now."

Mother developed a routine. She would rise early and light a small fire and get herself ready for the day. She toasted bread for us and made tea. She didn't eat until evening, apart from the crusts of our toast, and then, when she saw that we wanted the crusts, she left them on our plates. "Much too chewy for me, my dears." She washed our plates and cups and walked once around the garden. Then she took up her seat by the fire, with the screen shielding her gaze from the room. After the fire went out, she stared at the ashes in the grate. At dusk, when no one could see her, she walked awhile in the lane, and then she'd come in and light a second fire. We sat round it eating our supper, which became earlier as we grew hungrier with the increasing cold. Edward would stare at the flames like Mother and gently chew his knuckles. When the second fire went out we went to bed.

"Edward?"

"Hm?" He was rolled in a coat on the far side of our bed, dozing. Lit by a bright half-moon in the window.

"Do you think it was raining when Daddy died?"

He turned his head. Such a handsome boy he was. I was proud of him. He and I had blue eyes like Daddy but he had Daddy's chestnut-brown hair. Mine was blond as a stook of corn and much the same in behavior, bunching and sticking out however tightly I plaited it.

"Why do you ask?" He had a new, distant way of talking, now that his voice was breaking. I didn't mind. If anything it made him more admirable and manly.

"I'm just trying to imagine it."

The rain, and then a bang, and then more rain.

"The balance of his mind was disturbed," Edward said at last. "It overwhelmed him, alone as he was. The shame and dread."

"Is that the same as being mad?"

"Temporarily. Temporarily mad."

He started to sob without weeping tears, and even that was manly, in his new breaking voice. I sat up and put my hand on his crisp hair. In the morning he and I found an old potato bed and two rows of turnips among the weeds.

The tenth of December, and my twelfth birthday came. Mother gave me a book that she'd secreted among her things. For the first time since our fall, her cheeks and eyes glowed with pleasure. "This belonged to my mother, and now you shall have it." The book was leather-bound, old and very battered, entitled *Downland Flora*. All the plants of the chalk downs were in there, the color plates shielded by paper so translucent that the images beneath were visible as if through soft rain.

Mr. Dawes called on us. He carried a box containing a pudding and three Christmas crackers. "My sister will come on Christmas Eve with a duck, Mrs. Calvert. A few vegetables and you'll do handsomely." Miss Dawes duly came and we gave her fulsome salivating thanks. Then, later that same evening, there was a knock at the door. I opened it but there was only darkness outside. Then I saw a paper bag, and in it a bottle of beer. As I picked up the bag, the gate clicked and I looked up to see Lucy Horne vanish behind the hedge.

That first Christmas Day we polished our shoes, brushed our coats, and went to church. We weren't going to sit in our hole like mice. We slid to the end of one of the back pews and stared straight ahead. Behind me Daddy's strong voice rang out in the bass variation to "O Come, All Ye Faithful." O Come, Daddy, O Come. Edward sang the hymn loudly in Latin as he'd been taught at school. *Adeste fideles, laete triumphantes.* We left the church without looking back or stopping, even though Miss Dawes blurted, "Mrs. Calvert, Merry . . . ." as we passed. We walked on down the lane, and when it came to the turn for the Absaloms we halted, all three of us. At the Stour House there'd have been dinner waiting for us, guests gathering in the hall. Cries of delight at our tree with its glass balls as big as a man's hand and red as a man's blood, its tiny brass bells, its lights glimmering through angel hair like stars through cirrus cloud.

Mother clasped our hands together. "I can't go back to the cottage yet. Not today."

"No. A Christmas walk is in order." Edward was using his stout voice. "We can always have dinner later." And we strode on as if we were normal people, not creatures so clemmed that our stomachs were wringing inside us.

We went all the way out of the village to where the land spread out and up toward Beacon Hill. It was dry underfoot and Edward and I ran to and fro along the track, again and again, for the pleasure of being in the open, of being back on the hillside we'd known since we were able to walk. Edward inhaled lungfuls of downland air. "I don't know why we didn't come out here before, instead of staying cooped up in the cottage!" But I knew. It was because so much had become forbidden to us. Even as we ran and panted and laughed, there was a sense of truancy.

We helped Mother over the stile. Her legs had got so thin that her stockings were wrinkled at the ankles. We held her hands and pulled her to the top. Edward sang, *"Fal-de-ree, fal-da-ra, my knapsack on my back."*

At the top it was silent. We sat on a hillock that Edward said was made in the Iron Age. Then one by one we lay down on the soft springy turf among the dry rabbit droppings. We were warm from the climb, and the weather was mild. I tried to identify some of the downland flora but only managed buck's-horn plantain, a humble rosette of pointed leaves. It was edible, according to my new book, so Edward and I nibbled like rabbits. Like bitter parsley, we decided. Then I rolled onto my back and stared up at the bands of still winter cloud that blurred into the blue. A long time of peace elapsed.

Edward touched my cheek. "Ellen. You were nearly asleep."

In January I grew out of my boots. Edward put newspaper in his so that I could wear them to school. He found a pair of wooden clogs in the outhouse. When I came home we changed shoes. But soon it became clear from Edward's pigeon-toed walk that his feet had grown too. He went to look in the cash box under Mother's bed.

I went out into the garden. My feet slid over the ruts at the edge of the vegetable bed. I stamped and blew out a plume of white breath like a fire-eater. I tried to sing, but it turned into a sob. Edward came outside again. "I've been thinking."

"Oh Edward." I knew something was going to happen.

"There's not enough, Ell, not for three of us to go on like this—"

"Don't leave us. We'll die without you—"

"Nonsense. You'll do very well on the Parish money, and then—"

"Where will you go?" I was crying.

"Southampton."

"Oh, God—"

"There's a fortune to be made on the steamers, everyone knows that. And adventure. Who knows what I'll send back? Come on, Ellen. You'll live like kings."

"Edward. Oh, Edward."

He turned away. "I must tell Mother."

I wiped my face on my sleeve. My cheeks and eyes felt raw. I heard Mother give a broken sort of moan, a sound like a roosting hen.

In the morning I felt the first stubble on his chin graze my temple, his bony jaw and ear as he bent lower to whisper, "Keep Mother safe and study hard."

"Good luck, Edward. Don't forget us."

"It's for you I'm going, my dearest Ellen. So that's hardly likely."

He set off in his clogs down the lane. I watched him until he turned the corner. It was agony, but I had to, in case he looked back. He didn't look back.

Three weeks later came a letter. With a stamp like a tiny stained-glass window, there were so many colors in it. *Dear Ellen*, it read, *they used to call this land Darien. We have all been sick from the Atlantic swell. We are bound for Puntarenas and thence to San Francisco and then my hopes are for the Far East though it will lie in a westerly direction for me.*

Mother seized the envelope, raked the inside with her forefinger. "How could he send no money?"

I handed her the bank note, five American dollars, which had been enclosed in the fold of the letter. "In future we can get it from the company. That's what he says."

9

SPRING CAME, hot and late, and then a cloudless summer. Mother and I walked to Waltham and took the bus to Southampton, and made our way, at two in the afternoon, to the shipping office of Raymond & Rose, where we sat on hard chairs in the blessed cool and dimness of the wood-paneled room.

"So." The man behind the desk turned the pages of a ledger. "Edward Calthrop."

"Calvert." My mother spoke sharply. "He said his hopes were for the Far East."

But I didn't even know if that was true. I could imagine him in front of the mirror, thrusting out one leg, shading his eyes from an imaginary tropical sun, and saying "Edward Calvert, who took ship for the Far East."

"Calvert, Calvert." The man turned another page. "Ah. Here he is. Siam, ladies. Bangkok, Swatow, Hong Kong. Rice out, general cargo on return. On our *Queen of the Straits*."

My mother folded her hands together so that they could each comfort the other. She seemed unable to speak so I did it for her.

"It's simply that we haven't heard from him for so long."

The man nodded. He knew what it meant, for a seaman's family, to *hear from* him. "I'm sorry. He gave us no authority to stop back a portion of his wage." He dipped his nib in the well, pecked at the page. "There," he said, with satisfaction. This had been an easy task. "A note. Family inquired. It's all I can do."

. . . . .

I inked the holes in my stockings but when I sat down at my desk the holes slid to reveal crescents of white skin. Like the clock face that showed the lunar phases; Daddy sliding the brass lever to make the moon wax and wane, wax and wane. Temporarily, perhaps just for ten seconds, my father had lost his wits. Shot himself in the heart and got out of everything. No more pain and certainly no hunger.

"You've got half-moons peepin out on your legs," said Lucy.

"I know."

"You want to do them patches bigger. Or get yourself some darning wool like everyone else."

If $2a$ equals 10 what is a? Clearly a is for asinine, Miss Yarnold. Can there be a person alive who cannot see that a is 5? But yes, there are such persons, John Blunden and Daniel Corey for two, and Lucy for a third, and others, who all cry in protest, "But, miss. We've gone an learned two *fives* was ten. And now you says it's two a's that make ten!"

I met Miss Yarnold's eyes and saw a glint of tears.

Lucy nudged me. "Or you could try soot. It spreads better."

One Sunday in autumn I left the house, leaving Mother unfolding three yards of calico on the kitchen table. There'd been a discount on five yards but we couldn't run to five. Nonetheless she'd galvanized herself, taken herself to the haberdasher's in Waltham, and she was going to make drawers for us: "The light's good, darling," she'd pleaded, but I was too hungry to sit sewing. "I'm so slim now," she was saying gaily as I swung the door closed, "I can squeeze an extra pair in, I'm sure."

That gay tone I hated even more than the pleading.

I went by the back lanes even though they were wet and my left shoe leaked. The clouds broke late in the afternoon and I stopped by a field in the low sunlight and leaned on the gate, the field a wet vivid green, and a large pale cow rocking her head by the fence halfway down the hill. Lucy Horne was in the next field, leaning on the fence watching the cow. Beside her was a boy with a shock of walnut hair. When he sprang up onto the fence, I recognized him as Daniel Corey. Before I could move they saw me.

"Ellen," Lucy called, "come here."

I could have darted on down the lane, pretended I hadn't heard. I would have been hidden by the hedge in a second. But I was lonely.

Daniel was at the top of the fence when I reached them. He was wearing an enormous pair of breeches, so long that the knee cuffs came almost to his ankle. He didn't turn his head or say hello, just swung each leg over and sat on the top rail. "Dorc," he was saying. "Ready, Dorc."

"He's going to get up on Dorcas, if she'll let him." Lucy grinned at me. It was a sight. She had so many top teeth missing.

The cow stood, still rocking her head although there weren't any flies. Daniel perched his feet on the rail below the top, leaped up into the air, where he seemed to hover for a moment before falling deftly with his knees each side of the withers of the cow, who did not move. Lucy squeaked.

"Good Dorc," Daniel breathed.

Dorcas had deep folds on her pale neck. Her muzzle was the color of the lining in my mother's kid gloves.

"She's beautiful in't she," said Lucy.

"What would the farmer say?" I whispered. I didn't want to startle Dorcas.

"She's Daniel's. Well, his dad's. Do you fancy coming to ours for tea, Ellen?"

Lucy lived at the far end of the village street, on top of a high bank. I had always known there were cottages up there, but had never mounted the brick steps that led to them. Now I followed Lucy and Daniel up, placing my feet carefully, for the light was going.

Outside Lucy's door we took off our muddy shoes and went into a kitchen, where a gas lamp fizzed on the table and a man and a woman were packing eggs into cones of newspaper.

"Ellen, this is my dad and my nan," Lucy said. "Nan and Dad, this is Ellen."

"Three dozen and five," said the woman, without lifting her eyes. "Excuse us, dear. And six, makes three and a half dozen." She placed the newspaper cone into a wicker basket in the middle of the table. Lucy began a long, thorough bout of coughing.

"George Horne," said the man, who was as slight and dark as Lucy, raising his voice above the noise Lucy was making. "How do, miss. And four dozen," as he added another cone to the basket.

Lucy's cough tailed off into a deep sigh. "Oh lor, oh lor."

"Do you want the linctus, dear?" said her grandmother, without turning her head.

"Nope. Don't do any blimmin good." Lucy went to the oven and pulled out a metal tray, tutted at what she saw. "You didn't turn them."

"We can't think of everything," her father said. "And four and a half."

I realized I had not returned their greeting. "Good evening, Mrs. Horne, and Mr. Horne." I was going to add some pleasantry but the pies were there in front of me, lying in rows, the back ones dark brown, the front ones pale. It didn't matter; I was gobbling up the smell alone. My stomach fluttered, and I gasped through lips that were suddenly numb. As Lucy turned to look at me, I grabbed the door handle and ducked out into the garden. By the path I retched, the dusk abruptly deepened, and I sank to my knees. The stone of the path was cool and rough on my forehead.

A clink of knives and forks, and the gaslight very low. Lucy and her grandmother were sitting near the stove, tea towels on their laps. Lucy was sewing. And I, I realized, was sprawled under a blanket, taking up the whole of the couch. The embarrassment was instant: I struggled into a sitting position and saw Mr. Horne and Daniel Corey eating at the table. They'd been joined by another man with a square face in shadow. Daniel paused in his chewing but didn't turn his head. Lucy's grandmother held out a cup of tea. "Start with this, dear, and see how you go on."

My eyes drifted to a lone pie, a golden unburned one, on a plate edged with purple painted pansies. I couldn't imagine getting it into my stomach.

Lucy noticed. "We could put it in a bag for you, Ellen, if you don't fancy it now."

The tea was hot, barely milked, and as sweet as syrup. I held it in my mouth, afraid that I would retch again, and swallowed it in tiny scalding increments. Lucy sat down next to me and continued with her sewing. Her grandmother took a jug of gravy to the table and poured it over the men's helpings. They had mountains of mashed potato next to their pies and the gravy splashed over the crags and left high steaming lakes. "Capital, Betty," the square-faced man said, digging his fork into the mash. He was holding the fork in a strange pincer grip between thumb and forefinger. He met my eyes and lifted the fork as one might a glass, in salutation. He was missing the remaining three fingers on his right hand. I realized also that he had no pie on his plate.

"Evening, Miss Calvert," he said.

"This is Mr. Kennet," Lucy's grandmother said.

I took another hot gulp of tea. "How do you do, Mr. Kennet."

The man gave one slow blink and returned to his conversation with Mr. Horne. "Twin lambs." He shook his head. "Back last spring. Dead in their caul."

"And the pair weighing ten pounds," said Mr. Horne. "I'd have shot that dog."

"The vicar's lurcher, and all," said Mrs. Horne.

Lucy was doing a needlepoint panel of a bird perched upright on a twig, with a bright black eye and a questing beak, and currently no breast. "It was going to be a robin but we've got no more red thread. I could make it into a wren now or wait till Nan goes to Waltham. What do you think?"

"Do you enjoy embroidery, Miss Calvert?" Lucy's grandmother asked me.

I thought of the flowers, the white buds I'd stitched with Mother, the silk white on the rough white of the linen, that you could only see when the light fell on it a certain way. "Yes, Mrs. Horne. But there are . . . so many things to do in the day."

"Nan sells her decorated linens at the Women's Institute market," Lucy said. "Down the village hall on Thursdays. This one"—she nodded at her work—"he's going to market too."

Daniel threw himself onto the couch beside us and wiped his mouth. "That's the wrong shape for a wren, Luce. A wren's a little tub with her tail cocked up."

"And the vicar's only just paid Harvey Corey for the lambs," Mr. Kennet said. "Took him six months. Hasn't he, Dan? Paid your dad? Sit up, Dan, like a gentleman. These young boys, they do loll."

Daniel ignored him, and if anything spread his long legs further. "Hold your horses, Lucy, and wait for the red. Mrs. Horne, Ellen can eat her pie now, I'm sure."

Underneath, the pastry was just firm enough to hold, breaking when your teeth closed on it to divulge meat and onion and juices. The lid crackled. "Nan does flaky like no one else," Lucy told me.

The gas lamp fizzed. The kettle purred and Lucy filled the pot. Sleepiness dragged at my eyelids but I ate on, cramming in progressively larger bites of pie. The people in the room sat, sipping tea and digesting. Finally my plate was empty. The pansies had flecks of gilt in their centers and the edge was gilded too. I licked a finger and dabbed at the remaining flakes of pastry and put them in my mouth. Only then did Lucy's grandmother stand up and take the plate away from me. I rose slowly to my feet, and so did Daniel and Mr. Kennet, who hooked his lone finger under the handle of the egg basket and lifted it off the table.

"George. Betty," he said, sliding a brimmed hat onto the back of his head over a crown of hair the color of bleached corn.

"Goodnight, Bill." Lucy's father and grandmother spoke in near unison.

Then Lucy's father suddenly addressed me. "He had a good seat, Master Edward."

I'd seen Mr. Horne before, of course I had. Knee-deep in the waving sterns of hounds on the edge of the crowds at the Boxing Day meet, impassive as the jouncing hindquarters of my father's dock-tailed bay hunter wheeled in front of him, and Edward's gray pony started and stamped. A bowler-hatted man in the corner of my eye, because my gaze was on Daddy and Edward.

"You're the kennel man!" Hastily I tried to cover this gauche remark. "Thank you for the compliment, Mr. Horne. The compliment to Edward. I'll pass it on in my next letter."

Daniel turned to me. "Mr. Kennet and I will walk you home."

"Thank you so much for the pie, Mrs. Horne." I stepped out into the night hearing my mother's voice, in the singsong tone of "so much," and my face burned in the darkness.

In the morning I sniffed my fingers for the smell of gravy.

When dinnertime came at school, I began going straight to the lavatories, to keep well away from Lucy so that she wouldn't feel obliged to ask me to her house. Then I sat with Amy and Airey, the fatherless twins from the cottages by the river who, I had learned, wrote one with her right hand, the other with her left, so that they could lace their free hands together. Now that it was colder they leaned their folded arms not on their desks but on the top of the iron cage that enclosed the hearth, and laid their heads down to sleep so that by the time the others came back they each had one cheek rosy and creased from their sleeves. I'd have stayed there all night if I could.

≈

Winter came, and with it, my thirteenth birthday. Mother gave me a silk fan in a silk bag. The silk was the color of a tea rose and the fan opened to show a sepia line-drawing of an oriental scene: pagodas, bridges, long-tailed birds in the sky. The birds looked fat and good to eat.

"It's beautiful, Mother. Thank you." I folded the fan and returned it to its bag.

That Christmas there was no duck from Miss Dawes, and Mother and I didn't attempt to celebrate the feast. For a large part of the afternoon she paced up and down the lane. I lay on the bed and remembered last year, drowsing in the mild sunshine on Beacon Hill, the turf against my cheek and Edward lying beside me.

A letter had come from him recently, along with a pitiful amount of money, disbursed to the grocer, paying off half our mounting bill. *We've all been taken with dysentery and I have had to buy quantities of kaolin and morphine. Extremely unfortunate but not without comic aspects. I became so thin that when I sneezed my trousers fell down around my ankles. Stouter now however.*

"Is there something funny about a young man's trousers falling down?" my mother had asked when I laughed. "Both vulgar and flippant."

She'd stared at me; she had a new way of staring, unblinking and oddly concentrated, as if she were trying to bore into my mind with her tiny black pupils.

On Boxing Day the pipe froze outside, and split to show a wink of granular ice. I climbed over the rickety fence at the end of the lane to a well half-hidden by the nettles. I hauled off the cover in stages, resting by leaning against the well. The bucket thudded down onto ice, so I pulled it up and threw half a dozen large stones into the well. When the ice was broken up, I sent the bucket back down. When I pulled it up for a second time water streamed from a split in the side I stood, panting, watching the water pour back down the shaft.

I heard a clang and looked up to see someone closing the gate on the far side of the waste ground. It was a man in a wide-brimmed hat, moving slowly: as he raised the hat I saw that it was Mr. Kennet.

He came and stood beside me and we peered into the now empty bucket.

"Hello, Mr. Kennet. I broke it when I threw it down on the ice."

His maimed hand stretched into the bucket and inched crabwise over the split. Then he stepped away and stood for a moment, casting his eyes around. "Ah," he said, and went over to a fallen-down shack, a hen house, I thought, and tore a wide square of the tarred material off the roof. "Put this in and push it well down. No, the other way up. The underside is clean, look."

I did what he said.

"Now some string." He delved in his jacket pocket and handed me a bundle of twine. "Whip that around the outside, tight like a pudding. And then a stone in the bottom."

I bound up the lining and let the bucket down and filled it. He took the rope from my hands and began to haul. Soon the bucket was standing on the edge of the well. Water slopped, but only from the top. The repair was sound. The sun danced on the water and I realized what a beautiful day it was, clear and mild.

"Where did you come from?" I found myself asking.

"I work for Lady Brock." He jerked his head to the north. "At Upton Hall. My job's the kitchen garden, but sometimes I walk out this way."

Beacon Hill lay high and quiet beyond the flat fields, the sheep tracks on its sides sharply lit by low winter sunshine.

"It was your pie, Mr. Kennet." I realized it almost as I spoke.

"Pardon?"

"That evening at Mrs. Horne's house. It was your pie that I ate. You gave it to me."

"Oh yes." He nodded. "So I did."

"Thank you for that. It was extremely kind. Sometimes I feel faint, you see. It's just because I'm growing so fast."

He gave me a smile. "I was the same, your age."

"And thanks for mending the bucket."

"It won't last long."

"Neither did the pie!"

"Ha! Ha!" His eyes went into slits when he laughed. I laughed as well, too wildly. I couldn't remember the last time I had. Then we stood quiet again, but he continued to smile at me. He had such a nice smile, square at the edges like his face, showing good square teeth.

Someone far away started chopping wood, the ax blows carrying clear through the cold air.

Seeing that I had brought no container, he untied the bucket from its rope and walked with me to the fence. I had a sudden dread that he'd come to our door, perhaps see inside, how we lived. But he stopped as we reached the boundary. "Give my regards to your mother, miss."

I climbed over the fence and took the bucket from him. "You know her?" I was instantly ashamed at the surprise in my voice.

"I pruned your apple trees, once upon a time, at your old house," he said. "I expect it was before you were born." Then he turned his back and set off again over the waste ground.

"Who did you say?" Mother tipped her head at the mirror, this way and that.

"Mr. Kennet. He said he used to work for you and Daddy."

"Oh, William Kennet. Yes. We used to know him . . . What about him?"

"I just told you. He mended the bucket."

"Should I shingle my hair, darling?" Her hair was in a loose, greasy bun; she raked it with stiff fingers.

I was used to Mother's ways but this was too much and I snapped at her now.

"Must you be so offhand? He was very kind. Not only did he mend the bucket. He gave me his pie at the Hornes'—"

She wheeled on me, her face contorted by a sudden fury. "You went to George Horne's house? George Horne, who cleans up dog mess for a living. And his daughter a cretin, unable to write her own name." She went to the door and jammed her hat on her head. Loops of hair hung down unevenly on either side. I watched her make her way down the path, her shoes slipping off the backs of her feet so that the heels clopped on the stones. Her feet were so thin. Perhaps the hunger had shrunk her brain as well.

In the second week of January, Mr. Dawes sent Mr. Blunden to mend the pipe. It thawed enough to give us a trickle of icy water, and froze again. A yellow rime grew around the windows and the sink. I dragged in wet mossy logs, damp sacks of leaves, sticks, swathes of ivy and shards of bark that ran with woodlice. I dried it all as best I could but it still smoked. We sat by the smoke, feet propped on a chest because it was painful to set foot on the icy floor. I found an old sheepskin we'd brought from the Stour House and put it in the bottom drawer of the chest, and then I put my feet in the drawer and wrapped the sheepskin round until I could feel them again. At night we lay in our coats, side by side under a quilt with a carpet laid over the top, a Turkey rug, historically dark red, now brown, saturated with the smell of mice.

One afternoon I came home to find my mother kneeling in front of a sorry little heap of kindling and a dead match, and nothing in the scuttle but a smear of soot.

In the morning I went to Lucy.

"Lucy, we must have coal."

Her face was yellow in the winter light, her eyes very dark and blank. She twisted her mouth. "Wait for me after school at the top of your lane."

She appeared out of the dark with a lantern and a sack. "Come on." She spoke without breaking her stride.

"Where are we going?" I fell in behind her.

"To the sidings."

"The sidings?"

"The say-dings?" she echoed, mimicking. "May dyah. Not only does Ay have to show you *where* the say-dings are, but tell you *what* they are. You're the bitter end, you truly are."

I kept on following her through the dark. I didn't care what she said, as long as she led me to the coal.

"And your ma too. If she's so good at sewin why don't she come down the hall with Nan and Mrs. Broad and sew for George and Emily Rail, that lost the whole back of their house when the rick caught fire? Five children and not a stitch between them. Instead of prancin along the lane with her hat on sideways."

"We didn't know about the fire."

"Didn't know. Didn't know. The whole bloomin village saw it go up. Lady Brock ran up some nighties. And Mrs. Daventry from The Place. They turned up. *She* don't even go to church." She meant my mother. "She don't do nothin."

"No," I agreed.

"And now you've got no bloody coal."

"No."

"You take the biscuit."

"I only wish I could." I sighed. "I'd love a biscuit."

Lucy stopped, so abruptly that I bumped gently into her back. She turned round, holding the lamp so that it made dark hollows of her eyes. "What did you have for your tea?"

"Tea."

"Yes, tea," she said impatiently. "What did you have?"

"I just said. We had tea. With milk in."

"Holy Christ, Ellen."

In the dark we slid down over frozen mud and chalk onto the railway line. Above us there was a tangle of branches where the trees closed in, and down at the end of the line, a blockhouse and a square window filled with yellow light. Next to it, a coal truck, silent and black. Lucy doused her lamp. "Sam Pearce is in there. We don't want him to find us. No, we don't. So you just keep your mouth shut and your head down, and he won't see us at all."

Sam Pearce was young and fat with a small stoker's cap on the back of his head and shaven stubble above his ears. I could see one small eye, oddly thickly lashed and a thick eyelid too, like a pig's. He turned his head quite regularly, his jowl bulging over his collar. I realized that he was reviewing a spread deck of cards. We were in full darkness, keeping to the bank where our footfalls were soft.

At last we got to the truck. Up close it was a behemoth. I couldn't see how we were to reach the coal.

Lucy was picking her way down the bank onto the line. The track was bedded on sharp chunks of granite that ground together under her boots, making an electrifying *crick-crick-crick*. I crouched, paralyzed by the noise, and Lucy kept stock-still. Sam Pearce didn't look up. Lucy was waiting for me to give the all-clear: she couldn't see the window because the truck shielded her from the blockhouse. I made myself wave, and then crept sideways down the bank and onto the line. My eyes had been dimmed by the strong light from Sam Pearce's window but now I could see pieces of coal everywhere on the ground, under the truck and beside it. Lucy was already busy filling the sack. We laid each coal in as if it were porcelain.

A sudden, horrifying screech: a door, being forced open over a cindered step. Then the blockhouse light went out. Pitch-black, and heavy feet descending. Along the ground, the sweep of a torch beam in time with the same footsteps. Lucy fumbled for my hand and I clutched her fingers.

The beam traveled over the sharp stones and toward the truck. I squeezed my eyelids shut and saw a golden glare that dimmed and flared. But then I heard the scrape of shoe soles on grit as he turned on his heel. The torch beam swept away. The footsteps receded and the door squealed once more. Lucy's fingers slid from mine. The blockhouse light came on again and her face was before me, white as a chip of chalk.

"We're all right. Let's get a bit more in."

"Oh no, Lucy, please, let's go now—"

"I'm not shittin myself for half a bag of coal."

We filled the bag and sidled out from under the truck. I wondered how black my hands and face were. The soot seemed sticky; I'd have to get rid of it somehow with our sliver of soap. The door screeched open again, the feet tramped down the steps, and the torch flared over us, over my black hands, over Lucy's knee and a patch of raw skin the size of a halfpenny. And Sam Pearce a phantom behind the torch beam, laughing.

"I thought I heard some coal rats. Never thought it'd be you, Lucy Horne, and with such a fair friend and all."

He had a little rasp of a voice that came from high in his nose. He bent down and put his large warm hand around my upper arm. His huge fingers and thumb met. An odor came off him far deeper and ranker than any classroom air at Upton School.

"Get your sweaty paws off her—" Lucy yelled, throwing herself at him, but he caught her by the collar. The torch fell to the ground. In the gloom he swung us both toward the blockhouse. "Pick up the torch, Lucy Horne."

My voice turned to a high babble. "Please don't please don't touch me, Mr. Pearce, you may take the coal, please—"

"Not before I've had a bit o' company."

Lucy picked up the torch and began a shocking refrain. "Fuck you, Sam Pearce. Fuck you and your fuckin disgustin ways. You won't touch that girl, nor will she touch you—"

He laughed, the torchlight playing over his jowls, his eyes hidden. "Or what? Your little ferret of a dad'll come and see to me?" He gave a buzzing snort. "He wouldn't find the guts, not if he had till kingdom come." He pushed us ahead of him. "Now light our way or you'll dash your brains out on them steps."

We climbed the stairs to the upper door, Sam Pearce pushing in the small of my back and hooking Lucy's coat in his fist so that her collar fairly choked her. My knees were shaking too much to go at any speed. He shoved us ahead of him through the door and shut it. A kettle dripped and wheezed on the hob, and on the table by the window, next to the telephone, gnawed sandwich crusts were scattered over his deck of greasy cards. Every square inch of air in that room stank of him.

He stood there dwarfing the doorway. "Make yourselves at home," he said and sniggered.

I looked sideways at Lucy. She was licking her thin lips like a fox. I'd never seen her scared before, and the fear leaped higher in me too.

Just then the telephone rang. For an instant he took his eyes off us. Straightaway Lucy sent her foot shooting out to land between his legs. He screamed, buckling and burying both hands into his groin. Lucy danced in front of him. "That's what you get for being a filthy fucker!" She grabbed the coal bag as Sam, roaring, lunged at her. She fell with one of his huge hands clamped over her leg. I picked up the boiling kettle and swung it down on his head. Bellowing, he let go of

Lucy. She scrambled to her feet and we hurtled down the steps and into the dark.

We took a shortcut through the woods, lugging the full sack between us, stumbling over the hollows. Our breath sawed in our throats and we looked back and stumbled again, fearing a lamp beam swinging through the trees behind us, but all was dark. In the end Lucy came to a halt, her hands on her knees, coughing.

A weird high keening came out of my throat.

She put her hand on my shoulder and rubbed rhythmically, sucking her teeth. "Sorry, old pal. We should have gone when you said. I just wanted to get you more than half a bloomin bag. God damn Sam Pearce. Good work with the kettle. If only he'd got his privates scalded. That would put paid to him."

The white shape of an owl flitted along the treeline at the edge of my vision. It brought no comfort. "Oh, how . . . how revolting! We should report him!"

"*Report him.*" She creaked like a door. "Oh lor, oh lor. And who would believe us, you chicken? We were the ones thievin on the track. Sam Pearce would most likely say we were flatterin ourselves. 'As if I'd look twice,' he'd say."

We reached the Absaloms, and in the dim light from our window I saw my stockings were utterly torn.

"They were done for anyway, those stockings. Sell a bit of this coal to Bill Kennet, get yourself a new pair." Her own legs were scratched and bare.

I shook my head. "I couldn't sell the coal. I didn't come by it honestly. And I'm certain that Mr. Kennet isn't short of coal."

She was sardonic again, sucking her teeth, shoving her hands in her pockets. She bent to pick up her lamp and took a couple of backward strides down the path. "Try and wash your face before mornin. And don't you worry about men, dear. They ain't worth it."

10

ONE DAY IN FEBRUARY I woke to a liquid cheeping and chirruping and wondered why a warbler would come from the riverbank to our garden. But it wasn't a bird, it was water issuing from the pipe that served our outside tap, the pipe the ice had split during the freeze. And now came the thaw, its silence rent by the illusion of birdsong.

We moved carefully through the weakening cold, Mother and I. Meticulous with our coal, scrupulous with our firewood and kindling. Because at times we were sorely tempted to burn it all up at once, in one great fire festival, on a pitch-black night. Then, on a quiet March morning the sunrise shifted at last from behind the rowan tree out on the lane and my room was filled with new yellow light.

Mother and I lay, our hair frowsy on the pillow, our limbs trapped beneath the mouse-saturated carpet. Mother was blinking in the sunlight. The face she had now was a sunken version of her former face, with skin the color of unbleached flour falling into deep grooves either side of her mouth, and oddly huge nostrils. I watched her eyes wander over the ceiling and around the room as if she'd never seen it before.

"I think she's become a little unhinged," I confided to Lucy and Daniel. "The way she stares about."

Lucy looked somber. "She wouldn't be the first to go that way. That lived in the Absaloms, I mean."

Unexpectedly I found myself laughing. "Thank you, Lucy. How heartening."

"I'm just sayin," she said, already shame-faced, quailing under Dan's beetling glare. When he'd finished silently admonishing her he turned to me.

"She'll perk up come the spring, Ellen," he said. "I'm sure of it. Now, Saturday afternoon you're to come along with us. You need a change of scene."

On Saturday I followed them down a lane that ran along by the river in the lee of a high wall. We came to a halt beneath a line of elms, their branches still leafless against the clear sky, their tops untidy with the bundled nests of rooks. Lucy drew a key from her pocket.

"Where *are* we?" I said, but she took no notice, struggling as she was with the lock of a wooden door set into the wall. After a shove from Daniel, the door creaked open and we filed into a kitchen garden where the newly turned beds lay black in the sunshine. On the other side of a hedge at the top of the kitchen garden rose the upper story and peaked roof of a great brown house.

I clutched Lucy's arm. "This is the back of Upton Hall. How on earth do you come to have a key?"

"Lady Brock gave it me. She got sick of us climbin over." Lucy pointed. "There she is now."

And indeed there she was, a tall woman in a mackintosh pushing a man in a wheelchair along a stone path between the beds. She glanced in our direction, raised a long arm in a salute. The man in the wheelchair, a wraith tucked into coverlets and rugs, also lifted his hand.

"That's Sir Michael," Daniel said. "Gas got him in the War."

"Oh! Sir Michael!"

I gasped the name. I knew about the gas—everybody did. But he'd been upright the last time I'd seen him, greeting his guests in the ballroom of Upton Hall on Boxing Day. Beside him had stood a suit of armor polished to a brilliant silver, one gauntlet thrust out for the guests to shake. And I had done so, pink-cheeked and nicely plump in my tartan Christmas dress, well nourished on my father's rapaciousness—on Sir Michael's money, truth to be told, since my father had died owing him upward of three hundred guineas.

I sidled behind Daniel. I could have been carrying my father on my shoulders, his dead body in a peddler's pack, so enormous was my shame. I wished it would press me into the earth. "They mustn't see me," I whispered.

Lucy tutted. "They won't take any account of us. Look, they're goin now and all."

I watched Lady Brock turn the chair. The two figures receded and then disappeared through the gate at the top of the kitchen garden. "I don't care. I still want to go home."

"No, Ellen." Daniel was firm. "Not till you've had a look at our bolt-hole."

The shed stood among the greenhouses at the top of the kitchen garden. The light came from one small window. A polished charcoal stove, bearing an equally gleaming kettle, squatted in the middle of the room. There was a scuffed leather armchair and sundry folding camp stools and milking stools, as well as a wide flat tree stump. A low shelf bore a panoply of objects—lanterns and gas lamps, boxes and chests of wood and tin, enamel mugs. And there was a clean wholesome odor of compost.

Daniel picked up a tall cylindrical container bearing a scratched color picture of a girl in a white dress alighting from a horse-drawn carriage. He shook it by his ear, seemingly satisfied by the rattle.

"What's in there?"

"Lickrish." He went and crouched by the stove to light it. Lucy took the kettle and ducked outside, and I heard her filling it at a garden tap. "Whose shed is this?" I asked her when she came back.

"Mr. Kennet's, of course."

"Oh!"

"Didn't we say? We've been comin up here since we were little ones, Dan and me. When our folks wanted us out from under . . ." She spoke in an offhand manner, busy rummaging in her bag. Daniel sat without speaking on the tree stump, intent on levering the lid off the licorice tin. After a moment Lucy produced two school exercise books and held them out to me.

"I can't get the hang of the work, dear, you know that. I never could. And Daniel's got no patience with it anymore."

Daniel was still trying to open the tin, so bent on the task, it seemed, that he couldn't meet my eyes. His cheeks, though, were crimson.

I turned the books in my hands. Both were wretchedly dog-eared and ink-blotched, the arithmetic branded with red crosses, the grammar sentences petering out like tracks into desert sand. The owners would turn fourteen this year, as would I, and school would be finished for us all. Miss Yarnold had spent seven years trying to teach Lucy to read and write, and she had failed. Daniel was already far more use at a cattle auction than he was behind a rickety deal desk that was starting to squash his sturdy knees.

"Do help us out, dear."

Lucy's voice was soft. I looked up, but she wouldn't meet my eyes. She too had a rare dark flush on her cheekbones.

I sat down on a milking stool. "What will we do for pen and ink?"

The lid popped off the licorice tin, and I was given two pieces, along with a nib pen and a vial of dried-up brown ink, which we woke with a drip from the kettle. I started to write up Daniel's lesson, making sure the numbers and letters were as tall and wavering as his, my jaws fused by a glorious black salty sweetness that seemed to run directly into my veins. "Oh, this is delicious," I told him, somewhat slushily, from between clenched teeth. "Now, I'm making some purposeful errors—"

"Oh, Ellen!"

"Come on, Dan," Lucy said. "Miss Yarnold don't believe in miracles. We don't care about the marks. We just can't stand to do it ourselves."

Lucy's figures I made small and hatched and oddly spaced, the spelling carefully idiosyncratic. Pausing to deliberate how Lucy might spell "harbor," I stared up at the far wall of the shed, behind the armchair. Great towers of earthenware pots had been stacked there—long ago, it seemed, for the ones at the bottom were greened with lichen and moss, and some were cracked and crumbling. Lucy followed my gaze.

"I don't know how Bill sits there, under that lot," she said. "They're an accident waiting to happen."

"All our days are numbered, Lucy Horne."

Mr. Kennet was standing smiling in the doorway. He tipped his hat at me. "I see they've collared you at last, Miss Calvert."

I nodded, rendered mute by licorice and a sudden shyness.

He took four mugs and a teapot and caddy from the shelf. I started up to help him, afraid that the things would fall from his few splayed and cradling fingers, but Daniel gave me a shake of the head and I sat down again.

"Did you know," Mr. Kennet went on, "I found that lickrish tin in the wood at Dammstrasse, in 1917?"

Lucy was gaping. "So it's—how old, Dan?"

"We're in 1934," said Daniel, "so it's . . ."

"Seventeen," I supplied.

"Seventeen years old," Lucy said, "and you're givin it us to eat? That's disgustin. Shame on you, Mr. Kennet, for never tellin us."

Mr. Kennet arranged the tea things on the tree stump and sat down in the armchair, his eyes half-closed in quiet mirth.

"Do you want some baccy rolling, Bill?" Dan said.

"Don't you 'Bill' me." A friendly growl. Dan ducked his head, smothering a grin. Mr. Kennet returned to his story. "I found that tin in the grass and tucked it in my pack on our way to Messines Ridge. We were still deaf from the mines, so we were a pack of ghosts, it seemed like, with boots that made no sound."

Dan and Lucy nodded, quiet and attentive. They had heard this before, and it was not a time for questions.

"Sun rose higher, and soon it was a broiling hot morning. Seven o'clock we went forward. Then came my bit of shrapnel. Dan's father, and Lucy's, they went on to Passchendaele, but I came home. All three of us came home in the end."

Daniel rubbed his chin. "I've always thought how funny it is, Luce. That both of us had uncles that copped it, and both of us had fathers that lived."

Lucy cackled. "We couldn't have had dads that copped it, could we. 'Cause then we'd never have been born. You great lummox."

"Colonel Daventry came back all right," Daniel went on with his thoughts, unperturbed. "But Sir Michael was properly crocked up. There's no sense in it."

"No sense or meaning." Mr. Kennet cast his eyes at the ceiling. "Who else, now? Mr. Parr, of course. Of Parr's Mill. He drove ambulances, got a medal for it too. Old Mr. Parr, who had the mill before, was his uncle. But old Mr. Parr lost both his sons at the Somme, and so now that he's dead too, the mill has fallen to the present Mr. Parr, his nephew, being the survivor of that generation."

I knew who Colonel Daventry was; we used to see him on Boxing Day when the hunt left from The Place, his house with its huge courtyard at the front. A bright, friendly ginger-haired man offering a stirrup cup to the Master of Hounds. Mr. Parr was less distinct. Tall, I fancied, perhaps fair-haired, standing next to Lady Brock in church. I couldn't be sure. There were a lot of such men in the front pews. Mother and I went so seldom that I never got to tell them apart. It wasn't as if they were going to speak to us.

"Miss Calvert, I would like to say . . ." Mr. Kennet cleared his throat. "I would like to say that Captain Calvert fought very bravely at the Cratern. At St Eloi."

The kettle burbled slowly to the boil. My father was not singled out for valor but all the same I had heard it before as a young girl, that he had shown courage under the guns. But I had only a grain of pride left, the rest blasted away by my searing embarrassment at the mention of his name.

"I'd very much prefer it if you called me Ellen, Mr. Kennet."

"Right you are." He proffered the tin. "More lickrish, Ellen?"

"No, thank you." It was still clinging to my teeth. My tongue felt stained dark with it. I started to smile. "It's only the tin that's seventeen years old, isn't it. Not the licorice itself."

He winked. "Bassett's," he whispered. "Bought it in Waltham."

From that day on, I completed homework for Lucy and Dan. We would meet in Mr. Kennet's shed, and sometimes he would join us for a cup of tea. At other times we'd see only his back bent, digging, or the shadow of his hatted head in one of the greenhouses. We could come and go as we pleased, eating everything as we traveled the lanes. Our diet changed with the seasons: we nibbled the stalks of fresh long grass, pulled honeysuckle flowers, then blackberries. We fell upon the hazel trees, eating the nuts unripe, the green shells bending between our molars, our tongues and teeth seeking out the sour white flesh. Even the squirrels had more continence. One day I went with Daniel and Lucy back to the Stour House. My old house, that I hadn't seen since we left: I agreed on impulse. Dan's friend John Blunden, who used to mow the orchard with his father, came too. John told us that a family who made marmalade lived there now: nobody liked them, and I was glad of that. So I joined them, and we took apples from the orchard that used to be mine, climbing the wall and bagging the windfall cookers. We did our thieving down at the far end where the brambles grew and I tried not to raise my eyes toward the house. But all the same I caught a flash of red brick through the trees: the back of the laundry, it was, and it hit me in the heart. And afterward I couldn't smile, not even when we baked the apples in Mr. Kennet's stove and Dan tried to make John eat a piece of cooked worm. As they scuffled on the brick floor, bringing Mr. Kennet from his planting in high dudgeon, I wondered what I had been thinking of, to visit that house again. As if it could ever be all right.

When we went back to school I continued to sit with Amy and Airey at dinnertime, but now Miss Yarnold took to supplying us with dry rolls, one for each of us. But not every day, and not on regular days either, though we tried to work out a pattern. Then I overheard her with Miss Dawes in our playground at break time. "I don't have a great deal of surplus, in my personal economy," Miss Yarnold was saying, "but sometimes I confess I overbuy on dinner rolls, and they do end up here in school for the fatherless girls."

And Miss Dawes replied, "That's very warm-hearted and commendable. Just make sure"—and she leaned closer to Miss Yarnold—"that they don't come to *rely* on them."

"My dear, what do you mean?"

"Simply that the families in question, assuming the girls are fed at dinnertime, give them even shorter commons at night."

"Oh," said Miss Yarnold.

I was in the corner by the fence but my loitering stance caught her eye, and I blushed for shame at eavesdropping. She cleared her throat and bustled inside, and the next day summoned me. "Here is threepence from my purse," she said, holding out the coins. "In return you shall assist me in the classroom. Start by taking a little lesson with . . ." Her eyes traveled over the classroom as she listed the names. That afternoon I took charge of the twins Amy and Airey, and the Rail boys. Ernest and Stanley Rail were the children who'd lost everything in the fire that had consumed the back of their house when the rick caught alight—the boys for whom my mother and I, to my shame, hadn't provided a stitch of clothing. They'd been thrown from the top window into waiting arms like a pair of puppies. Ernest Rail was the older and smaller of the two, with knobbed shoulders and a tiny triangular mouth.

We huddled in a circle near the fire and I returned to the problem of 2a. "Consider twin lambs in their caul," I suggested. "Together they weigh ten pounds. So how heavy is one of the lambs?" Silence. They fastened their eyes on their boots. I put out my hands to Airey. "Ten fingers, look. Ten pounds. Two hands. Two lambs." But Airey clenched her own hands in her lap.

"Are they dead or alive?" asked Stanley Rail.

"It doesn't matter."

"It does. If they was dead, I wouldn't bother weighing 'em."

Amy sucked her teeth. "I bet they was dead. Mr. Corey had a lamb that weighed ten pound on its own. So two lambs that didn't weigh more 'an ten pound wouldn't be worth bothering about. Stan's right."

Airey put up her hand.

"Yes, Airey?"

"Ellen, what will you buy with your threepence? Will you get a lardy cake from Mundays? I could go a slice of that."

There was another silence. I was about to let my spread hands fall when Ernest Rail reached over and tapped my right palm. "Five, miss. One lamb weighs five pound."

Thanks to Miss Yarnold, I managed to set our grocer's bill on a downward slope. Mrs. Legg, the grocer's wife, was pleased. "Because of your worry, dear, as much as the money. Because of it being on your shoulders. I'm not allowed to write it off, you do know that, dear?" Although my coal was husbanded in a couple of barrels out by the fence where Mother couldn't find it, there still wasn't enough, and as it grew colder once more, Mother started to go to bed during the day. Mr. Kennet roasted chestnuts for us and I came home in the dark with sooty fingers, already hungry again by the time I reached the Absaloms. My birthday came, my fourteenth, and this year Mother gave me her Bible. It was a true lady's Bible, the white leather cover embossed with silver. Her confirmation cards were tucked inside.

"Mother, really, you shouldn't. At least keep these. They're from your old friends." The cards mostly bore pictures of lilies, and the girls, who were called Ianthe, Vera, Gretel, wished Mother almost identical sorts of good luck for her confirmation, which they were sure would go swimmingly.

Mother took the cards from me. "Those girls . . ." Her eyes wandered around the room. "I can't remember who they are now."

After Christmas I took to walking to keep warm, and while I roamed the lanes I pondered my future. Lucy was going to the kennels when she turned fourteen—she was three months younger than me—but I was staying at school, filling inkwells and tutoring the likes of Amy and Airey and the Rail boys, until something else happened to me. Perhaps nothing would, and I would remain there at Miss Yarnold's side forever. I couldn't allow that to happen.

One day in February I climbed up into the attic, thinking that there might be some unfound books or papers there to distract me from my empty belly. In the gloom I first laid hands on a sheaf of magazine pages featuring women displaying underwear and had a sharp memory of Edward, young, mocking, red-lipped. How long, now, had he been gone? Over two years, and the money orders he sent were scant and rare as April snowfalls and as quickly melting. I wondered sometimes, had I been the high seas adventurer, if Mother and Edward would have loved me as she and I loved him.

Underneath the magazines there was a dark board book disfigured by the droppings of insects and mice. I brought it downstairs, in a shower of muck, cobwebs, and dust.

Typewriting. A Practical Manual Based Upon the Principles of Rhythm and Touch. By W. R. Sedley. I turned it over. The back had been eaten off but there was an odd-smelling oiled paper sleeve that the mice had not liked. I drew out a folded keyboard made of thick card, and laid it flat on the table. The first eight pages of the book had been fused together by damp, so I began at Lesson Three. *The top row of letter keys. 1. The letters E, R, U and I. Place your forefingers on the starter keys and engage them in reaching up from F to R and J to U.*

"Look, Ellen." Mother was coming into the room, her hands held out flat and wide apart in front of her. Across her spread palms, a yard of Nottingham lace.

"This is for you, dear. For your birthday." She smiled. "I had it on my dressing table, do you remember? The green velveteen cloth underneath and then this runner of lace. I put my tortoiseshell tray next to it, with my two tortoiseshell brushes, the hairbrush and the clothes brush, and my comb."

The lace floated on my palms. When I shut my eyes I could hardly feel it. In a shaft of interior light I saw the open doorway to her bedroom, the brushes gleaming in the morning sun, and through the sun came a sweet caramel odor, because downstairs in the kitchen Jennie had let the milk catch in the pan.

"Mother, I've had my birthday. It's ages till the next one."

Her chin quivered with impatience. "I don't care. I want to know if you remember this lace." Her fingers dug into the crook of my elbow. "Do you?"

Her eye sockets were an alarming lavender. She was wearing a thick dressing gown over a draggling skirt. Her calves stuck out as thin as young coppice poles. As I looked, she belched surreptitiously and rubbed her hand over her stomach. She had been bilious frequently of late.

"Mummy, I don't think you're quite well—"

"It's simply indigestion, a little bit of indigestion, that's all."

She was far too prompt.

. . . . .

Dr. Bell had large hairless hands of the palest pink, with fingers so fat they appeared to have no knuckles. He laid Mother on his couch and placed the hands over her stomach. One by one, and then in pairs, the fingers gently dug until Mother gave a yelp and drew up her knees. The nurse produced a shining bowl and Mother raised her head to spit into it.

The doctor patted her shoulder. "You may rest there on your side, Mrs. Calvert, while I ask your clever daughter if she knows what the pylorus is."

"Sounds like a kind of snake." I spoke unsteadily. Here in the clean room, with its white-sheeted couch and shining bowls, Mother seemed far more wretchedly sick.

"Ha, ha." Dr. Bell smiled. "Not bad. The pylorus is a ring of muscle designed to keep the stomach closed. With certain digestive problems the pylorus, or pyloric sphincter"—his fingers bunched like a hand of bananas—"goes into spasm, like so"—the fingers rippled unnervingly—"and the result is . . . nausea!" The last word spoken triumphantly, as if he'd performed a magic trick. His fingers were white where he had bent them.

My mother was leaning her head on her hand, a whimsical smile on her face. As I watched, her lids fluttered: she was preening at the doctor. Even in these circumstances she had found a way to be embarrassing.

"Mother, for heaven's sake listen!" I hissed.

Dr. Bell lifted his head. "Nurse, please fetch Mrs. Calvert a cup of tea. Miss Calvert and I will sit next door for a chin-wag."

"The mass is the size of a grapefruit," he said. "And she's emaciated. How did it come to this?"

I turned my shoulders away from him. "We aren't big eaters," I said finally. "And we have to . . . we both wrap up warm. I couldn't have *seen* anything. And she's never complained!"

Dr. Bell sighed, then smeared his bulky fingers over his shiny black-clad knees. "Well. I'll send her to the Borough Hospital in Southampton."

I had half a crown in my pocket, and nothing else until next week. "How on earth will we pay?"

He soothed me. "There is provision at the Borough. A board, for funding cases like these. I must advise you to prepare your mother— and yourself, for that matter. We're not miracle workers."

"Look at her. I can't *prepare* her!"

Dr. Bell's eyes were blue, watery, and devoid of offense. "I'm sure you'll do your best, Miss Calvert."

Mother became very excited at the prospect of the Borough. Immured in damp, cold, and silence as she was, her main entertainment walking to a village where no one spoke to her and whose shops she had no money to patronize, the hospital represented cleanliness, warmth, bustle, and above all, kind people—people who'd take notice of her, care for her, and address her without sneering or poking their tongues in their cheeks. For my part, I was chiefly interested in the possibility of food. When I mentioned it, Mother licked her lips. "I'm quite sure they'll serve liver," she said. "It's so nutritious." She'd taken to rubbing the top of her stomach tenderly, with a certain amount of pride. "You won't be able to eat before the operation, Mother."

She snorted, and I looked up. She was smiling at me, her proper smile, not the crooked smirk of recent times, and I saw for an instant the woman she had been years ago, when Daddy was our rock and mainstay and her true love. "Goodness, Ellen. That *will* make a change."

"Miss Yarnold wants you," said a classmate, a girl called June Broad, as we buttoned our coats to leave school for the day. June gave me the usual up-and-down stare that she and her friends had now perfected, as if to say: What an *object*. They were all growing busts, June and the other girls, and June's overflowed the tops of her brassiere cups like dough rising from a bread tin.

"Did Miss Yarnold say why?"

June shook her head. Her curls were tight today, and they wobbled against her slabs of cheeks. "But she doesn't look pleased." Looking very pleased herself. There was very little wrong in June's world today.

Miss Yarnold was sitting behind her desk, sideways on the chair, lacing her boots. She waited until the boys had gone before doing this, because she needed to flip her skirt up over her knees. Alone of all the women in the village, she favored these voluminous skirts, full, of an uncertain length. She raised her head, cheeks pink. The room was now empty save for us. "Ellen, I hear that your mother's ill."

I nodded. "The operation's on Thursday. Dr. Bell says there's a mass." I hadn't spoken that word to anyone. My eyes burned, and I closed them. I felt her hand on my arm.

"I'm so sorry, my dear."

"Thank you," I blurted, and opened my eyes just enough to hurry from the room.

I swung through the doorway and clattered down the path. I ran home, faster and faster down the lanes, sobbing and splashing through the puddles, until I was throwing open our gate, with a taste of metal in my throat from panting so hard, and Mother was at the door, saying, "Whatever is it, whatever is the matter?"

"Nothing." I scrubbed at my eyes. "The wind was in my face. I went at a gallop!"

And she suddenly laughed. "Oh, Ellen, honestly, you are a card!"

We sat side by side in the front of the bus to Southampton. It was young Mr. Staveley driving: he'd not long passed his test, he told us, and took a good run-up at the hills. It amused us, how he leaned into the corners as he turned the wheel. He was lame from birth and put his whole heart into the driving.

It was mild now and the blackthorns dripped in the sunshine.

I thought of the last time Mother and I had come together to Southampton like this, in quest of Edward and his money. One of his recent letters had contained a photograph of a tall young man with the sun almost bleaching out his head and shoulders. "Like a sea god," Mother had said, and stroked the face. I didn't care about the photograph. Edward was alive in every sentence of those letters. I took out the last one and read it aloud to her now.

"*Dearest Ma and Ellen,*" I read, adopting the usual slightly gruff tone for verisimilitude, "*Today at five in the morning we went through the Sunda Strait. Steaming hot needless to say. My cat jumped overboard after a flying fish, poor soul. Probably the best fate for him, since the Skipper has ordered a muster of ship's cats at first light. He will line them up on the quarterdeck and keep the best three mousers. All others will be given their papers and sent ashore.*"

I stopped for Mother to giggle in her usual place, but she sat quietly, with a smile, staring out of the window.

"Go on, Ellen."

"*Where, no doubt, they will be either 1. Captured and held to ransom by the local rats; 2. Satayed by the warehousemen and sold diced, on peeled sticks, to unsuspecting travelers; or 3. Made into the softest furry hats for those babies born in the three days of fresh breezes they comically refer to as Winter . . .*"

We both laughed indulgently at this, veterans of winter that we were. General Winter, Napoleon had called him. I held Mother's hand. Her fingers tightened around mine.

"Will we see the sea soon?" she said.

11

A SISTER WINGFIELD ushered Mother smoothly away. Forty-five minutes, she told me, "to give Mother a wash and brush-up, and for Mr. Fairchild to see her. Have no fear, Miss Calvert." She accompanied me halfway down the corridor, adding, "Ladies get more upset when they have family present, so let's spare her that, hmm? There's a lovely view from the new garden."

I walked the length of a laurel hedge, pacing in what I took to be a mature, collected fashion, my hands clasped in front of me. I stood and sniffed the salt in the air, and wondered how I would get the money to wire Edward, and what I'd find to say. That would depend, of course, on the operation tomorrow. Dr. Bell had told me that Mr. Fairchild would "open her up and have a look-see." What he saw, I gathered, would determine whether or not he would perform further surgery. Dr. Bell had made to pat my hand again but I'd removed it hastily from my lap, diving for my handkerchief. "So we'll have to play the waiting game for now, you and I, Miss Calvert. Ha, ha."

Mother was sitting bolt upright with her legs shrouded in the sheets, straight out in front of her, her arms by her sides and her hair shockingly loose. "All neat and presentable," said the nurse. "Sister will be along to fill you in, and then you'll have to start thinking about your bus."

I sat down beside the bed and the nurse went out. Mother had her eyes closed, mercifully. Without opening them she said, "Oh, I think they gave me something nice in that tea. I do feel awfully woozy." A strand of hair fell across her mouth. Rather than lift her hand she blew it away. I reached out and tucked it behind her ear.

Suddenly she opened her eyes. "Do you remember Edward and the sherry trifle?"

She talked about this from time to time, how when Edward was four he'd gorged himself on sherry trifle in the kitchen while Cook was cleaning leeks with the tap running and didn't hear him come in; and how he'd wandered unsteadily through the sunroom where she and Daddy were having cocktails, saying, "Lay I down, lay I down and don't bend I," before being heartily sick on the steps outside. I was a babe in arms at the time, and often told her so, but she always asked me if I remembered.

I forced myself to smile. *"Lay I down and don't bend I."*

But she just blew out another breath.

Sister Wingfield came in and consulted her brooch timepiece. "Time for Mother to have a sleep. Mr. Fairchild will operate first thing tomorrow and his secretary will telephone Dr. Bell during the course of the morning. If you go to the surgery at twelve, you'll be able to speak to him before coming back."

"Mayn't I just come anyway?" I got to my feet. "And not wait for the call?"

The sister ushered me away from the bed and removed a pillow from behind Mother's back. She lowered Mother onto the remaining pillow before hooking her arm under Mother's knees and shifting her down the bed.

"Ah." Mother sighed. "That's comfy. Bye-bye darling."

Sister led me to the door. "Wait for the call, my dear. Visiting hours are three till five."

I'd never been alone at the Absaloms before. For a short while after Edward left, I feared that if Mother had to stay somewhere else overnight I'd be left among the brambles and nettles and the gaping sink in the kitchen. But I'd been young then. When I got home I put a small fire in and toasted the leftover bread, which I ate with an entire tin of sardines. Afterward I typed for a while on my cardboard keyboard, leaving fingerprints of fish oil. Then I made tea and had it in bed, where I reread Edward's letters, followed by *Downland Flora*. I fell asleep at "horseshoe vetch."

At a quarter to twelve the following day, I got up from my desk and went to wash my hands. Lucy followed me to the cloakroom. "Miss says I can walk you to Dr. Bell, if you need the company."

We met each other's eyes for the first time that day. Her gaze was currant-dark, unreadable.

"Why don't you come with me as far as your turning?"

We set off, our hands in our pockets, through the thin sunshine. There were spats of water shining on the road. Neither of us said anything until we got to the turning, when Lucy spoke. "Nan says you're welcome at ours for your tea tonight. Or tomorrow night, if you prefer."

"Thank you."

"It'll be poached egg either way, so take your pick." She smiled and set off, coughing merrily on her way. I never knew anyone so vigorous who did so much coughing. It was as normal to her as breathing. I kept waiting for her to grow, and get pink in her cheeks, but it never happened. She was who she was, it seemed. Small and high-shouldered, sallow in the face, and missing in the teeth, which you would never know if you weren't familiar with her, because she only let herself grin and guffaw with those nearest to her. I was one of those nearest to her, and I counted it a privilege, because I could not ask for a better friend.

The surgeon shook my hand and kept his friendly piercing eyes on me as he spoke. "We need tea, Sister Wingfield. Tea for all of us, if you please, and a goodly supply of your delicious ginger parkin, what say you, Miss Calvert?"

An orderly came in with a loaded tray. Mr. Fairchild and the sister distributed tea things with medical efficiency. Then the sister sat down beside me. "You must prepare yourself," she began in a hollow voice, "for some very grave news—"

"The growth can't be removed." I swallowed. "That's obvious."

"Thank you, Sister Wingfield." Mr. Fairchild lifted his hand. "We're a certain way beyond that, it seems. Yes, indeed. Miss Calvert's ahead of us here."

"How could she . . . ?" My voice wouldn't behave, it warbled up the scale. I cleared my throat. "How did it get this far?"

"Well, now." Mr. Fairchild stirred his tea. "This is a very sad matter. A gastric tumor produces no particular distinctive symptoms, do you see. A little indigestion, a little nausea, a little bloating: all everyday ailments, which is quite what your poor dear mother took them for. The cancer spread too far and too fast for me to produce any good result by taking it out. I'm very much afraid it is a case of comfort and solace, in the form of care and strong medicine for her, and for yourself, young lady, the consolation of your good friends in the Parish."

The sister leaned forward, put a hand on my arm. She began telling me how they would move Mother to the Old Infirmary at Waltham for her "last days with us," a place "simple in the extreme" but one more suited to her needs than our home, and where I could go to visit her whenever I wished. But I wished only that the sister would shut her mouth. I clamped my knees and teeth together, trying to keep it away from me. But it was in vain. I was in it up to my neck. She'd been clean and young and beautiful and now look at her. Look at us, living in filth and dreck, with Edward gone and a carpet on our bed. Daddy wasn't mad. He was just a wastrel and coward who had taken a coward's way out after robbing us. Left us in our coal dust and our filthy worn linen and our dry potatoes. I stood up, and a huge sob escaped me.

"He's done for her," I cried. "He's killed her at last."

They stood up too, but I pushed past them and ran down the

corridor. "Mother!" I cried. I reached her door before the sister. The curtains made her bed a battle tent and she a shrunken general. I slapped my own cheeks and screamed.

Sister Wingfield bound me across the chest with a heavy forearm. A nurse came and drew the curtain.

"Who's to say if she'll be alive or dead," Lucy said, as she sat with me by Mother's bedside one Saturday. "By the time he comes, I mean."

For the first month or so Mother had spoken every day, swimming up from the depths to say, "Good morning, darling." But as March moved into April, it took her longer to surface. Edward was on his way, but nobody could say how long his journey would take.

I sighed. "Who indeed."

We were both doing embroidery, Lucy with unthinking facility and I with a laboriousness I welcomed, since something had to be done with my mind and fingers while I took a rest from reading aloud. I was working my way through *Ivanhoe*, which, Mother used to lament, she had never read.

"Where did those biscuits come from?" Lucy asked.

The bag sat on Mother's bedside cabinet, giving off a gorgeous buttery smell. My tongue was already tasting the delicious crispness of well-toasted shortbread. "Mr. Kennet. I didn't see him—the nurse told me. I suppose he didn't realize she was beyond eating. It was extremely kind of him anyway."

"Ellen. For someone with brains . . . they're for *you*."

I walked the five miles to Waltham, sat at Mother's side for two or three hours, and then walked home again, reaching the Absaloms as the late April dusk fell. Mother began to sink more deeply into slumber. One evening Miss Dawes pushed delicately at the gate of the Absaloms. I was by the front door, having only just returned from Waltham.

"Miss Calvert. I've come about the move."

I turned and went back to her. There was no question of her entering my house. "I beg your pardon?"

"You can hardly stay here," she went on. "With no one to look after you."

I laughed. As if there'd ever been anyone to look after me.

Her dry fingers closed over each other, twisting her heavy silver rings. One had a ruby, which on that day was a dull black. "Miss Calvert, you can stay with us. And we'll help you to consider your future."

"You're terribly kind," I told her. "But I can't consider moving until Mother dies. This is our home, you see."

Edward arrived on the tenth of May. I went to Waltham to meet him at the Buck's Head. I entered into the gloom of the public bar, a place I had not visited in my life. There were no women, and no one sitting, for all that there were plenty of chairs and tables. As I made my way through the standing men, one of them turned from the counter and said, "Ellen." I stepped back and put one hand to my face, I couldn't help it, because he was six foot, walnut-brown, and endowed with a scar that plowed across his cheek and pulled his lip down.

"A cable parted." His voice was the same but deeper. "I was lucky it didn't take my head off."

"Good God. Edward."

He laughed. "Would you care for a shandy?"

"I certainly would not." I had no idea what a shandy was. "Where's your belt?" I demanded, because his trousers were held up by a piece of thick twine. "The one you made a hole in with the awl?"

"I sold it to get home. Ellen, you're weeping." He himself was half laughing. "Now, for pity's sake. A cup of tea, Maisie," he called. "A cup of tea with sugar, please, for my sister here."

There he was, a man, calling "Maisie," offhandedly, though he must have known her not more than an hour. Of course he knew how to make himself at home. He'd done so in all the seaports in the East. He pulled a chair out for me. I sat, the tears flowing down my chin. He proffered a handkerchief. I placed it squarely over my face and nearly choked with the effort of keeping the sobs from braying out. "I'm making a spectacle," I mumbled.

"This is the Buck's Head, not Bishop's Tearooms. No one's even looking."

He'd been crying for Mother on the boat, in the Channel, to leeward, convinced she had died already. "I don't know if she'd want me to see her. The state you say she's in." He looked into his tankard. His lip drooped further. It dawned on me that he was afraid.

"She just looks like a thin little old woman." I was gentle. "Nothing more alarming than that. I expect you realize they've been giving her morphine. That's a drug—"

"I know what morphine is, Ellen, thank you."

We stopped at the butcher's, another place I'd never seen the inside of. Edward fancied a stew, one like Cook used to make, he said, with everything melting. Then to the greengrocer's: he was astonished to learn that I had no onions at home, that Mother and I had never put in a vegetable garden, that we had no stored provisions. "No wonder you're about as fat as a hat stand," he said, buffing me on the elbow as we walked home with our meat and vegetables in a hessian bag slung over his shoulder.

"You don't look overly prosperous yourself."

"*Pruss-press.*" He hooted. "That's quite a burr you're getting, Ell."

I was looking away from him when he spoke, and it felt for an instant as if my old young brother, the one I knew, was by my side. The voice a little lower, a little hoarser.

"It's this way." I pointed down Rule Street. "For the Infirmary."

He cried when he saw her, as I knew he would, shoulders rising like a bellows, a long series of breaths forcing themselves through his pursed lips. In return she rolled her head from side to side on the pillow, eyelids fluttering, blowing a little white scum onto the edges of her lips. I had to put a stop to this. "Try to be quieter," I said gently. "You're upsetting her."

He collapsed sideways onto the chair, smearing the tears across his face. She continued to roll her head.

"Take her hand, Edward."

He turned himself toward the bed. Her hand was on top of the covers. He gathered it in his own large brown hand, as careful as if it were a shrew mouse. "Where's her ring?" he muttered.

I gestured at her neck, at a fine chain. "Her fingers are too thin."

Her head became still. She closed her mouth and the breath whistled through her nose.

"Mummy," Edward said after a moment, "it's me. Edward."

He bent his head to cross the threshold at the Absaloms. I followed him into the cave of the parlor. I'd made a great effort in recent days with the mold on the walls. He set the bag down on the floor, picked it up again, and stood motionless. I blew on the embers in the range, added kindling and coal, shut the door, and opened the vent.

"Did no one help you?" he said at last.

I took the meat out of the bag. It was heavy and damp in its grease-proof paper. "Mr. Dawes—you remember him, the Parish officer?—he's been very helpful, he and his sister. Miss Dawes." I pushed the blunt knife through the tough outer layer of an onion. "We need some water. Will you go?"

He cast about, looking for a tap.

"Outside. Remember?"

While the stew was cooking, he wandered round the derelict garden. I saw him stand kicking the furrow where we'd found the turnips that first autumn when we came here.

He gulped angrily at the food, lashing gravy around his mouth, wiping his face with the back of his hand. Belching. To reprove him I turned down the paraffin lamp so that the performance was not so clearly illuminated, and took dainty, soundless forkfuls. By and by I realized that it was tears he was wiping away. "I made fun of you, for being so thin. I called you a hat stand. I had no notion of . . . all this. It's terrible. All a terrible mess. I should have done more."

The hollowness of his voice, the barely controlled sobbing, had an irritating air of drama.

"You were young, Edward."

"But you'd have done it, Ellen." He sobbed again. "If you'd gone instead of me. *You* would have found a way, to raise more money."

"How on earth do you know?" I placed my knife and fork together. "You have no idea what I'd have done. Gone to the South Sea Islands and lived on breadfruit, maybe. Stayed there until I was entirely tattooed." His weeping tired me. I stood up.

"Ellen—"

"I'm going to bed. You can take the lamp. Be very careful turning it down, or the screw will fall out."

I woke with my knees under my chin, aware of a strange ticking. I strained my ears, and the ticking became a scraping. I rolled over. The door was ajar, and I saw Edward sitting at the table in shirtsleeves, whittling a peeled stick with a flat blade. His scarred side was toward me and I could see how it vanished under his hairline. His knuckles were huge, gripping the knife handle. He glanced up: my eyes were almost closed but he knew I was awake.

A sudden flurry of scraping. "There," he said softly. "A hawk for you."

He held it up. A perky upright bird with crest, wings, and tail made of peeled papery curls.

"How beautiful . . . That must be a sharp knife."

"It is. But this is balsa wood. I learned it from a Japanese carver I met in Lantao. I didn't have time to finish this one before I left. I'm going to ink in his eyes, and his body feathers—"

"Edward, please stay. She won't last much longer."

His face crumpled, as I knew it would. He set down the hawk and covered his eyes.

"What can I do for her now?" His voice quavered. "Having failed her completely!"

The anger shot through me. "You can at least wait for the end with me, and go to her funeral! After everything else I've done, on my own!"

He came to my side and embraced me. A mouse came into the bedroom. It paused to quiz us, its eyes drops of black dew. We began to smile at the mouse, and it darted away.

Outside the air was like milk. We had these fogs from time to time. This morning it lay so low that Edward and I rose head and shoulders above it. As we walked out along the lane, we saw some children in the field, bobbing up to see where they should go, like seals, and shrieking in delight.

We went to Beacon Hill as we'd done that first Christmas Day at the Absaloms. There was clear sunshine at the top and we sat and watched the fog melt away. We came back down through Pipehouse Wood, where the beeches were in their full glory. He laughed as we plunged through the shadows.

"I've dreamed of this, Ellen."

On the way home, he said he was planning to set up his own company. "My friend Frobisher and I, we'll be partners. Import export, out of George Town, Penang."

"What will you import and export?"

"That's not quite clear yet."

"A minor detail. Do you have funds, then?"

"That's a bit of a stumbling block too. What about you, Ellen? What will you do now?"

I came to a halt and so did he. He was smiling down at me, this brown boy, his eyes shockingly blue, teeth white. The chestnut hair bleached to a rich gold by a bigger sun than ours. He was just as handsome in spite of the scar, and just as young as he'd been when he clopped away in those wooden clogs. Perhaps the bright sea-light stopped one from growing old, from learning. He'd seen how we lived. Did he imagine we were just camping? That I could now jump up and choose my path in life?

His smile faded.

"I can typewrite, actually. I expect I'll find a job typewriting."

The smile returned. "Capital."

That night we baked two onions and had them with bread, and gravy from the stew.

She died on the fifteenth of May. We were there at the end, her children, but by this time she was nobody's mother, not even a being. Merely a rickety machine, a pump and a pipe. On and on it rattled, while we took it in turns to hold her hand. Finally, that afternoon, a crack, creak, cough, and then silence.

The coffin had been ready for a long time. Edward carried it, with Daniel Corey and John Blunden. The fourth man was the funeral director's assistant, a young man by the name of Hedley Hooper who muttered, "Hup she goes" as they lifted her onto their shoulders. It began to rain but the vicar continued imperturbable, turning the page of the prayer book with a flourish of his surplice sleeve. The headstone read *Susan Calvert*, and beneath the dates, the words *A Loving Mother*. These were extra but I had pleaded for them and Mr. Dawes had paid for them out of his own pocket. As well as the Hornes, and Daniel's family, William Kennet came bearing a sheaf of irises. "These weren't her favorite flower," he told me. "But they're abundant now, and Lady Brock said I should take all I want." I wasn't sure if I had ever known what her favorite flower was.

. . . . .

In the morning I walked with Edward to the bus stop.

"I've got a twist of demerara sugar in my kit bag." He rummaged. "I've been saving it for you. I nearly forgot."

I took the sugar and put it in my pocket. I raised my eyes to his but hot tears were flooding out, obliterating him. I shut my eyes and saw a red hull and a bright blue sea, and smelled salt and rust. "Let me come with you."

I felt his arms tight around me. I was almost rocked off my feet. His rough chin grazed my forehead as it had done before. "Ellen, Ellen. I'll try to help you. I'll—I'll come back rich."

"Yes, darling Edward. Of course you will."

12

MISS DAWES WENT BEFORE ME up a long flight of stairs. She led me into a bathroom and drew a deep steaming tub. I was about to ask why I was having a bath in the middle of the day when she added some drops with a chemical odor to the water. "Please make sure to wash your hair, dear, and leave your clothes in that laundry bag."

It had been so quick. Mother was tucked into her grave, Edward set sail for the East—and the next day Mr. Blunden had brought a cart to the Absaloms and taken my furniture away. His son John, my friend, had come too, and chopped up the chairs with a small ax, saying, "Sorry, Ellen C." Using my school name. "They're only good for firewood." And now here I was, in a strange scrubbed house, removing my clothes to order, stupefied by the passage of events.

When I was clean and dry, I put on the dressing gown Miss Dawes had given me. There was a knock on the door and I admitted a housemaid holding a black bottle. She bade me sit in front of the mirror while she examined my scalp.

"Yes." The maid nodded. "I do believe you are lousy. No offense, my dear." She dribbled the black mixture along my parting and combed it through. Then she made another parting an inch away and poured the mixture along the furrow. Four, five partings she made, with a hard metal comb, plying it over my scalp, and with each pass of the comb I blushed deeper. She smiled at me in the mirror.

"Don't worry, dear. The black bottle will do for them. I'm Elizabeth."

"How do you do, Elizabeth."

She was tall, spare, dark, with down on her upper lip. I'd seen her sometimes in Waltham, pushing a wicker basket on wheels, but never in the village. "I didn't know you worked here."

Elizabeth smiled. "Sixteen years. I was sorry about your ma."

The comb caught on a knot, my eyes filled.

"Oh, you poor lamb."

"It's just the comb. It tugs rather."

Elizabeth picked up a pair of scissors. "I don't like to do this, dear, but Miss Dawes says." And before I could speak she began to snip until all my tresses fell away leaving a boylike creature with thick brows darker than my drenched hair. My face was pasty, spattered with freckles. A few black drops ran down my neck

"What time is it, Elizabeth?"

She considered. "About eleven o'clock, I'd say."

I sat on the bed, my head in a towel. My face felt numb, my eyes salty and sleepy. After a moment I lay down sideways and closed my eyes. A knock at the door woke me from a heavy, uneasy doze. Miss Dawes was there holding me in a troubled gaze. "Your friends have come to visit you. Young Miss Horne from the kennels, and Harvey Corey's boy."

I pushed myself upright and bound the towel around my head. I was convinced that the lotion smelled of tar.

Daniel came in first. "By gum, Ellen. You look like the Queen of Sheba. Feel this carpet, Luce." He wriggled his stocking feet, his toes a seething mass of darns. I blotted my temples carefully with the edge of the towel, and then closed my eyes and leaned back against the wall. Instances of sleep visited me, each a second or two long, and after each one I came awake with a jerk.

Finally I heard Lucy say, "We came to see how you was farin."

"John Blunden broke up our chairs." The sorrow wrung my heart. Two tears coursed down my cheeks.

I felt Lucy's hand take mine. Her hands were small, the fingers slender. I knew them well by sight but seldom felt this light, firm, tender clasp. I opened my eyes. "Lucy, did I ever tell you, you've got very pretty hands? And nails." Because they were, the nails, naturally oval and the color of tea roses.

She sucked her teeth, smiling. "Get away."

I closed my eyes again. I heard Daniel say, from the other side of the room, "Bear up, Ellen, bear up." He said it several times, in the same manner, unhurriedly, and so it was soothing, like a pigeon calling on a summer morning.

I heard their voices distantly, bidding me good-bye.

When I fell asleep I dreamed of my rocking horse. The pony skin was bald around the neck and jaws where the red reins rubbed. In my dream I leaned my face against the horse's neck and whispered in his ear, and he dipped on his rockers as if to answer me. I leaned and sucked my thumb and stroked the bald patch. I turned my head and saw myself, a small child, and the rocking horse in the tall mirror. "I love Mummy," I told the horse, and wiped my thumb on his fur. The sunlight flashed in the mirror and my love was fixed in the bald patch, the fur, my wet thumb, the flash of light, forever.

The ham was so thin that I could see the pattern of the plate through it, a willow tree with puffy blue curlicues rendered violet by the overlaying film of pink. Even so, it was hard to insert this ham into my dry mouth, and thence down my gullet into a stomach that was shut like a clam. There were also potatoes to tackle, as inedible to me as boulders and similarly greenish on the underside.

This was luncheon of the following day. I'd slept unmoving for twenty hours or so.

Mr. and Miss Dawes ate ruthlessly, quartering their potatoes and impaling each quarter on their forks, cutting their ham into strips of equal width.

"Some sort of live-in position." Mr. Dawes broke the silence. "You're a clever girl and you sew well enough. With a little brushing up, you'd make a very nice companion."

"I want to stay at the school. I'm a good teaching assistant."

"The school can't support you."

"I could live here with you."

"My dear, that's not a permanent solution." Miss Dawes put down her knife and fork. "Now the first step is the Girls' Home in Bitterne. A place falls vacant on Tuesday. They'll teach you sewing, plain cooking. Every week I can take you to tea with Mrs. Daventry for conversation. You've got good manners and a nice voice. Soon the world would be your oyster. I can quite see you with a quiet lady, or even a nice family in Southampton."

I thought of Southampton. A place of gunshots and ships and bright sea, and hedges whose leaves glittered in the wind. Southampton had taken all of us.

"You have a life to build, Ellen," said Mr. Dawes. "You have everything before you."

I pushed my chair back and rose to my feet. "Apart from your kindness, I've got nothing in the world."

"But you will, dear," Miss Dawes said. "You'll make something of yourself."

I wondered how on earth she could know. Could those stones of eyes see into the future? She'd just eaten a meal, thin ham and hard potatoes but a meal nonetheless. How could she tell me about what I would make of myself? "Thank you. I think I'll go for a walk now." I left them sitting motionless at the table.

I made my way to the front gate and strode, as fast as I could without running, down the village street. My chin and lips trembled as I panted. I left the village on the road to Beacon Hill. I would go there and lie down like I had with Edward on that mild Christmas Day before he left for the first time. "*I will lift up mine eyes unto the hills,*" I said aloud, as sobs began to constrict my throat. "*From whence cometh my help.*" But I could see no help, just the hump of Beacon Hill, the quiet line.

The lightning started, planting itself here and there on the plain of fields beyond the hill, white and silent. A herd of cows, small in the distance and the color of pale sand, ran this way and that. I strained my ears and caught their terrified lowing, a tiny, faraway sound. I started to low like an abandoned calf, for my father, my brother, my mother. But they were gone. I didn't know where I would be, or who would know me, or whom I would love, in the years and years to come. I lowed, like a sand-colored calf, and my throat ached. "Oh, help me," I sobbed, "help me."

It began to rain in earnest, leaden coins drumming onto my scalp and shoulders. I ran up the lane toward the wall of a barn and cowered under the shallow eave. A lightning bolt sprang onto an iron gate five yards away. I screamed against the instantaneous crack of thunder, and turned round to embrace the wall. *Crack,* another bolt. I pressed myself against the wall. The rain flooded from the gutter and drenched my back, bringing a sensation of such violent cold that I screamed again.

"Ellen."

I thought the voice was in my head. But there was a hand pulling at my sodden sleeve. I turned to see Mr. Kennet in an oilskin, the rain battering the brim of his hat. "Come round the back." He sounded gruff and calm. "The barn door's not locked."

"I can't move." My teeth chattered. "I might get struck."

"You won't get struck. Come—" But the rest was lost in a white flash and a bang. The drainpipe at the end of the wall fell away into the yard. Mr. Kennet seized my arm and pulled me round the corner and into the barn.

. . . . .

The rain roared on the tin roof. I sat on a bale of hay. Mr. Kennet put his oilskin over my wet shoulders. The barn door was slightly open and through it I could see the walls of rain sweep up the line of Beacon Hill. I was still sobbing but my cries went unheard in the din of the rain on the roof. Mr. Kennet stood with his back to me, doffing his hat and striking it lightly against the edge of the door to shake the rain-drops from the brim. His hair was coarse, pale blond, like stubble in a field. The rain began to fall in large drops from the roof. I hugged my knees under the heavy oilskin, then rested my head on my folded arms. Great rhythmic shivers ran though me.

By and by I noticed that Mr. Kennet was gazing upward at the raf-ters, mouth half-open, chest rising and falling, slow blinks closing his eyes. Some kind of vagueness or otherworldliness seemed to be over-taking him, a strange, rapt solemnity.

"What's the matter, Mr. Kennet?"

"Wondering about those drips," he said after a moment. "I should tell Harvey Corey. It's his barn."

More light was beginning to shine in through the door. The rain had eased and the clouds were breaking up.

"You looked as if you'd seen a ghost."

"Fair few ghosts up here on the chalk, I reckon." He gazed out at the hill. "Along with the flints and bones from those ancient people. And they all had their troubles too. There's never anything so bad you can't be soothed by that, Ellen."

I disagreed, thinking that an empty belly put paid to all soothing. But did not say so.

"Thank you, Mr. Kennet," I said instead. "I think I was too fright-ened to move."

"Lucky it was my afternoon off. I always come up to take a look at the Coreys' sheep for them." He smiled at me. "So who did that close crop?"

I blushed to the roots of it. "Elizabeth."

The roof was silent. The rain had stopped. He stood up and pulled the barn door wide. I felt my tears rise again. "I'd much rather stay here."

He laughed. "You'll catch your death."

Desolate, I began to shrug my way out of his oilskin, but he shook his head. "Keep it on while we go down the lane. We'll go to Upton Hall and have a warm by my fire."

The cow parsley in the verges was drenched, the road shone in the sun. My head felt dull, my face and eyes sticky. I sniffed, to bring cool damp air into my lungs. Suddenly Mr. Kennet laughed.

"What is it?"

"Nothing." He smiled. "I have a great deal to think about. That's all."

Then he stared ahead at the water shining on the puddles.

We reached Upton Hall and the potting shed. The crying had exhausted me and I was still chilled to the marrow. Mr. Kennet kneeled down to attend to the stove. I sat down on a milking stool, thinking I would never be warm again. But it wasn't long before the coals glowed and he was passing me a cup of hot tea.

"What's in store for you now, Ellen? Where will you go?"

"I'm at the Daweses." I bound my fingers around the tin mug.

"After that?"

"Well." I fixed my eyes on the brick-colored tea. "I've been learning to type. I haven't got a machine, but I've got a cardboard..." It sounded pitiful spoken aloud. He turned round, still on his knees. I struggled on. "I've got a keyboard made of card. And I practice putting my fingers on it. According to the principles of rhythm and touch."

"Have you told those Daweses?"

I shook my head. I imagined their dismay as I showed them my typewriting book. I could see Miss Dawes picking it up by one corner, between finger and thumb. I had got rid of the mildew and the wood-worm frass, but could do nothing about the chewed parts. They probably contained vital information about typewriting techniques. There might very well be additional apparatus, dials, and levers about which I knew nothing.

"No one'll believe you can do it. Don't take on." He chuckled, because I was hanging my head, my eyes welling. "I meant, you'll have to have a go on a real one first. An actual typewriter."

I looked up. He was staring into the distance again but this time his eyes were sharp, narrowed, as if scanning a strange new landscape. But he was intrepid. "I reckon Lady Brock's got one," he went on. "It's in the farm office. Len Norris, the farm manager—he don't use it, but his girl does. Evie Norris. She might show you a trick or two."

"Yes, she might. Oh, Mr. Kennet. How will I find the money?"

"What for?"

"Evie Norris. She won't do it for free."

"Cross that bridge later. Let me ask her first."

We sat at rest. He lit the gas lamp. I gazed at his hand, the forefinger and thumb braided scar tissue and the truncated palm, in its pincering strength somewhat like a crab, in its silvered puffiness somewhat like a quilt. He followed my line of sight.

"When I was a young man I beat copper for a living," he told me. "I made the weathercock. The one on the clock tower of Waltham Town Hall."

I had seen the weathercock many times, jibing with a flash of red-gold in the wind. I had never considered it as a thing to be fashioned, or that there were people who knew how.

"That beautiful, shiny bird? How wonderful!"

"My cousin Mottram is a steeplejack. He brings it down every year, puts a polish on it." William grunted. "I wish he'd let the sun and rain turn it green, as is natural. So people would forget about it. So I could forget about it. But I can't tell him to stop."

"Because he's doing it for your sake?"

He nodded. "He thinks it's a kindness."

"Well," I said, "*I'm* glad he does it."

William smiled at me. "Then I shan't mind so much."

I hugged my knees, feeling the chill leave me. I knew that I ought to go back to the Daweses' soon. But it was peaceful here.

"Any road," William continued, "after the War Sir Michael gave me this job. One day I was in here whittling a birch twig, trying to get the knack of pruning, when your mother came by. On her way up to the Hall, she was. We sat and talked awhile in the shed. She didn't mind my hand. In those days, you see, people flinched at it."

To think of my mother, young, before our ruin, in this shed where I was now. Perhaps she'd sat on the milking stool, like me. Or would he have given her the armchair? Surely, yes. In all our years at the Absaloms she'd never mentioned it. But then conversation on any topic had been beyond her in the Absaloms.

I looked out of the window. Venus rippled beyond the pane, as bright as a lamp. I thought of my mother sitting here, being kind.

"I'm sorry, Mr. Kennet. I never invited you back to our house, after all your hospitality here. I'm afraid it wasn't suitable . . ."

He leaned forward to adjust the vent on the stove. "Don't you mind about that." His voice was deep. "Your mother was a lady. She preferred to entertain in style."

13

EVIE NORRIS'S TYPEWRITING MACHINE sat black and shining under a lamp with a hooked brass neck and a green glass shade. I was right: there were levers and rolls, things foreign to me. Evie bade me sit down and bent over me. She had warm warty hands and smelled of Parma Violets. She placed these hands on mine and I pressed the key of Q. *Bang*, went the machine. "Not so hard." Evie gave a violet giggle. "But better too hard than too soft."

I went to Evie twice a week after school, where I continued as assistant to Miss Yarnold, handing my wages to Mr. and Miss Dawes for room and board. They had agreed, reluctantly at first and then with good grace, to me extending my time with them until I was fifteen, a matter of six months or so. When the school closed for the summer, Miss Dawes found me piecework making clothes-peg bags and hemming dishcloths. "The fabric's from the Fallen Women. You know. The home for *unmarried mothers*," she added in a whisper, when I stared in confusion. "But you won't mind that, dear, will you?"

I did not mind that.

One day in September, Evie Norris said, "You're about ready for the Misses Spall and Benn in Waltham. You need your shorthand, and I can't help you with that." She gave me a contented smile, looked at the window where the sun made a muck of the glass and I saw lines at her eyes and on her cheek, lines I hadn't noticed when we were cooped over the typewriter.

· · · · ·

The shorthand course cost ten shillings. I had nothing to sell but *Downland Flora,* so when the time came I asked Mr. Dawes what I should do with it. "I believe Colonel Daventry's an expert on antiquarian books," he said. "It is antiquarian, isn't it?"

I turned it over. The cover had always been battered but it had survived the Absaloms remarkably well, collecting only a few spots on the flyleaf. The pages were so often turned, of course. The damp hadn't got to them, to glue them shut. "I don't know," I said. "It could be."

Colonel Daventry and I hadn't acknowledged each other since the Boxing Day meets of my early childhood, and it was with a stiff embarrassed little bow that he took the book from me. I didn't like to see his fingers briskly flicking the thin paper from the color plates.

"Those papers are fragile, Colonel Daventry. They might tear."

His eyes met mine, a pained light blue. "Quite right, Miss Calvert. This isn't the railway timetable, after all. I stand corrected." He turned a few more pages, for form's sake, and then he closed the book and placed it in a leather satchel. "I'll take it to Bradwell's in Southampton. But I'm so certain of a good price that I'll advance you fifteen shillings, my dear."

"I only need ten."

In unison, the Daweses broke into a ripple of discomfited laughter—at their charge's rude tone, at the comedy of an indigent young person rejecting an offer of money. But Colonel Daventry gave a genuine wide grin, and stepped back, rummaging for his billfold. Then he took my hand, and I felt the crisp pressure of a note folded into my palm.

"Ten it is, then. Be certain, you'll get the balance, if there is any."

"What if it goes for less than ten shillings?" Panic rose inside me. "How will I pay you back?"

Colonel Daventry laughed. "Out of your wages, Miss Calvert. Your wages to come."

· · · · ·

Miss Spall of the Misses Spall and Benn called me her Halley's comet. "Here you come blazing out of nowhere, Miss Calvert. From your farm office." She said the words with the scent of slurry flaring her nostrils. "But there we are." She handed me a stiff cream card. "Necessity, in this case, has evidently bred resolution."

I didn't tell her that I couldn't even claim the security of a farm office. Simply looked at the card, which stated in copperplate, under the stamp and seal of Spall and Benn's Secretarial College, that Ellen Calvert had obtained a Preliminary Certificate in Typing and Shorthand, Grade One, on the 29th November 1935. "There's a post opening up at the Town Hall," she went on. "In the typing pool. Don't get your hopes up. June Broad is also applying."

Smug June Broad of the blooming bustline. I had no idea she was even training. I'd never seen her here. But then I'd been coming to the evening class, full of yawns and wet umbrellas and workworn faces, older people by and large.

"Do I have to pay to apply for the job?"

Miss Spall's lips disappeared entirely as she smiled. "You do not. And I'll put in the application for you." Her gray, small-pupiled eyes flicked to my feet. "You'll go to the Town Hall for a test along with all the others. You'll have to lay your hands on some decent shoes, however."

Elizabeth went to see Deirdre Harper at the village post office. Mrs. Harper's daughter, Patricia, had a pair of black shoes with a low heel. "They're still in their tissue," Patricia told me. "Don't bend your toes. I don't want a crease in them."

"I'll try not to."

Patricia sniffed and handed the box over.

I walked together with Lucy down the lane. "Would you like to come and have tea with me at the Daweses?"

I pranced over the puddles. I was full of life today. All that ran in

my mind were the words, *Dear God in Heaven, please let me get this job.*
"I've got to get across Waltham Square without bending my toes!" I
burst out joyously. "Patricia's shoes have to be kept pristine!" I crossed
my fingers behind my back in hope, and let the giggles stream out.

"I shan't be able to, I don't suppose."

I turned. Lucy was dragging some way behind me, swishing a stick
in the hedge.

"To what?"

"To come to your Mr. and Miss Dawes. You just invited me, remember? Anyway, I can't. I'll be taken up with my job, you see. It's not
just you that's busy," she added.

The string broke. My exhilaration was whipped away, a kite in
the wind.

"Well." My throat was tight. "Be like that, then. After all your kindness, your family's kindness . . ." For there had been a fair few teas and
suppers at the Hornes', over the years. ". . . I wanted to repay you, that's
all. But have it your own way."

"It's all right for you." Her stick slashed at the verge. "You with your
full set of teeth and your fair hair and blue eyes, and all the rest. You're
tall. You're clever. And off you go now, and never mind that Lucy
Horne is shoveling—"

"Oh Lucy," I cried, "it's not my fault! What else should I have done?
Tell me!"

But she turned away, raising one hand daintily, palm outward, as if
to shield her face from my outburst. I saw Mr. Babcock approaching,
wheeled in his wicker chair by Marcy Berry. "Some people have no
manners," Lucy said to Marcy, who then tutted at me as she passed.
She was a tall girl with many moles. Mr. Babcock, stone-deaf and dozing, was undisturbed.

The morning of the test was fresh and we felt the breath of winter as
we boarded the bus. It arrived late, and the clock hand sprang to the

top of the dial as I started across Waltham Square. The sky was bright blue but the cobbles in the square still shone from the rain, and in the lower corner by the chemist, each cobble was ringed by cold blue water. The sharp new heel of Patricia Harper's right shoe clipped my left ankle as I stepped forward, a tiny sting. I tried not to bend my toes.

I took a breath as Lucy's voice grated again on my inner ear. *All right for you. Off you go now.* I shook my head. I didn't blame her for her resentment and fury but I couldn't afford, today of all days, to be upset by it.

"Ellen Calvert to see Mr. Renfrew," I announced to a secretary.

She gave me an owlish look and put a tick next to my name. "Please take a seat."

I turned to see, appearing out of the dimness, several girls on a polished bench at the back of the lobby, handbags on knees and feet together. I perched on the end of the bench. We were jammed like roosting hens but my neighbor surged back and forth in her seat for a few seconds, as if she were making room, to show willing. "Have you got your piece?" she asked, and I was hit by a blast of halitosis. "They'll make us do another," the girl added, and I swooped forward to duck the second wave of odor, as if to brush something from my shoe. When I saw the blood on my ankle I remembered the sting as I crossed the square.

"Of course. Otherwise we might have cheated." My voice on the word "cheated" rang out. The other girls breathed, and fastened their stares on their handbags.

"None of us would cheat," said someone, and straightening up I saw June Broad. Her large, puffy face was impassive. "Your hair's sticking out something shocking."

It had grown well since Elizabeth's shearing, back in the early summer, but still it could barely be called a bob. I raked my fingers through it, to little avail. Just then the secretary beckoned for us to follow her to a bright high-ceilinged room set out with six tin tables. Six tin tables and six typewriters: we were going to wake the dead. I sat down, June in front of me and the girl with the monstrous breath behind. As soon as we were seated, the secretary began: "Traveling in South America . . . requires a strength of constitution . . ." A battering cacophony as I had predicted, gone in an instant. One girl sobbed as her sheet was ripped from the roll by the secretary; another gasped: "I put the wrong *there,* all the way through . . ." We sat, wondering, until it became clear that the secretary, as she went through the texts, was separating the wheat from the chaff.

"June Broad. Elspeth Dixon." A pause. "Ellen Calvert."

We followed the secretary up the stone steps and into an unlit corridor. The door of Mr. Renfrew loomed at the end. I sat as June, and then the unknown Elspeth—a pole-thin pigeon-toed girl with a great tuck in the back of a vast sky-blue frock, her mother's without a doubt—went in by turn. June whistled and simpered behind the oak door; Elspeth was inaudible. June did not pause as she left, passing me without lowering her eyes, which I was astonished to see were glassy in the half-light, as if welling with tears. Elspeth said, "Good luck" cheerily, as if she had the job already, and sailed off with her dress bagging out behind her.

The door opened once more, four inches. Light lay behind. A male voice said, "Miss Calvert."

Remembering afterward my own typing test thrust into my hand: remembering the dizzying white light in the room, full sunlight streaming in through two immense windows, and glimpsing the square below, the expanse shrunken from this height, the drenched cobbles no longer intimidating, the shop fronts on the far side neat and domestic in scale. Just a glimpse; one second for each thing: light, typing test, windows, square—

And in the corner of my vision, the pillar of a man, grave, unspeaking. It was the secretary who said, "Take a seat, my dear," and I did so, unfolding the test to see a single fault, "atmisphere" for "atmosphere," circled in red crayon. Right ring finger straying inward. How elementary.

"You went to the Misses Spall and Benn, I gather," came the voice, after a long, quiet, light-filled expanse of time.

"Yes," I said at last.

"Take some shorthand, please. Miss Moss, give her the necessary."

A pad and pen were thrust into my hands and I seated myself on a stool indicated by the secretary.

"'Much as I delight in your company . . . '"

I stared wildly up at Mr. Renfrew. A thin man appeared in the fog of sunshine: an ordinary middle-aged man, a head already doming through thinning hair, a pair of direct dry eyes behind spectacles, a nose pointed at me.

"Take the words down," exhorted Miss Moss, in a tone somewhere between a whisper and a hiss.

I began my stenography, feeling a flush of perspiration on the sides of my neck and cheeks. I couldn't help seeing, as he sat down behind his desk, a hairless white shin and a sock reminiscent of Edward, baggy, wrinkled. Edward as a young boy.

"'Much as I delight in your company I feel bound to let you know that I am nothing but a simple parson and not the rich nobleman I so insolently pretended to be. The time has come for me to be honest and truthful even if it means the confounding of all my hopes which, embarked on such a frail pinnace as this, by which I mean a pinnace constructed out of my own lies, could not but be dashed on the implacable reef of reality. With that, my dear lady, I must release you from your vows though it breaks my wretched heart to do so.'"

My squiggles came to a stop. To my own great surprise, my shoulders were shaking with laughter. "Perhaps I can guess the outcome," I said. "She turns out to be a seamstress herself."

"Something like." He tittered. "I always use romantic novels for the new young ladies. It injects a lighter note into the proceedings. Now. Miss Moss, take a peek at those squiggles, please."

"I've been following," said Miss Moss, somewhat wearily. Perhaps she was tired of romance. "No errors."

Now Mr. Renfrew was spreading a crackling paper on his desk, one long middle finger pinning the edge. "These are your terms. Your conditions and holidays. Miss Moss will show you where you can take your luncheon. All our new young ladies take luncheon after their tests."

At the word "luncheon," Mr. Renfrew's person swelled and swam. I felt a soft, slightly warm handkerchief pressed into my hand. "Congratulations, Miss Calvert," he said, in his nut-dry voice. "Compose yourself. There's nothing to fear."

"Christ, it'll be a hole in the ground at that price," Lucy said. "Porridge in the morning and potato pie at night, I shouldn't wonder."

My new home was a hostel at the back of the Town Hall. It was described as a place for young ladies in the employ of the municipality whose home circumstances were unsuitable due either to remoteness from the workplace or to another cause. Supervision in matters of economy and welfare to be undertaken by Miss Moss—Mr. Renfrew's secretary—and an as yet unknown Miss Careless. The words "full board" preceded a dotted line on which was written a figure in black ink, followed by the phrase "per calendar month." It was this figure, the only part of the document that Lucy could understand, that had prompted her comment.

"I shan't mind," I said.

I folded the paper and put it in my pocket. We were sitting by the range in her kitchen. Old Mrs. Horne sat up at the table so that the window light could aid her sewing. Lucy was doing cross-stitch, neat and small. A linnet with a palest flush on the breast amid apple leaves.

The needle seemed to emerge from the fabric into her small fingers as if by its own power.

"Lucy, I'm sorry about our quarrel—"

"It was me that started it." She sniffed. "I was in such a corruption that day." Her eyes were distant.

I looked again at the cross-stitch fabric and reflected that the linnet was her favorite bird. She'd said so, or at least written it, asking me the spelling, on my first day at Upton School. "You could come to the Town Hall, Lucy, and have tea with me in my room."

"Yep." She ducked her head. "I reckon I could."

Mrs. Horne put down her embroidery. "You will still come to church, won't you, dear? On the Sunday bus. You could eat your dinner with us afterward, if you cared to."

I hadn't thought what I would do on Sundays. But Mrs. Horne had. "I can bring . . ." I had no idea what I would bring.

"They do lovely treacle tarts at Priddy's," Mrs. Horne said. "Wait till late Saturday afternoon. She'll sell them at any price."

After tea I went to the door with Lucy. "You know, Ellen, if we could, we'd have you here."

"I know that, Lucy—"

"Only we can't get two beds in my room. Not even if Dad made a bunk. He's measured and all. And it would cost you more in bus fares than your rent for your basement room. So that's that."

I was unable to speak, so I touched her on the arm. She suddenly grasped my hand and squeezed it.

"You were the only one," I found myself saying, "the only one who spoke to me."

"I told you about Vic Small, didn't I." Her eyes were shining. "Just to het you up." She did a rattle of a laugh. "You was so easy to tease."

"Good-bye, Lucy—"

"Give over, or you'll start me. Go on. See you Sunday." And with a little push on my arm, she sent me off.

It was time now to fetch my things from the Daweses and say good-bye. I had pressed some violets back in the spring and now I used them to decorate a card in which was written in copperplate *And now abideth faith, hope and charity, these three, but the greatest of these is charity. With boundless gratitude, Ellen Calvert, 15-xii-35.* It crossed my mind to include instead the verse about God loving a cheerful giver, but I wasn't a good Bible scholar and I couldn't find it, and anyway, it would have been cruel.

That afternoon I took my last journey out of Upton. The bus left the tree-lined lane and we breasted the first high bare hill on the road to Waltham. It wasn't really my last journey, of course. I'd be back on Sunday. But I'd be a visitor then.

Miss Moss took me to my room. A basement room, a long slit of a window at the top, where people's feet tramped by on the pavement above, which I could open and close with a hooked pole. There was a bed, a desk, a chair, a chest, all diminutive. A mirror, even, and a rug on the linoleum floor. A thick red blanket on the bed, and a white pillow.

I was led without delay to the kitchen. "Milk and so forth, any perishable extras you may buy go in the cold cupboard in the wall there." Miss Moss pointed. "That cupboard is common to all. Put your things in a brown paper bag with your name written on it. Nothing spoils my temper like girls bothering me with accusations of filching." Across a tiled corridor there was a lavatory and a bathroom. "Be brisk in the mornings," Miss Moss continued. "There are four of you down here. We want you all at work on time, neat and presentable. There is a tendency to linger, due to the proximity, and then at eight o'clock what do we find? Girls dashing along the corridors with hairpins falling out. Have you a clock?"

I shook my head, dismayed.

"Tsk." Miss Moss showed two square front teeth. She had a thin, deeply freckled face, narrow hazel eyes, a narrow body. She looked as if she'd rather be in a woodland glade, a powerful place with blasts of magic and other elves as irritable as her. "Miss Careless will wake you, then."

We went back to the bedroom. She caught sight of my bag and my box on the floor. "When will the rest of your things arrive?"

"Those are all my things."

She allowed herself a sigh. Then she said, more quietly, "I suppose you're saving your good black shoes for work." She was looking at my feet, in their boots.

"I had to give those shoes back. They weren't mine." I was gripped by a sudden fear that they'd take it all away from me, the job, the room. "I'm sure I can borrow some others."

She sighed again, this time a strong sigh of exasperation. "Lack and Son, in the square, will let you buy shoes from them at a small sum each week. Take your wage packet and sign in their book. I made this arrangement personally with Mr. Lack Senior, for you girls. Please do *not* let me down."

Or I shall blast you with my faerie power. "No, Miss Moss."

"There are rules on the door, please acquaint yourself with them. Supper's at six. Your time's your own until eight o'clock tomorrow morning when I shall expect you outside my office." I listened to her patter up the stairs and let herself out of the street door. It slammed behind her surprisingly loudly. Perhaps caught by the wind.

I shrugged myself out of my coat. Where was the heat coming from? There was no radiator. I unlaced my boots and kicked them off, and turned round in the small floor space. Everywhere was warm. The window pole was leaning upright in the corner of the room, so I took it and opened the window. Looking up, I saw the pipe. It was fat, painted white, and ran along the inner edge of the ceiling. I got up onto the bed and put my hand against it. It was hot, dry, smelling slightly of paint.

I opened my door and peered out into the corridor, which was dark, swept clean, and seemingly deserted. Somewhere a bell rang. Shortly afterward I heard footsteps, and a door at the end banged open to reveal a large woman in a crumpled apron who came hurrying toward me. "Are you on tea duty, dear?"

"I don't know. I'm new."

She sniffed hard. "What's the betting it's Polly and Esme. If they were mine I'd put each one over my knee and spank them. Can you make pastry?"

I shook my head.

"You girls. When I first came here I was flabbergasted, the amount of girls who didn't know how to make a good piecrust." She began to hurry off again and I followed her to the kitchen Miss Moss had shown me earlier. "It can't be your brains, can it, since you're all bright enough. You'd better start on the potatoes. You can peel a potato, I expect?"

"Yes."

"Off you go, then. In the cupboard there. My name's Miss Careless, if you haven't already been told."

"I'm Ellen Calvert." I pulled a large earthy sack of potatoes from the cupboard.

"Ellen. Good. I shan't bother with the surname, dear, if you don't mind. The rate you girls come and go. I'm not meant to be cooking at all, you realize. But you lot wouldn't even get a pie in the oven unless I pitched in. Nowadays I even bring my own blessed apron, see? About a dozen, dear." She was cutting lard into a bowl of flour, and pointed with her greasy knife at the potatoes I was putting in the sink. "Never mind. I suppose it must be your home backgrounds. If you had good homes to live in, with mothers who brought you up to make a proper piecrust, you wouldn't be here, would you. Which room have you got?"

"The one with the pipe." I ran the tap onto the potatoes. I was sway-
ing, whether from sleepiness or plain dislocation, I couldn't be sure.

"Oh, the boiler pipe. The new ones always get that." Miss Careless
plunged her big pink hands into the bowl and began to smear the lard
into the flour. "You'll die in there."

"Maybe." I turned the tap off. "But I'll die warm."

Miss Careless began to expel a series of billowing breaths. "You'll
die warm. Oh, that's funny." She exhaled some more. "Die warm. Bless
you. You'll be all right, I think. Peel away, now, dear."

When the pie was made, Miss Careless put it in the oven. I went
back to my room to wait until suppertime. I let my knees go and
slumped down onto the bed. My eyes felt swollen and sleepy. My bag
and box lay quietly on the floor, patiently. They looked so dirty. We
were thrown up at last on the beach, among tangled rigging and spars,
with boulders for pillows. But this pillow was soft. It was all that
counted.

Ellen

Early March, 1944

14

I WOKE, Selwyn beside me, a long form like a ridge of the Downs. I stroked the back of his head. He didn't stir. I got up and went through to the dressing room. Pamela was soused in sleep, sucking her thumb.

Eight years old now, and her emerging big teeth pushed out a little by this endless sucking; no good, no good at all. That perfect curve in her nose straightening but her eyes seemingly big as ever. The lashes trembled on her cheek. Freckles like those on a bird's egg covered her nose and the tops of her cheeks. There was no crease in her wrists anymore, but her arms, especially when she raised them above her head to shrug off a singlet or blouse, were still babyish smooth, the forearms rounded, the hands soft and stubby-fingered. I still brushed her hair as it straightened and thickened. The color of it dry was the same as mine wet—gleaming dark honey.

I pulled her blankets aside and dragged her sleeping legs to the edge of the bed. She obeyed me and rose and walked, eyes tight shut, down the steps from the old dressing room into our bedroom. She followed me into our bed, still sleeping, and lay half on top of me, utterly senseless. I lay squashed, uncaring that I was squashed. Her cheek was hot and damp. Her thick hair at the back of her neck smelled heavenly. Hot, clean, slightly salty, like baking bread with a breath of clean linen. That was it: clean dry tea towels covering loaves fresh from the oven. Or was it that? Was there more sweetness in it, something like honeysuckle nectar? Whatever it was, I could live off this aroma.

Selwyn rolled over. I couldn't see if he'd opened his eyes. "Uncon-scionable," I heard him say, with a smile in his voice. "What was that dream about? *Going up the old battery with Bobby and Ruby?*"

I laughed. "She can't help talking in her sleep."

"Well. She's given herself away this time."

"There aren't any guns up there any longer. Well, none that work."

"It's still dangerous. Rusty barbed wire is not a plaything." Selwyn pushed himself into a sitting position, put on his spectacles. "I must go and look at the level. This soft rain is deceptive." He reached over me and ruffled Pamela's hair. "Morning, parrot."

Pamela slurped, her cheek pressed against my neck. Selwyn got out of bed. I rolled her into the warm trough in the mattress left by him.

It was early March, 1944. We were nearing the end of a mild dry win-ter, roaring blue skies that brought no rain. The previous winter had sent a brief flood, widening onto the water meadows by the church. But the mill still turned, and our house was a weatherly little boat that floated on the highest tide.

This year, fine drizzle, and then clouds whipped away by the wind.

Selwyn had relented at the end of 1940, a month after Pamela came. I'd expected him, after Christmas, to resume his search for a home for her. But he hadn't. "I don't know why," he'd said, fingering his chin. "I think I've placed her in your charge. Mentally, I mean. I think you'll know what to do." For I had told him all of it, every jot of my young life, a long, dogged account of all those days of cold and dirt and privation during which, at times, he closed his eyes. He did not say if there was a particular thing that had moved him. Edward's de-parture, the death of my mother? Something small, like the frozen tap? Perhaps none of these things—I didn't ask. At least now he knew I was the bucket in the well, the bucket Mr. Kennet had mended for me after I'd broken it on the ice. I was made of old staves and tarred felt. Water poured from my seams when I was filled but I held enough, for long enough, to be serviceable. This knowledge made him gentler, which was touching but unnecessary since my mends were sound. Cautiously he'd let his mind creak open, like an old sluice gate, to the idea that he need not remain obdurate for my sake, that he too could dare to love Pamela a little. Bad days still came to her, even now, when she lay motionless and speechless, embracing a pillow on our bed. Sometimes she tied my dressing gown cord around the middle of the pillow to make a waist, and laid her head on the upper part, which had become a bosom. Selwyn, if he found her like this, would take her small cold feet in his hands and rub them, saying, "There now. There now."

So had three years and three months passed: we began to mill barley flour along with the wheat, and then we had to mix potato flour with the barley, and Pamela was still with us.

The wind was strong at seven o'clock, rattling the handle of the kitchen door. Last night I'd dropped a dish of steamed cabbage on the stone floor and there were still glass fragments, treacherously small, unfound. Nobody went downstairs in stockinged feet. Elizabeth and I had plucked a great deal of cabbage out of the larger slivers and served it without mentioning the incident to Selwyn or Pamela.

"This is exactly why we need that soft brush back from Lady Brock, Mrs. Parr," Elizabeth now spoke reproachfully.

"I'll ask her again. I'm sure it's just slipped her mind." I had a strong suspicion Lady Brock had lost the brush.

Elizabeth sliced bread and put it onto the range to toast. "And the hole in the bellows has got atrocious. I might just as well blow on the kindling with my own lungs."

I inspected the bristles of the insufficiently soft brush for glistening particles, gave up. We'd find them all in the end. Perhaps in six months' time, in the soles of our feet. Then I let the brush drop and rubbed my face. "I'll look out for those chammy leathers we had for the car. Pamela, put your slippers on your feet."

Because here she was, my heart, my joy, with her slippers on her hands like paws. "Are we going to see Lucy after school?" She sat down to her unadorned porridge, poked it with her spoon. "I wish I lived in her house. She's always got sugar."

"What's this about going 'up the battery'?"

I said it artlessly, but she wasn't gulled into telling me. No longer five years old. "What battery?"

"You said it in your sleep."

She gave a delicious display of little and big teeth. "I expect it was just a dream then."

"Pamela, I think you know what I'm talking about."

Her eyes sparkled with guilt.

"Don't rise to it, Mrs. Parr," Elizabeth said. "You're a cheeky girl, Pamela. I would put you over my knee."

"I'd escape by springing into a forward roll. Bobby and Ruby and I, we've been practicing. We can do it straight off a chair, like this."

There was no such thing as a single unchanging child. They altered as fast as clouds across the Downs. A month ago she seemed a placid moon-faced creature reciting her tables, the month previous elfin and fey. Now she was effervescent, particularly in the morning. The sunrise uncorked her and up she fizzed, this time to pitch toward the stone floor and lithely curl into a rolling ball.

"Pamela! Careful!" Elizabeth and I cried out together, mindful of the glass. Pamela got up unharmed, rosy-cheeked from being up-side down, and sat on her chair again. I glanced out of the window. "We're going to see Mr. Kennet this afternoon, Pamela."

"Oh good, I want to borrow something from him."

"What?"

"Something."

Out in the hall the letterbox flapped. "Will you fetch the post, darling?"

She hurried back, handed me a long white envelope. "What lovely stamps. Please may I have them?"

"I expect so." I couldn't see the stamps properly—they looked black in the gloom of the kitchen. I took the letter over to the window where I made out a grim silhouette of brown tanks mounting a dusty, identically brown escarpment. "I'd hardly call these stamps lovely, Pamela . . ."

Suid-Afrika, they said. South Africa.

So long I'd imagined it, this letter. Deep in a mailbag on an airplane droning its way north, fragile as an insect, casting a tiny wavering shadow over the veldt. And now it had come. I opened my mouth, thinking to call Selwyn, but my fingers were already fumbling at the envelope.

Dear Mrs. Parr,

Thank you for your letter regarding the child you refer to as my niece. Please know that I have had no contact with my sister since her divorce. I know nothing of the father of this child, never having met him. My sister led a dissolute life and I have therefore consulted a solicitor, whose note I attach and who confirms that I am not liable in law for the child's upkeep. My husband will arrange for the sum of £10 to be made available to you at Barclay's Bank. This is purely in recognition of your kindness and in no way constitutes an acknowledgment of future obligation. I now regard the matter as closed and any further communication from parties acting on behalf of the child will be treated by my solicitor as harassment.

Yours very sincerely,
Marjorie Lord (Mrs.)

That final viper's bite, the forked teeth sinking into the ball of my thumb, made me drop the letter. There was another sheet beneath, the solicitor's attached note, on blue paper. They both dimmed and descended as if into water, and the air around me darkened, teemed with sparkles, became unbreathable.

Pamela and Elizabeth were looking down at me. *She's grown old,* I thought of Elizabeth, as I noticed the folds around her mouth, the wiry gray hair springing from under her scarf. When on earth did that happen?

"Jeepers, creepers, now you've opened your peepers," Pamela burst out in a tuneless chant. But her mouth was puckered in anxiety.

"Darling, I simply fainted." I felt a stab in my scalp. "I've found a piece of glass. Quite a big one, I think." I gave a watery giggle.

Selwyn appeared in the corner of my vision. "Good grief. Darling."

"Oh my lord, the toast." Elizabeth sprang away.

"She fainted," Pamela told Selwyn. "She read a letter and fainted."

Selwyn bent down and took my hands. I allowed myself to be helped up into a chair. "I'm really quite all right."

He picked up the two pieces of paper, one white and one blue, from the floor. He read with his back to me. Pamela stood beside me, leaning against my side. A long, long while passed, and my head pounded. I felt the back of my scalp, retrieved a shard of glass the size and shape of a fingernail. There didn't seem to be any blood.

"Who on earth is it from?" said Pamela to Selwyn.

His eyes flickered from the letter to Pamela and back again. "A thoroughly cross and silly person. Nothing for you to worry about." He bent down to Pamela. "Don't lean so hard against Ellen, sweetheart. She's feeling faint."

"Selwyn . . ." I said.

"Sit still, Ellen. Let me—let me take this to my study."

He made to straighten up again but Pamela grabbed his tie and pulled him down. "Please will you give me a kiss on my parting?" Elizabeth turned from rescuing the toast to see Pamela battened to my side, Selwyn tethered, kissing the top of her head.

"Mr. and Mrs. Parr. For goodness' sake, will you eat your breakfasts."

Elizabeth left the house soon after, for Judd's in Waltham where she made shell nose-cones alongside a bombed-out company workforce from Portsmouth who ragged her for her country burr. She preferred Judd's, she said, for all the teasing and backtalk, to looking after those "rapscallions of boys," Jack and Donald and their cousin Hawley. They had gone home after the worst of the air raids, their mothers no longer able to do without them.

That morning I took the lorry out to collect the orders from the farms, leaving Selwyn kneeling in a boiler suit and goggles, chipping at one of the Derbyshire peak millstones with hammer and chisel. The odd spark flew out unheeded, which always worried me, but, so far, I had never returned to black smoke billowing from the mill roof. I traveled at speed across the high land where the chalk came close to the surface of the soil and the sheep nibbled short tough turf. The mill was low-lying, tree-shrouded: I loved being able to see in every direction, the clouds in fleets all the way to the sea.

I reflected on what to say to Pamela about Marjorie Lord. Pamela had never met her, nor even mentioned her since those first days with us. Good God, but the woman was monstrous. Could she have children of her own? Perhaps they hatched from eggs in her swampy lair, fully formed, with teeth. *Pamela, dear, your aunt . . .*

The aunt she did not know, whom she did not remember, had repudiated her.

I would not allow myself to venture any further along this path. I simply let the facts settle in my mind. They didn't weigh heavy. Instead, a lifting sensation took hold of me, as if there were more air in the lorry's tires, more light among the clouds spreading away to the horizon.

As the school day came to a close, I went out to the garage for the bicycle. William Kennet had made us ropes of straw to fill our outer tires. The original inner tubes were packed in chalk dust and kept for very long journeys, rubber being rare and costly now.

Edward had written twice in 1942. The first time was in February. *All the world has come dashing over the Straits, Indians, Aussies, etc., Japanese hard on their heels but we plan to blow up the Causeway and in this way raise the drawbridge. Fear not, drst Ellen, I'm a wharf rat of long standing as you well know and have got myself out of any number of tricky spots.*

By the time I received it, the causeway had been destroyed, but this hadn't stopped the Japanese. Singapore fell and there was no word from my brother. Then in April 1942, to my immeasurable joy, another letter had arrived, this one crumpled, filthy, and water-stained. The only legible words were . . . *to Ringat in a terrible old* . . . *annot believe how they missed* . . . *Padang* . . . *Nurses* . . . *n Ceylon now* . . . *tea the best in the world.* And after that more messages had followed, clearer ones, detailing his escape to Ceylon, his journey to India and thence to fight in Burma. Pamela, thrilled by these letters, plotted his progress in drawing pins on her map of the world. I was never wholly happy with this ritual, imagining the day when a distraught Pamela would climb onto the chair—because she would insist on doing it—and push in the last pin. But he'd told me, my darling Edward, he'd told me not to fear when he was fourteen, when he took himself far off into the shocking dangers of hurricane seas and fever coasts. It was the least I could do to trust him again now.

I rode to the school, collected Pamela. She climbed onto the makeshift backseat of the bicycle. The rolled sheepskin that served as a cushion was well squashed down now. I doubted it would ever recover.

I strained on the pedals and she breathed in, as she often did, to make herself lighter, and we set off for Upton Hall and William.

"You'll have to pedal me, soon," I said.

"Let me do it now, Ell."

"Wait." A rumble was approaching from behind. "Soldiers coming."

Two army lorries passed us at thoughtless speed, each one creating its own diesel gust, making me weave. A parcel of eggs nestled in my wicker bicycle basket. Our ducks had been laying well and we were taking them to William in exchange for four young apple trees. I was to give two of the trees to Lucy. Her old apple tree, which kneeled like a camel to the ground, produced only fruit the size of large marbles now.

"Where are they going, all these soldiers?" Pamela was clinging to my waist, creating a drafty gap beneath my jacket. I wished I'd worn my long coat.

"To the camp." Which occupied the long narrow field under a wood known as Jeps Hanger, where sheepdog trials took place in happier times.

"I mean all the soldiers *in* the camp. They aren't on holiday, are they! They must be off *somewhere*. Ruby says it's France."

"We don't know, Pamela. Nobody knows, and we don't talk about it."

"I bet you do, really."

We caught up with the lorries as they halted at the camp gates. The tops of Nissen huts and mess tents poked above the high new fence. People were starting once again to voice the unspeakable word: *invasion*. Only this time the tide had turned and the invasion was running the other way, from England to France. Gales were sweeping down the Channel and yet all those men had to be got covertly out, over the sucking bottle-green waters of the docks, in moonless secrecy, to face the chop of the open sea. The very idea sent nerves shooting down my arms.

The driver of the first lorry was opening the wide gate. The men in the second lorry had pulled up the canvas shield at the back. Pamela cupped her hands to her mouth. "Got any gum, chum?"

"Pamela! Really!"

One of the soldiers, a black-haired boy, rummaged in his pocket and a tiny white package whistled across the road to land in the verge. Pamela leaped off the bicycle, pounced on the package. "Oh, gosh! Thank you!" she yelled, and the young soldier grinned. They were all young, and all quiet, sitting obediently in two rows facing each other. Their hair was indecently short, the scraped skin of their necks pink, damp tufts sticking up from their crowns. The lorries moved forward into the camp and the gates were closed behind them.

"That is *the* most coarse way to behave, Pamela."

She climbed back onto her bicycle pillion. "Bobby does it all the time."

"I don't care what Bobby Rail does."

Mrs. Rail had produced so many children that her elder boys were grown up—Ernest and Stanley, who'd been thrown from their house when the burning hayrick set it alight. Stanley had come home from Dunkirk and was now waiting like these soldiers, in another camp somewhere in the South of England. Small Ernest, too frail to pass the board, was clerking in Southampton Docks. I feared for him as much as I did for Stanley.

"*Hey, ho, nobody at home, Meat nor drink nor money have I none*
Yet will I be merry, merry, merry, Hey, ho . . ."

Of all our songs it was this mournful little rhyme Pamela loved best. We sang it in a round. It had taken her weeks to learn to sing against my melody, and even now her voice would merge with mine from time to time. "No! Not that tune!" she cried.

I'd broken into the descant. "I'm sorry. I can't help it. Don't you think it sounds nice?"

"It's nice but *wrong*." Her voice sounded mushy.

"Are you chewing that disgusting stuff? Take it out before we get to the Hall, if you please. *Hey ho, nobody at home. Meat nor—*" The bicycle lurched and plunged.

"Ell! You're jolting the eggs! We must get off!"

We were plowing along the drive to Upton Hall, over ruts as deep as coffins. I braked and dismounted. I hadn't even noticed. I *always* dismounted on the drive to the Hall, which was impassable on straw-stuffed tires. And today we had eggs, of all things. No wonder Pamela slept so deeply: every incident of the daytime inspired an orchestral level of emotion. I had fainted; she'd got some chewing gum; and now I was about to smash the *eggs*. And it wasn't yet teatime! I walked the rest of the way and Pamela rode. When I reached William's shed I leaned the bicycle against the wall and, at her insistence, lifted her down. She clung, briefly, like an infant monkey, and the shock of delight was accompanied, as always, by a white flare of pain in my lower back. "This is ridiculous, darling, you're eight years old."

Her eyes twinkled. "Yes, but *extremely* light." I set her down, kissed her cheek.

William Kennet was in the small greenhouse with a barrow of compost and what looked like a hundred thumb pots. He looked up, said, "Hm," in a mild, contented way, and jerked his chin at a clutch of four larger clay pots, each with a thin lively stem and thrusting leaves. "Those are your pippins. I raised them from seed. Go slowly home. They won't like to be rattled in the breeze. Don't worry about Lucy's trees—her dad will come for them." He speedily filled another dozen pots. "So, young Pamela, how are the onions progressing?"

William was president of the Upton School Onion Club.

"The little ones are such lazy weeders." Pamela pouted. "'Why should we grow onions to give 'em away to the sojers?' That's what they say. May I borrow your *Art of Prowling*, Mr. Kennet, please?"

"You may not. You can read it while you're here. A young child like you with a good memory, you can get it by heart if you try."

Pamela suddenly gasped. "Oh! Guess what happened this morning! Ell got a letter from a cross, silly person, and then she fainted! She did! And after she'd finished fainting there was a piece of glass in her head!" Pamela spread her arms, triumphant, at the splendor of her story.

"I dropped a dish, the night before." I was laughing.

He broke into a broad smile. "That tale deserves a cuppa, and a toffee."

The toffees were the color of polished walnut: fat discs, all of different sizes, with smooth, rounded tops and flat glassy bottoms. Lady Brock stored up her sugar and her land girls made them, dropping them from a spoon onto a marble slab.

Pamela took William's pamphlet *The Art of Prowling* from a battered wooden box, flipping up the lid with an insolent familiarity.

"Those are Mr. Kennet's things, Pamela."

"Don't mind her, Mrs. Parr. It's just some bits of old rubbish, anyway."

"Licorice isn't rubbish." Pamela shook the tin. The fine lady was still there on the side, alighting from her carriage in a blizzard of dents and scratches. "Oh, Mr. Kennet, you've restocked!"

"You leave that be." William was stern. "You've got toffees today." He gazed past me, out through the open door where Lady Brock was walking on the path, followed by Nipper. "Out, damned spot! Out!," she was saying.

"They're doing *Macbeth* at the Hall," William told me. "For the Canadians."

"I know." I thought of Macbeth's ineluctable, prophesied defeat. "It's hardly the most apposite story."

"No, my dear. The idea is, Macbeth is Adolf. Doomed." He smiled his square smile. "So you had a letter, then."

Pamela was creeping on hands and knees, or more accurately elbows and knees, out of the door and onto the path, glancing every few moments at William's pamphlet, which she was holding in one hand. "I did indeed, William." In a soft voice, one that merged with the hum of the kettle on the stove, I told William about Marjorie Lord. "It really seems Pamela's got no one," I concluded. "Not a soul."

The hills of the morning rose in my mind's eye, speckled with chalk, and the bare line cut the brightening sky, and peace broke out, and Pamela, aged ten, twelve, eighteen, strode up ahead of me with her skirts flapping in the wind.

So you might get to keep her.

I laughed. "Who knows?"

"Pardon?"

"Didn't you speak?"

"No."

I was sure I'd heard his voice.

Beyond him the doorway grew bright: the sun had come out. Lady Brock was still striding up and down the path, rubbing her hands together. Pamela, unnoticed by her and by Nipper, crept along the flagstones in the lee of the greenhouse. William offered me a mug of tea. The thin enamel handle dug into my fingers. I raised the mug to my mouth and the rim burned my bottom lip.

"Hold hard," William said. "It's way too hot." Surprised that I should even try to drink yet.

I blew on my tea. William blew on his, his eyes almost shut, eyebrows raised, mouth in an "O." This gave him a somewhat angelic air. A rather careworn, older angel, just now a little fatigued, I learned, from a long night patrolling bridges and culverts along the railway line. "No chance of a brewup, and brambles this high. All we saw was some Canadians coming back from banging their heads on the beams at the King's Arms. We properly apprehended them. Why do they grow them so tall over there? It can't be good for their brains. I'd get down to Southampton while you can, if there's anything you need. They're going to shut the whole coast off soon."

I felt a strong inward sucking at my sternum. "Oh lord, lord—"

"Bear up, my dear."

"I suppose we can pray."

"We can. For the Canadians, and ours, and all of them."

I lifted my mug back up to my lips.

"She still has got a father, though," William said after a moment.

"What?"

"Pamela. She's got a father."

I gulped the burning tea. "Whoever he is, he's not interested in fathering. He scarpered long before the war, remember? I'm sure I told you." I pictured Constable Flack in our kitchen back in 1940, running his finger under his chinstrap. "Anyway, we've hardly been dilatory—goodness, we've gone through the Forces, the police, the Wounded and Missing, and no one's come up with the right Pickering. Quite honestly I don't know what else you expect us to do."

"I'm not expecting you to do anything—"

"Good, because we can't." A heat was spreading over my cheeks to my eyes, unconcealable. Silence fell. Outside, Pamela shrieked, "Oh, Nipper, you naughty, naughty boy!" and Lady Brock, more indistinctly, echoed the sentiment.

"Ellen. I didn't mean to offend."

It wasn't often these days that he called me Ellen. More and more, it seemed, I was becoming Mrs. Parr. "No offense taken."

He gave a single soft laugh. We drank up our tea. "Well, then, my dear," he said, as we rose to our feet. "Thank you for the eggs. A duck egg omelet can't be surpassed."

Outside, Pamela and Lady Brock were both speaking to Nipper, who was lying with flattened ears on the path. "Bad dog," they were saying. "Bad, bad dog."

William lifted up the pots containing the saplings and I lodged them carefully in my wicker bicycle basket. "I'm sorry your rehearsal was interrupted by Pamela," I called to Lady Brock. "Pamela, it's time to go."

"But we haven't finished telling off Nipper. He was digging."

"Pamela was a welcome distraction." Lady Brock came up the path toward me. "I'm sick to death of Lady Macbeth."

"That rhymes. Sick to death, of Lady Macbeth. Sick to death—"

"I had a dream," I found myself saying to Lady Brock. "That you and Pamela were eating Christmas cake." Remembering the dream as I spoke: their faces pink with pleasure, the plate containing only dark rich fragments of dried fruit and aromatic crumb. "And you hadn't"— I felt the indignation now—"even asked me to join you!"

Lady Brock was smiling, her wrasse-like mouth still a lush red. Where on earth did she find such lipsticks now? Nobody knew, and nobody begrudged her. "My dear girl, I do apologize. Cake, now. I'll have to look that one up. I've got a dream book, you see. The man who wrote it must have been raving, but one's quite gripped all the same." She turned to Pamela. "Now pay attention, you young rascal of a girl. Enough prowling. Obey Mrs. Parr all the long day, d'you hear?"

At the tone of command, both Pamela and Nipper ducked their heads.

Pamela sang on her way home, a long song of her own invention, psalmlike, each phrase ending with the same fall of notes. "*And we we—hent to Upton Hall. But we did—not, no we didn't, see-hee the knight in shining ah-ah-armor . . .*" There was a light curtain of rain behind us, I felt its damp breath first and then turned my head to see it sweep over the army camp. The tiny trees wouldn't mind it. They fluttered in the basket in front of the handlebars. I hoped we weren't "rattling" them.

"Pamela, don't lean sideways. How many times."

"I'm peering past the apple twigs. It's practice for prowling. Tom-tits and jays give warnings, you know."

"Do they?"

"They're alarmed by the enemy, you see, coming toward you."

The wind blew at our backs all the way home.

15

A WEEK PASSED. George Horne planted Lucy's pair of trees, and Selwyn and I planted ours. Lucy developed a cold and a cough so incapacitating that Harry Parker ordered her off the tractor and into bed. By the time I visited, she was on the mend, sitting up peevishly. Old Mrs. Horne was taking away a half-finished bowl of soup. "I do hope you've brought her something to do, Mrs. Parr."

"Yes." Lucy gave a sigh. "I'm bored to blimmin sobs."

I unpacked a blanket from my bag, the middle gnawed away by mice. "I'm cutting a waistcoat for Pamela. Perhaps you could help me with the stitching."

Her small hands rose and fell in fists. "I dunno."

"I thought you needed occupying."

"I'm dying to get up but Nan won't let me. You'd think I was seven years old." She sighed again. "Oh, give me the pattern." The "pattern" consisted of rather ragged calico shapes I used for all Pamela's top-half clothes. Lucy and I pinned them into an economical corner of the blanket. Lucy drove in the pins quicker than me and spread out the rest. "What are you going to do with this bit?"

"I hadn't thought."

"You hadn't thought." She looked up, grinned. "Sometimes you sound like your ma."

Nobody else could say this to me. "Do you want one, Lucy? A waistcoat?"

"I wouldn't mind." We cut out another series of shapes, using Pamela's pattern but clearing it by two or three inches each side. Lucy couldn't be that small. I glanced from the pattern to the span of Lucy's shoulders and the narrowness of her chest, and saw that she was, indeed, that small.

We began on the sewing, whipping the pieces together with a tough yarn. Then we would bind the free edges with a close blanket stitch. The waistcoats were a dusty midblue and the stitching would be dark red. "I've still got Edward's wooden toggles. You and Pamela can have three sets each."

"Bill Kennet dropped by."

"That was nice of him, to come and see you."

"Hm. Came to inspect the planting, more like. Dad can't be trusted to put a couple of trees in, see." She coughed. "Oh, yes. I know what I was going to tell you. This chest has made me so forgetful. There was a lady, looking for you at the WI last week."

"At the market?"

"Yes. Last week."

"Oh, blast, it's Thursday today, isn't it." I looked at my watch. "I was going to get some oven gloves." The old ones had turned to such rags that I'd burned my hand through a worn-away patch in the palm. "What sort of lady?"

Lucy laughed. "The sort that isn't a lady as such. String bag and slits cut out of her shoes for her poor old bunions. She bought a tea cozy off of me."

I bit my thread and knotted it. "So what did she want, this nonlady?"

"All she said was, that she'd been to the mill but you weren't at home, so she popped by the village hall. She said, 'I've come from Southampton to have a word with Mrs. Parr.'"

"Southampton?"

Lucy nodded, took another wheezy breath. "I told her you and Mr.

Parr was in Waltham, and she said, 'Oh well, I'll get home then.' And she took the bus back to the city. I saw her gettin on when I came out with Deirdre Harper to flap the tablecloths,"

It was true. Selwyn and I *had* been in Waltham last Thursday. Selwyn needed a stopping in his tooth and I was hunting for herrings and paraffin. Lucy was slumping back on her pillows, tired out by her tale. I slid my needle into the blanket fabric, bewildered. I thought of saying, *You could at least have asked her name.* Following it with *Why on earth didn't you find out what she wanted?* But Lucy ill being even more intransigent and touchy a creature than Lucy well, I let it pass. She was watching me now, her black eyes soft, curious. "Don't you even have one single inklin, Ellen Parr?"

"Lucy, I swear, if I did I'd tell you. I can't think what any woman, any *bunioned* woman—you're sure about the bunions?"

"They was the size of pickled onions."

"Ha, ha. There's a rhyme for Pamela . . . I should go. It's nearly time to fetch her." I folded my blanket pieces into my bag and stood up. "Is there any news from John or Dan?"

Lucy shook her head. "Marcy's not heard for a while now. Nor has Ted."

Daniel Corey and John Blunden were either in North Africa or Italy. We didn't know which. I knew Dan and John weren't together, and I was glad of it. During the Great War a single shell-burst had killed all the boys who had gone together to France from Fair Mead, a hamlet the other side of Waltham. All that was left now of Fair Mead was a handful of dilapidated houses and a vast memorial. And yet somehow, a bare twenty-five years later, we were once again toiling toward the end of another war. It was inconceivable. Toiling, mending, digging, waiting, waiting. The fear and dismay of all these years, the craving for release, gathered and roiled in me like smoke above an oil fire, and I let loose a long sigh.

"All right, dear?" Lucy was gazing up at me, the blanket fabric bunched in one hand, a needle gleaming in the other. A Victorian or-phan, put to work.

"I do so want this to end. For everyone's sake."

Pamela came out of school with Bobby Rail and Ruby Sutton. "We're going to club together and buy a lardy cake at the market next week," she told me.

"Good heavens. How are you going to get there? It's during schooltime."

"We're going to play truant!" All three children spoke together, elated by their foolproof plan.

I laughed aloud. "I think you'll be spotted. Come on, Pamela, it's time to go home."

Pamela, somewhat crushed, said good-bye to her friends. We were on foot today and it was lovely to walk holding her hand. "Tell you what," I said. "You club together, and I'll buy it for you."

She brightened. "I'll get their ha'pennies tomorrow."

"Is that all they're contributing?"

"Bobby and Ruby are poor. They don't get pocket money." She used her patient voice. There were a great many things she'd been obliged to explain to me, *viz* how to make a loop out of a plantain stem and snap it tight so that the black head of the plantain shot off, preferably *at* someone; or trap a grass blade between your upright thumbs and blow on it to produce a shocking squawk; or shove hairy rose-hip seeds down an unsuspecting neck, where they would pro-voke violent itching. I'd never discovered these tricks. At Pamela's age I was still governessed and starched and ironed. I didn't run the lanes until I was eleven and too old, or at least too sad, to learn them. "Bobby only had the money in the first place because he got it off some Yanks."

We reached the head of our lane and crossed the road. As I glanced to the left, I saw a woman walking behind us with a shopping bag.

Trudging for the bus, no doubt. I tightened my clasp on Pamela's soft warm palm. "I wish you wouldn't say Yanks."

"Well, Bobby told the Ya—the Americans that the beer at the Stour Hotel was watered and they'd be better off going to the Buck's Head in Waltham, and they gave him two ha'pennies. But I didn't ask for the whole penny even though Bobby offered it. Just half."

My old home had been a hotel since I left Upton for Waltham. In keeping with its tainted past it had become a funk hole at the beginning of the war—a refuge for rich individuals too frightened to stay in London. Now most of these fearful types had gone, and the bar was open very late to the visiting soldiery—though it was apparent that the servicemen hadn't inspired honesty, let alone generosity, in the staff.

"In point of fact, the soldiers around here are Canadian, Pamela. It's an important distinction. It was nice of you not to take all the money..."

We got home. I put my sewing bag away, washed my hands, and knocked back some risen bread dough I'd started after lunch. I baked only two loaves at a time now that we were four small eaters instead of the seven that we'd been at the beginning of the war. But the bread tins were nowhere to be found. Searching every shelf and drawer in the kitchen resulted only in irritation and dust. How on earth could I have lost the tins? I shaped the dough by hand into two long loaves and left them to rise on a baking sheet. Regular heavy thumps crossed the ceiling from the bedroom above: Pamela, somersaulting. The doorbell rang. I covered the loaves with a cloth and hurried to the door.

A woman was standing on the step.

"I was walking behind you," she said, as if nothing else were required. "I'm so glad to find you in, this time."

Her face was jowly, patient, her teeth few when she smiled. She folded her large, ringed hands, and then I remembered. Those fingers, feeling along the waistband of Pamela's knickers. When we were all in the sitting room, the morning after the bombing. Her face, of course, was less puffy, the bruise vanished from her eye.

"Mrs. Berrow."

She smiled wider. "Phyllis. Phyl to my friends."

She'd done her hair smartly too, in a sort of domed style with an obedient row of curls across her brow. Set with sugar water, no doubt. Conscious of my own slatternly locks, I rammed the pins in across my crown. She watched me do it, and when I had finished she continued to stand on the step, waiting. Her feet cumbersome in her slippery-soled shoes, the bunions noticed by Lucy. But not by me, the first time, back in 1940. I hadn't seen them then. I hadn't looked at her feet.

At last I said, "Do come in."

"I will indeed. Thank you."

I gave her the armchair she'd sat in that morning when Pamela had told us about the candles for her cake. Her carapace of hair caught the light from the window and briefly sparkled.

"Where's that little girl of yours, then?"

I was transported to the horror and the cold of that night, the glare beyond the battened blackout curtain. "Oh Mrs. Berrow, how brave you all were."

She permitted herself a delicate snort. "We was petrified."

As if to answer her, there was a thump on the ceiling. I said, "We couldn't let her go. Not at Christmastime," and she smiled, a slow, kind smile with lips closed, acknowledging the three years and more that had passed since that Christmas.

"I'll make you some tea." I started toward the door, but then turned. "Her mother's dead. She died on the second night of that raid, in the cellar of the Crown."

"I know," said Mrs. Berrow.

• • • • •

Elizabeth back from Waltham, nipping in by the back door.

"Elizabeth I'm making tea."

"You'll be lucky, Mrs. Parr." She shrugged off her skimpy coat. "I let the fire go right down."

The range was cool. In my haste I hadn't noticed. "I've got Mrs. Berrow in the sitting room. One of the ladies from Southampton, on the night of the bombing, do you remember? She had a black eye."

She frowned. "Was she the one that found Pamela's address? What's she doing here?"

I listened to Mrs. Berrow's voice in the sitting room. Pamela had come down. "Hello, dearie," Mrs. Berrow was saying. "Remember me?"

Elizabeth reached for the coal scuttle. "I'll mend that fire. We'll need it hot, for the bread. Though with these bellows . . ."

"I'll see if I can find those chammy leathers," I promised her. "I expect we'll need an awl, to make holes in the bellows for sewing. Perhaps we should ask George Horne. He's an expert home leatherworker . . ." I was babbling, the blood starting in my veins.

"Go next door, Mrs. Parr," Elizabeth said softly. "See that Pamela doesn't annoy the lady." The chief effect of Pamela on her elders, in Elizabeth's eyes, being annoyance.

Mrs. Berrow was sitting leaning forward, hands spread out. Pamela was pressing down on each of the gnarled old fingers. "This one has a ruby ring, this one has a gold ring. They're the queen and the king, I think. This one's crying, he's a prince but he doesn't have any rings at all. Boo hoo, I'm a sad prince. Why don't you give him a ring, Mrs. Berrow?"

So she'd introduced herself.

"He's too little for a ring, dearie. Look at him, he ain't hardly grown up at all."

"Tea will be some time, I'm afraid, Mrs. Berrow."

"Please don't go to any trouble. Your good woman doesn't want to put her range up and I don't blame her." She turned to Pamela. "I suspect you've got some dollies somewhere upstairs. You go and dress them all up properly for me, and when they're ready I'll have a look at them."

"I've got my old peg dolls, that I had when I was that small." Pamela flattened her hand in the air, somewhere near her knee. "I never finished inking their faces and now there's no ink. I can fetch—"

"Go and play, my love. Go on upstairs and play."

How did they do it? Mrs. Berrow, Lady Brock. Two voices less similar one couldn't imagine, and yet both had this kindly, blunted edge of iron that brooked no opposition. Pamela left without anguish, at speed. "Now what I came to tell you, Mrs. Parr," Mrs. Berrow went on, "was that I've been in Southampton all this while, and I've been cleaning the nurses' hostel since last year. I'm a char, dear, I always have been. I don't mind anyone knowing. This hostel is just down the road from the Crown, as it happens, and I live round the corner, and it's the best job I ever had. Those nurses keep everything clean as a new pin, it's in their nature. Sit down, dear."

I obeyed, taking one corner of the sofa. And I was so glad to sit, because I suddenly felt very weary. "This was about ten days ago. I'm out shopping, just opening my bag wondering if my old feet can stand to queue for a loaf, when I see my purse has gone. There was ten and six in there, along with a photo of my late husband, and I was bloody furious. So, sore feet or not I head off to the police station. But."

She stopped. Elizabeth was coming in with a tray. "Ah, my dear." Phyllis Berrow viewed the tea things and the plate of thin toast with a scrape of butter, and sniffed in the smell of strong tea. "That *is* splendid." She waited through Elizabeth's silent retreat before continuing.

"So I go up the cop shop and report it. And afterward I'm standing in the lobby with tears in my eyes, I don't mind saying, because I know full well I won't see my money or my photograph again, and it was just the principle of it—I'm standing there, and this nice young man asks me what's up So I tell him, and blow me, he gets out his wallet and hands me ten and six. 'I can't let you be robbed,' he says. 'There's enough wrong with the world already.' And then he asks me if I know where the Crown Hotel is. 'I should say I do, dear,' I tell him. 'I live and work in spitting distance, but I hope you don't want to stay there, because it's bombed to ruins.' 'I know,' he says to me. 'My wife died in that raid. But my little daughter survived, as far as I know, and I've come to look for her.'"

Mrs. Berrow set a teacup down in front of me. "Are you grasping it, dear? What I'm saying?"

I shook my head, and she lifted the teapot and poured for both of us. Then silence came. I sat very still, knowing I would have to speak.

"How can you even think it?" My lips felt swollen. They rubbed together strangely as I moved them. "He could be any man, any man. There could be any number of children in that hotel. How can you come here and say it's, it's Pamela's . . ."

She poured milk into her cup and then lifted her face to me. Battered, wrinkled, sharp-eyed. "He's still young," she said. "So you can see it full clear. She's the spitting image of him."

My fingers found the piping on the arm of the sofa and pinched it. In my mind's eyes I saw Pamela's hot cheek marked by the raised seam of the bus seat. Where she'd slept on her journey out of Southampton, alone in her dirty blanket.

Mrs. Berrow handed me a cup of tea. It rocked on the saucer as I took it, but didn't spill. I set it down. Her eyes were trained on me. Small, bright blue, almost triangular under the sag of her old eyelids.

"It can't be."

She gave a slow shrug, as if to say: *I am but the messenger.*

"Do you know that this so-called father disappeared from her life before the war? Pamela doesn't even know him. Why has he left it till now, to come out of the blue?"

She took a gulp of tea, sighed. "His wife kicked him out after a year. Took the child away and didn't want any more to do with him."

"There's bound to be a good reason for that. Some men aren't made to be fathers, or husbands—"

"I would say, listening to him, it's his heart's desire to find that little girl." She rolled her eyes, gave me a sweet, colluding woman-to-woman smile. "And I've listened to a lot of people, Mrs. Parr, in my time. It's surprising what ladies and gentlemen tell the char."

That had been my last shot, my last shell, and it had exploded in midair. I leaned my head back, suddenly drowsy with shock. Nauseated, too: even the milk in the tea was unwelcome, greasy in my mouth.

"Would you care for a cigarette?" I heard myself say. "My husband keeps some for visitors."

Selwyn didn't smoke but he didn't mind if other people did. He'd just remark on the smell as a way of inquiring about our guest. *Oh,* he might say. *Who dropped by, darling?* But what would I tell him this time? I held the heavy lighter in both hands but the spark jumped in vain.

"Here, love. Let me." She produced a floppy blue flame, buried the tip of the cigarette in it. The plume of smoke she directed courteously at the ceiling, holding the cigarette pinched in the V of her first two fingers. "Ah, Turkish." She shut her eyes. "Takes me back."

Her hand was dangerously close to her head. I hoped she wouldn't catch her hair. It would caramelize in an instant.

"They're probably rather stale."

She opened her eyes. "I've seen him again, you know. He's taken to walking by the Crown. Up the street, down again, and into the Lyons on the corner. Waiting for those coppers to pull their fingers out, is my guess, and in the meantime he don't know what to do with himself. I ain't spoken to him—ducked out the way, in fact."

"And you still hold to this, this resemblance?"

She didn't reply. The sitting room door was opening with its usual tiny creak. Pamela came in. "I've dressed them up. Guess what they are!"

In her hands, bunched against her belly, eight or nine wooden clothes-pegs, each swathed in one of Selwyn's white silk handkerchiefs. As she kneeled, some of them tumbled onto the floor. She laid them out in a line, pushing and patting the folds of silk into position.

"Roman ladies?" I forced a smile onto my face. "Those dresses look a bit like togas. No—of course not. Roman ladies don't wear togas." But neither Phyl nor Pamela was listening to me. Pamela was picking up the peg dolls one by one and placing them on the generous double hump of Phyl's knees.

"They're ghosts," Pamela was telling her. "*Oooh, oooh.* See?"

"I do see."

Her eyes met mine over Pamela's head, just as Pamela turned and said to me, "Is Mrs. Berrow going to stay the night again? She was telling me all about it earlier."

"No, Pamela. We're going to finish our tea, and then I'm taking Mrs. Berrow to the bus stop."

I walked with her down the lane. The evenings were lengthening now, and she'd be back well before dark. She went surprisingly fast for a heavy woman with avowedly sore feet, rolling from side to side in such a way that her elbow occasionally jogged mine, with no shortness of breath.

"He was invalided home from Italy," she said as we walked. "He went to Plymouth to see his wife and it was the Plymouth coppers who told him the story. So up he came to Southampton. Our police will get round to him in the end, and then he'll be arriving in Upton before you can say knife. I'm just trying to warn you, dear."

We passed under a tall dank hedge. "Thank you, Mrs. Berrow. I'll consider myself *warned.*"

"I don't blame you for a bit of temper. Call me Phyl, by the way."

"Likewise, Ellen. I do beg your pardon. I should be reimbursing you for your bus instead of making rude remarks. Especially as you've made two journeys on my behalf." My words were dull in the still air.

"I won't hear of it, Ellen my dear."

We sat in the bus shelter, safe from the fine drizzle that had begun to fall as we covered the last hundred yards. A loop of river lay beyond the fence in the bottom of the field opposite, and the cows churned the bank as we watched, muddy to the hocks.

"I hates the country," Phyl said.

"It can't be him." The words burst out of me. "It's just too ridiculous, for you to tell me a man looks like a girl child. That's all you've done, talk to a man in a crowd who told you he'd mislaid a daughter. Did he say her name? Did he?"

"No."

"There. And now you've formed this ridiculous opinion. I won't countenance it."

She leaned forward on the seat, looking back toward the village. "If you want to take a look at him, come down to Southampton one afternoon, get a bus to the Crown stops. Come at four o'clock, we can sit in the Lyons together. We'll have a bit of a chat if he spots me. Write to me care of the nurses' hostel and tell me when you're coming."

"I'll do no such thing—"

"The bus is coming, dear."

So it was, a motoring burr beyond the trees. I rubbed my knees like a schoolgirl. "He can't have known her. They can't have been a proper family, ever. Why should he suddenly care now?"

She patted my arm. "Why don't your old man give you a baby," she said, almost to herself.

"He's given me himself. That's enough."

That tickled her: she gave me a sharp, mirthful glance. "He must be one hell of a chap. How did you two bump into each other, anyhow?"

"We did precisely that. Bump into each other. It was an extraordinary piece of luck."

The bus drew up, came to a stop. In the quiet, the door swished open. "Thank you," I said as she mounted the step. She turned to speak to me once more.

"I ain't said nothing to the man. Nothing," she repeated, meeting my eyes. "Do you understand?"

Pamela and Elizabeth were kneeling on sheets of newspaper by the back door, polishing shoes. Elizabeth turned her face up to me, her expression one of a person who had listened to a solid forty-five minutes of Pamela's chatter. "Oh, it's times like these I miss the boys," she told me. "If you slip yours off, Mrs. Parr, we'll do them now."

"*Buff buff buff buff buff.*" Pamela plied the brush over Selwyn's toe caps. "*Buff buff buff.*"

"Stop that now, young Pam. Did the lady go off all right?"

I stepped out of my shoes. Found a bright tone to reply to Elizabeth. "Oh yes! She caught the bus with plenty of time to spare. We had a nice chat. I think she simply came to say thank you to us. She said she fancied an outing. Oh, lord, Elizabeth, I forgot the bread."

"I didn't. Look, they've kissed." Elizabeth nodded toward the cooling rack where the two baked loaves sat, fused together down the long side. I'd put them too close together on the tray.

"So they have. Never mind. I'm sure I'll find those wretched tins before the next time." As I went to the larder I caught sight of Pamela's face, a secretive moon of guilt and glee.

"Pamela? Do you know where the tins are?"

She squirmed, but it was with pleasure rather than apprehension. She was safe in my love and she knew it. "I'm very sorry, Ellen. I just borrowed them for a short while. They're completely perfect for doll beds."

"You're the absolute limit. Please go and get them."

"But the mattresses fit in exactly! What's wrong with the bread kissing, anyway? We can just eat double toasts. It would be fun. Oh— I got you a present." She jumped up and left the room, returning a moment later with a newspaper parcel.

I took it from her while she stood, beaming. "What on earth?"

"Open it."

I pulled aside the newspaper. It was a pair of oven gloves, made of a heavy coarse yarn the color of porridge. Made all of a piece, two pockets for the hands joined by a wide strip. The most useful, durable, practical kind.

"Oh, Pamela."

"Elizabeth told me you needed some, and Suky fetched them from the market for me." She beamed wider. "I used up half my pocket money savings." Bathed now in munificence and self-congratulation. Her small face glowing.

"Darling heart, come here."

She smelled of fresh air, boot polish, and sugar, and I clung to her.

Selwyn was lying on the bed, fully clothed. Everyone in the house was asleep except us. When he felt me watching him, he turned his head, held my gaze: surprised, perhaps, at the way I stood without speaking.

"We had to repair the block on the beam today. I had to bicycle over to the forge at Barrow End and get Edwin Lusty to beat a new pin. It took the best part of the day." He sighed. "It's exactly like living in medieval times."

"Except for the bicycle, I suppose."

He smiled. A small coal fire hissed in the bedroom grate.

"I got very cold, up there on the beam."

"I don't begrudge you a fire, my darling."

The letter from Marjorie Lord was lying on the bedside table along with the solicitor's note.

"Pamela will have to know, eventually, I suppose," Selwyn said.

"What?"

"That her aunt disowned her . . . Oh, yes. Look." He reached for the second sheet and held it out to me. "This is what I noticed. The solicitor identifies Marjorie Lord as *née* Pickering."

I peered. There was the phrase exactly, in brownish-black ink on pressed blue paper. *On behalf of Mrs. Marjorie Lord (née Pickering)* . . .

My understanding was slow. I thought suddenly of the young trees William had given me a few days ago. I should go and tend them tomorrow. Watering was vital at these early stages. The wind had dried out the soil a great deal.

"Don't you see?" Selwyn's eyes were wide and earnest behind his glasses. "Pamela's mother, Amelia's, *maiden* name was Pickering."

"No. No." I gave a slow shake of the head. "Don't you remember, she was *Mrs*. . . ."

Selwyn tutted. "She would merely have called herself that. She mightn't have been married at all." He sighed. "We've been barking up the wrong tree, haven't we. Looking for Mr. Pickering all this while. He could be called anything."

"Mr. Anything." My voice was tight and dull. "Yes, he could."

"Well, whatever his name is, he's still the same renegade. I doubt any authority will bring him to heel after all this time." When I didn't reply, Selwyn looked at me once more. "Ellen, darling, are you all right?"

"Tired."

The house was quiet. We both listened to the soft roar of the water outside as it coursed into the spillway. Unending, unending, except in flood. He propped himself up on one elbow and tossed the solicitor's letter back onto the bedside table. "What were you thinking of just now? When you were gazing at me."

"Do you remember that girl you bumped into? The bright-eyed thing with her long stride and her Trollope from the library?"

He sat up and held out his arms. "You still are that girl," he said. "You always will be, to me."

I moved onto the bed and accepted his embrace. "I can't even remember her."

"Because you have so many cares. My sweetheart, you'll find her again after the war."

"Yes, maybe." I closed my eyes. "After the war."

I remembered the first time we lay down together on this bed. We were fully clothed then, and I had just put the new sheet on, tucked it tight.

"Selwyn," I said.

"What?" He stirred beside me.

"I'll always love you."

"Excellent."

"No, I mean it," I said. "Come what may. I'll never regret loving you. Saying yes."

He propped himself up on one elbow, searching my face. The white sheet sailed out and hovered in the air, foursquare, and it would settle in a second. In a second, it would alight on the bed.

Ellen

1939

16

MAKING MY WAY along Castle Road in the shadow of the printing press, I looked up to see a gull flying down the street above me, lower than the rooftops. I realized that it was spring—sensing it in the warm breeze, since there was nothing to guide me in the way of trees or flowers.

I was returning from the library, where I'd exchanged *The Eustace Diamonds* and *Phineas Redux* for *The Prime Minister* and *The Duke's Children*. When I got back to my room, I would stand the books, spine outward, on my table, using my boxes of cotton reels and elastics as bookends, and pretend they were mine. At the age of six I'd been the owner of two entire shelves of books. I could still see the sunlight striking the titles, some bright gold, others, belonging originally to my mother and father, a deeper bronze.

But I was eighteen now, and perhaps it was simply adulthood, or perhaps it was also the insulating effect of three meals a day, but I was now able to remember my old books, to wander freely through the Stour House of my memory without feeling that jolt of shriveling pain. Even more so now that it was a hotel, its outbuildings prettied up and its graveled drive rutted by motor cars. Lucy and I had peered in through the gateway one Sunday. The Stour Hotel, Lucy opined, looked "a bit racy." I had searched the brick façade for signs of raciness but could see none, wondering later if it was the sleek shining line of parked motor cars that had given her that impression.

The Absaloms, however, was another matter. My thoughts refused to dwell there.

I also had a volume called *Heroic Feats of Animals.* This was for Lucy. "I'm fed up to the back teeth with stories," she told me. "I want something about real life. Real life, and with dogs in." She railed about her life, the dirt, the cold, but over the past few years she'd come to love the hounds. I still spent most Sundays in Upton, and occasionally she took me up to the kennels to see them. They pressed their noses against the wire and yodeled at her, their bellies pale, like the inside of tree bark. She put her hand out and bade them "clam up." She was no longer even trying to read, so after Sunday dinner I read to her. If she especially loved the book, we'd go together to the bus stop and sit on the bench and continue until my bus came. Whenever anyone passed by, I was to fall silent. She didn't want them to hear me speaking the words aloud to her.

It was nice to be out. My working life was spent in cacophony, a noise like hundreds of thousands of small nails falling onto a tin roof, the typing pool at full stretch. I unbuttoned the collar of my coat in the fine warm breeze. Reaching the corner, I turned into Waltham Square, glancing up at the gull that was now winging ahead of me.

And stepped straight into the arms of a man.

We buffeted each other, sprang back gasping. My books flew from my hands.

"Oh!" We bent simultaneously to the pavement. I felt a sharp clout to my temple as his head hit mine, and I fell to my knees in agony. *"Ouch!"*

"I'm so sorry. I do beg your pardon. I was looking the other way." His voice was fine and light. I didn't know what he looked like. My eyes were squeezed shut. "My skull," I heard him say next. "My skull is thicker than yours. The male brow ridge. I'm so sorry."

I clasped my hand to my temple. "I'm lucky you aren't a Neander-thal person," I managed to say. "You would have laid me out."

I opened my eyes. He had spectacles, fixing them carefully to his face as I watched. Making him recognizable. "You're from Upton," I blurted.

He was smiling broadly. Sandy hair tufted on the top of his head. A gentleman somewhere in his thirties. "I am indeed. Of Upton, and not, as you say, of Neanderthal stock. Yes, they did have the most co-lossal brow ridges. Although I feel we malign them. Brains aren't everything."

"Oh, they had extremely large brains."

He raised his eyebrows. "Did they indeed? Clearly it's how one uses one's brain that counts, then, rather than its absolute volume. It seems you give yours a great deal of exercise."

"I spend most evenings reading. In the library. And in my room."

We were both still kneeling on the pavement. I looked up to see people skirting us, smirking. He rose to his feet and held out his hands. They were warm, dry, thin, strong.

In Bishop's Tearooms they gave me a compress and a little bowl of iced water. I sat holding the folded damp linen to my brow.

"My name's Selwyn Parr. And you?"

My name, trailing after me like a soiled slip. But there was nothing for it.

"I'm Ellen Calvert."

The tea came. He took over the task of pouring from the fluted metal pot. "Was there a—was there a Captain Calvert? In that splendid house the other side of Beacon Hill, beyond Barrow End . . ." I watched him make his way toward realization, embarrassment.

"Yes. I was his daughter." The past tense felt better.

He filled our cups and set the pot down. "I'm so sorry. I was abroad at that time. I heard, afterward. And now I'm repeating it back to you. How dreadful of me." He blinked behind his glasses, at a loss.

"It's a hotel now, of course." I put down my compress.

"I know." His lips turned down. "They attract a rather fast crowd, I believe."

"Do they?" I repressed a smile. Lucy had been right.

He had long fingers. They held his cup as if it were porcelain rather than thick tearoom china. The tea was strong and brown. "So where did you go after the Stour House?" he persisted. "Your family, I mean."

It had to be my youth. People thought they could ask a person under twenty-one anything they liked. "We came to Upton," I told him. "My brother went to sea. My mother sadly died. But I was helped a great deal by Mr. and Miss Dawes, and managed to get a post at the Town Hall, in the typing pool. And this is where I live now, in Waltham, at the hostel at the back of the Town Hall. And today's my afternoon off, which is why I was walking back from the library." I knew I was beginning to sound pointed, piling detail upon detail. But he seemed not to notice. He was staring in distraction, at my hair, my hands, into my eyes.

"Drink your tea, Mr. Parr, or it'll go cold."

A smile caught his lips. "I've been awfully rude."

"Not at all."

"How old are you?"

"Eighteen. And you? Since we're forgetting our manners?"

He laughed, a peal of light laughter. His teeth were white and regular. "Thirty-nine."

"And you own the mill in Upton." A memory pricked me— William, speaking to me in the potting shed. "Old Mr. Parr was your uncle, wasn't he, and—"

That's right." He picked up his cup. "Fine flours and animal feeds. I inherited it when my uncle died, five years ago now, and I'm at last starting to make a fist of it. In spite of my secretary, who is hopeless, even more so now she's about to leave and get married. Every day she comes a little nearer to telling me."

I'm a good secretary, I nearly said.

"I suspect that you're a good secretary, Miss Calvert."

I laughed aloud.

He accompanied me back to the hostel. "Any headache, any dizziness, alert somebody. There is someone who looks after you all? Miss Careless? Not a very propitious name. Be aware, Miss Calvert. Concussion can be dangerous." He handed me my books. "Enjoy your Trollope. And"—raising his eyebrows—"*Heroic Feats of Animals.*"

"That one's for a friend." I was smiling. "She's not so fond of fiction."

"Good for her." He glanced again at the cover. "I knew a horse, during the War, who would be a natural study for this book." As we shook hands, he cleared his throat. "I'm in Waltham once a fortnight or so. Perhaps I could take you to tea another time? When we've not been so violently struck on the head."

I felt a warm blush of amazement and delight all over my face and neck. "That would be very nice."

"May I leave a note here?"

I nodded. "This door's unlocked in daylight hours. We've got pigeonholes inside, with our names on. And then there's another door—that one's always locked."

"So I should hope." He was smiling back at me. "Good-bye, Miss Calvert. Until we meet again."

There was now a lump, pinkish, on his temple. Was there somebody to watch over him? "You must take your own advice, Mr. Parr," I said, lifting my hand toward his face. "About concussion."

He gave a slight bow of obedience, and turned away.

I didn't watch the pigeonholes. I merely bought another slide for my hair. A practical one, from the chemist's, to hold it more firmly in place. It had taken a month of walking, in Waltham, to beat its bounds, to cross the square and perch on the step of the market cross, to sit in the bus shelter when it rained; to visit Mrs. Priddy in the baker's shop, Mrs. Royle in the chemist's, Mr. and Miss Barker at Barker's Outfitters for underwear and stockings. I had to erase my former life, my grimed and lonely memories, from every yard of the streets, and put in place a new Ellen, well-fed, contented, and strong. The principal—indeed, the only—objection in my mind to seeing Selwyn Parr again was the fact that he came from Upton.

A tall figure in the main aisle of Upton Church. I knew him now. My church visits had become so much more regular now that I was clean and respectable and visited the Hornes for lunch. Sandy hair, a carrying tenor voice: yes. He was the good singer.

"Yes. I do sing." He did so, quietly. *"Because there is none other that fighteth for us . . ."*

Two ladies at the next table turned their heads and smiled at him. Their gazes traveled benevolently from him to me, and I smiled too. Uncle and niece, they probably thought. Or godfather and goddaughter. We were having tea at Bishop's Tearooms, as he had promised, a fortnight later. The note had been well sealed. One of my fellow typists, Polly, had snatched it from me but I'd foiled her with a sturdy grab of her wrist.

". . . but only Thou, O Lord." Even *sotto voce* the notes were floating and true.

"Why aren't you in the choir at Upton?"

"Ah, but I am. Clearly you've never attended Evensong. I don't sing at Matins because I take Lady Brock to church on Sunday mornings and stand with her. As much as a person like Lady Brock allows herself to be taken anywhere."

"How is Sir Michael?"

He looked away. His eyes were almost square with sadness. "I don't think he'll leave the Hall again." He looked back at me. "It was gas, you know, during the War."

A memory pricked me. "Mr. Kennet told me that you drove an ambulance."

He took off his spectacles and began to polish them. "I did." He held the spectacles to the light, squinted. "They said my sight was too poor for combat. Though good enough to fling one of those vehicles through the ruts, it seemed." He cleared his throat. "It did for my nerves, rather, afterward, and I departed for the Holy Land. But that's another story . . ." He glanced up. "I didn't know you were acquainted with Mr. Kennet."

I nodded.

"Splendid chap. A copper beater, you know, before he got his hand blown off, half of it, anyway."

I nodded. "At Dammstrasse," I said. "The Battle of Messines. I also know Mr. Horne, and old Mrs. Horne. Lucy Horne and Daniel Corey, Harvey Corey's boy, were my schoolfriends. They're still my friends."

His brow wrinkled. "So do I gather . . . that you went to Upton School?"

His incredulity made me smile. "Most of my education I got from a young lady called Miss Fane, who was my governess before my father ruined us. But then, yes, I went to Upton School."

An episode of rapid blinking. I'd shocked him at last. "Dear girl. Dear girl."

"It's a good school. Miss Yarnold worked hard on us. And there was a huge fire, lit in October and put out in April. That was the main thing. The fire."

He placed his warm, dry hand over mine. "And where did you live, while you were at Upton School?"

I didn't particularly want his hand over mine, but I didn't take my hand away. "Do you mind awfully if we change the subject?"

"Of course. Of course. I do apologize." He cast around. "Look. Have another scone."

I shook my head. I was still unable to eat very much food at one time. But I dearly wanted to take that scone away in a paper bag.

"I'll ask Mrs. Bishop to pack it," he said in a low voice.

There. Every inch a godfather.

"Why are you smiling?" he said.

"No reason. Except that I'm happy."

I realized it was true. And so was he. I looked into his eyes for anything veiled, troubled, guarded, but there was nothing except a transported blue gaze. Not innocent, like Edward's: these eyes were older, and they had seen the Great War. I could tell that, by their sharpness. He was a man who, before looking at me, had looked at many dreadful things. But he was delighted now.

We were visited by a sudden moment of delicious serenity.

"I can't believe we've only met twice," I found myself saying, and just as I did so his eyes left mine, and then he rose to his feet as I heard a middle-aged female voice, slightly hoarse, cut of solid lead crystal.

"Selwyn! I thought it was you!"

I got up out of my chair and turned to face her. She had a large, long red mouth, and she was seemingly incapable of hiding her feelings, because it dropped open in astonishment. The long red mouth had an unusually fat and featureless top lip, which reminded me of one of those large tropical fish that graze on coral—wrasse, I thought.

"Heavens, it's Miss—"

"Calvert, Ellen Calvert." I saved her from pronouncing the soiled name. I put out my hand. "How do you do." Feeling the new hair-slide bite at my nape. So glad that it was dependable.

"Althea Brock," she said. "A pleasure."

"I love Bishop's. The scones are quite gargantuan. Look at that." Lady Brock held up the remaining scone between thumb and forefinger. "You could feed a family of four on it. You don't mind if I pinch your plate, dear, do you?" She took my plate and knife and slathered the remaining butter over the scone, divided each half into half again and set about dispatching the resulting four sections into her maw of a mouth. I met Selwyn's eyes. They were keen with amused embarrassment. He lifted his shoulders in the slightest shrug.

"Any tea in that pot?" Lady Brock said through crumbs.

Selwyn laughed. "At least let me get you a cup, Althea." He signaled to the waitress, was ignored in the crowd, rose to his feet, and left the table.

Lady Brock turned to me, chewing. "I'm absolutely famished. I've been up at the farms all day. Nothing like a silage clamp for dulling your appetite. One never wants lunch as a result, so by midafternoon one's ready to boil up one's own shoes and eat the soles with brown sauce. I'm on my way to Mrs. Pettit for a fitting. She used to come to me, but last year she told me there are too many calls on her time now, if you please, so I have to get out the motor and flog into Waltham. But there we are. Everything changes, doesn't it, Miss Calvert. You in particular, I think."

She had brown eyes the color of coffee, mobile, rather liquid, rather close-set. The span of her mouth almost exceeded that of her eyes. While she was eating, they had been sliding all over my face, my hands, my clothes. Now they looked directly into mine.

I folded my napkin, edge to edge. I'd expected constraint, anxiety, but after the initial surprise of her arrival—and of her consumption of the scone—I realized she held no fear for me. "I've had the greatest good fortune, Lady Brock. I have a job at the Town Hall, in the typing pool. I live in the hostel with some jolly girls. Our meals are nourishing. My room's very warm."

I had kept the room with the boiler pipe. The first time Lucy came to Waltham to see me, we had spent a deal of time standing on the bed in stockinged feet, caressing the pipe in awe.

"Oh yes. Evie Norris helped train you, isn't that right? My farm manager's daughter. That girl is a terrific horticulturalist, you know."

"Really?" I was confused as much by Lady Brock's pointed tone as by the news itself.

"Indeed. There was quite a traffic in slips and scions that year—the year you had your lessons, I mean. From my greenhouses to her little cloches and propagation beds. Some of the plants were really quite rare."

I searched her long, sardonic, deeply amused face. I was utterly bewildered, and then, a second later, bewildered no more.

"Mr. Kennet," I said slowly. "He paid Evie in cuttings—!"

Lady Brock held a gloved finger to her lips. "It's a huge secret. William hates his good deeds to be bruited abroad."

"Surely *I* should know, as the recipient!"

"Perhaps. Thank him in private, dear, and make it brief. He would hate fuss."

A waitress came with a cup and saucer and a fresh pot of tea. Selwyn followed her. He was holding a brown paper bag, folded at the top and grease-specked, which he placed without comment on the table between us.

"Mr. Parr and I collided in the street a fortnight ago," I said. "Now he's giving me tea, by way of apology."

"I wasn't looking where I was going," Selwyn told her.

Lady Brock rummaged in the pocket of her mackintosh and produced a battered packet of cigarettes. She offered them to me: I shook my head. Selwyn, suddenly, was holding out a cigarette lighter with a small flame dancing on top. Lady Brock inhaled deeply.

"Selwyn's always been rather distracted." She emitted a blue jet of smoke. "Even as a child. He'd go out for a stag beetle and come back with a slow worm."

"Simply because the slow worm was more interesting. Not because I'd forgotten about the stag beetle." He was smiling broadly, fanning the smoke away from his face. "Althea, kindly direct your fumes elsewhere. I've got Compline in Barrow End tonight."

She ignored him. "He and I have known each other since he was small enough to hide among the gooseberry bushes. I was like a much larger teenage sister. Never mind, I should be on my way. Mrs. Pettit will be having a seizure." She got up from the table, and so did Selwyn, and I. Lady Brock shook my hand. "A pleasure," she said, and then, still holding my gaze, "Selwyn, darling. Do look out. Do look where you're going."

He nodded, smiling. "I will, Althea. Good afternoon."

We watched her stride past the window, mackintosh flapping. Selwyn handed the brown paper bag to me. "Another scone."

"You shouldn't have."

"But you might like it, later."

"No. I mean that *she* should have replaced it. She was the one who ate it."

He sighed. "She knows no better."

We walked back to the hostel, agreeing that we would meet in church at Upton on Sunday and perhaps visit Lady Brock for a cup of tea in the afternoon, after my luncheon date at the Hornes.' "I'd have to take the late bus, though. The last time I did that, I squeaked in a minute before curfew . . ."

"Ellen, I have a motor car. I can drive you."

The street outside the hostel was empty, and there was a dusty breeze that tugged at my hat. "Yes, but should you?" I blinked, my eyes suddenly gritty. "You heard what Lady Brock said. You should look—"

He laughed in a forced way. "I'm hardly going to bump into you again, am I!"

Could he really be so stupid? I stared up at him. There was a faint flush at the top of his cheeks. He was pretending he hadn't grasped Lady Brock's meaning. He and she had stood there, imagining they were speaking in code, as if in front of a child. "You needn't fear on my account, Mr. Parr. I've become quite resilient, what with one thing and another."

That evening I wrote a letter to William, care of Lady Brock at Upton Hall, thanking him for his great kindness in the matter of the cuttings. *I shall always, always be in your debt. If in the future I can render you any service, Mr. Kennet, please let me know.*

I had a reply two days later. Well-spaced small capitals, sitting solidly on lined paper. IT WAS NOTHING I ASSURE YOU ELLEN. I LIKE TO DO FAVORS WHERE I CAN. I KNEW YOU WOULD WORK HARD AND THAT IS REPAYMENT ENOUGH. YOURS WM KENNET.

I told Lucy about Selwyn before church, as quietly as possible, as we walked up the lane to the lych-gate. She often met me at the bus stop but today she was late, so we only came in sight of each other at the head of the lane where a dozen or so people were filing through into the graveyard and the church itself. I told her what had happened and she came to a standing halt, as I knew she would. "Mr. Parr?" She was gaping. "Parson Parr of Parr's Mill?"

"Why do you call him that?"

"Everyone does. 'Cause he wanted to be a vicar, but then he changed his mind." She gave a long, throaty chortle. "Ellen. You *are* having me on. What the hell do you want with Parson Parr?"

"Don't say 'hell' here, so near to the church."

She sucked her teeth. "You can see that he's about a hundred and five."

"He's thirty-nine."

"*He's thirty-nine.*" She mimicked my plaintive tone. "Oh, good God above. You've got it for Mr. Parr. Who would have thought."

I glanced up at the church door, hot with irritation. "I knew you'd be like this. I only told you because I need to excuse myself after dinner. He's taking me to tea at the Hall."

She walked a small circle, her hands on her hair. Another laugh, this one harder. "Tea at the Hall. *Tea at the Hall.* Well, I never."

Mr. Price, the verger, was at the church door, his hand on the bolt. There was no one behind us. "Lucy. Come on." I started up the path.

On the way to the church she stopped again, twice, once to say, "Can he see without his specs on?" and then, "Make sure you don't miss your bus, after *tea at the Hall.*"

I didn't tell her he was driving me back to Waltham. It would have finished her.

I marked the page with the silk ribbon and closed my prayer book. If I raised my eyes I could see Selwyn with Lady Brock the scone thief, today in a startling hat, a winged sort of turban. One of the wings was lower than the other, as if the hat had flown in and just that minute settled on her head. Lady Brock cared for her good friend Selwyn, and less than nothing for me. She already knew who I was. What on earth did she have in mind, inviting me to tea?

As they left the church, they both turned their heads and smiled at me, and I couldn't help it. I was not the person in Upton that I was in Waltham. I blushed, and blushed, and even my lips were hot, and I kept my foolish burning eyes on the floor like a stupid schoolgirl. What was I thinking of? What was Selwyn thinking of?

I produced the fruit tart from my bag. "There weren't any treacle ones left," I said to old Mrs. Horne. "This is gooseberry."

Mrs. Horne nodded. "Very acceptable, dear. Thank you."

After we washed the dishes, we sat in the parlor as we usually did. I was secretly recovering from the sharp pain in my stomach which invariably came after eating so much delicious food, sharper today because of the impending tea. Lucy's father sat outside on a stool with his pipe. Lucy and her grandmother embroidered. We enjoyed a spell of quiet, and then Lucy said, in a thick voice, "Ellen's got to go."

"I know," Mrs. Horne said calmly without raising her eyes. I watched her deft, calloused old fingers stabbing and looping. An apple swelled in gradations from green to gold to deep pink. Lucy was talented but her grandmother's work was glorious. The older her hands became, the more beautiful the result. I cleared my throat.

"Lucy, would you care to walk with me to the Hall?"

She shook her head. "I should get up to the kennels."

"You're not wanted there till evening time," said her father from the doorway.

"Go on, girl," Mrs. Horne told her. "Get your sulky face out of my sight."

Selwyn met us at the door in the wall of the estate, where Lucy and Daniel and I had entered when we were young. Selwyn shook my hand and Lucy's. I wondered whether she would suck her lip down over the gaps in her teeth, as she tended to do with strangers, but she didn't this time because she said nothing at all, simply giving Selwyn a brief black stare as he said, "How do you do?" and then turning away. We both watched her stiff back retreating. I was confounded by her rudeness. But Selwyn just said, "She's a shy little thing."

We passed in under the high elms that were loud with rooks today and walked up the path toward Mr. Kennet's shed. Selwyn chuckled. "Bill gets up a tremendous fug in that hut, doesn't he, with his charcoal stove. It must be the warmest place in Upton Hall. Do you want to look in on him?"

"I think not today."

Two sparrows in the birdbath wriggled and flicked water with their wings. We walked on toward the house.

17

"Nipper," shouted Lady Brock, as the dog flung itself to the end of its chain. "Nipper, for God Almighty's *sake*."

We edged past the limit of the chain, Selwyn laughing. "Hello, Nipper," he said. "So nice, to be greeted this way by an old friend."

"He's losing his marbles. He doesn't recognize you. Everyone is new. Imagine that." Lady Brock gave me a wide grin. The hat was still roosting on her head. "Look at this thing," she said, following my eyes. "It needs to be put out of its misery. Come in. Mrs. Hicks has commanded us to go into the sunroom, since she burst a cushion in the drawing room and the air's full of feathers." She took us inside and pointed across the hall. "Ellen, my dear, desport yourself in there. I shall go and order tea. Selwyn, would you be kind and play to Michael?"

"It would be a pleasure." He mounted the stairs, glanced back at me with a smile.

"He won't be long," said Lady Brock. "Sir Michael's been looking forward to some Chopin all afternoon, but he'll only want a quarter of an hour or so. We moved the piano upstairs a month ago. It had to go through the gallery windows. Ted Blunden and Ernie Mount couldn't budge it with their block and tackle, so we got the firemen over from Waltham and they inserted it in a trice. I have great confidence in them should we ever be ablaze."

She disappeared down the hallway. I went where she'd bidden me. The air in there was sunlit and shaded, cool and thick and green with the smell of earthenware pots of alyssum that were ranked, shelf upon shelf, along one portion of the rear wall. A cactus grew up the edge of the huge glass doors, metal-framed and the metal painted black, which led out to the steps and the garden. The wicker chair creaked as I sat in it.

Dimly through the green the single notes came down from above, rounded, dropping. I hadn't known that Selwyn played the piano. It floored me. He'd only told me words. I hadn't seen or felt anything of his life, his world, until now.

I couldn't stay still. At the other end of the sunroom was another set of doors. They led into a gloomy dining room where the curtains were drawn. And beyond that, through another doorway, the hall, and somewhere beyond, the clink of crockery. I followed the sound and came upon the kitchen where a woman was pouring boiling water from a kettle into a teapot, face set upon the task. "I believe you must be Mrs. Hicks."

She glanced up, and down again. Her face mumping around toothless jaws. "And I believe you must be Ellen Calvert." She took a tea strainer between thumb and finger and placed it on its pot. "I know about you. You and the Horne girl, pushing your dirty little bodies at my nephew."

She was surely raving. I opened my mouth to tell her, but she was quicker. "Samuel Pearce on the railway line. His ear and his neck scalded cruel. I wouldn't serve you so much as a cube of sugar if it was up to me, so you're lucky it in't."

She set down a white milk jug. The rim and spout and handle decorated with forget-me-nots. No, they weren't. They were speedwells. I stood, once again pied with chalk and coal dust, stinking and trembling.

Lady Brock came in. "Ah, Ellen. You've come to admire the copper. Good. Let me show you William's. It's better than his apprentice master's, though he would never agree."

I followed her silently into a buttery. I glared up at the shining pans and kettles hanging in rows from the ceiling. My hands were shaking, so I made them into one large fist and held them at my waist. "Those are most fine." I found my voice shaking too.

"You mustn't mind Mrs. Hicks. She—"

"It wasn't even true. I did not *push* myself—"

"She can be the most vicious animal." Lady Brock reached up, took down a pan. "Look. A fish kettle." She handed it to me and bent to a cupboard. "Here's the drainer and the lid. Look at the handles, look how the lips are rolled." She turned the pan, letting the light play over the beaten, rosy gold. "William made that when he was sixteen. He'd barely been apprenticed a year. And then the Boche blew off his hand, or most of it." Her eyes met mine, her mouth in a level line. The top lip protruded as before. "I knew you came to William's shed. With Lucy Horne and Daniel Corey."

"Yes." I still felt sick from the attack. "I used to do their sums and spellings for them."

She smiled. "William's a sweet man, an unimpeachable man. Unlike some, gross people, who take advantage of good girls. Despicable people." She held me in a steady gaze, and Sam Pearce was condemned. "The worst of it is," she went on, "the good men must all carry on, even though the War did so much damage. William. My husband . . ." She took the kettle from me and reached up with her long arms to suspend it from its hook. "Selwyn," she added lightly, turning toward the door.

"Selwyn?" I said to her back.

"He never thought he'd come to the mill, of course. He wasn't the heir, you see, it was his poor cousin Victor. But Victor and Henry both died at the Somme. Selwyn wanted to be a priest, but the War made everything harder. He abandoned his training."

She began to walk back through the kitchen, now empty of Mrs. Hicks and the tray. "He went to Jerusalem, taught in a school. Oh, I missed him dreadfully during those years." We crossed the hall and traveled into the gloom of the dining room. "I was glad when his uncle died, because I knew it would bring him home." She came to a halt in the doorway of the sunroom. Above us the notes of the piano continued to fall. "Ellen," said Lady Brock, "I'm telling you all this because you're very young. Selwyn's not a demonstrative man, but he's very much in love with you—"

I closed my eyes as a glorious golden blush washed from the crown of my head to the soles of my feet. "Oh . . ."

"He's in love with you, and he's never been properly in love before. His life has been—dreadfully dislocated. It's left him . . ."

I opened my eyes as the music came to a stop above us.

"Somewhat damaged."

I shook my head, bemused. "I've seldom met a more . . . undamaged person."

She covered her mouth with her hand, as if to stem laughter, but I realized it wasn't that. She was trying to keep words inside her.

"Do tell me, please, Lady Brock."

But she turned and walked ahead of me into the sunroom. She started pulling down the blinds at one end of the room, intensifying the green of the shade. "Don't you adore alyssum?"

It might have been chickweed for all I cared. "Lady Brock. Please. Whatever it is . . ."

"Have you heard the expression *mariage blanc,* my dear?"

I pondered the words. "Is it the French for 'white wedding'?"

"No, it is not, my dear." Footsteps sounded in the hall. Lady Brock bent to the tea tray as Selwyn came in.

"Sir Michael wishes to sleep." Selwyn gave a wan smile. "He won't have Nurse Fletcher give him his dose. He'd prefer his dear love, he says."

Lady Brock poured milk into each cup before standing up straight. She turned to me. "Come up with me, my dear. Sir Michael has a rather glorious bedroom ceiling."

I followed her up some dark stairs to an oak-paneled corridor with a door at the end. She took a few paces, then came to a halt. "Ellen, a *marriage blanc in good plain* English is a marriage without any breeding going on."

A hot blush rose up my neck. "Ah. Oh. I see."

Lady Brock shook her head. "Oh God, Ellen. I've said far too much. I'll leave it to Selwyn . . ." She trailed off with a sigh. "He's such a bally fool."

She pushed open the door and a barrel-vaulted ceiling yawned above me, cross-hatched with heraldic beasts and symbols, a checkered pageant of the Middle Ages. In each square, a sword, a griffin, a shield, a dragon, all wound about with leaves, rare lobed fruits, crested birds. I held my breath along with the curved inbreath of the ceiling. Reflected in a long mirror was a slanted shard of a man, a face white above dark bedclothes, lips dry and parted. "Darling?" whispered the lips. Lady Brock patted my arm, and went in, closing the door behind her.

When I returned to the sunroom, I found the French windows open and Selwyn sitting outside, on the third stone step, clasping his arms around his knees. I went and sat beside him. His fingers clenched and unclenched. He was a thin man, his wrists, where they came out of the sleeves, all sinew and bone. I placed one hand upon his clenching fists to stop him saying what he was going to say, but he spoke anyway. "Ellen, I've done something very stupid. I should never have asked you to tea. I'm sorry. I can no longer see you."

I took my hand away and fixed my eyes on the tops of the elms. The sky was blue behind the rooks' nests, pale blue, and the nests straggling. It was astonishing, how much it hurt.

"Is it something to do with breeding?" My lips trembled as I spoke. "I'm afraid I didn't understand what Lady Brock said. I mean, of course I know about that sort of thing, but . . ."

He buried his head in his hands and laughed in despair. "It appears

Althea has blundered in on my prepared speech. Preempted it some-what. I don't blame you for being confused—"

"Can't you explain it to me?"

"Not now. It's become a bit of a mess. I would need to write it in a letter."

"A letter?" Anger seethed unbidden up the column of my torso. "What am I, a fainting maiden? Selwyn, I'm old enough for you to be frank."

"It's not a matter of age."

I got to my feet and shook my skirt out. I took the remaining steps down with caution, as my knees felt unstrung. Even so, it was un-gainly. His shoes scraped on the step behind.

I turned back. "So we won't meet again?"

"No."

"Then let's not prolong it. Please take me back to Waltham. I'll send a note to Lady Brock and apologize for spoiling the tea."

He went into the house, spent five minutes there in conversation. Then he did as he was bid.

He drove faster than before, running through the gears, his hands alive on the wheel. We barreled through the light and shade of the lanes, and my anger and pain were lit up by the beauty of the day.

"Ellen, you are absolutely splendid—"

"Oh, shut up."

We screeched to the junction. He stared at me. A man who'd never in his life been told to shut up.

"Be careful, Selwyn," I said with satisfaction. "That was a skid." I sat back in my seat. "My father used to skid the car on purpose, to make my mother scream. She loved it. Anyway, what you did was hardly worth the name. My father would have called that 'a mere wheel protest.' I doubt you're capable of a real skid."

He said nothing. Gave me a sudden white smile and put the car into gear. We tore out onto the road to Waltham. The corner approached but he didn't brake. A girl appeared, leading a donkey. Girl and donkey whipped toward us, the donkey skittering on the bank, the girl clinging to its halter. "I think that's Dan's sister, Esther Corey." I craned to look. Esther was mouthing, her face crimson, "Selwyn, you road hog!"

In answer he put the hand brake on. The rear of the car swung round. My head brushed the door frame. We curtseyed against the hedge and bitter smoke funneled up into the window. I gave a ludicrous, wobbling scream of delight. "You'll ruin the tires."

"They're my tires," he said calmly.

We set off in the direction we had come. I hid my face from Esther, who shook her fist as we passed. He took another turn. The road burrowed through the trees down to the river. Then a sharp right turn, and we were on a track above two sunken hay meadows where the grass grew thick, and there, on a rise, was a cottage with a wall to one side and a great high building beyond the wall. We were at Upton Mill.

He brought the car to a halt. A fine perspiration shone on his forehead. His eyes were once again bright blue. "Come on in and wash your face." He smiled. "We shipped a little dust during our antics."

The front door closed with a soft puff of air. "This door fits beautifully," I said. "What a silly thing to notice at a time like this."

"Not really," he said. "You're a sensible girl. A sensible girl who likes fast driving. This is Elizabeth."

And so it was, Mr. and Miss Dawes's Elizabeth, standing at the end of the hall.

"Good heavens." I was embarrassed. "Elizabeth. How nice."

"Mr. and Miss Dawes moved to Bournemouth." She smiled. "Too far for me."

I scrubbed at my face with my handkerchief. "I'm sorry, I'm in such a state . . ."

"You was in a state the last time." She was still smiling. "I'll show you where to wash and then I'll put the kettle on."

"Take her upstairs," Selwyn said. "I'll just be in the sitting room."

Elizabeth led me up to a spartan stone bathroom where I washed my face. My hair was coming out of its bun. I pulled out the clip and the combs and ran my fingers through it as it fell around my shoulders. I glared at my reflection, and my reflection glared back.

When I came out, Elizabeth was on the landing. She was carrying a large brown paper parcel. "I was just going to put these in the airing cupboard." She set the parcel down on a chest on the landing and untied the string. "We send them to Peck's Laundry. They're the best." Inside the parcel was a bale of four white sheets, the crispest linen. She pulled them out. I followed her to the airing cupboard and we passed a room with a half-open door, and inside it a mirror, and in the mirror a bed with a golden-brown polished headboard and a bare mattress. "I'll do his bed this afternoon," Elizabeth said. She opened the airing cupboard and lavender washed out on the warm air, fresh and clean, and I was transported, a young child again in all my riches, sliding my hot summer legs into the scented cool of laundered sheets.

Elizabeth put the new sheets onto the shelf. She tucked lavender bags, flat gauze pleated bags tied with a purple ribbon, between the fat folds. "I make them fresh every year. Smells nice, doesn't it?"

There were pillowcases too, ironed into squares. I wanted to bury my face in them. "It's gorgeous." I took the sheets from the shelf. "I'll do the bed."

"Oh, Miss Calvert. It's hardly proper."

The lavender bags fell onto the floor. I picked them up. "You can tell him, Elizabeth."

The sheet floated out before settling foursquare onto the bed. Even before our fall began, I used to help Jennie, and Mother used to watch.

Hospital corners, miss, said Jennie. I pulled out a sharp triangular fold and drove it deep under the mattress. The sheet was tight, a level plain of right-angled fields. Selwyn was in the doorway. I saw him as I straightened up, moving toward me, toward the bed. He was taking his glasses off. His eyes were wide, bright, haunted.

"Ellen, my dear, I simply can't—"

"I've nearly finished," I said. "Don't sit down on the bed. *Don't* sit down. Selwyn, you've ruined it."

I wept, my hands on my wet cheeks. He held out his arms.

There were so many things on a man, so many things to dig into one. Belt, braces, watch, cufflinks. Spectacles. And their heavy, iron-tipped shoes. Each and every one dug into me. He was warm, lean, lithe. He smelled of cotton, heated cotton. My heart pounded but I felt utterly safe. He pushed the hair from my face and smoothed it over my shoulder. "It's astonishing. Like a sheaf of wheat . . ."

His face, close up, was thinner, younger.

"What did you want to say, Selwyn? What can you not do?"

He swallowed, looked away at the window. "Ellen, do you know the story of Sara and Tobias?"

I shook my head.

"Tobias . . ." He closed his eyes. "And Sara . . . well, the crux of the matter is that on their wedding night they remain chaste."

"Chaste."

"Chaste." His eyelids trembled. His shoulder pinned my arm. Soon I'd have to move. "They pray . . ." He cleared his throat. ". . . and then they go to sleep for the night."

There was silence. The headboard creaked as I began to tug my arm from beneath him. "I'm afraid I missed a lot of Sunday School—"

But then he spoke quickly, eyes still shut. "I can't perform the physical act, Ellen, I'm sure you know the one I mean, and I've done a stupid, harmful thing in befriending you, because you're young, you need a family, and the joys of a full married life, and I'm not the man for that."

He sat up and swung his feet to the floor. His back was facing me. I pushed myself upright.

"Is it . . ." I squeezed my hands together. These, for me, were utterly uncharted waters. "I mean, isn't there some sort of treatment?"

"No. At the end of the War, I was hospitalized. They called it 'neurasthenia.' I started passing out at the wheel, you see. Seconds at a time, with no warning at all. My brain was no longer giving me permission to drive. Or eat, or drink, or speak. And then there was this final thing, the one we're talking about, that I discovered I couldn't do at all. I'm afraid that ability never came back."

"Are you sure?"

"Yes. I am," said Selwyn. "Believe me, I have tried."

I fought vainly against a bursting volley of giggles. He put his head in his hands.

"Oh, Ellen," he said. "Ellen, Ellen."

"I do understand, you know. You're describing a *mariage blanc*. I learned the phrase from Lady Brock."

"It's no marriage for you."

"Kiss me, Selwyn. You can do that, can't you?"

"No, Ellen. It would be wrong."

I kissed him on the cheek. Then he put his lips against the corner of my mouth. My entire left side was electrified.

"Now you've made it worse," he said.

We drove to Waltham. Selwyn put his hat and gloves on before he got in the car. Accoutred as he now was, it was impossible to believe that we had ever lain on the white bed. He drove in silence, craning forward to penetrate the shadows in the lane.

"So," I said as we crossed Waltham Square. "Thank you for a nice afternoon."

He laughed in spite of himself, a lovely light sound. He slowed the car to a halt. The hostel door drew level with my window.

"I've got no desire to have children, Selwyn."

He gave a tired smile. "You say that now."

"I do say it."

"In a year you'll change your mind—"

"How do you *know*!" It burst out of me. "Why do people even *think* they can know about me!"

I grabbed at the door handle and got out of the car. He peered up at me, his hat low on his brow. Selwyn Parr of Parr's Mill. Fine Flours and Animal Feeds. "It's a pity you're determined to finish this," I said. "Because you're ruining your life, and mine too, by turning down the one woman who'd suit you."

Ten days, and then a note in my pigeonhole. Copperplate, spare and neat. I read it with what little light penetrated the heavy clouds of early summer, in the lobby of the hostel, propping the door open with my foot. I didn't want to take his letter into my room, where I'd keep chancing on it among my things. The hurt would take my breath away.

Please try to understand that the last thing I wanted to do was cause you unhappiness. Someone like you, a young woman of great beauty—

Hyperbole.

—will prompt the rashest acts in men. It is one of life's unfairnesses.

Balderdash.

Ever yours, Selwyn.

Arrant falsehood.

Crumpling the letter in my pocket I wandered through the streets of Waltham, watching women hoist babies out of perambulators, plug their mouths with bottles. I might turn into a thousand things—who could tell? But I couldn't live my life according to what I might be, or might want. I was myself, now. And he was here, now. A man who wouldn't just hold me and kiss me, but a man I could say anything to and be understood, a man who could open the world to me with his heart and mind. How many women had that? Didn't he realize what we could be, together?

I tried in vain to swallow a great hot lump in my throat. Stupid, *stupid* man.

The following morning I inserted a fresh sheet of paper into the roller and began to type. My eyes were smarting, the keys of my machine spattering the letters onto the page.

Dear Mr. Parr, Thank you for your note of Wednesday last. It will probably gratify you to know that I am at present walking out with a Mr. Robert Coward, a bookkeeper at the Town Hall. His name does not suit him and might better be adopted by another of my acquaintance. Yours sincerely, Ellen Calvert.

I then hammered *Mr. S. Parr, Esq., Parr's Mill, Upton, Nr Waltham, Hampshire* onto an envelope and sealed the letter inside it, and thrust it into the typing-pool mail sack with a single loud tearless sob that went unnoticed in the din.

I had not lied. One of my fellows, Polly, had asked me to make a four with her and two young clerks, Tom Dallimore and Bob Coward, at Bishop's on Saturday afternoon. I'd willingly have paid a high price to go to another tearoom but Polly refused the notion. "It's so clean in Bishop's. All those virginal lace doilies. It gives a tremendously good impression. And Mrs. B is quite the chaperone, should a boy lean too close. The moment you feel his breath on your neck, she appears soundlessly at your table. Perhaps she runs on castors."

She was a witty girl, if not wholly likable.

We had tea. I answered Bob's compendious list of questions and watched Polly eat Tom alive. We could rob a bank this afternoon, I thought, as long as Polly was in charge. She'd just make Tom do it, and he'd go to jail with the same enraptured smile on his face. Bob was a stringy boy with too much of the looks of Selwyn and none of his mind. As the afternoon wound to an end I excused myself, saying that

I had to pop into Priddy's for a tart for Sunday. I'd go to Lucy and Mrs. Horne as usual, for my Sunday dinner, though I might excuse myself from church.

The air was fresh, rinsed with recently fallen rain, and there were rough, uncertain patches of blue in the sky. Water lapped the cobbles in the lowest corner of the square. It was on a day like this, one after rain, that I had hurried toward the Town Hall in Patricia Harper's shoes, late, full of hope.

Selwyn was coming toward me across the cobbles. His glasses were misted. Had he even seen me? But then he gave a shaken smile. "Ellen. I was making my way to find you."

I put out my hands and he took them tightly.

"Robert Coward shall not have you. I can't bear it."

I stepped back, my hands still in his, my arms extended. "Don't I have a say?"

"Beautiful Ellen. I love you." He was laughing, and so was I.

In the street we embraced. My head lay comfortably against his shoulder. I was a tall girl. His hand was deliciously heavy on the back of my head, my shoulders, my back. I shut my eyes and the cobbles pressed through the thin soles of my shoes.

Lucy scraped a spoon round the pie dish and stuck it in her mouth. A moment's noisy sucking followed. "I just wanted to get the most out of it," she said. "We shan't see another one of these for many a long year."

"How rude," said Mrs. Horne.

"Lucy, honestly. I don't have to work in Waltham to bring you pies." I laughed. I had to laugh every so often, to release the sparkling happiness that brimmed inside me.

Lucy's father, George, rose to his feet. "Miss Calvert. Let me offer you my congratulations." He held out his hand and I got up too, and shook it.

"Thank you, Mr. Horne."

He turned and left the room. I saw his back bend outside the window. He was putting on his boots to go up to the kennels.

"Go on, Nan," said Lucy. "Into the parlor with you."

Lucy and I cleared the table. I put on the apron that Mrs. Horne called "Ellen's pinny," a long, starched affair rejected by her and Lucy because the hem brushed their toes. I began washing the cutlery. Lucy leaned against the drainer and tugged the knives and spoons from my hands to dry them. Something about the way she placed them carefully, one by one, into their slots in the drawer, glancing up at me all the while, caught my attention.

"What is it, Lucy?"

"I don't know if I should say this, Ell."

"You're not usually so hesitant." I smiled at her. "Spit it out."

"All right. You know Ivy Sutton, who cleans for Dr. Bell? She told me something about your Mr. Parr. She didn't mean to overhear but she was polishing the brass plate on the surgery door."

"And the keyhole too, I expect. So what did she *overhear*?"

"She said . . ." Lucy cleared her throat. "She said Mr. Parr can't do it. Because of the War. The War affected his, you know. His private parts." Her eyes shone black with embarrassment. "I'm only thinking of you, dear. That's the only reason I'm repeatin this."

I slid our dinner plates into the sink and let my hands rest on them, pleasantly gloved by the hot water. "I already know, Lucy."

"So it's true?" She gaped. "So it'll be just . . . just room and board?"

I laughed aloud, that the riches that had poured into my lap could be termed so. "Oh, Lucy. Would you like to be my bridesmaid?"

≈

Selwyn and I would wait half a year or so. He needed to let me be sure. He would never hold it against me if I reconsidered. I grew more certain every day that we spent together, walking in the beech hangers and the high tops of the Downs, or motoring to the sea, or reading in his sitting room, me with my hair down around my shoulders and my bare feet propped on the low table, and he looking up from his book and smiling at me. And all the while the small diamond burned its quiet determined fire on my finger.

But it was 1939, and we couldn't live isolated in our warm little nook. In the summer of that year people were still professing their great faith in Mr. Chamberlain. He would save us from these growling warmongers. "You're trusting the wrong person," Selwyn told them. "Your fate doesn't lie with Mr. Chamberlain but with Herr Hitler."

And so it proved. We married shortly after the war broke out, in December, amid the turmoil of those early months. Our wedding took place at Waltham Town Hall, a stark building now in wartime, denuded of its railings, the tall windows crisscrossed with blast tape. Lucy attended as bridesmaid, and her father and grandmother accompanied her. Daniel Corey came, in uniform: he had a two-day pass from Aldershot and he'd brought his new wife, Marcy, Marcy Berry that was, whom I'd seen pushing Mr. Babcock in his wheeled wicker chair. John Blunden came, and his father who had taken my things to the Absaloms and taken them away again. Polly and my other pals from the Town Hall. Mr. and Miss Dawes. Some very distant female relatives of Selwyn's, cousins of his late father, who looked sideways at Lady Brock's lipstick. Lady Brock came with William Kennet, who was astonishingly dapper in a suit once the property of Sir Michael, whose God had finally shown him mercy back in September, right at the beginning of the war.

I wore a white satin dress that came to my ankles. I had made it myself on Lady Brock's machine. For a veil I had my mother's yard of Nottingham lace.

Selwyn, allowed to kiss the bride, took me in his arms. Something extraordinary happened to the room then. It seemed to be flooded with a sudden buzzing light, very fierce, as if a piece of Heaven had been torn down to earth to land all around us.

We had cake and champagne afterward in Bishop's Tearooms.

Lady Brock had supplied the champagne. Daniel read out a telegram from Edward in Singapore. DARLING SISTER STOP OVERJOYED STOP HUSBAND CLEARLY MAN OF GREAT DISCERNMENT STOP HOPE MEET SOON STOP MUCH LOVE EDWARD.

Daniel read aloud in capitals, and included all the stops.

We came out into the square. Those holding champagne glasses toasted us. I shook hands with Selwyn's bevy of very much removed cousins, who then fitted themselves decorously back into a long black automobile and departed.

"Dear girl," said Lady Brock at my side, and gave me a carmine kiss on the cheek before going toward Selwyn.

Lucy loitered nearby, and I went to her. "You look so nice, Lucy."

She did, in a cream linen jacket and skirt, and a cream cloche hat with a small lilac rose. We had chosen the fabric together, my gift to her as bridesmaid. She chewed her lip. "Don't forget us, Ellen."

I laughed. "I'm moving back to Upton, silly!"

Suddenly she put her arm in mine. We drifted away from our companions. "I do love Waltham Square," she said. "It feels like freedom to me."

"I never knew that."

"Oh yes. Coming out on the bus, those Saturdays, to visit you. I never go anywhere, you see."

I smiled. "Neither of us are great travelers, Lucy."

"You will be now. He's got the wanderlust, your Mr. Parr."

Selwyn wanted to take me to Italy, Greece, the Holy Land. "We'll have to wait until this is all over."

"One day though."

"Yes."

Selwyn approached us, took our hands, mine and Lucy's. The breeze bowled the few clouds along. Mr. Kennet's weathercock swung overhead and caught fire.

Ellen
Late March, 1944

18

"I REALLY CAN'T get it at Waltham. They don't stock it."

As I lied, I slid the pin of my pearl brooch into the placket of my high-necked blouse. Put my cotton handkerchief in my skirt pocket and fastened my watch around my wrist. Arrayed in these gifts, all from my husband, I stood up. The dressing table mirror tilted on its spindles, swinging out of the vertical, so that I looked disconcertingly up my own nose. My lying nose.

A week had passed since Mrs. Berrow's visit. I had endured two days of anguish; then, when I began to jump every time the telephone rang, I'd written back to her. *Dear Mrs. Berrow, I have come to think it would be best if I came down to Southampton as you suggested.* A hasty scrawl, the stamp pasted on askew, shoved into the letterbox furtively, trying to hide the deed even from myself. I had no idea what would come of this. I simply couldn't remain in limbo, waiting for the blow to fall. Not even certain if there were a blow to fall.

The man might not be there, of course. What would that do to me? I had no idea.

"Surely they can send it," Selwyn said now. "What sort of item is it, anyway?"

I was ready with my fabricated excuse. "The sort ladies buy in person. From the chemist's shop."

In the corner of my eye I watched him pull the white shirt over his head. When his face emerged it was still flushed. "Ah. Well. You must do what you must, my love. Indeed."

I dragged the brush through my hair, out to the side and let it fall. "I could cut half this hair off and still make a bun." Even to my own ears I sounded brittle. "Some poor woman might need a wig. Perhaps I'll ask in Southampton."

"Don't you dare."

I turned from the mirror and pulled my jacket on. "If I'm not back, send Pamela to Lucy's after school. To spare Elizabeth."

The wind had dropped and masses of cool air hung motionless under the trees. I was glad of my heavier canvas skirt. In my handbag was Mrs. Berrow's reply to my letter. I was to meet her, as she had suggested, at the Lyons teahouse near the ruined Crown, and our appointment was at four o'clock. I had not been able to tell Selwyn about what Mrs. Berrow had said. I couldn't even broach the subject to Lucy. Every word uttered would bring the unthinkable closer into reality.

And here I was, pushing the unthinkable closer. But I couldn't do otherwise.

The driver pulled up at the stop, shaking me out of my daze. I climbed aboard. "Goodness, I didn't hear you coming! A return to Southampton, if you please."

"I was coasting." It was Rick Staveley from Upton, the man lame since birth who had driven this line since before the war. He put two warm coppers into my hand. "Twopence change. Do you want the bus station, Mrs. Parr?"

"No. The Crown stops."

"Right you are." He put the bus into gear. "Funny the way we still call them that, even though the Crown's been smashed to smithereens. You know we shan't be allowed down there in a few days? The company told us. They're shutting the whole coast off, all the way along." He swept his arm from west to east.

"Mr. Kennet said."

"I'm to turn round at Fair Mead and come back. That's what the company says."

The bus swung through the lanes under the budding branches that were on the point of releasing their freshest green, and I remembered sitting with Mother—Rick had been driving us then, too—and reading her a letter from Edward. The one about the ship's cats, the superfluity thereof. When we reached the coast, the water flared in sudden sunshine. *Will we see the sea soon?* my mother had said, like a child on holiday. Now we were passing along the mauled High Street, the piles of masonry still strewn about like a carnivore's leavings. I used to imagine the enemy rebuilding the High Street after our conquest, but now people were clearing rubble, sweeping it down to the shoreline for hard standings and new quays. Caissons, jetties, fuel channels to feed the gathering boats and trucks and tanks, and surely every yard of it photographed by the Luftwaffe. I imagined them cruising with glinting wings over our skies, the maps silvered as if by moonlight, our little streets outlined. The mixture of hope and alarm curdled in me, nauseating.

I went into the Lyons and found a table by the window with a clear view of the hostel and the ruin of the Crown. The entire top story, the roof and the upper set of windows, had slid down and sideways, as if the building were sinking like a doomed ocean liner.

"There's nothing behind," said a man. "Just this façade. The rest is a heap of rubble."

I turned my head and saw instantly that it was him. A chubby, childish face with a rounded chin and Pamela's light, peat-brook eyes, wide-set and clear. Light eyes and dark honey hair, his a little wavy where hers was straight, glossy. That was the only difference. A pulse pounded in my throat, made me afraid to speak.

He continued to stand by my table, looking out at the Crown. Some time went by. Finally I managed to say, "It's horrible."

He blinked, slowly like his daughter, as my words took him from his reverie. "Yes." He seated himself at the next table. "It is."

We sat in silence, both facing the street. Then a waitress came over. "If sir and madam could share a table? We're chock-a-block today."

We said in unison, "I'm waiting for a friend," and she tutted in disbelief. "Really, I am," I told her, but she'd already taken herself off.

"People have become so rude." Gingerly he pulled his coat from his shoulder. I saw a sling and a bandaged hand.

"Anzio," he said, and I nodded.

Once I started looking at him, I couldn't stop. I should forget about Phyllis Berrow, and leave. Just then he lumbered to his feet. "There she is." Mrs. Berrow, laden with a heavy shopping bag, was pushing at the café door. She pulled a scarf from her head in the throng, gave a bleary glance toward the window and smiled at me. Then her eyes widened as she saw him but she was tough and handy and she smiled at him too. "Goodness, it's that young man from Plymouth!" She jostled her way to the table and he stood and pulled out a chair for her. "I see you've already met my friend here. Mrs. White."

"We've had a little chat!" I said, in the tone of a Mrs. White.

"I can't stop long, dear," Phyl said to me. "If you knew the errands and suchlike I had to take care of. You wouldn't believe what a job it is to keep everything clean and respectable and make ends meet at the same time."

The same tame. She polished up her accent for him. I noticed even through the heartbeats pounding in my ears.

I watched him rummage in his jacket pocket. "Here." He put three packets of cigarettes on the table. "I'm only sorry I couldn't snaffle more. It was awfully nice talking to you that day. I don't suppose you've heard anything on the grapevine? In the locality—?"

A vigorous shake of the head released a thick curl of hair from her set. She cupped it back into position. "Oh no, dear, no."

"We met in a fearful crush outside the police station." He turned to me. "Poor Mrs. Berrow had had her purse stolen. Such venal coward-ice, in a way. And I'm on the hunt for a small missing person."

I could neither speak, blink, nor swallow. He smiled at me and then addressed us both. "Well, I'm on my way, but may I get you ladies a pot of tea?"

We, or rather Mrs. Berrow, declined. He picked his coat up from the chairback, hitching it clumsily over one arm. As he put on his hat he bowed his head to me, locked my eyes for a second, and then made his way to the door. I felt a pain in my palm, looked down to see my hand in a fist. I released my fingers to see four dark pink dents along my lifeline.

Phyllis stuffed two of the cigarette packets into her shopping bag and took out a box of Cook's matches. "Bloody hell." She lit her ciga-rette. "That was close to the wind."

I stared out into the street, at some young women whose thin skirts were being pulled out behind them by the sea breeze. In unison they turned round, clutching at the sides of their heads, to save their hats. Their screams of laughter were transformed into thin whines by the plate glass. My heart was sinking into the depths of my body.

"What a mistake." I swallowed again. "An awful blunder. I was like a rabbit paralyzed by a shotgun barrel. He knew it was me."

Mrs. Berrow's small blue eyes roved over the possibility. "Any road, I didn't help him, I promise you."

The door of the café swung open, bringing a gust of wind. Bills flut-tered from tables, chairs scraped. It was the laughing girls, in their skirts, patting their hair. Suddenly the room was unbearably full. I stood up.

"Don't you want to have tea, dear?"

"I can't stay. Good-bye, Mrs. Berrow."

She grasped at my arm, a hard, sudden grip, as if she were in a heavy sea and I in a lifeboat. "Give that little child a kiss from me."

. . . . .

The blasting wind whipped at my eyes, made them leak. Like the girls, I put my hands to my hat. At the bus stops there was a milling crowd of children under the care of a single elderly schoolmaster. He funneled them in through the doorway of the bus with a shepherd's long practice, and smiled at me. "I don't suppose you want a couple, do you?"

It was astonishing how often people said things like that to me. *You're welcome to her, my dear. Have one of mine, I wouldn't miss him.* "Yes. I'll take . . ." I glanced over the flock. "Those two boys there, the ones hitting each other with their caps."

He laughed in good humor. I imagined Pamela's father saying to me, *I don't suppose you want her, do you? Keep her. She's yours.* I followed the schoolmaster into the bus. The children were sitting in their seats, if bouncing and jostling could be called sitting. The noise, rather like that in an aviary, abated as he held up one flat hand. "Lower Fourth," he intoned, "*Tacete,*" *be silent,* and they were. He stood aside to let the rest of the passengers on, and I filed down the crowded bus. The driver was in a hurry: he lurched away from the stop while we were still on our feet. I staggered against the person behind me who gasped in pain. "I do beg your pardon."

I sat down and so did he, next to me.

He took a moment to reposition his arm in its sling, and then smiled into my face. His candid light brown eyes ran over me. "They bombed us in the Bay, you know. A hospital ship, and they bombed us. At one point we were fighting four simultaneous fires. That's how I came a cropper. The surgeon in Naples dealt very well with my fingers." He gave me a steady look. "I'm not an idiot, Mrs. . . . White?"

A shade of contempt in his query. I blushed to my hairline.

"Parr. Ellen Parr."

"I wasn't lying in wait for you today. I had no idea that you'd come. But I knew Mrs. Berrow would let drop some sort of clue in the end. She's a slightly better liar than you, but still not very good. *A little girl?*

Oh no, dear, I don't know nothing about that." It was a fair imitation, gravelly, lower than his natural tone. "I told her I'd pay fifty pounds for the information but she held firm. I thought you might like to know that."

He was regarding me with a clear, benign, interested gaze. "I should introduce myself. Aubrey Lovell, naval surgeon."

So it was Lovell. Why not? A nice name, elegant. Competent.

"Pamela thinks she's called Pamela Pickering." My voice was husky. "That's what she's been taught."

His eyebrows shot up.

"Yes." I swallowed. "Her mother called herself *Mrs.* Pickering, you see. It was only a few days ago that we discovered this wasn't right. So naturally we've been looking for a *Mr.* Pickering all this time. Not a Lovell."

"You have been looking, then?" He smiled.

"Oh, yes. The police, the Forces, Wounded and Missing . . . why do you ask?"

"Your face, madam. The sheer horror when you looked at me."

The way his lips thinned, even now almost mischievous. It was Pamela, and yet the downcurve of the mouth translated effortlessly into masculinity. I saw all this and struggled in vain for words.

"I'd have found her myself, in the end. It's simply a fact. If not now, then after we've finished with all this." He gestured clumsily at the battered frontages beyond the window. "Sooner or later the constabulary would have got round to me. How long must it be now?"

"Must what be?" I was stupid, my lips numb, the margins of my vision dim. I wondered if I was going to faint again. I did hope not. That would be so embarrassing.

"Since you found Pamela."

"Let me see. Three—three years and three months."

"Are you all right, Mrs. Parr?"

The sunshine glanced along all the windows of the bus as we turned north. "I'm quite well, thank you."

. . . . .

The city streets seemed to stretch and hold us in their grasp. There were so many ponderous military vehicles; they swung out onto the highway and we gave way every time.

"How did you know to go to Plymouth? You said you were estranged. You didn't know where she was, did you?"

Even to my ears I sounded odd, needlessly interrogatory. As if I were still testing him, as if he might still turn out to be the wrong man. He seemed not to notice.

"She wrote from that address, asking for money. I sent her some. This was at the beginning of the war, and we'd been apart for four years or so. Then I left England. When I didn't hear from her, I simply assumed she was in funds, or had found someone to keep her in funds." He glanced out of the window at a row of shops, half-intact, the other half a smashed and blackened mound of brick. "God, what a mess they've made of us, the bastards. Excuse my language, Mrs. Parr. I'm afraid we do an awful lot of cursing in the navy."

"I don't mind it." We were crossing the river now, winding our way through the battered city. "That was the entrance to the gasworks." I pointed at a blasted weed-run expanse in which a hulk of deformed ironwork had collapsed to its knees, rivets crying rust. "They hit Cold Storage. Did you hear about the butter fire? It burned for nine days. And the ice rink. The ice rink," I repeated, at the absurdity of it.

"And so when I came back to England, I went to Plymouth first. They told me she'd come here. So how did you end up with my daughter?"

I told him about the raid, the fleeing buses, and the well-meaning women. In my mind I picked Pamela up from the backseat, in her dirty blanket, and felt her hot cheek against the side of my neck.

"What a shambles. What the hell was she doing in Southampton?"

"I believe her mother . . . I believe there was a man."

He nodded, fingering his chin. That part made sense to him.

. . . . .

"Amelia danced before she walked, she told me. Born to it. She hated being still. She was ill with Pamela, bed rest from the fourth month until well after the birth. She grew . . . baleful. Blamed us both, I think, me and the baby, for hobbling her. She fell back in love with Pamela the minute she set eyes on her. Not with me, however."

Southampton had released us at last and we had traveled into, and out of, Waltham. Now we were in open country. He gave a sigh and stared out of the window.

"We parted in 'thirty-six. Pamela was barely a year old. I came home from leave and the house was empty. Not so much as a hairpin. I tracked her down to a place along the coast—she hadn't gone far—but it did no good. We divorced soon afterward. She was happy to provide a co-respondent. She said she was sorry, she knew she was to blame. She'd blundered. I was a mistake. And sometimes the price of freedom is higher than we'd wish, but worth it all the same."

Freedom. What freedom was worth that, tearing a child from her father? Sending the child out alone to wreak havoc? Because havoc she had surely wrought.

He smiled. "To be fair, she was a good mother."

I found my voice, such as it was. A poor croak. "How do you know? If Pamela was only a year old when you left."

"When *Amelia* left." His correction was mild. "Do you have children?"

I shook my head.

"A year's long enough to tell." He looked around him. "This is a pretty place."

And so it was, on a breezy late March afternoon. The high brick walls lichen-covered, the meadows well watered, the houses with shining windows. One could hardly believe that we were at war.

"This is Upton. We get off here."

．　．　．　．　．

I stood for a moment on the triangle of grass by the bus stop in the main street. Pamela would still be at Lucy's house. "She's in the care of a friend this afternoon," I said at last. "It's this way." We began to walk up the road.

"She won't know me, of course." he said suddenly. "I'm worried I'll frighten her—with my arm in a sling."

He had no idea what she was like. How could he know? "Pamela won't be frightened of a sling. When she was six she had one herself, for a sprained wrist. A cartwheeling injury." I stopped walking. "Is that all your worry? Not one question about how she is?"

He turned back to me, stricken. "She hasn't left my mind since I arrived at the Crown Hotel. When I see her I'll know how she is."

We reached the steps up to the Hornes' cottage. He went first, climbing in an awkward way, swinging round toward the rail. The steps were steep, and he had one arm bound to his body. By the time we reached the top he was breathing much harder than the labor merited and I saw the apprehension in his face, the pallor and wide eyes, and he looked even more like his daughter.

Lucy and Pamela were in the garden, standing, both bending, and with their backs to us, in the long grass beyond the apple tree. "Maurice," Pamela was saying. "Oh Maurice, do eat your grass."

"My God, my God," Aubrey murmured at my side. At the click of the gate Lucy straightened up.

"Here's Ellen now," she said. "Oh."

Pamela came toward me, ahead of Lucy. "He won't eat it. He's a stubborn tortoise."

Lucy's eyes flicked from man to child, from child to man. The rest of her face unmoving.

Aubrey held out his uninjured hand to her.

"This is my friend Lucy Horne," I said hastily, because she was taking his hand with a stiff nod and no words.

Aubrey turned to Pamela. "Hello, Pamela. I'm Aubrey." He pointed at the tortoise. "Is this Maurice?"

Pamela stood, doubtful. "Beg pardon, but who are you?"

"Aubrey. I told you."

She frowned. "Yes, but who *is* that?"

Aubrey began to laugh, gently in delight. "I'm someone who's interested in tortoises." He moved forward and stood in front of me, and bent down to Pamela. "Did you tickle Maurice on the nose? That's the way to start. We need a long, juicy piece of grass."

"It would be nice if we could eat grass," Pamela said as she led him away. "It's not on the ration. Everybody knows that. We could have grass buns, grass cakes. Grass lemonade. Look at your poor arm. Did you get bombed? Grass jelly. Grass . . ."

It was liquid, like birdsong, her voice. They stood now where Pamela had stood with Lucy, in the wilderness beyond the apple tree. Except that he was with her now, and Lucy was beside me.

"Jesus Christ, Ell," she whispered.

We opened up the dining room, ran a duster over the walnut table, set out the pink Venetian glasses—a deep lucent pink, the color of ripe Victoria plums. "Don't wait up for us," I told Elizabeth. "I'll clean the plates and the pan while the water's hot." And her mouth set in a line, the lips almost vanishing: disapproval of this idea, and pity for me at the same time.

We ate a chicken we'd killed, the last of the kale, bolted and bitter, some potatoes. I cut up his portion for him in the kitchen but all the same he worked at his food. It was his right hand that was injured, and he wasn't yet clever with his fork.

Selwyn set down his glass with minute care, his face drawn. He'd listened to Aubrey's account, waved aside my apology for not telling him about Mrs. Berrow. That hardly mattered anymore. Now he began to address Aubrey.

"It's simply that—well, here you are, without . . . I'm sorry, it seems absurd to say it, but—"

"Without any actual evidence?" Aubrey said mildly. "I know. I don't even have her birth certificate. But I do have friends and family, of course, respectable people, who'd swear in court that I'm the Surgeon Lieutenant Commander Lovell who married Amelia Pickering, and that we had a child, a baby girl called Pamela."

"My dear man, I didn't mean to offend—"

"No offense taken. And then there's my face, of course. Give Pamela a short back-and-sides and she could be me at the same age."

I put my hand over Selwyn's, which was clenched around his silver napkin ring.

Aubrey was reaching under his sling, into his inside breast pocket. "I've got some photographs." He withdrew a small brown envelope, which he placed on the table. The flap was lifted. I could see that it was stuffed with photographs, too tightly for a single hand to take them out. "Mrs. Parr, if you'd be so kind."

I picked up the envelope and began to pull out the photographs. The first was of a baby for all the world like a small monkey, with huge eyes beneath surprised brows.

"Here she is." He smiled. "More bush baby than human being. She had a dreadful couple of months at the start, you know. She wouldn't feed. That's why she was so thin." More images slid out in my fingers. Pamela as an older baby, crawling. Now standing, feet apart, arms above her head, hands enclosed in the large fists of an elderly woman. They and a black Labrador were flanked by stone gateposts. "That is Ireland, County Waterford. My sister's house. The lady's her late mother-in-law. That dog I believe is called Winnie. Pamela was a year and a few days." He looked up at Selwyn. "My wife severed relations with me shortly afterward."

I withdrew another photograph, and there he was himself, smiling, carrying a once more tiny Pamela, holding the hand of a woman in a cloche hat. The brim shaded her face so that only her mouth was visible. The lips were parted, black in the sunshine.

"That's Amelia."

The photographs skated and spun on the polished wood. They were so little and light.

"I'm wifeless," Aubrey went on. "And a serving officer. Not to mention my injury. I can't look after her, as much as I want to. Pamela will go to my sister in Ireland, at least until the war's over. Hester—my sister—has four children. She was dreadfully hurt when Amelia left me and took Pamela away from us. She adored Pamela."

I might as well have been cloven in half with an ax.

The meal seemed to be without end. We were now eating an apple pie, the pastry thick, the apples dark and wrinkled, no cream. Selwyn and Aubrey were talking about Egypt, Libya, Malta, Sicily. I interrupted Aubrey in midsentence.

"I'd like to speak to your sister on the telephone."

He gazed at me, his face softening. My misery was too clear and too awful to ignore.

"I'd like to hear her voice. Hester's."

Aubrey nodded. "Of course, if it's humanly possible. The lines may be too busy."

"I'll make tea first." I pushed away my dessert. "Elizabeth has gone to bed."

I put the tea tray in the sitting room, where the remains of a fire hissed in the grate. Aubrey was in the hall, speaking to the operator. He was consulting a small leather address book, cradling the receiver between shoulder and ear. The sight of him brought me some way to my senses and my manners. "I do apologize if I'm disturbing her. If I've inconvenienced you . . ."

He gave a true, delighted smile. "I'd probably have asked to telephone anyway. There's no one in the world who'll be happier to hear we've found Pamela. Apart from me, of course. I'll speak first, if you don't mind."

"Of course."

I went back into the sitting room. Selwyn was crouched by the grate in rolled shirtsleeves, mending the fire. "It will be very hard for my wife." He stood up. "I blame myself, as much as anyone." He looked up and saw it was me.

I didn't enjoy his discomfiture. "Oh, Selwyn. You blame yourself, do you? How pointless."

He stayed where he was, his face peaked in sadness. The sitting room door opened and Aubrey put his head in. "Mrs. Parr, Hester would be so pleased to speak to you."

"My dear Mrs. Parr." The voice was deep, tremulous, brimming with tears. "I am Hester Browne, Pamela's aunt, and I thank you from the bottom of my heart. You saved her from the bombs—!"

"No, no, I didn't. I just picked her up in the bus, where she was sleeping—"

"Oh, my dear woman. Amelia never wrote back, you see, and they moved, and I never saw that little baby again. Aubrey and Amelia were utterly sundered, though it was the last thing he wanted. He was at sea, you know, and then the war . . . What's she like now? Does she still have those round eyes?"

"Yes, she does. She's very . . . very ebullient."

Hester gave a rich trill of laughter. "None of us Lovells ever shut up," she said. "Not even Aubrey, although what with the war, and his poor hand . . . Do you have any children of your own?"

"I do not." I closed my eyes. "And I'm sure Pamela will be delighted to be part of a big family. But she's . . ." I fought for strength, for some kind of mercy.

"Hello? Have we lost the line?"

"I was saying that she's been over three years here in Upton, with us."

"Of course, my dear. It won't be easy. We must speak again if we can."

I endured another bout of gratitude, and rang off.

I left the men murmuring with their tea. I didn't care whether they were discussing the Mediterranean theater of war or pitying me. I climbed the stairs and went into the old dressing room where Pamela was asleep. On her side, one leg flung out behind, the other bent up at the knee, the opposite arm crooked as if holding a baton in a relay. A child flitting into the next room of her life, and I would be gone, hidden by the closing door. She stirred, and blew a bubble, her fist closed around a peg doll that was still clothed in Selwyn's handkerchief. I pulled it gently away in case she lay on it in the night and woke up. Her fingers jerked and released it. She sighed, and stirred again. I sat down on the bed, with my hand on my chin, watching her.

Some time later I heard them on the landing, Selwyn showing Aubrey to his room. One of them, I couldn't tell who, said, "Goodnight." Then Selwyn came into the bedroom. I heard him move around, preparing for bed. Then he came up the steps into the dressing room and stood in the doorway.

"He's her father," he said. "We always knew he might come in the end."

When I didn't move or speak, he went away.

I undressed quietly and lay down beside her and watched on. She was a hot, industrious sleeper. I pulled the strands of hair from her damp cheek. It was still rounded, like her forehead, and her mouth was pushed out in the usual way, as if about to sing "O." I put my face against her hair at the nape of her neck, breathing in her extraordinary scent, so that it would nourish me in the years to come.

In the middle of the night I dozed and then my eyes opened again. She was breathing with regular little snorts. I put my hand on her back, for the warmth.

Selwyn's leather clock told me it was three, and then four. I liked that clock. It was the clock of an independent man, one who had traveled, who'd seen hot horizons, islands in a glittering sea. The case folded so beautifully into one's hand, like a leather egg. At five o'clock I sat up and went silently into the big bedroom. I took out a sheet of writing paper from the drawer and began a letter to Pamela. I thought I'd slip it into her suitcase with her clothes. *Dear Pamela, I hope that you will keep this letter after you have read it so that you can read it again because I have some very important things to say to you . . .*

I doubted she would read it again. She was too contrary. She'd make a paper boat of it and float it in the bath. A bath in Ireland, big and cold, with clear brown peaty water pouring from a single flared silver tap. And a great Juno of a woman with tumbling chestnut hair would be scooping the water over her back and her small pale rounded shoulders, trilling at her lovingly. I had no idea what Hester looked like but I felt that only a generously built woman could possess such a rich contralto.

I carried on writing. Perhaps I could give the letter to Aubrey.

Selwyn stirred and muttered, and almost immediately afterward I heard his voice.

"Ellen," he said. "It's six o'clock."

"Mm?"

"What are you doing?"

The sky was light. I felt light too, clear-headed.

"I've been writing a letter."

I heard him sigh. "I'll be back at eight for breakfast."

19

PAMELA ROSE INTO CONSCIOUSNESS with much lip-smacking, stuck out an arm as if hailing traffic. I grasped her hand and she opened her eyes.

"Mercy me, here you are," she said.

I made myself smile. "It's seven o'clock. And a nice springlike day already. I thought we'd wear our picnic dresses." I was already dressed in mine, a faded gray linen button-down dress with a shirt collar and wide pockets, one of them with an ink stain but never mind, it was the most comfortable thing I owned.

"Look," I said, holding out her dress. "Do you remember this one from last summer?"

It was a simple tunic of sky-blue polished cotton checked in thin white lines. Made out of a full-skirted overall I'd intended to use for cleaning grates and silver, but never had, on account of the fabric being too fine. I had put a trim, a ricrac of white daisies, around the bottom.

"I don't like those daisies anymore."

"They're pretty."

She pushed herself upright in the bed. "Why does that man want to be my daddy?"

"He's always been your daddy." I put the dress down on the chair.

"No, he hasn't! How can he be a daddy when I've never seen him!"

I reached out and touched her cheek. She was still hot from sleeping. "You saw him when you were a baby. You just don't remember."

"Mummy said he didn't want to be a daddy."

"Well. I think he did in his heart."

She nodded, somber. I heard the lavatory flush, and then footsteps, first over the landing and then on the stairs. "Anyway," I continued, "now he's back, and he's here, and he'll be expecting to see you for breakfast. It's lovely for you, to have a daddy." I stood up and began to get ready. In the mirror I saw her get out of bed and pull her nightdress over her head.

"So he can be Daddy," Pamela said when she appeared out of the nightdress. "And you can be Mummy." She sat down on the floor with her back to me and put her knickers on. Her hair was like a bird's nest where she'd slept against the pillow. "And we'll all live here with Elizabeth and the hens."

I unpinned my hair and started to brush it out. Some of it fell across my face so that her reflection, as she pulled on the tunic dress, was obscured by a golden sort of mist. "Oh, Pamela. What about Mr. Parr?"

"He'll be Grandpa, of course."

"Crack Daddy's egg for him."

The dining room was cool, an early sun edging toward the table. Pamela did as she was told, with concentration, tapping the teaspoon on the top of the egg. Steam rose from the egg and from the teapot.

"Now scrape it out carefully, in big pieces," I said. "So that Daddy can eat it with his fork."

His face was crumpled from sleep and he had a small red cut on his chin. He watched her wield the spoon, and then looked at me, smiling. "May I observe what an absolute pair of beauties you two are."

Pamela emptied the egg and put the shell on her plate. "Ellen's more beautiful because she's got yellow hair, not brown."

"No, I'm not, Pamela. Your hair is beautiful."

Mine was falling around my shoulders. He held my eyes. He had no tic: he noticed me noticing. "It's the one thing. Well, and shoelaces, of course."

"We'll see to that after breakfast. Pamela and Aubrey, do please eat."

"Did you get your cut in the war?" Pamela raised her hand toward his chin.

He grinned. "No. In the bathroom."

"But you are still in the war, aren't you?" She was making headway into her toast, lips and cheeks now shiny with butter and covered in crumbs.

"I am."

She slipped off her chair and came and murmured greasily in my ear. "Is it completely bombed off, his hand?"

I whispered back. "No. It's just a little hurt."

"Because if it was, we could get Mr. Kennet to come and show him a few tricks. How to do things with one hand. Like driving and making fires and so on."

"I can hear you, Pamela." Aubrey was smiling. "My hand will be completely better before long."

"In the meantime you'll want to work, though, or you'll get awfully bored." Pamela spoke through her munching. "You could do a job pressing buttons, couldn't you? In my book about London there's a chap who stays in the lift all day going up and down and pressing buttons. You could do that, I expect."

"Pamela, pop that crust in your mouth, and go into the kitchen to wash your hands and face."

She did as she was told. We ate, and I poured him a second cup of tea. The clock struck once, for half-past seven. He lifted up his cup saying, "You're very good with her."

"She's spent almost half her life here." I filled my own cup, my hand steady. "It was hard in the beginning, in the winter. You must tell Hester that sometimes she'll go to the bedroom and take a pillow and tie something round the middle, like a dressing gown cord, to make a person, and then she'll lay her head on the bosom of this person."

The sunlight had reached the table. He sat still, his cup in midair.

"'There's no talking to her during this time," I went on. "No cousins romping on the bed, please. And if Hester has Marmite, she should make toast fingers and bring them to her after a while. Those will cheer her up. She'll say they don't, but they do." I stood up and went to the window and pulled the curtain across, so that the light didn't shine in his eyes. "I'm assuming you'll be able to stay with them a little, in Ireland." I arranged the folds in the thin curtain. "That would mitigate the rupture. Not that she's overly familiar with you, come to that."

Outside in the garden a male blackbird jabbed for worms. I turned back to him. "When were you planning to take her?"

"I thought perhaps the day after tomorrow."

I nodded. Still grasping the bunched, soft linen of the curtain. "That would give you time to tell her, I suppose. For her to try and understand the idea, at least. I assume you *are* going to prepare her in some way?"

His face puckered. "Of course. I just don't know how to start." He cleared his throat. "Mrs. Parr—"

"Ellen."

"Ellen, please don't quiz me like this. Please help me."

I didn't speak. Simply sat down again, but this time on Pamela's chair, the one next to him. Pamela came in, clean. She climbed onto my lap and stuck her thumb in her mouth. Regarded him, blinking slowly. She hadn't sucked her thumb in a long time. I smoothed her skirt and mine, and held his gaze. "Pamela, you can practice your bows. Daddy's shoes need tying. Sit sideways," I bid him, as Pamela slid off my lap. She kneeled at his feet and pulled the laces tight.

"One loop's always bigger than the other one." She looked up at him. "Do you mind?"

"I don't mind."

"I could do a sheet bend."

"There's not a great deal to do, here in Upton," I explained. "Selwyn's been through the book of knots."

He grinned. "It's the same with Hester's children. Deep on a farm, no outings or treats."

"Is there a family likeness?"

"In myself and Hester, yes. The children take after their father. Rusty hair and freckles."

"Why is Hester in Ireland?"

"She was a nurse in Dublin. She met her husband at a dance. He's Church of Ireland, I should say."

As if I cared about their denomination. Why was I even asking, when each question brought another lance of pain? I couldn't manage anymore. He seemed to know it, because his voice was very soft. Pamela, chirping in self-congratulation, moved on to the second shoe. Then I said, "Have you got your tie?"

"Oh. Yes." He hesitated. I could see he'd been going to ask Selwyn to help him with that task. I waited for him to say so, but he didn't. Instead he leaned to one side, produced the tie from his pocket and held it out to me. It was thin, old, a dark maroon, with a coarse grain. With a single clumsy hand he tugged his collar up, and then bent his head forward. I invested him with the tie and he raised his chin.

"This may not be very expert, I'm afraid." My only experience of ties was watching Selwyn, when we were newly married and I lay in bed, in love, while he dressed. Those days were far off now.

"You'll make a better job of it than me." He was smiling.

I started to make the knot. The fabric slithered through my fingers. A fumbling novice. Out in the kitchen the back door creaked open. I heard Elizabeth say, "There's an egg for you, Mr. Parr," and Selwyn reply, "Splendid."

"Darling," I called, "help us."

Selwyn came in, grinned, finished the job. "Where's Pamela?" he asked, when Aubrey had thanked him.

She stood up. "I've just been lacing those big shoes."

We all laughed a little. "Ah." Selwyn sat down. "Good morning, Pamela. How helpful. You made a good breakfast, I hope." He turned to me. "Darling. Look at your hair in that flowing style. You look positively pre-Raphaelite. And Pamela. What a pair of beauties."

Aubrey smiled. "That's what I said."

Elizabeth came in with Selwyn's breakfast. "I can't answer for the egg, how hot it is anymore," she said.

"I'm sure it'll be perfectly good." Selwyn glanced at me and then at Aubrey.

"Pamela," I said, "will you go upstairs please?"

To my mild astonishment she did exactly as she was told.

"When are we going to tell her?" I said, when she was out of earshot. "We can't just leave it and leave it. She doesn't understand. She doesn't understand she's going."

Aubrey stiffened at my wild tone.

"Perhaps you could introduce it into conversation," Selwyn said. "Gently, without scaring her."

"She'll be upset whatever you say." I faced Aubrey. "She will. She's known you for a space of hours, and she's to go to Ireland—"

"London, actually, first. I need to go to London. Tomorrow."

"The day after tomorrow. You said she'd go the day after."

"I've changed my mind." His mouth twisted with the unpleasantness of his duty. "Look, Mrs. Parr, I have to be honest. I won't be going to Ireland. I can't travel to a neutral country. I'm not allowed. And as I'm sure you're aware, living so near the coast, all routes are going to be shut down soon, for the invasion. So I'm going to London, where I'll hire a nanny, a proper registered person, to take her immediately to Ireland."

"You're not even going to take her yourself?"

"I've just explained that I can't."

We stared at each other. My face flamed. Selwyn's hand enclosed mine. I looked away from Aubrey and down at Selwyn's hand. My eyes were glassy with tears but I wouldn't let them fall. Inside me a fortress crumbled.

There was a thumping on the stairs. Pamela's voice came, a great shout, as if we were two hundred yards away. "Ellen! I can't find Popsy! She was in my bed and now she's gone! Where's Popsy?"

Popsy was a peg doll. Perhaps the one I'd pried from her hand when she was sleeping. Aubrey rose to his feet. "I'll go and help her. See if I can't tell her. Start, at least."

Selwyn and I remained a few moments more at the breakfast table. I sat silently while he tried to piece together a last day for Pamela. We would all go to church, it being Sunday, and then I'd take Pamela to say good-bye to Lucy while Selwyn showed Aubrey the mill. "He might enjoy seeing the turbine, I suppose." He spoke unsteadily. I took his hand.

"After lunch you could take Pamela to Upton Hall," he went on. "Bill Kennet needs to see her, and Althea. In fact we could all go to the Hall for tea. Do you think that would be nice?"

His fingers tightened on mine. I couldn't answer for the tears raining down my face.

Pamela appeared, wearing her straw hat. I spoke to her in a soft voice. "Did Daddy tell you about Ireland?"

"Mm." She tipped her hat at her reflection in the hall mirror, swung away, turned back, tipped her hat once more. I realized she was trying to do it the way William Kennet did.

"Mm, he did, or Mm, he didn't?"

"He did."

She brushed past me and went out of the front door.

· · · · ·

Lucy had a dark blue beret slanting over her forehead. It suited her, made her sallow face and black eyes more dramatic.

"You should wear that more often," I told her as we went through the lych-gate of the church. "You look quite dashing."

"You've bin cryin."

"Thank you for pointing it out. Pamela's going tomorrow."

"Oh, God Almighty."

We filed into the shadowed transept. Pamela tried to keep her voice down in church but it was so clear, so piercing always. "Can we sit with the Hornes?"

"Shush, Pamela. Your voice is like a steam whistle." I glanced back at Selwyn. He was silhouetted in the doorway, a head taller than Aubrey. I couldn't see his face but he would see mine. I gestured toward Lucy and Mrs. Horne, to say that we were going with them. "Of course we can," I said to Pamela.

Old Mrs. Horne and Lucy's father were ahead of us. Mrs. Horne broadbacked in a yellow frock and leaning heavily on her son's shoulder as she walked. We followed them into a pew. "Sit between me and Lucy," I whispered to Pamela.

"I always sit with you, Ell. Let me go between Lucy and Mrs. Horne."

"All right."

She scrambled past our knees and wedged herself between Lucy and her grandmother. Lucy looked up at Selwyn and Aubrey, as they walked murmuring down the aisle with Lady Brock. Lady Brock squeezed my shoulder with her gloved hand as she passed. We rose to our feet and the vicar said, "*O come, let us sing to the Lord, let us make a joyful noise to the rock of our salvation.*" I mouthed the words. Tomorrow I'd be bidding Pamela good-bye at my front door, watching her leave, and then going back inside. It was unimaginable. How would I go through the house, in and out of all the rooms? The dressing room, especially, where she slept: I didn't know how I was ever going to go in there again. I'd have to move the bed, shift the little table. Make it different somehow.

How would Aubrey manage, with one arm? He wouldn't be able to hold her hand in London, not if he was carrying her suitcase. She'd have to be very good, and not run ahead among the crowds.

"*In His hand are the deep places in the earth,*" I recited. "*The strength of the hills is His also.*"

We left the church and made our way to the Hornes' house. It was extraordinarily warm for the end of March. The heat made the day strange, because the trees were still bare. Pamela shrugged off her cardigan and walked ahead of me and Lucy, between Mrs. Horne and her son. If one could call it walking: an hour in church, doing no more than sit, stand, and kneel, had built up an intolerable head of steam in her. Every step was a jump, every fourth step a leap into the air, accompanied by a shriek. "That's a fox," she told Mr. Horne. "That's what they do at night. They play about at night and go like this." She leaped and shrieked again, and I heard Mr. Horne, a kennel man all his life, say, "My word, Pam. You're a brave fox," as he took her hand. In that moment I honestly would have preferred her to go then, just to vanish in an instant, and spare me the agony of waiting the rest of the day and the night.

"Let's have a tot in our cuppa." Lucy sniffed. "Bloody hell." I saw her sharp little face, the wetness in her narrowed eyes. We grasped each other's hands, and then parted to climb the steps.

I watched Pamela bend over in the long grass, trying for the last time to feed Maurice, who was as recalcitrant as ever. The brandy hadn't been a good idea. Mr. Horne had said it would stiffen our sinews but it was only cloying my mouth, bringing me closer to tears. How close could one go to tears without actually crying? I had a pain in my throat from it.

"Oh Maurice, you are sweet," I heard Pamela say.

I went over to the long grass and put my hand on her shoulder. I'd been the one who'd told her that her mother was dead. I remembered her in the privy here, her face lit by the heart-shaped hole in the door. *Won't be long, Pammie,* her mother used to say. A smaller child, in the grip of a great grief. It was my job to tell her now. "Pamela, tomorrow you're going away to your cousins in Ireland."

"I know." She didn't turn her head. "We're going on a train to London, and then on a boat to an island, and another lady's coming with us. Daddy told me after breakfast. He said you'd probably let me take the Peg family, but I should ask. So can I?"

"Ireland. Not island. Though it is an island . . ."

"That's it. Ireland." Still holding the stem of grass, she straightened up and looked at me. "Can I take them?"

"Please," I said, as a reflex.

"Please?"

"Yes."

She took my hand, put the grass stem into it. "You try."

"No, I don't think he's hungry." I felt too weak, suddenly, to cry. "We'd better go home. The Hornes will want their dinner soon. Say good-bye to Maurice."

"'Bye, Maurice." We went back toward the house. "'Bye, heart lav," she said. "And black currants. Oh—Ellen. You'd better bring your other hat, the one that stays on, because we're crossing the sea. It would be a shame if that straw one got blown away into the waves. Nobody'd fetch it for you, that's for sure."

I heard Elizabeth's voice, when she said "that's for sure."

"I'm not coming, Pamela. I'm staying here and you're going on the boat with a nanny, a lady to look after you. Over the sea to your aunt. Aunt Hester."

But she was running ahead to Lucy, who was standing by the apple tree. I watched her walk along the trunk. One foot in front of the other now, toes pointed, steady. A big girl. Lucy held out her hands but they weren't needed anymore. Mrs. Horne came out of the cottage, followed by a warm breath of gravy and draining cabbage. She was drying her hands on a tea towel. "We're not sent more than we can bear," she said. "You know that, my dear." Then she turned and went inside. She didn't expect an answer. I wanted to thank her, for being so kind to me, always. But there would be time enough for that.

We had our light luncheon. I forced down a scrap of carrot, cabbage, and potato patty. After the meal I went upstairs to get Pamela's things ready for her journey. I met Elizabeth on the landing. She was holding the blanket waistcoat I'd made for Pamela.

"I don't know if he'll want you to pack this." Loyally, Elizabeth refused to say his name.

"I'll ask him." I took the waistcoat. "It rains all the time there, you know. Damp and chilly."

Elizabeth sighed. "Well, she'll have castoffs galore now, from the big family. She won't wear a new thing till she's eighteen and gets a dress for dances, and even then it's touch and go. I know what it's like, I had three older sisters. I thought stockings came with darns." She grasped my arm. "Oh my dear, I'm so sorry. I'm speaking out of turn."

Because my face was obviously stretched into some sort of awful mask, as I contemplated Pamela tumbling away into this flock of children.

"Never mind, Elizabeth," I told her.

There wasn't much to pack: it would take a quarter of an hour at most. I fetched together the few dresses, stockings, a pair of shoes, a pair of Wellingtons. Underwear. I checked under the bed in the dressing room and withdrew a few more peg dolls, some still dressed in Selwyn's handkerchiefs. She could have the handkerchiefs too. If Selwyn protested, I'd buy him more after the war ended. Surely it would, someday.

I heard footsteps on the stairs, and then Aubrey put his head round the door. I looked up at him, and then continued to lay out vests on the bed. "These will last the summer, I daresay. She'll need warmer ones in the autumn. But Hester will take charge of that."

"You've been terribly kind. Keeping her in clothes over the years."

"I was given coupons." My voice was lifeless, insolent. I moved around the room.

He came in and sat down on the bed. "I'm sorry about all of this."

My shoulders sagged. "Really, I can't see why you should be, since none of it's your fault."

He was silent for a moment. Then he said, "Thank you for the suitcase."

It was one of Selwyn's, awfully old. I thought he'd probably taken it to school. "You don't have to continually apologize and thank." My voice rose. "You have no suitcase. I'll give you one. There was no one to look after your daughter, so I did it. We all do what we must."

He said nothing, adjusted the sling on his shoulder. I turned away from him and began to put Pamela's clothes into the suitcase. The Wellingtons in a shoe bag, her winter boots: they might be too small by Christmas, but they would go anyway. Two of the three vests. All the stockings, all but one pair of knickers, all but one pair of socks. Small white socks, some irretrievably mud-stained however much we scrubbed, but serviceable. I would put in her nightdress and toilet things tomorrow, and shut the lid, and never see any of these clothes again.

"Will it be as warm in London tomorrow, do you suppose?" I asked Aubrey, in the same high voice. "She'd better take her hat. Shall Hester want this waistcoat?" I held it up. "It's made out of a blanket. Nice and cozy."

I glanced up at his reflection in the wardrobe mirror. He looked tired, discomfited. Catching my eye he forced an expression of manu-factured cheer. "The house is glacial," he said. "The children play upstairs in their coats during the winter. So I'm sure it'll come in handy."

I put the waistcoat into the case. It was almost full. Where would she fit her toilet things, the Peg family, her book about London? I'd have to find another bag.

"She thinks I'm coming too, Aubrey. We need to disabuse her." Despair passed through me like a breaking wave. I sat down next to him on the bed. "I did say. But you know how she runs off all the time. She didn't hear me, or tried not to, at least. How are you going to manage in London? She's not used to cities. I was thinking about it in church. You won't be able to hold her hand and the suitcase—"

"She *might* remember cities. She was in Plymouth, after all." He got to his feet so that I had to look up into his face. He seemed so young, this widower. It was almost ridiculous. I wondered how his face would change with the years. What sort of man he'd make, when he was Selwyn's age. His brisk words cut off my thoughts. "My half brother will meet us off the train. He's much older than me and Hester. He works in the War Office, he's an actuary. He's a terrible old stick, he knows nothing about children, but he has a flat, and two functioning hands."

We heard her feet on the stairs, and then she appeared in the doorway, beaming at Aubrey. "Guess what, we're going to the Hall for tea. The *Hall*." She echoed herself, dragging the word out. "To show you the knight in *armor*." She came over to me and looked in the suitcase. "Oh, there's my new waistcoat. I was looking for that." She picked it up and began to struggle into it, turning it upside down in her haste.

"Pamela." I pulled the hem away from her shoulders. "Sit on the bed with me. Take this off. It's too hot for today."

She was hogtied, her arms bound into the waistcoat, but nonetheless scrambled onto the bed. "No it isn't. It's perfect."

"I'm not coming to Ireland with you," I said. "Pamela, are you listening? I'm staying here, and you're going with your daddy."

"A mouse ate this blanket so it had to be cut up for clothes." She rolled away from me into a ball, kicking her foot against the suitcase. I got up and grabbed at the case before it fell onto the floor.

"Pamela darling, I'm not coming—"

"A family of mice. *Squeak, squeak.* Lucy's got a waistcoat too only hers is bigger but not much."

Aubrey stood, bewildered.

"You could help," I said.

"Pamela, Ellen's staying here and we're going to London, just you and me. Then we'll find a nice lady who will take you on the boat. She'll make sure you have some chocolate—"

"Stop talking. Stop talking, you horrible man." She sat up, threw off the waistcoat. Her cheeks were flushed, her eyes shiny and hard. "I'm going to the Hall with Mr. Parr. You can go wherever you want. Go to London or Ireland or Australia or Canada and see if I jolly well care." She scrambled off the bed and bounded out of the room, across the landing and down the stairs.

I put the waistcoat in the suitcase and clicked it shut. I still needed to find another receptacle for the rest of her things, but I wouldn't look now. Aubrey sat down again on the bed, shoulders slumped. "Oh dear."

"She doesn't particularly like chocolate. Chocolate cake, yes, but not chocolate on its own."

"I didn't know." He seemed to slump further.

"How could you?" I crossed the room. "I'll go and see where she is. Since you can think of nothing better than to sit there in that hopeless fashion." My lips were shaking with anger but it didn't weaken me.

"Ellen," he said as I left the room, but nothing more, and as I started down the stairs I glimpsed him hang his head.

20

I FOUND HER in the kitchen making tiny dough balls out of a piece of bread. The grime from her fingers graying the already gray dough. I firmed my mouth and said her name. She looked up.

"I know you don't want to go to Ireland," I said.

"Do you?" She shot me the same hard shiny look as she had given her father. "So what? It's not like either of you care the tiniest bit about me."

I kneeled on the floor beside her and put my arms on the arms of the chair. Gently she banged her foot against my thigh. "I hate you," she said in the softest voice. She gave me another small kick, and another. "Hate you, hate you, hate you."

The house was still. Elizabeth was in the garden, pegging tea cloths on the line. Aubrey showed no sign of coming downstairs. Selwyn could have been anywhere.

I pushed myself upright and fetched a canvas bag, one with a strap, that hung from a hook on the door. We needed food of some kind, and water. There was an army canteen under the sink—I brought it out and filled it. Then I wrapped a hunk of seedcake, dried out but edible, in greaseproof paper. That would do. Both these items I put into the bag.

Pamela was watching me, swinging her leg, pouting.

"Come on, Pamela. Come with me."

"Why should I?"

"Outside. Now." I went to the kitchen door without looking back, heard the scrape of her chair on the floor.

I wheeled the bicycle toward the double doors of the garage, pushing it fast over the uneven path. She tagged behind, recently caught up, whining.

"Why are you putting it away? I wanted to ride to the Hall."

"We need to put the real tires on. Take hold of the bicycle so I can tackle this door."

I opened one half of the door, lifting it so that it wouldn't groan on its hinges. Inside the garage the sheeted car was motionless in the gloom, the tank empty. The bicycle's inner tubes lay in their box on the shelf. I fetched the box down and gave it to Pamela, who watched while I stood the bicycle on its handlebars and saddle, reached for the spanners and removed both wheels. I loved this machine. It was never a labor, caring for it.

We used a couple of old spoons for tire irons. They worked perfectly well. The outer tires were off in an instant.

"Why are you changing the tires?"

Less whining now.

"We can't tackle the hill road on straw ropes."

I pried out the ropes that William had bound, that were properly made out of eight twisted strands. He and I had fitted them together, he pressing the straw neatly between the flanges of the wheel before I sewed the two ends together with waxed upholstery yarn.

"We won't be going on the hill road. We're supposed to be having tea at the Hall."

"That's not for an hour and a half. Do be quiet and bring me that pump. No. The black thing." She didn't know what a bicycle pump was, of course. I pressed the inner tubes into place, inflating a little to give them form, and worked the outer tires back on and pumped some more. "Now, on with the wheels."

Pamela was squatting by the bicycle now, holding the pump. "Coo. You should be a mechanic in a bike race, Ellen."

In my haste I tightened the front wheel-nuts unevenly and pushed the wheel out of true. It seemed to take an age before it was ticking round steady and free. I put the straw ropes in a dry bucket beneath the workbench, righted the bicycle, and wheeled it out to lean against the brick wall by the door. "Now a bit more air."

"Let me—"

"No." I grabbed the pump from her. "There isn't time."

"It's rude to snatch."

Behind us the front door opened. "Mrs. Parr?"

At least it was Elizabeth, and not Selwyn or Aubrey. "We're going for a spin, Elizabeth. Could you please tell the men we'll meet them at the Hall for tea?"

It felt right to say "the men," like that, airily, as one did at picnics or tennis matches, or, indeed, tea at the Hall. As if nothing untoward were happening. But Elizabeth silently wound her hands into her apron and stared at the bicycle pump.

I slipped it into my bag. "Come on, Pamela."

When Mother died, Edward and I walked through Pipehouse Wood together: the light green shadow, the small ups and downs of a beech wood. Now Pamela and I traveled through the same light and shade, unseen by people on the road. I pushed the bicycle over bulbous, silvered roots; she trotted and gamboled beside me. She'd forgotten about Ireland, I could tell from the spring in her step. She was still just young enough to do that. Let things slip entirely from her mind. The path led along the bottom of the wood. We would have to join the road in the end, but at least, for this first part of the journey, the trees hid us. I walked on, and the warmth here, even among the trees, recalled the summers when Lucy and Daniel and I used to wander in and out of the deep beech-shadows here, hungry and none too clean, and glad to be in the sunshine. But I no longer cared about heat and cold. I would endure ten of the winters of my childhood, ten in a row with no summer between them, if it meant that I could keep Pamela by my side. Let me freeze and starve in the Absaloms again if, at the end of it all, my girl could stay with me.

Once on the road, the land started to incline: a tough climb, but we made better going than in the wood. I labored from pedal to pedal. The breeze blew through the trees that lined the road. Pamela sang her song, *hey, ho,* but I had no breath to join her. I just listened to her clear little voice as Beacon Hill rose in the distance. The road started to level out, the air-filled tires spun along. I didn't remind her of the opportunity to pedal and she didn't mention it, and I was glad, because I was faster.

We traveled past a farm where nobody went. Only the dogs saw us and barked unheeded. Dry pats of cow dung littered the road.

"I don't like this place," said Pamela.

"We're not staying in it."

"Where *are* we going? I'm hungry. I want to get off."

"We will. We're just going over the back of the hill there. Look at those clouds, how puffy they are."

They were marshaled on the horizon, piled up and pearly on their flat undersides, almost still in the light breeze. We reached the back of the hill. There was a stile by the side of the road leading to the summit. I dismounted by the fence and bade her get down. The bicycle toppled away from the fence, striking my calf as it fell. "Stupid bicycle." I left it there. "Come on, Pamela. Climb ahead of me."

Over she went onto the other side of the stile, and then a neat jump to the ground.

"What a girl," I said. "I'll love you forever."

I watched her run ahead of me up the chalky path. I didn't know if she'd heard me.

. . . . .

We had our picnic in the bowl of the tumulus on the crown of the hill, its little ramparts sheltering us from the breeze, which had stiffened over the high ground. The turf was warm, peppered with dry rabbit droppings. Among the grass I saw buck's-horn plantain, tiny spread leaves flattened by millennia of nibbling teeth. "When I was twelve, Pamela, I used to read a book called *Downland Flora*. It was the only thing I had that was nice."

She didn't say anything, just bit into her slice of cake, chewed, yawned, chewed again more slowly. Her cheeks were rosy in the sunshine, her eyes sleepy.

"Will you come to Ireland, Ellen?"

"You know that your daddy and I told you that I can't."

"Not tomorrow. But in the future?"

The future. A high road on a chalk land.

"We will all do what is best."

She let her eyes run over me, considering my words, weighing them for truth or lies or any meaning at all. Then she seemed to give up on the task. We had told her so many things. Why should she take account of us now? She lay down on her side, pillowing her head on her arm. I lay down too, so that I could see her and also the sky on the brow of the tumulus, the clouds chasing. I shut my eyes, and then opened them to look straight up at the sky. The wind dropped for a moment, and I heard a high sweet rivulet of sound above us.

"Listen," I said. "A lark."

She turned toward me, screwing up her eyes against the bright of the sky. "I can't hear him."

"You will."

The wind guttered again, the lark wheeled. She opened her eyes. "Oh yes!" She pointed upward. "I can see him now too."

I lay back down on the turf. "I can't."

"You will!"

We both laughed, and then my eyes caught a small dot in the blue, the song reeling off him like thread from a bobbin.

The breeze was now gusting over the hill. My hair streaked across my face as I took her back to the bicycle. The sun was still strong, throwing a heavy horizontal light across the chalky fields. This was the upland where little grew. The lane led flat and straight toward the horizon, where another line of hills undulated and where the fleets of clouds, darker now, waited. Beyond them lay Southampton. When the clouds parted, the sea would gleam like a bar of metal.

"I'd like to get under those clouds," I said to Pamela.

"Where are we going?" Her hands were digging into my stomach, she was clinging so hard. "Ellen? Where are we going?"

"To the sea."

It was downhill from here. All we had to do was keep pedaling. The sun brightened ahead of us somewhere out beyond the clouds gathering on the coast. How beautiful they were, stately and opalescent. Underneath them a section of the sea duly started to shine. Pamela swayed sideways to look at it and we both laughed.

"Let me pedal, Ellen, I'm getting cold."

"Just a little longer."

The tires made a fine rushing on the smooth road and the wind buffeted my ears. We would be there in half an hour or so, I thought. A great big port city.

"If only Edward were here," I told Pamela. "He's a wharf rat of long standing, you know. He'd find all the nooks and crannies. Bolt-holes, and so on."

"What's a bolt-hole?"

I strove onward. The light was making my eyes water. The skyline swelled, the road became a blur. There was a kind of hatched shadow lying across it. A break of brushwood, or something. Why would anyone do that? I slowed, and as the wind in my ears abated I heard the hum of a car engine approaching behind us.

"A bolt-hole," I was saying, "is a place where—when people come looking for you—"

The engine behind us was louder. The thing in the road sprawled larger and darker. I braked and the water streamed from my eyes, which then saw full clear the barrier of barbed wire that crawled thick from one side of the road to the other and into the fields too. My fingers clamped down on the brakes, and the car came alongside. Pamela suddenly caught sight of the barbed wire and screamed, and pulled me sideways. I couldn't help but yank the handlebars round. We skidded over the light gravel on the edge of the road and onto the verge, and fell with the bicycle. Pamela shrieked and scrambled out from under the frame. I couldn't move my leg, and for a moment the pain in my ankle was so intense that I thought I'd broken it. I flexed my foot, cried out. Pamela's hands were on my leg. "Ellen! Ellen! You've broken your bones!"

I lifted my hand, saw a graze on the ball of my thumb. Beads of blood were springing.

"I've just twisted my ankle a bit," I heard myself say. "Honestly, Pamela. What a tragedy queen."

The car had halted just ahead of us. It was Lady Brock's motor. I waited for Lady Brock's feathered hat to emerge from the driver's door. But it was William Kennet who got out.

"Oh, William." I struggled into a sitting position. "We're all at sixes and sevens."

He lifted the bicycle off my leg and laid it on the edge of the road. Then he came and kneeled down beside me. "Can you move?"

"Yes."

"Good job you didn't hit that." We looked at the barbed wire. It was a nasty hedge, four or five foot high. "We laid it out to see how much we needed. Didn't you see the signs?"

"I had tears in my eyes."

"Tears in your eyes. You'd have had more than tears in your eyes." His voice was peremptory, bleak. "Get up now, girl."

I lumbered to my feet. William took not my hand but Pamela's, who allowed herself to be led to the car. I followed them, limping, and leaned against the car while he loaded the bicycle into the boot. The boot wouldn't close, of course, so he lashed the handle to the mud-guard with a piece of twine, his hands skillful, angry, and quick. He glanced up at me. "What a right mess you look."

Pamela climbed into the back of the car, her face frozen.

"What did you bump?" I asked her. "Does it hurt?"

"Nothing." She looked at William as she answered. "I'm quite all right."

I levered myself into the passenger seat. Now that I was seated, the pain in my ankle lessened. William turned the car in the narrow lane. We drove in silence for a mile or so. Then he said, "You were above Galley Down. That's how far you got."

"Is that all?" I spoke with difficulty, being suddenly terribly cold. "I thought it was further."

"They're frantic at the Hall. If you were younger I'd put you over my knee."

I started to laugh at that, a sliding wail of a laugh that rose and fell beyond my control. William took no notice, speaking on through the unseemly noise. "We'll say you sprained your ankle and couldn't move. You just thought you'd take a turn along the Beacon Hill road, and you lost track of time. But on the way back you fell off because of a—stop now, with that racket. Ellen. Stop."

I clamped my hand over my mouth and held it firm there until I was sure I had quelled the wailing. "Because of a farm dog," I said finally. "Which ran out. That awful dog that belongs to the farm nobody goes to."

"And you couldn't budge," he went on. "Never mind what the little one says. She's always full of stories."

I craned my head round toward the backseat. Pamela was huddled wet-eyed in the corner. My wailing had shocked her. I stretched out my hand in remorse: she considered it, and looked away out of the window.

William drove easily, his maimed hand a soft claw gripping the rim of the wheel.

"I suppose you drove all over the place, looking. I'm so sorry, William."

"I had an idea where you'd be. You like those top roads."

The sun lowered at last, striking the glass of the windscreen, hazing his hair.

Pamela was calm when we reached the Hall. Selwyn and Aubrey came out, followed by Lady Brock. William got out of the car and went to speak to them, the words indistinguishable. Then Lady Brock bent down to my window. "Just as long as you and Pamela are all right."

"She's unharmed. Only upset. By the accident, and the wait."

Lady Brock peered into the car. Pamela was sitting motionless, her hair across her face, her dress rumpled. "Dear little child. Did no one come by, on the road?"

"Not a soul. I was so glad to see Mr. Kennet."

Her small brown eyes held mine. I could hardly see her expression. "You must be cold. Sitting so long, immobilized. You'd all better get back to the mill." She glanced behind her and straightened up. "Selwyn, take the wheel. Lieutenant Commander Lovell, your daughter needs you. You're keeping the motor for tomorrow, anyway, so off you go."

I heard light male voices. I looked for William but he'd gone. "Please thank Mr. Kennet," I told Lady Brock, but she had turned her back and was walking toward the steps of her house.

Selwyn got in behind the wheel and started the car as Aubrey took his place beside Pamela. He put his arm round her shoulders and she leaned her head against his chest. Over her ruffled hair he met my gaze.

"I was silly," I said to him.

But it was Selwyn who replied. "Everybody does silly things from time to time, my love." His face was turned away from me as he reversed the car over the gravel.

We traveled silently in the heavy gloom of the car. When we reached the mill, Selwyn helped me out and we went haltingly into the house.

We had a supper of soup and the last of the bread. Afterward in the sitting room Selwyn and Aubrey began a long, slow wind through an A to Z with Pamela, the subject being Birds of the World. *Albatross, Buzzard*, they chanted, sticking for a long time at M before arriving at *Mallard*, and again at U. "There's a bird called an upland goose," I told them. "I learned it at school." When we had finished, Selwyn played the piano and Pamela fell asleep on the sofa. Selwyn carried her up the stairs and I followed him into our bedroom. He laid her on our bed.

"I'm sorry," I said again.

"I'm just glad that William found you."

He straightened up. I looked into his face. He knew what I'd done, tried to do, the knowledge was in his eyes, but he held it there. He didn't give voice to it.

"Selwyn . . ."

"I love you so much, Ellen. I'm so sorry—"

We clung to each other, dry-eyed. "It's not your fault," I told him, many times, because it wasn't, and the truth bore repeating until he understood.

Later I undressed and lay beside my small child. The night was short. I pulled the sheet over her cold, round little arms. For most of the night I watched her but my eyes and mind were worn out with looking and anyway, she had closed herself off from me now, it seemed, and lay like a nut in a shell with her back and her face turned away from me.

In the morning I gave her a bath, and squeezed the sponge over her shoulders. "I shall wear my dark blue dress," she said, with solemnity. "The one with red pockets."

I buttoned up the dress and brushed her hair for the last time. She was supposed to do it but today she let me, her head rocking backward with the strength of my brushstrokes, her eyes impassively trained on her reflection.

We went downstairs. I gripped the banisters, limping a little. She turned back and said, "Your poor ankle," and then walked on down.

I couldn't eat, so sipped at a cup of tea. Pamela had her porridge. There wasn't enough jam for a whole face, only for the two eyes. She shrugged and started eating.

Aubrey came in, followed shortly by Selwyn. She looked up at them. "What sort of woman is it, that'll take me to Ireland?"

"A nanny," Aubrey said. "One specially trained in traveling with children."

"Yes, but will she be a kind one or a bossy one?"

"I'm sure she'll be kind," I told her. "Only kind people do jobs like that."

After breakfast Pamela and I brushed our teeth and finished her packing. The nerves in my stomach were singing and I felt light-headed. I remembered that I hadn't yet found a bag for Pamela's remaining things, her peg dolls and her books. I brought out an old shoe bag of Selwyn's, but as I began to fill it an idea came to me. "I know. You can have my little suitcase."

It was the one I'd taken from the Stour House when we moved to the Absaloms. I removed the label that said "Ellen Calvert" and turned it over, and wrote "Pamela Lovell" on the blank side. The case was cream-colored with a pink inside, a pink I'd never liked, nasty and artificial. She laid in the dolls, and stuffed in a cardigan to keep them all lying down in position, and put her London book, and her drawing book and pencil, in on top.

I fetched my letter to her and tucked it into the side pocket. "You can read this when you get to Ireland."

"Is it from you?"

"Yes."

"Why don't you just tell it me now?"

"Because it's for Ireland, not now. Look, we can tie everything in with these little straps." There were two of them on the inside of the case, also pink, with brass sliding buckles.

But she shook her head. "The Pegs'll be comfier without them."

She hadn't smiled all morning, and I realized I'd seen the last of her smiles the previous day, and I wouldn't see another.

Selwyn called up the stairs. "Darling. It's time."

I carried the large case downstairs, she the small one. When she reached the hall, she said, "I need to go to the lav."

We went to the downstairs lavatory. I made sure she washed her hands well. "Don't neglect your hand-washing on the journey, Pamela," I said. "Just because I'm not there to tell you. And if you need the lavatory, always tell Daddy well in advance." She still dried her small hands so clumsily. It was astonishing how long it took, to learn the grips and turns of the fingers for washing and drying. I finished the task by patting the backs of her hands with the towel.

Elizabeth was waiting by the lavatory. She held out her arms. Pamela embraced her, putting her cheek flat against Elizabeth's belly. "Dear Pammie," said Elizabeth. "Little pet." Then she set her hands on Pamela's shoulders and bent to kiss the top of her head, and then she turned quickly and made for the kitchen.

The front door was open. Lady Brock's car was outside, Selwyn already in the driver's seat. He was wearing his motoring hat. He looked at me, but only to be sure that there was nothing amiss. He knew better than to do or say anything else. Aubrey was waiting on the path. I went to join him. I put out my left hand and he took it in his, clasping it rather than simply shaking it. Pamela followed me out and clutched my other hand. I was bound by them.

"You must both let go of me," I told them, and they released me.

I kneeled on the path in front of Pamela. "Be a good girl." I embraced her. Her arms came round my neck, gripping hard. I pulled her against me and breathed in, sniffling as the tears flowed down my nose. She gripped harder and I felt her sobbing.

"Come now, Pamela. You must be brave. We must both be brave."

"No. No." She began to cry loudly. "We haven't even fed the hens. You said we would."

"Never mind now. There'll be hens enough in Ireland. You'll see." I let go of her middle and took her hands in mine, tugging them from my neck. She was sobbing hard. "Come on. Good girl. Into the car." Aubrey tried to guide her by the shoulders but she twisted away from him.

"Ellen!" She clung to me again. "I don't want to go! I want to stay here with you and feed the hens!"

I put my arm across her back and led her forcibly to the car. She sat sideways on the seat and started screaming, kicking out at me. I caught hold of the flailing legs and pushed them round so that she faced the front. "Get into the car," I told Aubrey. I slammed the door shut on Pamela, who was still screaming. As Selwyn started the engine she held up her arms. "Ellen! Ellen! I don't want to go! Ellen!"

"Drive on," I said to Selwyn, as Aubrey got in. "Drive on!" I cried, when he hesitated. I stepped back from the car and Selwyn drove away. I watched them reach the end of the lane and turn. The car window was shut but I could still hear Pamela calling my name.

When the sound faded I went inside. Elizabeth was nowhere to be seen. I went upstairs to the bedroom. Pamela's dress, the one she'd worn the day before, was lying on the bed. It was too small to pack, she was growing out of it, and the trim of white daisies at the hem was coming off. I picked it up and held it against my face. The sky-blue cotton was still warm, and it smelled of her. I didn't know how long the smell would last.

I held the dress to my face and breathed in. I held the breath and the dress.

Some time later I looked out of the window. William was in the garden watering my apple trees. I went downstairs and out into the garden. I was still holding the dress.

I said to him, "I don't understand how I can still be alive."

William set down the watering can and embraced me. Rough tweed, stiff, against my face. "And yet you are," he said. "Come with me to Upton Hall, Ellen. Sit awhile with Lady B and me." The trees were damp at the knees, their leaves fluttered in the breeze. I saw Elizabeth crying in the doorway and beckoned to her. William took my arm. We left the apple trees to grow, and the three of us set off up the lane together.

Two

Ellen

1944–1973

21

15th March 1944

Dear Pamela,

I hope that you will keep this letter after you have read it so that you can read it again because I have some very important things to say to you. You're very young and you may not quite understand them now. But if you crumple up this letter and throw it on the fire, or make a boat out of it, that'll be the end of it, and when you're twelve or sixteen or eighteen you might wish you still had it so that you could go over it and understand it better.

Pamela, do you remember our blackout adventure? You were seven, I think, and we went to Waltham to buy you a pair of shoes. I was silly and disorganized that day so we didn't get to Waltham until half-past four, and when we came out of Lack's it was after sunset and the whole town was pitch-dark. And we set off carefully over the street toward the bus stop, but when we got to the other side it wasn't there! Do you remember? The bus stop I'd known all my life, that I thought I could find blindfolded?—Well! We shuffled up and down and round and round, stretching our arms out and peering like a couple of bats. I didn't tell you at the time, but I didn't have the faintest idea where we were. And then we saw the nurses—we spotted their white caps in the gloom. They were new to Waltham and they didn't know our bus stop, but they said they'd just come out of the teahouse. I realized we'd gone much further than I thought. So we crept back along the pavement until quite suddenly you said, "Ellen!" and there it was. You'd bumped into the pole, quite gently thank goodness. And the bus came, and we went back to Upton.

Pamela, you and I, we've been on a sort of big blackout adventure. The war came, and it set you wandering off your path in life. You lost Mummy in the air raid and you were brought to Upton. Nobody knew who you were and you had no one to look after you. So I took you to my house. I didn't know you were coming—it was all a huge surprise—and I didn't quite know what to do with you in the beginning, I must say! But I felt my way along, do you see? And so did you, and we held hands tightly all the while. But now you have found your way again. After all this adventuring you've found your father and a whole family of cousins who all love you.

Of course we shall miss each other for a while. Blackout companions become very close. But life will be so much better when peace comes, Pamela, I promise you. You can't remember what it was like before the war, I don't suppose. But there'll be so much to do and enjoy. Games and toys in the shops, and ice cream and bananas, and trips to the seaside. I daresay you'll find your aunt and uncle and cousins a little strange at first. But remember how quickly you and I got used to each other. In no time at all you'll be firm friends with them, just like you and I have been, because they love you.

Here is a kiss from me, darling. X.

> Ellen

18th March 1944

Dear Mrs. Parr,

I'm writing to tell you that Pamela has arrived safely in Ireland. Please be assured she recovered from her great storm of grief at leaving you and her eyes were not only dry by the time she reached London but *round and inquisitive. She was the perfect train companion and greeted the nanny, a Mrs. Cross, with a polite handshake and the words, "I do hope you shan't be"! The voyage was marred by seasickness—the Irish Sea is seldom merciful—and they had another long train journey once in Ireland but when she reached my sister's house she was only a little travel-stained and very sleepy.*

I wish once more to express my gratitude at your kindness to my daughter during this great crisis in her young life. I couldn't have asked for better "foster parents," if you'll excuse the term, than yourself and Mr. Parr. My pain at not being with her when her mother died is considerably assuaged by the knowledge that you were both offering her such comfort, especially during those dark days at the beginning of the war which tested everyone's nerves so sorely. She's a lovely child, rather more solemn than myself or Hester at the same age, but that is wholly to be expected. She is also far better behaved.

In short, I owe you a debt I can never repay. Please take this letter as an acknowledgment of that fact.

Yours sincerely,
Aubrey Lovell

March the 18th 1944

DEAR ELLEN

I shall NOT call you DEAR. You are NOT DEAR. Why are you telling me this RUBBISH about the blackout? I'm so sad I've TORN UP your LETTER.

I HATE YOU AND DADDY AND I HAVE KICKED HIM.

PAMELA

PS The letter is in little bits in the RABBIT'S CAGE. Because it is fit only for RABBIT BEDS.

25th March 1944

Darling girl,

Of course you're angry. I don't blame you at all. I can see you in my mind's eye, glaring at me like you did when you were very small. I wish I could do something to help. Darling, don't kick your daddy. It's not his fault that you're feeling sad. He's trying to do what is best for you. Why don't you tell me a little about your new home in Ireland? It seems that your cousins have a rabbit. That's nice, at least, isn't it?

Ellen X

March the 31st 1944

Dear Ellen

Nothing is nice.

Pamela

April the 2nd 1944

Dear Ellen

When I get into bed at night Aunt Hester gives me a nightdress with a string round the bottom so that I can pull it tight and sleep in a sort of bag. She gave me a little mirror that folded in half but I didn't want it.

We aren't in the war here. Instead we're in the Emergency so there's hardly any butter or sugar just like at home. But we do have meat. I don't know why.

I miss you Ellen.

Pamela X

9th April 1944

Dearest Pamela,

I'm so glad to hear that your nightdress is keeping you warm and that you've got plenty of meat. You see? I knew there'd be some nice things about Ireland. Perhaps you can tell me a little bit about your cousins?

I miss you too, darling. Of course we miss each other.

But we must put our best feet forward!

Ellen XX

April the 16th 1944

Dear Ellen

Today I went with my girl cousins out to the sheep fields to a place where the sheep leave tufty bits of wool on the wire fence, and we pulled it off and collected a bag of it. We're going to stuff cushions with it. Doll's cushions I mean.

There. That's about my cousins.

There's a map of England and Ireland in Uncle Jack's study. He gets furious if we go in there but I do it all the same. Because I can see Southampton on the map and I know that if I put my fingertip on Southampton the top of my nail is about on Upton even though it isn't written there. So at least a tiny bit of my fingernail is in Upton.

Ellen I've tried to like it here for WEEKS AND WEEKS. But I don't. I don't care about the sheep fields or the wool or the doll's cushions. Every day I go to the gate on the lane and I try and see you coming up on the bike, pedaling round and round with your bun coming out in the wind. And you call PAMELA PAMELA MY DARLING And you say IT'S

ALL BEEN A MISTAKE AND I'M COMING TO TAKE YOU HOME. But you never ever come!!

Pamela XXX XXXX XXXXX

May the 1st 1944

Dear Ellen

Why don't you write BACK TO ME? Have you FORGOTTEN all about me???

Pamela XXX

May the 4th 1944

Ellen I don't think you LOVE ME ANY MORE. If you DID you would WRITE to me telling me you will come and get me and take me HOME. I don't want to be here and I don't care if these people are my uncle and aunt and cousins. I don't know them and I don't WANT to know them. I don't even know Daddy. I thought I liked him but then he turned out to be FOUL and CRUEL because he took me away from you.
I thought you LOVED ME.

Pamela XX

11th May 1944

Pamela,

I love you above all things. But I can't come and get you. Firstly, nobody is allowed to come to Ireland because of the war. Secondly, even if I could come, it would be wrong. You may not care about your family yet,

*but you need to be with them now. My sweetheart, hold on. Their house
doesn't feel like home for you now, but I promise you it will. This is your
new life, my love.*

Ellen XXX

19th May 1944

Dear Mrs. Parr,

This isn't an easy letter to write, but I know that we both want the
best for Pamela, so I do feel I've really no choice in opening my heart and
feelings to you as one woman to another.

I know that my brother has written to you expressing his gratitude for
the great care and fondness you showed Pamela during her stay in
England following Amelia's tragic death. I concur absolutely with his
sentiments and no one could be gladder than he and I to receive once
more into our arms a little girl whose life had been so tenderly . . . can I
say, repaired, if it does not sound too odd, by yourself and your husband.
Amelia was not a conventional woman, certainly not one made for
marriage. I'm dreadfully sad for my brother, of course, that she made this
discovery at his expense, but I don't entirely blame her. I also have a
strong sense, for all Amelia's waywardness, that she loved Pamela
inordinately.

We all love her, you see—Amelia, Aubrey, Jack and myself, and her
four cousins.

Now I have to tell you that last week Pamela was found at a bus stop
in Kilkenny by the Gardaí who returned her to us completely unscathed
but weeping inconsolably. She had taken her cousin Richie's bicycle and
ridden it off to Waterford where she took the bus for Kilkenny.
Apparently she had boarded the bus amid a crowd of children and the
driver had not realized that Pamela was in fact traveling alone. Anyway,
Pamela told the Gardaí she was trying to reach Dublin in order to take
the boat from Dún Laoghaire to Fishgard, if you please, and then her

plan was to work her way back to Hampshire and to you. Found on her little person was the sum of 21 shillings, being the combination of a present from her father and the pocket money she had saved.

My dear Mrs. Parr, we're not cruel people, my husband Jack and I. We hate to see children unhappy. We weighed it up and decided it would do no harm for her to send a few letters to you in Upton while she got used to us. The alternative, cutting her off from you at a stroke, seemed counterproductive as well as brutal, since it would throw her into such misery as to make it even harder for her to settle in. But here we come to the nub of the matter.

We know that you're a wise and sensible young woman, Mrs. Parr, and it is to that wisdom and sensibleness that we now appeal.

I am wholly unsurprised to learn from your most recent letter to Pamela that you love her above all things. She is a lovable child even when angry and sad. But, as I am sure you will agree, the task—if you like—of loving Pamela now falls to Aubrey, and to me, and to my husband, Jack, and our children. As you told her so wisely and tenderly in your letter, Pamela's life is with us now. And I am sure that you and I both understand how much harder it will be for her to come to terms with that, if she is continually reminded of her former life with you.

So—I know I've been long-winded but verbosity is a hazard when speaking from the heart—so it is in her interests, Mrs. Parr, that I ask you now to consider that letter you wrote to Pamela as your last. I will keep the letter safe. I will assure Pamela of your love. I shall explain that it is because you love her that you need her to go forward, as you told her yourself, into her new life.

I believe it is time for all of us, not just Pamela, to go forward into our new lives. The war must end next year, it must. I hope that you too will rejoice, Mrs. Parr, and I trust that you will reap all you deserve of the fruits of the peace.

Yours most gratefully,
Hester Browne

· · · · ·

The first days passed. One, then another, then six, a dozen—trippingly, as if rattled off a spool.

Punctuated also by sunrise, sunset, bread. I could only eat scraps of bread. At night I lay on Pamela's small bed holding the dress, which was all I had.

I spent my days with Suky Fitch and Selwyn in the mill. Sometimes I felt faint and had to sit down or even kneel on the floor, but the humming of the turbine came into me through my knees. Selwyn spent much time watching the millstones turn, watching grain falling from the hoppers, and I watched him.

A fortnight—Aubrey's letter arrived, and Pamela's the next day. I entered a half-life, touching papers she had touched, crying over letters she had cried on. The bluebells came in Pipehouse Wood, and the small flowers on Beacon Hill. I took her letters to these places and read them over and over. Then Hester wrote, and the ax fell, and she was truly gone.

I was glad of the travel ban, really I was, it was an iron fence I could fling myself against. Without it I would have gone to her in Ireland, presented myself crying, screaming, trying to tear her out of the door.

Some time after I received Hester's letter, Selwyn handed me a small round leather case. Inside was a compass, a lively little thing with snapping lid and a dancing needle. I put it on the table and it settled, true and eager. He told me that when the war was over, we could go on a long trip. He said, "Why don't we get out the atlas this evening?"

I wanted to please him, so I said, "Yes."

And it proved to be comforting to run my eyes over maps free of the thick arrows and crosses and hatched zones that were the marks of war. Instead there were rumpled purple mountains, seas grading from turquoise to the deepest indigo, wide ocher plains, all with the barest of boundary lines. I turned only the pages showing the Mediterranean, the Adriatic, the Aegean. The Holy Land. Nowhere closer to home.

The idea came to me as I sat there. I could still write to her. Of course I could. I simply wouldn't send the letters. I would keep them in a pile in my desk drawer. Tied into a packet with ribbon and inscribed with her name. I would tell her everything that was in my heart, speaking not to the child but to the woman I would never know. Hoping that one day in the years to come the letters might fall into her hands, and she would read them and know that she was not forgotten.

7th June 1944

Dear Pamela,

The invasion has happened. The soldiers have gone. Hurling themselves out into the Channel, into a gap between two gales, grabbing their luck and courage in both hands, sending our hearts into our mouths. We knew it was coming by then—barbed wire sprawling and running everywhere, army tents pitched under Jeps Hanger and then under Pipehouse Wood. Even Beacon Hill was out of bounds. Jeeps flashing by, the sun catching the braid on unfamiliar uniforms. And finally, the rumbling. It rose, and swelled, until Selwyn and Suky Fitch and I heard it through the racket in the mill. We ran outside. I looked up but there were no airplanes. We hurried to the end of the lane and there they were, lorry after lorry after lorry passing, bound for the sea. Our road alone couldn't account for the noise. It was coming from all the roads in the south.

Suky and I waved at the soldiers, and Selwyn saluted them.

I wish you'd been there, Pamela, holding my hand. Not just for my sake, but for yours. You'd have been thrilled.

14th March 1945

Dear Pamela,

Dan is dead. He died in Italy. To survive so much and then lose his life like so many others on the Gothic Line. None of us can comprehend it yet. You might remember a brown-haired man with small blue eyes who came to Upton during your first Christmas with us. I think he danced a reel with you in the village hall. Lucy is more distraught than Marcy his wife—I wish you were here, to go to Lucy's house and eat bread and butter and climb on her apple tree. It would be a comfort to her. Her eyes are always dark but now they seem utterly lightless. The only thing rescuing me from similar grief is my fury that he's gone, that the war has taken him.

Edward is in Bangalore recuperating from malaria, dysentery, and an infected wound to the scalp. He is doing very well, he says. I try and hold him in my mind.

We still have the map you stuck drawing pins in, to trace his journey. We've run out of drawing pins so I put an ordinary dressmaker's pin into Bangalore for you.

22nd August 1946

Dear Pamela,

Yesterday I was arranging flowers with Althea Brock, cutting the stems of her dahlias, the stiff red pompons Sir Michael liked so much in his time: I was standing in the pantry at Upton Hall and pushing the knife down through green stem after green stem when suddenly I couldn't move. So I was motionless with the knife in my hand until Althea approached with a brimming jug and the words, "Ellen, have you turned to stone?"

In this room were cupboards and cupboards of glasses, some Venetian, and porcelain coffee cups, some Chinese. Ranked behind the glass-fronted panes.

I couldn't move because I saw you in the fluted perfection of that whorled red flower just as I still see you in the green arrowhead on a snowdrop petal, the blue bell of a bluebell, in the freckled gullet of a foxglove. Because they too are perfect, small, untouched; and because the season comes for them to be borne away.

Althea touching my elbow. My dear. Bear up, my dear.

2nd November 1948

Dear Pamela,

Edward came to Upton. Thin as a rail, brown as a toasted nut. Joyful to see me. His blood is half saltwater he says—he learned this in the war. It wasn't enemy fire that nearly killed him, but trudging through the dust and mud. He stayed with us a fortnight, and he and Selwyn spent a great deal of time in the mill, replacing the bearings in the turbine. He's back in Singapore now, tentatively—I think—looking for a wife. "If any woman in her right mind will have me." Despite the old scar, he is handsome in a lean wiry fashion and endearingly doesn't know it. This is the last bit of boyishness left. In all other respects he's grown up now.

He told me how sorry he was about Daniel. Then he handed me a page of a letter I had sent to him when he was in Ceylon. You had drawn snails and slugs down the margins, identifying them with arrows and titles. Snail, slug, slug, slug, snail. At the top of each margin was a duck with an open bill. "I thought you might like to have this," he said, and for a hideous moment it was as if you were dead and this was a relic. But then I took it, and was glad of it. I told him about the war here, how we'd lived. "We were mostly preoccupied with bread and potatoes, and coal."

He put his arm in mine. "A bit like the old days, then."

After he left I remembered what he said, and thought of you. Because you must be thirteen now, and I hope and trust your thoughts do not run as incessantly as mine did at that age on the staples of life. I picture you whirling through the days with your big cousins, the five of you gathering round a table of plenty. Where's Pamela? Ah, there she is. There she is.

12th May 1951

Dear Pamela,

I'm as indomitable as a spider creeping on a wall. In and out of the crevices of brick. Spinning silently in sunlight. Industry, industry. The mill. Selwyn. The Women's Institute. The illiterate children I help to read at Upton School, their fingers leaving smears of grime or butter or ink under the difficult words. The mill, the WI, the children, Selwyn: what industrious spinning. My webs hang glittering, drooping under dewdrops.

In the beginning when I looked at those children's small, soft fingers and saw yours instead, all my weaving was torn away by a dry heartless leaf-bowling wind. Nothing to do but start again, and I did start again, and now the children's fingers remain their own, and I learn their names. Robert and George and Margaret.

If it's possible to love Selwyn more than I did during the war, I do. I haven't said anything about how he missed you. We walked a lot that summer, out along the Downs beyond Barrow End. Just the two of us, hand in hand. Almost foolishly bereft. In the evenings we read aloud to each other as we used to before the war. We had begun The Count of Monte Cristo *in the summer of 1939 and now we took it up again, and as Selwyn read I felt not the blaze from our log fire but the sunburn on my face from that summer. And if I lay on the sofa, teetering on the edge of a doze, I could almost convince myself the war had not taken place and we, Selwyn and I, had somehow taken a different path through time.*

You must be sixteen now. A clever girl, I don't doubt.

12th February 1959

Dear Pamela,

*Lady Brock has sold Upton Hall at last. It will now be Upton Hall
School, a boarding school for girls. The new head is one Mrs. Margaret
Dennis, an army widow who has endeared herself to Upton society by her
enthusiasm for drinks, parties, bridge, racing, and the odd set of tennis.
The ballroom's a dining room now, the squash court a chapel, the stable
block full of pianos. William is now caretaker, a job he's been performing
untitled for years. He can't count the number of leaks he's plugged in that
infernal old roof, he says: he is so glad there's money in the place, so he
can have done with all this "makeshifting and stopgappery."*

*And Lady Brock? She hasn't gone far. Just to the Lodge near the top
of the drive. A small square house hidden in laurels—we used to pass it,
you and I. Selwyn, William, Lucy, George, John Blunden, and I helped
Lady Brock move in. We brought the knight in armor, you'll be glad to
hear. He stands guard in her new sitting room, looming beside the
window, not entirely steady on his feet. She never tires of telling everyone
how blissful it is to be shot of the Hall. "I was camping in the sewing room
by the end, you know," she says, and guffaws.*

*Now that she has grandnephews in New Zealand, Lady Brock
occasionally regales me with stories of their doings. Recently she told me
how after finishing their boiled eggs the boys turned the hollowed shells
over in the egg cups to make it look as though the eggs were still
untouched, earning a mock rebuke from their mother. But she brought the
story to a halt saying, "What silly stuff. Now—about the church
flowers . . ." Because she saw in my eyes that it was something that you
did, my child, when you were here.*

11th April 1963

Dear Pamela,

I have walked bareheaded under the Lion Gate at Mycenae, felt the sudden shadow cool on my face. The sky belonged only to Zeus, so blue it was. We'd forgotten our water canteens but we didn't care. Even our thirst was exciting. Selwyn rubbed a sprig of thyme between his fingers. I was given a great gift, which was to see him again as he must have been in his youth. Because it was a new person I discovered. And I told him so, and he said, "It's you. You've made me young again."

We've been to Mycenae, Olympus, Thermopylae. I can't imagine where you are anymore. Still in Ireland? Moved to Dublin? London, perhaps. You might even have been in Greece yourself on one of our trips. Could I have glimpsed you below me on a mountain path, a young woman with a rucksack, exploring?

Extraordinary to think that you're now older than I was when I first met you. Older than I was when I let you go.

10th January 1971

Dear Pamela,

Selwyn has gone. Mister Parr has gone.

Pneumonia took him. A cough turned to bronchitis, he recovered. Then he got worse again. One cold afternoon he became very agitated, wouldn't stay in bed, paced around the bedroom saying, "I can't see them, they're calling but I can't find them." I suspected that in his delirium he was back at Messines. Looking for the wounded men in the mud.

William came. He was magnificent. He said, "Lieutenant Parr, return to your bunk."

He drove me to the hospital in my Land Rover. We let the ambulance speed ahead of us into the rain.

It isn't called the Borough Hospital anymore, thank God. That name went after the war. It's Southampton General instead, a competent modern name. Though the injections and modern doctors did not make a difference, in the end.

Selwyn died before the winter dawn. I was almost asleep but felt him leave me. I pressed the bell and a nurse removed the oxygen mask. He had an expression I hadn't seen before, that of a traveler gladly alighting with no thought for the companions he was leaving behind. That expression didn't belong this side on earth but should only have been seen in the afterlife.

By now my friends were sleeping in the waiting room, propped upright on benches. Lady Brock was there—she had been reading to him in his last hours. She had long training in this task. Articles from the Hampshire Chronicle, the prices of grain and feed.

The moment I came in they awoke and rose to their feet as one.

William took us all home and I sat in the back with Lucy. Selwyn's watch and his toothbrush and copy of Edward Thomas's The South Country were in a plastic bag on my lap. I took the watch out, felt it smooth in my hand, the rubbed pale-gold back and rim, the soft brown leather strap, the biddable buckle. I slipped it on and the narrowest hole in the strap fitted.

I put it to my ear and heard him still, in the ticking of the watch.

23rd October 1971

Dear Pamela,

There are so many things gone, I clutch at what's left. Often I still touch the things he touched, the paperweight in the study, the clock key, because it's comforting to know his hand rested where mine is. I wear his watch, of course, the heavy golden penny of it snug beneath the cuff of my blouse.

I've been building my own way markers now for a long time, building them just as carefully as cairns on moorland. A scone and butter, a nap, three clues of the crossword, to help me beat a path through the day however low the fog rolls. They punctuated mourning in the beginning; now they punctuate work. I run the mill with Suky Fitch now, and pay her accordingly. But when she retires, which is soon, I'll lease the mill. I couldn't do it with both Selwyn and Suky gone.

When you left, it was different. I didn't want your things around. After the first agony I buried your small blue dress deep in the layers of a linen chest and extirpated everything else that I could because it hurt too much to see them. It was wartime, you never had a wardrobe full of clothes or a box full of toys, but you had left your mark everywhere. You took the Peg family but all the other clothes-pegs had to go too, because over the years you had put eyes and mouths on all of them. You had a child-sized fork and spoon, your own, and you had bent the tines of the fork trying to pull a nail out of one of the runners of your sledge. I had to put those in the attic. In the bathroom you had drawn a fox in the steam on the mirror, a fox that reappeared with every bath I took for days and that had to be scrubbed away.

I still find things. A pencil stub at the back of a desk drawer, the end chewed by milk teeth.

8th February 1973

Dear Pamela,

I remember you teasing Mr. Parr as he read the newspaper. He had the paper spread out in his usual way, as wide as a windbreak, and he was hunched in the chair behind it, eyes narrowed behind spectacles, wanting nothing more than a few moments' peaceful wandering among *the newsprint columns. And you could not give him that, you terrible, gorgeous girl, and you kept tapping and poking at the outer pages until he brought the paper down with a great flap and a howl of only-just-pretend annoyance that made you shriek in delight.*

You had a great deal of mischief in you, Pamela. I hope that mischief hasn't gone.

Three

Ellen

1974

22

I placed my feet solidly on the branch, held tight with one hand, and with the other reached for an apple. They were beautiful this year, large enough to fill my palm and spread fingers, excellent for peeling. The warm, rustling breeze swayed me gently to and fro. A mile away, the church tower peeped above the wall, and beyond, under strong sunshine, lay the recumbent flank of Beacon Hill. To be aloft in an apple tree, on a hot afternoon in late September: surely this was an instance of Heaven on earth.

Lucy was below, filling the barrow with windfalls. From my position I could see the inch of gray at her parting.

"I wish you'd come up, Lucy. It's simply glorious."

"My climbin days are done," she replied equably. "As you well know." She placed a palm over the top of her head. "I can feel you lookin at my roots, Ell."

I giggled, and picked another beauty. "I suppose I could always send the basket down with my eyes shut. If you don't mind it landing on your head."

She squinted up at me. "Have *you* thought about hair dye, dear? You don't want to end up like Miss Peacock. Remember her?"

Xanthe Peacock, who had been born in 1879 and who used to live by the ford before the war. A goatkeeper and cheesemaker, she had been famous for her long, looping, iron-gray locks.

"My hair is nothing like hers." I unwound the rope attached to the basket handle and began to pay it out. "It's simply a rather light blond after the summer. Particularly at the temples."

The basket began its dallying descent. I heard Lucy stifle a snort.

We took the kitchen chairs outside to do our peeling. Deck chairs were more comfortable but all you could do in a deck chair was loll. And lolling was a temptation, beneath this deep blue sky as hot as a brick kiln.

Lucy heaved a sigh of happiness. "We're owed this."

She was right: a rainy August had kept us damp and discontented. "Didn't the blackberries recover well, though? Jet black. Prodigious."

Lucy laughed. "Your Selwyn was the blackberryer. I remember him gathering at that big hedgerow behind Beacon Hill. Hooking them down with his stick."

Selwyn used to wear an old mackintosh, which he spread against the brambles so he could lean in and reach the high treasures. Tall and spare, his soft trilby on the ground next to an enamel bowl. I'd be homeward bound, calling him in a low sun but on he'd go, returning at dusk with his quarry. It was three years since he'd died—three times I'd entered into the dark tunnel of January and come out the other side, and each time the light came a little sooner, and now I could talk like this about him, smiling.

"Selwyn was no gatherer of blackberries," I told Lucy. "He was a hunter."

We worked on, throwing the apple parings into a bucket placed between us. The quartered apples, sliced of their cores, swirled in a plastic tub of water. A platoon of ants was trying to bear away a scrap of peel the shape of a tiny shield; they circled, unable to find direction.

Lucy grunted. "Them ants need a general."

I picked up another apple, smooth and slightly greasy in my hand. I should start peeling, but instead I closed my eyes in the sunshine.

"Do you know young Colin Bowyer, Lucy?"

Colin was the son of Barney Bowyer, an affable red-haired chap who had taken over the lease of the mill when Suky retired.

"Him that charges around in bell-bottom trousers? Strange flappin articles. Not a hornpipe dancer, is he?"

I had never heard Lucy describe a man born after 1945 with anything but censoriousness and denigration.

"I expect many people admire those trousers. And he charges around because he's busy and hardworking. Anyway, Colin told me his father Barney is nephew to old Evie Norris who taught me typing, about a century ago."

The sunshine was warm and rosy on my eyelids.

"Norris, now," Lucy said. "Norris. Oh, yes. Her with the warts on her fingers. From the estate office at Barrow End. And it was all down to Bill Kennet."

I smiled, and opened my eyes to the blue. "She was a terrific horticulturalist, it turned out."

"Lucky for you she was, Ellen. My word, what a piece of good fortune you had there. A husband. A house. Clean sheets and a roaring fire. All on account of Bill and his rare cuttins, and Evie Norris."

"Give me some credit." I laughed. "I worked jolly hard. Anyway, I'm not sure it's as simple as that. I met Selwyn by chance, after all. We bumped into each other in Waltham Square. I was looking at a seagull flying down Castle Street." The gull making its way down the street below the tops of the buildings, white wings flashing in and out of sun and shadow. Catapulting me into the arms of a tall man whose skull banged against mine as we kneeled to retrieve my library books. And we had spoken of Neanderthals. Brow ridges. Brain size.

Lucy tossed neat chunks of apple into the tub. "Just think. You might be there now, if it weren't for that gull. Typin away at the Town Hall."

"I wouldn't have minded. I was extremely happy, with my warm room and my independence."

"Or you might have married that boy who was sweet on you. Tom Coward—"

"Bob Coward."

"—Bob Coward, and got the full bowl."

"Bob Coward? Not in a thousand years." I wiped my hand on my apron. "I saw him at Waltham Show last year, strolling with his lady wife. A beer belly leading the way, and not a hair on his head. What do you mean, anyway, getting the full bowl?"

"The full bowl of cherries. You know, what life is meant to be."

"Actually the saying is, life is *not* a bowl of cherries. Or even a bowl of apples—"

A familiar engine roared at the top of the lane. It was my Land Rover. Lucy jumped to her feet. "Bill's back!" She rushed away, knife in hand, and disappeared round the back of the house to the mill yard.

I sat looking at the cut apples swirling in the glinting water. I wanted to follow Lucy but I couldn't. Something was stopping me from gathering myself together. I gazed up at the unending sky, blue vault opening upward into blue vault. My heart gave a series of strong thumps, as if demanding to be let out.

After a moment, I levered myself to my feet.

William was drawing into the yard, his tires dusty.

He hopped down in a semicrouch and unbent cautiously. "That journey was too long for my old back." But he was smiling. He was wearing sunglasses, which gave him a rakish look. Now, there was someone who'd never gone gray. He'd simply bleached, from wheat to white.

"Oh, Bill." Lucy, for the first and probably the last time, hugged him.

He patted her small narrow shoulder with his good hand. "Steady on." He put out his other hand to me and I clasped it. It had been a great trip, arduous and long planned, to the cemeteries and battlefields of Belgium and France.

"Welcome back, William."

Lucy released him. "I'll put the kettle on."

We followed her into my house, where he sat down at the kitchen table, took off his sunglasses, nodded toward the open back door. "You girls have been at your apples, I see."

I brought in the plastic tub and drained it. "It's a bumper crop." I put a jam pan on the stove and tipped the apples into it.

Lucy set the kettle on the other hot plate. "So what about those graveyards, then, Bill?"

"I visited all the Upton lads, then the rest of my old pals. Then I scarpered." William rubbed his fingers, easing each knuckle in turn. "I couldn't abide the numbers."

There were seven men from our parish who had fallen in the Great War. Frederick Broad; Ralph Corey, brother to Dan's father, Harvey; Ernest Horne, brother to George; William Rail; Henry and Victor Parr, cousins to Selwyn, offspring of old Mr. Parr; and George Yarnold. All of them absent and grievously incorrect on the memorial for Upton and Barrow End. From time to time I wondered about those boys: who would have stayed on the farms, who would have made money in town. Who would have stolen a pig and run away. And their children and grandchildren, who could not be imagined.

"I'm glad you didn't linger." Lucy shook her head. "I didn't want you traipsing for hours round all those headstones, not on your own."

"No. If I'd felt like viewing all the cemeteries, Lucy, I'd have gone with a pack of old codgers on a bus tour. But with Ellen's vehicle I was my own master. I went back to Plugstreet Wood, found some bunkers in the young trees. Looked at the mine craters at St. Eloi and roundabout Messines. Sat in a field awhile, near Dammstrasse."

I tried to imagine him there, chewing a grass blade, remembering the squall of shells. Was it in that field that he had wounded his hand? He was as quiet as if he'd just recounted a fishing trip. I stirred the apples and then sat down at the table, wishing I had one ounce of his boundless calm.

"And what were the craters like?" I asked.

"Full of still water, like great big dew ponds." He blinked. "How's George, Lucy?"

"Frettin. I don't know what to do with him."

The night William left for France, Lucy's father had broken his leg. He had caught his foot in a root high on the embankment above the disused railway track, falling and fracturing his thigh. He was now installed in the office at the kennels, on a couch, preferring this to isolation in his own bed at the Hornes' cottage.

"He'll be glad to see you, Bill," Lucy continued. "The days are ever so long, and he's gone off the wireless."

"I know he's bored with *me*," I said.

Lucy brought the teapot to the table. "He never is, Ellen, he's always glad to see your face."

"And my back, a short interval later." I was laughing. George and I could never have offended each other.

William raised a finger. "What about the pupils? Always volunteering about the place, those girls. A couple of them could run up to the kennels and read to him."

The apples puffed and sighed on the stove. I got up to stir them again. "There's an idea, Lucy."

Lucy cackled. "He'll only want the racin pages, Bill. Upton Hall girls, readin out, 'Golden Boy, two forty-five at Kempton Park,' to my dad. That would be a flabbergastin sight."

I laughed. "Why shouldn't they? It can't be all Wordsworth."

After tea my friends climbed into the Land Rover and I took the wheel. We went first to Lucy's cottage, dropped her off, then to Upton

Hall. On the drive I spun the wheel from long habit: the potholes moved, but they moved slowly. We reached the main building: it was still the Hall of my childhood, but these days it nestled grayly between two red-brick wings, faced down by the glittering science block opposite.

William was watching me with a particular look, one I'd come to know well. A sort of tender glare.

"Thank you, Ellen, for the loan of your vehicle. I'm a lucky man to have such friends."

"Oh, honestly." I put my hand over his scarred one, laughing gently. "We're lucky to have you."

I made my way back, faster, less careful of the potholes. The Land Rover pitched and rolled. Althea Brock used to say it was like the mine craters at St. Eloi, but of course it wasn't. I thought suddenly of General Lord Plumer. Not the man who had caused the mines to be set at Messines, but the croquet ball Selwyn's father had turned into a doorstop. I remembered the little girl who had transformed General Plumer into a doll, or the head of a doll. Hauling it onto her tiny lap and wrapping a tea towel round it.

What had she been saying? Some little phrase, some game about going shopping. She'd been very small then. At the beginning of the war.

The scrap of apple, the futile ants, the hot sun: all sucked away by low pressure bringing wind and front upon front of heavy rain. William's weathercock was flung this way and that before settling in the west; a green, storm-tarnished old bird now, as he'd always wanted it to be, for his cousin Mottram, the steeplejack, had long since lost his head for heights. My sandals were stowed in the cupboard, my heavier coats and skirts released from their trunks and presses. I'd had good clothes for nearly thirty years now, and a fire to dry them. The lovely wholesome smell of hot cotton and dry wool, *toasty-dry* as Elizabeth used to say: I breathed it in time and again, the smell of safety and content. Elizabeth had long retired to a bungalow on the new estate in Barrow End, still with her scarf wound about her head, these days not quite concealing soft white hair, which in turn did not quite conceal a pink scalp blotched with fawn patches reminding me of the belly of a Jack Russell terrier.

So it was October, and autumn was well under way, when I put on a full-length mackintosh and set out through the rain for Althea Brock's house with six jars of stewed apple in my bag.

The door to the Lodge, when I knocked, swung gently open. I went in, and took a few paces down the tiled corridor. I was about to call softly, so as not to alarm her, when I drew level with the open sitting room door. Althea was on the sofa, facing a small girl in a school mackintosh and a beret out of which poked a bush of untidy hair. I stifled an exclamation. The Lodge and its surrounding shrubbery were strictly forbidden to Upton Hall girls. But Althea was speaking.

"Bullies abound, my dear," she was saying. "Bullies abound. And the only remedy is to go back to them with your head held high. Go on. Show me now."

The child lifted her chin. A small soldierly form, eyes burning.

"Higher."

The child obeyed. There was a long, singing silence, and then Althea spoke.

"*That's* the girl. Now off you go."

The girl made a bobbing bow to Althea. "Thank you very much for the lime cordial, Lady Brock." Her voice was almost a whisper. As she turned to go she saw me, gasped, and ducked past me through the doorway and back down the corridor. By the time I reached the front door she was darting away over the mud of the drive, her white-socked legs flashing up behind her.

. . . . .

"Good lord, Althea." I was laughing—laughing, and rather moved. "Who was that?"

Althea hitched herself up on the sofa, one bony hand stabbing at her cushion. "A new girl. She arrived late, and the others are ragging her, the vixens."

On the coffee table were two cloudy glasses half filled with greenish liquid. I longed to bear them away to the kitchen and plunge them into hot suds but Althea's tiny boiler was grudging. The dishes piled up beside the sink rimed in dried-on food, waiting for the rare flood. "What are they doing?" I asked. "What kind of ragging?" I dug in my bag for paper and pencil. All my ladies had a list prepared when I dropped by, but Althea was emphatically not one of my ladies.

Althea snorted in disgust. "They told her to come and walk down here in the shrubbery, that a sweet old lady would invite her in for tea. I found her cornered by Stuart. I'd like some cod," she added, seeing me lick my pencil.

As if he had heard his name, Stuart sent us a long growl from his tartan bed. He was a terrier of uncertain temper bequeathed by Colonel Daventry, who was now too old to take his dog for walks. I wondered privately how long this arrangement could last. Althea had recently gone from one walking stick to two. But without slackening her pace, or hardly.

"With parsley sauce, Althea, or just plain cod?"

She stared. "*Parsley sauce?* The Mac Fisheries isn't a restaurant."

"You can buy it frozen. The sauce is frozen with it."

"Good God above. My mother preserved it, you know. Laid it down in layers of salt."

Her mother had done no such thing. It was understood that her mother's cook and undercook had performed the task. She struggled to her feet, and we made our way down the hall to the kitchen to stare together into her dark cupboards where tins gleamed.

She grunted. "I hate cod."

"Then why on earth buy it?"

"It's good for one. And Stuart likes the skin."

"I'll get you some trimmings for Stuart. And you might try a box of the new parsley-sauced cod. You must eat it this evening. I don't trust your icebox." I opened her fridge to see the tongue of a glacier, studded with peas, poking out of the plastic hatch. "Shall I ask Mrs. Ware to pop round?"

June Ware, June Broad that was, my old schoolmate whose bust rose like dough over the cups of her brassiere, and who had gone for the typing pool job at the Town Hall with me. Her bust was still good, and she had the strong, bulging calves of a woman who had never owned a car. She didn't hold it against me, that I had got that job instead of her, and she certainly didn't need my charity. She had four grown children, all married, and they took turns to roast her a Sunday dinner.

Althea flapped her hand at the icebox. "Oh, if you see fit. While I think of it, Ellen . . ."

"What?"

"Lucy's wondering whether she should collect her stewed apples, or if you'll deliver them to the cottage."

Slowly I started lifting the jars out of my sturdy bags. Almost a fortnight had passed since that blue September day, the last of that vanished hot pre-equinoctial world. I should have taken Lucy's apples to her cottage, but I hadn't, and I was at a loss to find the reason. Perhaps there was no reason, and I simply forgot. Althea, however, had spoken carefully, and with meaning, and she was waiting for my reply. Which meant that Lucy had made her feelings known to Althea.

"My God, who would live in a village?" I plonked a jar on the table. "One can't make the tiniest slip . . . All she's going to do is buy that blessed Angel Delight."

Because Lucy didn't eat her apples. She sold the lot at the Women's Institute market and used the money to buy packets of this dessert.

Althea picked up the jar, holding it by the neck in a slightly unsteady grip, appraising the contents as one would a vintage liquor. She chuckled at my rage. "What's that? It sounds literally heavenly."

"A powdered sweet you make up with milk. Tastes of butterscotch." I shook my head in bewilderment. "I know I should have gone to see Lucy by now. The change in the weather seems to have swept me off my feet, somehow. Time passing. And this rain . . ." Curtains of it were falling outside as we spoke.

"It's like that, on and off." Althea touched my arm. "For the first few years. You bash around your house looking for your specs, no one to ask where they are, and then things seem to settle around you . . ."

"Lucy thinks I should have married Bob Coward."

The words leaped out like frogs from a pail of water. Well might Althea stare—they surprised me too.

"You should have married—*whom*, did you say?"

"Bob Coward. He worked at the Town Hall. When Selwyn tried to turn me down"—we both smiled at the memory—"I went out to tea with Bob Coward and another couple. Anyway, Lucy thinks that if I'd married him I'd have got the full bowl of cherries."

Althea frowned. "Surely, life is *not* a bowl of cherries."

"Yes. That's what I told her. She got the saying wrong. She meant, a full life."

Althea's grin was not an altogether pleasant sight. A great deal of bridgework was on display. "My dear girl, are you sure? Lucy's no great handler of words."

"But she said it, she said, 'What life . . .'"

What life is meant to be. Six quick words flashed out on the blade of a paring knife, then covered by the dark roar of the Land Rover engine as William turned into the yard. But I had heard them.

"Good lord, Ellen. Don't tell me you're hankering after a life with this Mr. Coward. Ten to one he's a frightful bore."

I managed a smile. "I don't suppose it matters."

We finished her list and walked together to the front door. Suddenly she chuckled. "Did you know there's a discotheque this Saturday at the Stour Hotel?"

"A discotheque!"

"Mm. I was thinking of going."

"Who would partner you?"

"That's the beauty of discotheque dancing. You do it on your own." The wires on her teeth shone in the unlit hallway. "It's made for us widows, really. You should come with me."

We both started hooting gently, at the idea. Tears were leaking into my eyes, perhaps hers. I opened the door and the gale forced its way in, blew in our faces.

"Ellen, do go and see George. Lucy's worried about him. An injury like that is cruelty to a man who only ever sits down in church."

A long mental sigh swept through me. "Of course I will."

"Oh, and get me some of Lucy's angel pudding, if you please. It sounds wizard."

23

GEORGE WAS IRRITABLE, SHIFTING his plastered leg over the waxed cloth of the couch. Though he said the sound leg bothered him more. "This one"—indicating the poor limb—"he's content to lay. But this one"—slapping the undamaged leg—"he wants to be up and doing. He's getting cramped, stuck here on this settee."

"That's why you need to exercise it." I picked up the crumpled leaflet supplied by the hospital. It featured line drawings of an impossibly muscled man lifting his brawny thigh at varying degrees from his torso. "Gosh. He's a fit fellow. Not very encouraging, somehow."

George sighed. "I know it."

I glanced at his injured leg. Someone, to my mild amazement, had sketched a sailing boat on his knee in ballpoint pen. The boat was sandwiched between pinched little wavelets and bulbous clouds, all slightly bumpy from the plaster. Underneath was a signature, *PL*, and the exhortation *Get well soon Mr. Horne.*

"Who did this, George?"

"Girl from the school. They been up to read."

"Oh, I'm glad."

"It made a nice change. I might try those exercises."

"I'll help you." I stood above him, holding out my hand. He lifted his good leg about forty-five degrees until his heel touched my fingers. The heel was warm, dry, and small. The sock was clean. I could probably pick this man up.

The rain had not stopped at all in the three days since I'd gone over to see Lady Brock. People in Upton were openly talking about the possibility of a flood, which was sensible, of course, but sat ill with me. I never liked to tempt the river gods.

Outside, a barrow clattered to a halt. Lucy, heavily hooded, looked in through the window, gave me a grin of welcome. Then the outer door banged open and there was a stamp of boots, and in she breezed, bringing a gust of damp autumn air. "This bloomin rain puts me so behind. I've only just finished strawin the hot bitches." She coughed. "I'll put the kettle on in a sec, Ellen dear."

"Lovely. Now," I said to George. "It says to repeat ten times. Can you manage that today, or shall you just do five?" Because his face was shining with the effort, and had become the color of standing cream.

Lucy took off her working anorak and shook it out, tutting. "He's neglected them. Because he says the man on the bit of paper looks like a circus performer. Ain't that right, Dad?" She put a special emphasis on the words "circus performer," by which we were meant to understand that George thought the man in the diagram was homosexual.

"Oh, really, George," I cried, as he raised his leg again.

I followed Lucy into their new kitchenette, their pride, a galley with a shining fridge and Baby Belling stove. "I put your jars of apple under your porch, Lucy, on my way up. Lady Brock said you were waiting for them."

"Oh yes." She looked sheepish.

"I'm terribly sorry I forgot. I can't think how. But you could have reminded me, dear."

She filled the kettle and set it on the large ring of the Baby Belling. "Oh, I kept forgettin too. It's this weather. The river's bank high, you know."

"I do know."

"Course you do. With the mill channel and all."

There was a pause. I cleared my throat.

"Yes," I said. "It's hard to remember that lovely warm day when William came back. When was it? Two, nearly three weeks ago. Seems like a different world now."

She was tearing open a packet of small rectangular chocolate flavored biscuits, the kind she and her father relished. To me the chocolate cream filling was cloying, chalky. "Do you want a Bourbon, Ell?"

"Perhaps later. You were talking about how my life could have been different if I hadn't married Selwyn. If I'd married Bob Coward instead."

Her graceful little hands moved over a pink plate, arranging the biscuits. "When was this, again?"

"The day we were peeling the apples."

The kettle came to a boil. Lucy spooned tea into the pot. "Oh. When Bill came back . . ." She turned to stare at me. "You marry *Bob Coward*? Did I say that?"

"Mm."

"Why would you want to do that?"

"I've got no idea. It was you that suggested it."

"Well, I haven't the foggiest." She shook her head. "You know what I'm like, Ell. The things I come out with. Will you take those biscuits, dear?"

I picked up the plate. The biscuits were laid in a pretty pattern, pointing inward like the dark rays of a pink central sun.

George pushed himself upright on the couch and I passed him a cup of tea. There was a book lying open, spine uppermost, on the windowsill. I made out the faded gilt words, *A History of the Waterford Hounds*. "Is this what the schoolgirl read to you? May I?" I turned it over. The yellowing pages were spotted by flies. "*He showed tremendous sport,*" I read, adopting a squeaky, cut-glass tone, "*but I must say that when I took over the hounds . . .*"

George grinned, his teeth reminding me of Lucy's before she had her dentures fitted. He'd never been shy of them, so the black gap in his broad grin was familiar to all. "Don't make fun," he said. "The child don't sound like that. She's got a nice clear little voice."

"She does," Lucy agreed. "Scruffy little bint, though."

There. Why should I take any notice of what Lucy said? Words blew off her like a dustbin lid in a gale—you got struck, or not, at random. I was only bothered because her remark to me had been about Selwyn. And that was ridiculous, because like most of the hundred and one flippancies Lucy uttered in the course of a week, it meant so little to her that she'd forgotten it altogether. Absentmindedly I took a Bourbon, washing it down with a cup of brick-red tea. The biscuit was as horrible as ever but the combination was bracing.

A sudden muffled cry startled me from my thoughts. I looked up to see William Kennet at the window, his face stretched in a rictus of panic. A moment later he reappeared in the doorway and Lucy leaped to her feet as the cause of his distress became clear. Clasped in his stringy arms and covered over with a piece of sacking, a television. "Bloody hell! Why didn't you come and fetch me out, Bill? I could have got the trolley!"

William panted a reply. "She's a deceptive creature. The weight settles after you pick her up. And a damned awkward shape." His bad hand was flattened against one side, his good hand clamped like a bracket around a bottom corner between two of its piglike legs.

I gasped. "It's enormous!"

"Not at all." William bore it across the room and placed it with a metallic boom on top of the filing cabinet. "There are many far larger." He pulled the sacking away. "This was given to Mrs. Dennis and her aunt, Miss Wyatt. They never view, you know. They agreed we should put this one into service. I said I knew just the chap who would benefit."

"Strike me, Bill. Strike me. That is damn generous of you." George's thin face was alight with embarrassed pleasure. "I'll be sure to think of you, if you was ever to be laid up."

"Thank the schoolmisses." William took off his hat and shook it, wiped his gleaming temples with a handkerchief. "Lucy Horne, I could do justice to a cup of tea." He turned to me. "I got a lift with your Colin Bowyer. He was leaving the mill, and kind enough to stop." He bent to plug the television into the yellowed socket in the corner of the room.

"You mean you set off from Upton Hall," I began, "with the intention of carrying a television all the way along the lanes—"

"Stand off, Ellen." George held up a long finger. "We men like work."

William turned on the television, conjuring a buzzing warped grain of variegated grays onto the screen. "That we do." He fiddled with the aerial. "I wouldn't have gone along the lanes anyway. I'd have cut up through Pipehouse."

I choked on the last of my tea.

William and I made our way down through the beech wood in the dusk. I turned my face to the wind, sniffed the damp air. It had been raining hard to the west, in the higher hills, and that water too would come down to us. William walked beside me, a light band on his hat glowing in the half-light, sniffing the air along with me.

"There'll be a bump in your channel tonight," he said. "It wouldn't surprise me if we were awash, up at the Hall."

"What on earth will you do with all those girls?"

"The pupils have got their October furlough. They're not due back till tomorrow. There's only half a dozen in the school, poor creatures with no one to go to. Mrs. Dennis will stow them in the village, I expect."

The wind blew in the branches. "You know," I went on, "I've slept to the rush of a millstream for many years now, but I could nod off just as well to the sough of beech branches, if I were ever to move from the mill."

"Do you think you might?"

"I hadn't given it a second's thought, until this moment."

"I was wondering if you needed a change," he said. "You look careworn, Ellen. What is it?"

"Nothing at all. Really."

"If you say so, my dear."

We traveled down over the mounds and dips of the path, the spoil heaps and sinkholes of generations of badgers and rabbits who tunneled there. You had to know where to put your feet but we did, William and I, even in the dusk. We asked each other questions like this from time to time; always softly, in situations where we didn't have to look each other in the eye, and I had never strayed from the truth before.

"Really," I repeated, when we reached the bottom of the wood, "it's just a little thing, too small to mention. I've let it upset me. Stupidly."

He nodded gravely and ushered me ahead over the stile, his extended arm pole-like in the heavy coat. Both Lucy and I gave him supper once a week, piling his plate with mashed potatoes, pork chops. Other than that, we relied on the school cook to keep him fed, and she was a busy woman. "I'll have a shepherd's pie ready tomorrow evening, William. I hope you'll join me as usual."

"I would be very glad."

The flood came during the night, heavy and incompressible, loading and overloading the riverbed and the mill channel until the water stopped falling, being the same height everywhere. The special silence woke me at three in the morning, and I got up and went to the window. A blackness was conquering the fields on either side of the embanked track, moving pantherlike into the woods beyond. My mill cottage, on its rise of land, was as safe as ever. But I thought of Selwyn, his calm in the face of these moving waters, and I wished all the same that he was here to watch it with me.

I went back to bed and dozed until six-fifteen, when the telephone began ringing. It was William. "Water's in at Upton Hall," he said. "Basements and kitchen flooded and no electricity. Mrs. Dennis has called the fire brigade and now she's driving her girls to The Place. Colonel Daventry has got Marcy to open up the back of the house for them."

Marcy Corey was Daniel's widow, housekeeper to the Colonel.

"What a good idea."

"Meantime the teachers are ringing round, telling everyone to stay away till the water's pumped out and the electrics are back on."

"I'll go and see if Marcy needs any help."

"You do that, Ellen. I'm going down to have a look at Lady B."

"Remember I can bring her here if needs be. What about your rooms?"

"Dry," he said. "I'll sit it out."

"You can't stay there, with no power and no hot food!"

"I will so. I'm the caretaker, and I have a gas lamp and a stove. Someone must supervise the fire brigade. The laying of the pump hoses."

"At least let me fetch you for supper, as we arranged."

He agreed and we said good-bye. The telephone rang again almost immediately. It was Lucy, as I thought it would be, needing a lift to the kennels. I got dressed and ate a hasty piece of bread and butter. Pulling on Selwyn's waders, I left the house. In the lane to the village I met high water but the Land Rover cleared it. I reached the village to find the high street a fast-running stream. In the half-light I saw the flash of a torch at the top of the bank at Lucy's cottage. She nipped down the steps and opened the passenger door.

"I've got the Suttons up there, every single one of 'em including old Ivy. They've been in my parlor since two o'clock this morning. They didn't sandbag, did they."

"Oh no!" The Suttons were low down near the ford. "What are they going to do?"

"Clear off to their cousins in Barrow End, is what. As soon as I can make 'em. Shall we do a run of the village first? I want to see if anyone's got water in." She swung herself into the passenger seat. "This will be down by ten o'clock, I bet you. Look at the sky. Those ain't rain clouds."

The first light was coming in the east. I cast a doubtful look at the lowering sky. "I hope you're right."

We drove through Upton at a crawl, with the window open. Neighbors were gathered upstairs where torches flickered in the dark rooms behind them. They were all sandbagged, expecting the worst, but I wasn't sure the flood would come to them. The main street was a trough worn down by centuries of cattle herds and heavy drays, and nearly all the garden paths climbed to their front doors. It was the lack of power that would chill them. We called back and forth, and they insisted they needed nothing. I crossed the Green and reached the turning to the church, where I came to a halt. We looked over the wall at the submerged meadows beyond. Our little river was, just now and just here, the width of the Rhine. Lucy whistled between her teeth.

"I'm going to The Place later," I told her. "Colonel Daventry's taking in the Upton Hall girls."

Lucy gazed unseeing over the river. "I wish he was out and about."

Suddenly I knew she was thinking of the war and the day Southampton was bombed, when the crowds came to Upton and Colonel Daventry drove cartloads of them to village houses and surrounding farms. This was what happened when you knew a woman for over forty years. You knew her thoughts, the way they ran, almost as well as you knew your own.

I let my mind dwell for a few bright seconds on that long-ago day. "Yes," I said. "He was indispensable, wasn't he."

I put the Land Rover into gear and moved off. We'd only traveled twenty yards when I heard the hoot of a horn. A small lorry carrying sandbags was coming up behind us. I reversed alongside. The window wound down to reveal the driver, a black-haired man with a black beard.

"Morning, vicar," Lucy said. "Bloomin heck."

Belatedly I recognized the Reverend James Acton, new to the parish and hardly known to me.

"I wonder if you could assist?" he said. "Church Walk is nearly under."

"We'll follow you, Reverend," I said.

Church Walk was bounded by a flint wall on one side, on the other by a terrace of half a dozen houses that were home to some of the frailest and most elderly souls in Upton. There was no lane just now, instead a brawny flood sucking at the terrace steps. I got out and met the reverend in the middle of the water.

"We don't have much time," he said.

"You're right."

Lucy could barely walk without the water overflowing into her boots. The reverend gave her a leg-up onto the flatbed of the lorry and she began passing sandbags to him. I took each one in turn and laid them in the first doorway. Brown water swirled over the step whenever I approached, but retreated again. We worked fast, the reverend moving the lorry steadily up the terrace. The faces of the elderly appeared in the windows, some pale and confused, others mouthing thanks and messages we couldn't make out.

"They'll be awfully cold," I said, "with no power."

"I have paraffin stoves," said the reverend, breathing hard.

Soon all six doorways were barricaded behind a wall of small, snugly brick-laid sandbags.

"Let's hope that's high water," the reverend said.

I shook my head. "We can't be sure. There might be another bulge coming down the river."

He held out his hand. "I'm sorry, we haven't met. My name is James Acton."

"Ellen Parr."

His hand was cold, and so was mine.

"Of course. Althea Brock has mentioned you," he said. "She told me you were a miller's wife. You would know about rivers."

I smiled. "My late husband was always careful to point out that I was a miller."

"I—we—stand corrected." He was giving me a slightly perturbing stare, his eyes wide, dark blue, almost lidless.

"Where did you get the sandbags, Reverend Acton? I thought they were like gold dust."

"Requisitioned from the soldiers. The camp up on the hill." He nodded at the lorry. "I've got contacts."

"That's good of them."

He broke into a white grin. "I don't think the quartermaster is fully aware of how generous he's been."

I laughed, and laughed again with surprise.

"Reminds me of a pirate, that man," Lucy said as we drove to the kennels. We were taking the back way, a track up the spine of Pipehouse Wood.

"Ha. You're more right than you know. Those sandbags are pinched from the army. It shows what a poor churchgoer I've become, that we've only just met."

"Why don't you come anymore, Ell?"

I considered her question. Perhaps I had always drawn more comfort from the body of the church, the frost-fractured brick and lichened stones, than from the liturgy or the doctrine. And it was only now that I felt free to act accordingly.

"Selwyn's not there to sing." It seemed as good an answer as any.

Lucy cleared her throat. "Ellen. You know I would never think badly of Mr. Parr."

I shot her a bewildered glance. The track to the kennels was a treacherous gully in the wet. "What do you mean?"

"I wouldn't say anything bad about him." She began a small, tentative, twisted smile. "Or if I did, it would be by mistake. I wouldn't mean it. You know, if it seemed like I suggested that somebody else . . ."

"Oh, so you've remembered, have you?"

"Yes. Ellen—"

"You did *indeed* suggest somebody else. Someone who would have given me the full bowl of cherries. So what *is* the bowl of cherries, Lucy? The one I missed having because of Selwyn?"

A shocked silence followed. My voice rang in my ears, leaden and vicious. I hardly recognized it.

Eventually, Lucy cleared her throat. "I told you, dear. I didn't *mean* it—"

"Even better. Next you'll say it was only a joke."

"I shan't talk about it anymore, Ellen." Lucy turned to face the window. "I think that's for the best, don't you?"

"If you say so."

The silence descended again, dreadfully thick, and lasted until we reached the kennels, where she jumped down and hurried away without a word. I turned the vehicle, my hands unsteady on the wheel. She'd been saying sorry, and what had I done? Run her to ground like one of her hunting dogs.

Slowly the thrills of anger died away. Bewildered and shaken in equal measure, I drove to the Place.

"I've got eight girls already," Marcy Corey said. She jerked her head toward the back of the house. "The staff didn't manage to ring all the families in time, so they've come trailing back to school. Mrs. Dennis has been directing them here. Goodness knows how many we'll end up with."

She and Dan had married two months before us: their wedding had been full of joy and jokes about cradle snatching, since she had a full seven years on Dan. She'd never remarried after he was killed, though it wasn't for lack of offers. She looked youthful still, unbowed. I was glad of that, for her sake.

"Do you need help, Marcy?"

She grinned. "Those girls, it's like they're on maneuvers. Bedding rolls, picnic supplies—I haven't had to lift a finger. They've even swept out the back bedrooms."

My spirits, depressed by my shameful altercation with Lucy, began to lift. "That's Mrs. Dennis for you."

"She's a trouper."

Through the doorway to the drawing room I saw Colonel Daventry sitting in his armchair. He saluted me wordlessly, lifting a hand, his cardigan sleeve baggy round his thin wrist. "Lucy and I were talking about the Colonel this morning."

"Come and tell him," Marcy said. "Take those great boots off and have a cup of coffee with me. I'm ready for a sit-down."

Colonel Daventry's once russet mustaches were wispy and gray and he spoke very high now. "I've been invaded by girls," he chirped. "It's absolutely splendid. A detachment is coming in for a hand of whist this afternoon."

I couldn't help smiling. "It's very kind of you, Colonel. I'm sure Mrs. Dennis is grateful."

"Nonsense. Keeps a chap on his toes."

"Lucy and I were talking about the war earlier today." I smiled. "Everything you did, on the day of the air raid."

He harrumphed. "That's going back a bit. We only did what we were supposed to. How is it at the mill?"

"Snug. The Bowyers run a tight ship."

He nodded, very satisfied. Then he said, "Ah. Marcy, dear, will you fetch the book?" Marcy got to her feet and left the room, returning a few moments later with a battered brown volume. "I found it a few months ago in my library. I've been meaning to return it to you ever since. But one's memory fails."

Marcy handed the book to me. It was dog-eared, foxed, the spine broken. It always had been. Looking at it now, the book I'd not seen for nigh-on forty years, I knew that it would never have fetched more than a handful of copper coins. The Colonel would have seen that instantly but he had taken the book from me, with a small bow, when I was fourteen years old. It was my copy of *Downland Flora* that I had given to him to sell for me, to pay for my shorthand course at Spall and Benn's.

"I wasn't sure if you'd want it," the Colonel said. "Then I decided you should be the judge."

He was right not to be sure. I turned the book over in my hand, looked up at him. "Thank you, Colonel Daventry."

His thin shoulders lifted, his gaze widened and drifted over an inner landscape, one that seemed to sadden him. "You deserved more than what we gave you."

There was a moment of silence while I searched for a reply. "It was a different age," I told him. "We're living in a better one now."

"Here's to that," Marcy said. I opened *Downland Flora* and she and I looked together at the brighter plants, the bird's-foot trefoil, the mouse-ear, the early gentian. "They're so delicate and pretty!" she exclaimed, but the sight of that misty shielding paper made me feel cold, and I smelled mice as I turned the pages.

The trees closed above me, hollow and wind-whipped, spattering leaves across my windscreen. Above the trees, the low ceiling of the clouds, glimpsed occasionally when my cover broke, a malicious iron-gray. We would be sunk if there were more rain. My hands, chilled by the sandbags or by *Downland Flora*, I was not sure which, gripped the wheel of the ancient Land Rover. I crossed the bottom of the main street, looked up the road toward Lucy's cottage. Because of the power cut, not a single house was lit. The street looked much as it had done during the war.

I turned for home, plowed toward the dip in the lane. The hedges thinned out here and I could see clear across flooded fields squared out by half-drowned fencing. Some creature was perched on the fence on the other side of the field, across the vast expanse of water. I brought the Land Rover to a halt and peered out in the lowering light.

It was a figure, definitely. A person in an anorak, hood up, back to the road. The person—a child, I was certain now—clung to the gate with an air of great anguish, frozen in fear like a bear cub or infant monkey at the top of a swinging tree.

It, the child, must have waded through the field.

My feet were made of ice, my hands numb, and I was hungry. All I wanted was a bath, a cup of tea, and a crackling fire. Perhaps even a small luxurious nap, before heading out again to fetch William for supper.

"Oh hell," I said aloud. "Oh, absolute bloody hell."

24

I OPENED THE DOOR and got out and down into the water. The road gate, I saw immediately, was padlocked.

"Hello there! Are you all right?"

Perhaps my voice hadn't carried. Or perhaps the question was too ridiculous to answer. Either way, no reply came. I screwed up my eyes. I could see the small body was quaking with cold. Or fear, or sobs, or all three.

I climbed over the gate, landing with a splash into soft mud, and set out across the field. The water rose only to my knees but inside the waders my legs rapidly began to chill. My boots swished through the water as I approached, but the child didn't move. The sight of its mud-caked shoes, entirely soaked trousers, was appalling. I didn't say anything. To ask, *What on earth are you doing?* was almost as stupid as *Are you all right?*

I came closer and leaned over the top of the fence to get a better look. It was a girl—a pinched little face, hanks of hair protruding from her hood. She shrank away from me, shaking so wildly with the cold that I thought she might slip off the bar and tumble down into the mud.

"I don't know what's happened," I said, "but you need to get down off this fence."

She shook her head vigorously. "I'm absolutely fine here, thank you very much."

I gave a laugh of exasperation. There was such a thing, it seemed. "What are you planning to do next?" I was genuinely curious.

"Cross this next field." Her teeth chattered. "And keep going."

I leaned farther over the fence, glimpsed a violet edge to her lips.

"Did you know that the cold can be dangerous?" I said. "It can stop you thinking straight. I think that's what's happening to you. You're too cold to think straight. If you were warmer, you'd realize that wasn't much of a plan."

Her head turned then, and as her body twisted she lurched sideways and clung on. Her fingers whitening against the wooden rail.

"Mummy will be irate."

"Where *is* Mummy?"

Silence.

"Listen," I said. "I'm going to try and carry you to my Land Rover. Piggyback style. Okay?"

She stared at me, blinking. I recognized that hypothermic fogginess. At last the message penetrated. She lifted one cautious leg, and then the other, over the top of the fence, staring hard at the swirling water below. It made me shiver simply to imagine her walking through it. What on earth could have made her do that?

Now her feet were firmly on my side of the gate. I stepped in front of her and reached behind me.

"Come on," I said. "Put your hands on my shoulders."

Her arms yoked me, pulling back against my neck. Her knees dug viselike into my hips. As her weight settled on me, I felt the bones of my back pressing down, one upon the other, and my feet were driven deeper into the mud. Now I wasn't even sure if I could walk at all. I hooked my hands under the backs of her knees and started to move. Just then she shifted, pulling herself up over my shoulders and I staggered sideways, my foot skidding out from under me.

"Keep still," I hissed from between my teeth. Her forearm was jammed against my larynx.

"I'm going to fall off—!"

"You won't." My left leg, carrying all her weight, was threatening to buckle now. "I promise you."

Surely the rashest promise of my life. I regained my balance and managed a proper step, then another, dragging a weight of mud and pressing water each time I put a foot forward. The field seemed immense, the water leaden as the sun lowered. I was slow as an astronaut. Strange, since they were weightless and I was carrying—what, four stone of child? A gray wagtail landed on the road gate: I focused on it, counting the dips of its tail, and made headway. Every half minute or so, the child was racked by deep shivers, and I had to slow down for each bout and endure the delay. The only sound was our breathing, mine harsh and regular, hers whiffling in the region of my right ear.

We reached the road gate and she scrambled off me to cling to the bars. After a pause, where I hung my aching arms over the gate and heaved in any number of strangled breaths, we negotiated the last few feet to the Land Rover, where I pulled the door open and let her down onto the driver's seat. Relief flooded me, and with it a heady mixture of incredulity and near indignation.

"Now," I said, still panting. "What on *earth* did you think you were doing?"

She scrambled away from me into the back of the vehicle, where she sat gasping and squeezing her hands together. "Running away."

A high little voice. Of course she was. She hadn't gone out there for fun.

"Who from? Mummy?"

She made no move to answer. But there was no time. There was a car coming up the lane. I ducked out of the Land Rover to see it breasting the floodwater, headlights on. It was small and white, and as it toiled through the rising tide toward us, I realized that the driver wasn't going to stop. The water, already churning around the tops of the hubcaps, would flood the engine at any moment. I ran with a heavy splashing stride out into the road, waving my arm. "Stop! Stop!"

The car came to a halt, its mud-brown bow-wave settling and stilling. The driver, a woman, wound down the window. "I'm looking for my daughter." She spoke in a sort of controlled shout. "I was trying to get her to Upton Hall, and—"

"She's in my vehicle. She was sitting on a fence, so I helped her down." I didn't say which fence, or anything else. I didn't have enough breath.

"For crying out loud. I slowed down for the water, and she jumped out. She's the absolute bitter end." She peered reproachfully up at me. A strange frowsty odor emanated from the interior of the car, rather as if bottled fruit had gone off.

"Her lips are turning blue." I spoke slowly and with emphasis, for the only course of action was rapidly becoming clear to me. "She needs to get warm, now. You must both come to my house. It's not far. Please turn round and follow me." I began to walk back to the Land Rover.

"You don't understand," she called. "We're going to Upton Hall School—!"

"Forget the school," I said over my shoulder. "It's closed. I'll explain later. Now please turn your car."

It was a relief to simply give orders. The girl's mother glowered at me for a moment longer, and then yanked her steering wheel round.

I kept an eye on the white car in my rearview mirror. She chugged along competently enough. Soon we'd be on the track to the mill, and safe. Occasionally I glimpsed the child's pale little face, her wary eyes.

"I should have carried on," she whispered. "Even if the mud had got to my waist."

I pictured a small lone figure traveling over a distant field, struggling through the mire.

. . . . .

We crowded into my hall and removed our coats. I sloughed off my waders and hurried upstairs, returning with two thick blankets, long socks, a toweling dressing gown. The girl obediently removed her wet shoes, trousers, and socks. I was glad to see she was wearing a woolen polo-neck jumper. I stoked the sitting room fire and put coal in the kitchen range. There was no electricity, as I had feared, but we would do well enough without.

The girl's mother stood clutching her handbag. "Shouldn't we put her in a bath?"

This truculent tone, I thought, must be her natural manner of speaking. "No." I spoke tersely, pumping the bellows until the logs in the grate flared into life. I pulled my small armchair close to the fireplace. "Come here . . . what *is* your name, dear?"

Now swathed in my robe and socks, she stepped forward and sat where I bid her, and I folded the blankets around her. She was still wearing her school beret. "Penny," she whispered.

"Well now, Penny, don't worry. This is a watermill, and I know what to do when people get cold and wet. Wrap up and sit near the heat. You'll feel better in a jiffy, especially with a hot drink inside you. It won't be long until the kettle boils." I turned to her mother. "I have a solid-fuel range. It's a boon at times like this. I expect you'd like a cup of tea as well, Mrs. . . ."

"Lacey. Veronica Lacey." The mention of tea seemed to mollify her somewhat. "Awfully decent of you. This whole thing. Rescuing, and so on."

"Please don't mention it. It's nothing more than any villager would do in a flood. I'm Ellen Parr, by the way."

"Nice to meet you, Miss Parr."

"It's Mrs., actually."

"Beg pardon. Just thought you looked like a Miss. Don't know why."

I searched in vain for a civil reply to that comment.

. . . . .

I went into the kitchen and started to prepare tea. After a few moments Penny slipped into the room.

"You should stay by the fire, dear. You must get warm."

"It's warm next to this stove."

No truculence here. The words came out soft in her little treble voice. And it was true: she was spreading her hands over the closed hot plate. As pale as before, but the violet line had disappeared from the edges of her lips. She watched me from beneath the brim of her beret. The hat, and the wary look, were familiar.

"I saw you at Lady Brock's house, didn't I."

Her eyes widened. "You're the lady who came in. How do you do." She darted a look toward the closed door to the sitting room. "Sorry about the fuss."

Her voice had dropped back to a whisper. That, and the light of fear in her eyes, stopped all the questions in my mouth.

"Look. We'll have toast." My voice was almost as quiet as hers. "And then we'll think what to do." I fetched down the hot-plate toaster. It was a simple thing, made of two round grills joined by a hinge and furnished with wire handles. "Would you like to make it?"

She picked it up. "What a funny contraption." Under my instruction she loaded the grill with four slices of bread, folded the top half over, and slid it under the lid of the hot plate. "How can you tell when it's done?"

"The room fills with smoke."

She allowed herself to smile. I hadn't expected the word "contraption" from so small a person. I wondered how old she was. They took them as young as eight, at Upton Hall. When the toast and tea were ready, I draped her wet trousers over the closed hot plates and put the shoes on a piece of newspaper in the bottom oven. The hems of the trousers were frayed, the shoes hardly visible through their coating of mud.

"Well now!" I said, as I put the tea tray down in the sitting room. "Hopefully we're all a little warmer?" This sort of brisk inanity being the only course in the face of such bizarreness, such daunting cold and distress. I remembered William telephoning before dawn, the sand bags in Church Walk, my savaging of Lucy, Colonel Daventry's cheerful chirping. I could hardly believe it was still the same day. As if in response, my lower back began to ache, a compressed feeling around the cradle of my hips.

My guests were hungry, I was certain, and so was I. For a while the only other sounds were the crunch of toast and the series of noisy gulps made by Mrs. Lacey. The teacup empty, she set it down.

"That hit the spot," she said. "Sorry to be a barbarian."

She was sitting with her coat round her shoulders now, a cigarette held jauntily between two fingers, as if it were the morning after an all-night party. Not a good party, I felt: there was a sort of accidie emanating from her, something compacted, an impasse reached. Her eyes swiveled, her pearls were dirty. A tideline of tan makeup scuffled along her hairline.

"Don't apologize, Mrs. Lacey." I pushed an ashtray toward her. "This is rather a trying time for you."

"I'll have to take her all the way home again, I suppose. They could have phoned."

"They did try. Anyway, all is not lost." I explained about the girls' refuge at The Place. "You'll have to go back to the main road, though, and enter the village at the other end. The water this side is too deep for your car."

She grunted. Not a single word, kind or otherwise, had passed between this woman and her daughter. I turned to the child.

"The others are having a grand time at The Place, Penny. They're all fixed up on those inflatable beds, the ones you can float on. People loll about on them now, instead of having a proper swim. What are they called? Lidos."

Penny stared at her hands, rubbed them together. "Lilos," she offered.

"Lilos. Of course. Because you *lie low* on them. That *is* clever."

Mrs. Lacey abruptly stubbed out her cigarette and stood up. "Right. Well, if you give me directions to this house, we'll get out of your hair."

There was something odd about the way she was standing, feet planted wide apart, giving her daughter a stony, befuddled stare. I couldn't tell what she was thinking. I wasn't certain she was thinking at all. I pondered this for a second or two, and a strong impression began to form in my mind. I rose to my feet.

"Mrs. Lacey, you can't go yet."

"I'm sorry?" She frowned.

"Penny's clothes are still wet."

"So what. She's got more in her case."

"Mrs. Lacey." I looked her full in the face. "Please sit down again, and I'll bring you some black coffee." For it had dawned on me, what the problem was.

"I'm absolutely *fine*."

A warm intimate blast of fermentation, the same fruity odor that I had smelled in her car and that I now recognized of course as half-digested alcohol, hit me full the face. I breathed out, hard.

"Of course you are," I said. "I'm simply suggesting you wait awhile, before taking the wheel."

"And *I'm* simply suggesting it's none of your business."

I stood silently, Penny's miserably hunched outline in the corner of my eye, my heart racing with the sheer nastiness of the scene. Suddenly Mrs. Lacey let loose a startling bray of laughter.

"Okay, if that's how you want it." She began rummaging for her keys. "*You* can take my daughter into the village. And I'll clear off."

She turned and left the room. Dismayed, I listened to her striding

steps on the hall floor, the creak of the front door. By the time I came
to my senses and hurried after her she was opening her car door.

"Mrs. Lacey!" I ran toward the car. She was getting in now and
starting the engine. "Mrs. Lacey!"

"You've been very kind!" she shouted back. "Very kind!" Then she
pulled away with a squirt of gravel from her tires, some of which spattered over my legs. I watched her lurch out onto the track and proceed,
engine roaring, up to the lane. The car disappeared, and I heard it
gather speed as she made her way back toward the main road.

A small blue suitcase lay on its side, dumped on the damp gravel. I
picked it up. I swallowed convulsively, two, three times, to get rid of
the sordid taste on my tongue. Slowly I made my way back inside.

Penny was still curled up in the small armchair near the fire, knees
by her chin. She didn't move as I came in. I didn't want to look her in
the eye, because then I would be openly seeing her shame, and I
needed to spare her that. I put her suitcase down and stretched out my
hands to the warmth. My fingers were trembling. I wondered what to
say, but only came up with tritenesses, not to be uttered. In the end it
was Penny who spoke.

"Some people hate home, and some people hate school." She dug
her chin down between her shoulders. "But I hate home *and* school."

I listened to the crackle of the fire, the occasional *phutt* as a pocket
of water in the wood turned to steam. I rubbed my hands together, just
to make friction, to get a purchase on this absolute despond. "I'll go
and see if your trousers are dry."

They were. I took them off the top of the range and remembered
the shepherd's pie for this evening. William was coming to supper.
The pie was ready in the larder. I put it in the oven to heat through.
When I brought the child's trousers into the sitting room, she wedged
herself deeper in the chair, binding her arms around her knees. "You
need to get changed, Penny," I told her. "Not into these muddy things,

but into some of your clean clothes. I'm going to tell Mrs. Dennis you're here, and then take you to join your schoolfriends."

She pressed her lips together, said nothing.

"You can change here by the fire." I went toward the door. "After I drop you off, I'm collecting a friend for supper."

"What are you having?"

I paused. "What?"

"For supper. What are you having?"

"Shepherd's pie."

She unfurled the polo-neck of her sweater and pulled it all the way up over her nose. Above the woolen ribbing her lower eyelids were a flat line, the upper lids semicircles. It was the perfect shape of sadness.

The number for The Place, when I dialed, was engaged. I tried twice more, at intervals of about half a minute, but the line remained busy. I went back into the sitting room to find Penny still lodged into the armchair as tight as a whelk, her suitcase unopened on the floor beside her.

"Dear," I said. "Come now."

"Have you spoken to Mrs. Dennis?"

"Not yet."

She lifted up her chin, as Lady Brock had taught her. I opened my mouth, shut it again. The implication was clear. When summoned, she would get ready to leave. But in the meantime she would sit by the fire.

I retreated to the window and looked out into a featureless, settling dusk overlaid by the reflection of the room behind me. Running my finger down the side of the window frame I felt a little dimple in the wood. Two, three—a whole line of them, about three inches apart. They were the holes made by the hooks we had screwed into the frame, the hooks that held our blackout curtains taut to the window. We'd never filled them in properly, those little holes. Just added a coat of gloss paint, then another as the years went by. I had no idea that they could still be felt, after all this time.

The firelight silhouetted the child's snubbed little profile, the fuzz of hair beneath the beret. She'd pulled her polo neck down so I could see individual tears reflected in the glass as they tracked down the side of her nose. What had I said to her mother? How we looked after people in floods? Well, then. Let there be a moment's truce in the world, a natural contract between two human beings, one the owner of a warm house, the other clinging to a gate in a flooded field. I thought of the lilos, the drafty barracks of bedrooms at The Place.

"Come, dear," I said. "You shan't stay in that chair."

She looked up, startled, with the same fearful light in her eyes as before. I made a sound, something between a sigh and a laugh.

"No, Penny," I told her. "I'll give you a bed."

25

IN THE BATHROOM I turned on the hot tap and left her sitting on a towel on the lip of the bath, her suitcase on the floor at her feet.

"Don't let the bath run over. I'm going to fetch my friend William."

"Okay." Her voice, small and high, came through steam.

I telephoned The Place again. Margaret Dennis answered this time, and I explained the situation. "I met Mrs. Lacey coming into the village. She didn't get the message."

I didn't mention the woman's shunning of her daughter, her precipitate, outrageous departure.

"Thank you, Mrs. Parr. That *is* helpful. We're filled to the gunwales here. James Acton's been singing your praises, by the way. I gather you saved Church Walk. He says we need more practical people like you!"

I laughed. "Lucy Horne helped too. But that's very kind of him."

"Look after young Lacey. She's a miserable little thing."

"I think there's a reason for that."

"Yes." Mrs. Dennis grunted. "Mum's on the sauce."

"I'm glad you know."

"Major Lacey's stationed in Ulster, you see." She sighed. "These modern army wives. Half of them aren't remotely cut out for it. Look, I'd better ring off. We've got games to plan for tomorrow. Beanbag relays, that sort of thing. I'm staying the night here so Marcy can look after the Colonel. I've brought my own camp bed, of course, and a hot water bottle."

I fought back the urge to giggle. Althea had appointed the right kind of headmistress.

I plunged down the wet lanes toward Upton Hall and William. Selwyn had taught me to drive in the days when men wore gloves at the wheel. He'd bought me a pair the first time I successfully double-declutched. I'd driven this road with headlamps slitted for the blackout, knew it better than the back of my hand.

Practical. *Ellen has such strong fingers. She's so practical.* Who had said that?

Mrs. Daventry and Miss Legg, of course, in the village hall. They couldn't deal with the knot on a bale of blankets. Southampton was engulfed in fire, and they hadn't been able to untie a simple reef knot between them. Mrs. Daventry had none of her husband's courtesy, Miss Legg none of her mother's kindness—her mother being the grocer Mrs. Legg who had steadied my nerve, in the face of our mounting bills for potatoes and cheese, during the time of the Absaloms. That was why, on that day in the village hall, I had said, *I simply know where to pull,* coldly, as the rope loosened in my grasp. Uncaring, in the face of their complete ignorance of life, of how rude I seemed. I had released that knot one-handed, of course, because my other arm was bearing the sacklike weight of a small girl.

William was among the firemen outside the school building. A wide hose snaked across the flagstones, its origin in the basements where a banging, hectoring engine was driving the pump. A chute of stinking brown water erupted from the mouth of the hose into a tank.

"The boiler rooms are nearly empty," William said to me. "They won't get much more out with this great sucker." He kicked the hose gently. "The rest will be done with shovels."

The cloud bank was at last passing over, it seemed. The horizon was a clear dimming blue in the eastern quarter beyond the elms, their enlacement of branches bare against the sky. We negotiated the drive and the first part of the journey in silence. I hoped that Penny had turned off the bath tap.

"I've got an Upton Hall girl at home, William." I described my encounter in the flooded lane, the ensuing debacle. "She's such a wretched little thing, I simply couldn't say no."

He was nodding. "That'll be young Lacey. Her mother's already famous."

"Oh dear."

"Mrs. Dennis will appreciate it, any road." He shook his head. "Nobody understands how unbudgeable water is, not till they grapple with a flood. Barring you millers, of course. Water being your stock-in-trade. I always thought Mr. Parr took to the job exceptionally well, being that he never expected to inherit the mill."

"Selwyn would have been gratified by your compliment."

"It's the truth."

"Do *you* think he gave me what life is meant to be?"

I didn't take my eyes off the lane ahead of us, the headlights probing the mist that was gathering over the tea-brown water.

"I've always had the impression," he said at last, "that Mr. Parr gave you everything you wanted. But it's hardly a matter for another person to judge. Friends may not understand that, of course, and speak out of turn."

So Lucy had already talked to him. Of course. I could tell from a lightening in the corner of my eye that he'd turned his head to look at me.

"Lucy doesn't feel she's quite been forgiven," he continued. "And it can be wounding, when forgiveness is begrudged."

"I see." I gave a short laugh, no humor in it. "She casts aspersions on my husband, and so I should apologize for wounding her."

William was shaking his head several times slowly, not in negation so much as sorrow. "There's no call for bitterness, Ellen. She meant nothing by it."

Penny was creeping down the stairs in her dressing gown, her beret pulled low on her brow. That, and the way she froze when she saw us, gave her the air of a small, unsuccessful burglar.

"Come down, Penny. Don't be shy."

In the kitchen William greeted her. "Hello there, lost sheep!"

I put a pan of peas on the heat. "Lost sheep?"

"She couldn't find her classroom. So I showed her the way."

I stared from William to Penny. "Surely the teachers showed you your classroom on the first day?"

"She didn't arrive on the first day. Isn't that right, Penny?"

Penny looked up at William and nodded, pressing her lips together.

"Oh, yes," I said. "Lady Brock did say you arrived late. What happened?"

"Her ma never received the letter. The one that told 'em when to come, and what to bring, and so on." I could tell from his steady stare that William thought the letter was lying unopened at the bottom of Veronica Lacey's handbag.

"What bad luck. Now, could you lay the table, dear?"

The shepherd's pie came out bubbling with a black rim. My guests sat, their eyes trained on the small fumaroles of steam escaping from the crisp mashed potato. I dug in with the serving spoon and they lifted their plates in due reverence.

"Wait a while," I pleaded. "It's so hot." But it was hard for them to resist. There was much blowing around mouthfuls, and great care taken when loading the fork with peas. Soon the plates shone, and second helpings were distributed. "I haven't fed such hungry people for a long time," I told them.

Similar short work was made of an egg custard. William and I were exchanging a few words about the Upton Hall basements, the age of the boilers, when Penny suddenly said, "Granny made egg custard for me."

She had been quiet all the way through the meal. I hadn't expected conversation, after the day she had endured.

"Did she, dear? That's nice."

"Yes. She was wearing an overall with poppers on the side. I was about three. Anyway, Granny was talking to Mummy, and Mummy said to her, 'Yes, Mummy.' And that's when I realized that mothers had mothers too. It was an extremely interesting fact, and kind of a delicious one too, because I was eating egg custard at the same time."

It was like a burble of fresh spring water, suddenly stopped up. Her cheeks went pink under our gaze.

"That *is* interesting." I smiled at her. "Do you know, when I eat flaky pastry I always see a lady called Mrs. Horne in my mind's eye. She was kind, and so I taste the kindness in the pastry."

She nodded, the blush fading, and picked up her spoon again.

When I returned from dropping William back at the school, I found Penny had gone upstairs and curled herself up on my bed, on top of the blankets and counterpane. The single bedside lamp was on. When she saw me she stirred in the yellow light, raised her head, and struggled upright, hampered by her dressing gown.

"Were you asleep?" I asked.

She shook her head. "This is your bed, isn't it. I hope you don't mind. I wanted to be cozy. And the fire went out."

"It's fine, Penny."

"Where do you want me to go?"

The room was saturated by a thick quietness. My limbs felt so heavy.

"Get under the covers, dear." I nodded my head toward the step up to the old dressing room. "I'll make up another bed for myself next door."

She lay still, following me only with her eyes as I passed back and forth with bed linen. Her deep fatigue made her gaze clear and dreamlike at the same time. I fetched a thick blanket from the wardrobe and swung the door closed. The mirror caught the reflection of the bed and the child lying there. I glanced at her, away, and back again, and now her face had a dense, creamy pallor, and it was rounded like a small moon. A face I had not seen since wartime.

I stared into the glass. A pair of shining hazel eyes looked straight into mine. I held this extraordinary gaze. Three, four, five seconds passed, counted off by a pounding pulse in my ears.

At last I turned and looked back at Penny. Then once more to the mirror, where I saw her reflected exactly. The vision had gone.

"Are you all right, Mrs. Parr?"

I sat down heavily on the end of the bed. Eventually I found my voice. "I'm fine, thank you, dear." She blinked slowly, with a sudden solemnity that made the hairs rise on my scalp and fall again. She had brown eyes, hair a similar color. Beyond that, she was nothing like. We sat in silence for a few moments.

Eventually I cleared my throat. "Penny, can I ask you something?"

She nodded.

"Do you always wear that hat?"

"Yes."

"Even in bed?"

"Especially in bed."

She snuggled down, and soon lay as still and swaddled as if she'd fallen and become covered in drifting snow.

I tidied up downstairs, listened to the wireless. There would be no more rain. That, at least, was a blessing. Later I crept past Penny to the dressing room and lay wakeful on the narrow bed. I hadn't slept here since Selwyn's final illness. I picked up his clock, set it, and put it down. It rocked back and forth on the hardwood making a tiny high-pitched rumble. Through a chink in the curtains, Southampton glowed dull orange from the sodium streetlamps, turning the night sky blind and dusty. Next door Penny stirred, muttered something, a repeated phrase, but I couldn't hear it.

I was tired, that was all.

At seven in the morning the sky was clear. Penny didn't move when I fetched clothes and left the bedroom. I had breakfast and took a telephone call from Lucy. "Water's down," she said curtly. "I can make it up to the kennels through Pipehouse. Ta for yesterday." I opened my mouth to reply, but she had already rung off.

I stood at the foot of the staircase and listened. It was strange to be in my own house, waiting for someone to wake. Selwyn had nearly always risen before me.

I climbed the stairs, glanced down the landing. The bathroom door was open, no one in there. No answer when I knocked on my bedroom door. I pushed it gently open to see the bed empty.

I moved into the room and approached the steps up into the smaller bedroom. There she was, standing by the window in her pajamas and beret, holding the balsa-wood hawk in her hand, the one that Edward had carved for me. She was weaving it back and forth through the air so that it dipped and swooped. Tilting her head and murmuring to the hawk in a private undertone, gesticulating with her free hand to make sure he understood. She said, "Good bird," kissed him, and began to dance him along the deep windowsill. Then she saw me, started, and blushed.

"Good morning, Penny. Don't worry, he likes conversation, and flying. They all do."

There were twelve birds now, a variety of budgerigars, peacocks, parrots lined up on the windowsill, one for each time Edward had visited. The most recent one, a merry little chicken, had been carved in 1971 when he came to stay with me after Selwyn died. He'd made that chicken while teaching the technique to William—I remembered them both hunched over the kitchen table, chips and chunks and curlicues of balsa wood everywhere on the floor, and Edward's brown hands moving under William's watchful craftsman's eye.

"Do you like them?" I asked her.

She nodded. I waited for her to say more.

"Look," she said. "The person who did this, they must have started with the smallest top curl." She passed me the hawk. "And then peel, peel, peel, all the way in, to the longest feather."

I turned it in my hands. "Just think, if you snapped one feather off. You'd have to start all over again with a new piece of wood. My brother made these, you know." I ran my finger along one wing, and felt an unwelcome sharpness. Three or four feather tips had been amputated. "Oh, look! It's broken!"

Penny jumped. "I know. I saw that. I didn't do it. It wasn't me."

"Of course it wasn't." I could see the breaks were old, there was dust clinging to the brittle stumps. "Oh, the rascal. How could she."

"Who did it?"

"A naughty, naughty little girl."

"You don't sound very cross."

I met her inquiring gaze. She was trying to raise her eyebrows but the low brim of her beret squashed them down. The effect was comical.

"I'm not cross anymore."

At the time I would have been. The entire household would have witnessed my sharp cries of annoyance, the dressing-down that would have followed, the list of chores to be done as recompense.

"Who was the naughty girl?" Penny asked. "What happened to her?"

I pictured her coming up the village street toward me, her arm linked in Bobby Rail's. The day's dirt, mostly ink and mud, smutting her face and knees. Her mouth moving. What had she been saying before I came into earshot? Something about a lardy cake they were going to buy. A silent speaking, never forming into words.

"She was called Pamela," I said. "She went to Ireland."

I looked out at the flooded field. Here and there, tufts of pasture could be seen, islands in a reflected sky.

"North or South?" said Penny.

I turned to her. "South. A long time ago."

"My dad's in the North. He's in the army." For a moment, her mouth formed a perfect upside-down U.

I nodded. "Mrs. Dennis mentioned it."

She looked away. I considered her.

"Do you know what I think, Penny?" I said. "It's time to take off your hat."

Shutting her eyes, she hooked her fingers under the brim of her beret and yanked it off her head. The hair tumbled out, falling around her face and shoulders, a mass of knots and snarls, great hanks of it matted inextricably, inexplicably together.

"Gosh." I swallowed. "Gosh, that's quite a nest."

She placed her hands over her head, but they were too small to hide this prodigious, embrangled growth. "They call me Pigpen at school."

I didn't entirely blame them. "Oh, Penny. How on earth did it get this way?"

"I went on hair strike."

I smothered a smile. "Why? So you wouldn't be sent to Upton Hall?"

Silence.

"Well. Reason or not, you'll still have to go to Upper Cuts in Waltham."

"That's what Mrs. Dennis said." She started to blink rapidly, shaking the horrid tresses away from her face. "Just think of all the customers pointing at me and grimacing." She pronounced it, grimace-ing. I was about to deny this but I couldn't be sure, looking at this awful growth, that a few people wouldn't grimace.

I flexed my fingers. I had trimmed Selwyn's hair on occasion, using the long sharp scissors I kept for fabric, and the results had been perfectly acceptable. "Why don't you let me cut the worst tangles out? You can always visit the hairdresser when I've finished. At least it won't be so embarrassing by then."

Her eyes welled. "It'd be the end of the strike."

"I'm afraid so." I went to the door. "After breakfast you can decide if you want me to cut your hair. What would you like for breakfast? I have porridge, eggs, or porridge and eggs."

"Haven't you got any Alpen?"

"No, I haven't got any Alpen, madam."

She gave me a sudden grin, and the rain cloud was torn from the bright sun. No little teeth left at the front, and the big ones yet to be grown into.

26

I PUT A CHAIR by the kitchen window, fetched the scissors. From the bedroom I brought down my free-standing dressing table mirror, the kind that swung in a sturdy frame. She sat obediently upright for me to put a tea towel over her shoulders. In the good clear light of the window the mess reminded me of homemade felting. I found myself quite light-headed with anger. A dog in this state would be rescued from its owner.

"It was because of Dad," she said.

"What? The hair strike?"

She nodded. "I thought if he knew what a state it was in, he'd come home and tell me off. But when I wrote to him about it, he just wrote back and said not to be so silly. So it's obvious he couldn't care less about me."

"Penny, I'm sure it was because he simply couldn't come. Not that he didn't care."

She folded her arms. Cautiously I embarked on the task, working in silence until curiosity got the better of me.

"Will you like school better now, Penny? The girls won't be able to call you Pigpen anymore."

"Oh yes they will. They don't need a reason to be awful. They're horrible, stupid people. None of them even know who David Bowie is."

I couldn't help chuckling.

"I knew you'd laugh." She was laughing too.

I continued to cut, delicately parting the locks and pruning where I could. "*I* know who David Bowie is."

"You don't!"

"Keep your head still, dear. There's a young chap called Colin, who works at the mill here. He's got a T-shirt with 'David Bowie' on it, so I asked Colin about him. What a striking young man he is, I must say. You seem a bit young for pop music, dear."

She sucked her teeth. "I'm nearly ten. That's old enough."

"Colin's favorite song is called 'Space Odyssey.'"

"It's *Oddity*, actually. Would you like to hear it?"

It was a dirge-like melody, reproduced in a wavering soprano. "That was very nice, dear," I said when she stopped.

"Wait. That was just the first verse."

The story of the troubled lone astronaut and his obscure demise lasted until I had cut away all the larger pellets of hair. The few knots that remained were too near her crown to be tackled without scalping her, so I began to shape the rest. She had fallen into a contented daydream, and there were no sounds now except the snip of my scissors and the crooning of the hens outside, and the tick of the railway clock that hung on the kitchen wall. Althea had given it to Selwyn when he was a young man, after it had served many years in the kitchen of Upton Hall. I heard the deep, measured tick, the seconds falling away.

The blades had come so close round my neck and ears, the black ointment had dripped on my neck. Elizabeth's face was above me in the mirror, a thin face, a shadow of down on her upper lip, eyes on her work. She never said an unkind thing, not even to Donald of the shaggy locks, our most mutinous evacuee, when he refused to have his hair cut. *Donald, you're a proper disgrace.* They knew she didn't mean it.

Snip, snip snip. No sound save the deliberate tread of the clock.

Donald got a pudding-bowl like the other boys, and in the New Year Selwyn took the boys to Waltham, to Suggs the barber for a short back-and-sides. He took Pamela too, even though she was so new with us, for a trim. I thought she might not like it without me. But he brushed me aside and proceeded to manage four children on the bus, four children successively in the barber's chair, effortlessly keeping order and providing distraction.

And Elizabeth said, *Your Mr. Parr, he's a natural with them.*

Her hair was shining now, soft, a bobbed style with a slight wave in the short locks at the front.

"There we are, darling. Done. Look in the mirror."

She did so, turning her head this way and that, wriggling in her seat with pleasure. "Oh gosh, Mrs. Parr. It's *groovy*." She looked up at me smiling.

"Is it?" I smiled back. "I'm very pleased. You can see what a nice color it is now."

She wrinkled her nose. "It's annoying. Too dark for blond, but I can't call it brown, either. What color do you think it is?"

She pushed the mirror and my child swung into view looking heavenward, her hair curling on her brow, her sublime pallor that of a bored cherub, the light catching her eyes. There was a strong bright silence.

"What do you think, Mrs. Parr?"

I looked away, saw a patch of blue sky beyond the window, widening between ragged, running clouds.

"I don't know," I said at last. "I don't know at all."

Penny was gazing up at me. The tea towel caping her straight little shoulders. When I said nothing else she shifted in the chair. "I suppose I should be going."

"Yes." I spoke deliberately. "They'll be waiting for you at The Place."

She got up out of the chair. "Thank you very much for the haircut, Mrs. Parr. And the shepherd's pie—"

"Wait. Penny."

"What?"

"I'm thinking. Perhaps you don't absolutely have to go. The school is still closed, after all. If I ring Mrs. Dennis, and she says it's okay, would you like to spend the rest of the day here?"

"That would be terrific." Her eyes were sparkling.

"Wait till I tell you what we have to do." I smiled. "Feed the hens, and then go on the bike to visit Lady Brock."

"I love biking."

"More than beanbag relays?"

"We have to do them in the gym when it's raining." She lowered her voice. "I prefer death to beanbag relays."

Mrs. Dennis, effusively grateful, allowed it. The number of refugees at The Place had risen to fourteen. I gave Penny my wooden hen-run clogs and a bucket of peelings. Going upstairs for extra socks I saw her out of the bedroom window casting the scraps wide, like a sower in a field. The beret was back on her head, but more rakishly set.

Neither of us was heavy, but together we probably weighed as much as a corpulent man. The bicycle tires needed more air. I handed her the pump and she worked it vigorously, her face turning a faint rose. At last I'd got her blood going round. I tied an old hassock to the bicycle rack. Much darned and finally thrown out by the church worthies, I used it as a kneeler for weeding and scrubbing. William's sheepskin was kept upstairs again, hanging on the back of a little chair in my bedroom. It was so old, the hide cracked and frail. It had done good service.

Penny climbed on. I put my weight on the front pedal and, with one fearful wobble, we moved off. I laughed aloud and so did she. Soon we were going apace. Momentum was vital in the water, and we took the bends of the lane in style. "You're a good passenger, Penny. You lean the right way."

"Charlie takes me on his motorbike when he's on leave. My big brother."

"Is he in the army too?"

"Mm. He's in Cyprus."

We came to the Absaloms. There was a neat path of floodwater up to, and inevitably under, each front door. The concrete walls looked at home in the wet, since they were already green from sucking up decades of damp from the ground. There was nobody left inside.

"Look at those houses, Penny. They're prefabs. Not yet thirty years old but they're empty. Condemned."

"Prefabs?"

"Prefabricated houses. They arrived on great lorries after the war. Whole walls and roofs. Men put them up in an afternoon or so. Plumbed them in, ran the electricity along the lane, and hey presto. They thought they'd get rid of poverty itself." I drew breath and worked my legs harder. "I don't know how anyone thought it would be a saving, to buy cheap housing. Look. Number One. That was where I lived, but not in that prefab. This was long before *they* came. My house was a brick house, and nearly a ruin."

There was a silence, broken only by my breathing. Then she began talking, her voice so soft I barely heard her.

"I'm sorry about Mum, yesterday. Dad's just gone back to Northern Ireland, you see. And what with Charlie as well . . ."

I considered this, the life that her mother wasn't cut out for. I doubted I could ever reach the stage of pardoning Veronica Lacey, but understanding her—that, perhaps, glimmered on the horizon.

"Penny, you don't have to explain."

"Dad says it's more dangerous to cross the road in London."

"I'm sure he's right."

I was too short of breath to say more.

"Let me pedal, Mrs. Parr."

"Really? Do you think you can?"

"I could have a go."

I guided us to a damp field verge and we changed places. She pushed off and careened to the other side of the road, as if she were breaking in a black metal steer, one with a bell on his horns.

"Wheee! This is the biggest bike I've ever ridden. Ha, ha! We could go off on an adventure, Mrs. Parr. Why don't we? We could have a picnic!"

"Perhaps when the water's lower." I was laughing. "Keep left, I implore you, Penny.'"

Lady Brock's front door was locked this time, but we couldn't summon her. Our second more imperious knock only alerted Stuart, who could be heard working himself into a frenzy somewhere within the house. I slid my hand inside a broken flowerpot on the step and took out a key. When I opened the door, Stuart came racing down the hall, barking so hard that he almost fell off his feet. From the sitting room came Lady Brock's voice, shouting, "Stuart, hold your blasted tongue," through the noise.

"Althea?"

"Ellen." Lady Brock sounded hoarse. "Come through."

The sitting room was gray and cold. Lady Brock was sitting on the floor surrounded by pieces of the suit of armor. She flourished a nonchalant hand at them. "I thought I'd give my knight an overhaul. Who is this creature?"

"It's Penny, Althea. From the other week. I'm not surprised you don't recognize her."

"Good lord, so it is." Althea guffawed appreciatively. "Is that your work, Ellen? Bravo. Very *gamine*."

Only now did I see how Althea's other arm was braced rigid behind her back, her legs splayed straight out in front of her. "Penny," I said. "Go and put the kettle on, do you mind?"

When she was gone from the room, Althea groaned. But it wasn't a beseeching look in her dark eyes. Althea would never beseech. "I'm cast, Ellen. Like a mare in a stall."

"I know." I brought a footstool near, and then bent over her. "Lift your arm if you can. And now the other. Round my neck."

"I'll bring you down, my dear."

"No, you won't. This is how I got Selwyn out of bed in the last week. Now hold fast."

I swung her gently onto the footstool and thence to the sofa. She was so easy to lift, for all her height. Her bones had to be as hollow as a bird's. She leaned back, mouth open, alarmingly like her own death mask. Then the carmined lips moved. "Good God. It's come to this."

"Althea, please think about a daily woman. Suppose I was busy and couldn't call?"

"Oh . . ." She lifted her shoulders. "Someone always drops by eventually."

I turned my back, which was sometimes the only resort in the face of such pig-headedness, and went to the kitchen.

Penny and I brought tea. Then she and I sat on the floor and worked on the knight's dismembered limbs. I watched her dashing away at a greave, buffing it to a mirror shine. The bike ride had thawed her: she was quickening, all elbows and eagerness. "I wouldn't mind if Upton Hall was washed away in a tidal wave. Oh, Lady Brock, I forgot it used to be your house . . ."

Althea, snorting with mirth, agreed. "I have felt the same at times, my dear . . ."

Penny's light cotton jeans were stretched over bony knees. No wonder she shivered. I could take her to Waltham, buy her some warmer clothes. "Penny, I've had an idea. This afternoon, if you like, we could—"

A heavy rapping at the front door provoked Stuart once more into clamor. Althea cocked her head. "Must be William. Why everyone feels they have to beat my door down I can't imagine. Penny, do go and let him in."

William entered, wild, damp, and gaunt, and full of life. "Hello again, young Lacey," he was saying to her. "You've had a shearing, I see. I'll bet that's Mrs. Parr's doing. Ah, I thought I could smell metal polish. No, Lady Brock, I don't want a sit-down. Let me at that armor." He took his jacket off and kneeled with us on the floor and began work. I watched Penny observing the grips and squeezes of his ruined hand. He glanced up at her face from time to time, tranquilly, without disapprobation. She was unaware of these glances.

He gave his report on the state of Upton Hall. "The basements are drying out now. There's two generators up there, and the electrics will be back on tonight, they say. Esther—that's Mrs. Staveley to you, Penny, your cook—she's lost a roomful of stores, so you girls will be having soup in packets."

"Cup-a-Soups," said Penny.

"Cups o' soup. That describes them fairly. Lord." He gave a high yipping laugh. "We could have done with them! Oh yes! They'd have gone down a treat in Plugstreet Wood!"

"Were you camping in the wood, Mr. Kennet?"

"We were not, my dear." Courteously he turned to her. "We were fighting. Or waiting to fight."

She smiled. "Cup-a-Soups would have been perfect, then. Just boil the kettle and there you are. You could pounce on the enemy while they were still heating up their old tinned stuff."

"Yes indeed."

When all the pieces of armor were equally shining, William got up, flexed his knees. "Let's put the old chap together again. After that I'm off up to the kennels. See George about some snares."

"I am shutting my ears," announced Lady Brock.

"Can I come?" Penny blurted. "I could read to Mr. Horne again and have some Bourbon biscuits."

"You were the one," I said, as it dawned on me. "Who drew on his plaster. You're *PL*."

She nodded. "I thought it was sad that no one had written a message."

"Go on, William," said Lady Brock. "Take her with you. She's going to be bolted up in the Hall by tonight."

I clambered to my feet, making a business of pulling my skirt straight, hanging my head so that no one would see the fast-rising tide of ridiculous disappointment that was flushing my face and making my eyes burn. I cleared my throat. "Yes, go, dear. I'll pop home and start collecting your things together."

Penny sounded uncertain. "Is it okay, Mrs. Parr?"

"Of course!" I manufactured a cheery smile. "Why on earth not?"

"You said something about this afternoon."

"No, it wasn't anything. You go on, dear."

William raised his good hand, judgelike. "We'll go up the kennels, but we won't be long. She'll have had enough spoiling by then, skiving off all this time. Mrs. Dennis will be wanting her back in the fold."

Without speaking I passed Penny and William the pieces of armor for them to hang on the frame. Soon the knight stood whole and shining, his metal fists fielding beams of light and bouncing them onto the walls. "Behold the High Middle Ages," crowed Lady Brock, and Penny lifted his visor and looked inside, and I bid good-bye to no one in particular, and received a flurry of distracted good-byes in return, and in no time I was outside, getting back on the bicycle again alone. The air was sharp and the road more slippery than it had seemed earlier. I was lighter now, of course, spinning along on my pumped-up tires.

Her belongings were dropped and scattered everywhere. I started to pick them up. What was it with children? Did those young fingers suddenly become nerveless, lose their grip? How could one girl strew so many things across a bedroom floor? Trousers, hairbrush, slippers, rabbit, hat. I performed the bendings and straightenings, dip and up, just like before, each time with another small object in my hand, a child's garment or toy. Years of such gleaning. My body began to insist, to push and nudge. *You don't fool me. You remember.*

In sudden anger I tossed the clothes and hairbrush into the suitcase, banged down the lid and snapped the catches shut. I didn't have to be a maid to this child.

I stood, breathing hard. The counterpane of my bed was thrown back and the bottom sheet bore the imprint of her curled body, a comma-shaped trough. Without thinking I lay down there, and stared at the ceiling with smarting eyes.

"For heaven's sake," I said aloud, and got up again.

Opening the case I took everything out and repacked it, one garment after another, folding and tucking. Vests, knickers, small mudstained socks. A Viyella blouse, the yoke narrow for narrow shoulders. A pair of sad cotton trousers, thinner even than the ones she was wearing. The case was blue, eggshell on the outside, grimy and battered at the corners, the inside a slightly darker dusty blue, an old-fashioned color, with interior straps to hold everything in place. I fastened the straps and then tightened the gilt buckles with care.

When the knock came at the front door I brought the suitcase downstairs and met Penny on the doorstep. William was waiting by the Land Rover, transfixed by Venus hanging aglow among the lower branches of the ash tree. The jangle of my keys awoke him from his reverie.

They both sat in the back, passing a few words to each other, something inconsequential about the kennels. Beacon Hill rose against the darkening sky.

"Gosh," Penny said. "Look at that beautiful hill."

"That's Beacon Hill. You can see the sea from the top. The sea, and Southampton." I glanced in the rearview mirror. Her light brown eyes were wistful.

"Southampton's a major global port, you know," she said. "Mrs. Dennis told us. You can get a ship to anywhere in the world."

"Mrs. Dennis is right," said William. "Mrs. Parr's brother did that very thing. He ended up in the Far East. He's had some great adventures."

"And he carves birds."

"That he does."

"That would be my best job. Bird carver and adventurer."

At Upton Hall I came to a halt on the gravel and got out along with my passengers. Two minibuses were disgorging pupils and luggage. William sketched a wave and hastened away to the mews and his quarters. Penny stood facing me, shivering in the wind, away across the gravel from the horde of pupils, her teeth clenched with cold and distress, and I saw again the girl I had found on the field gate.

"Don't worry, Penny," I said. "You've come back with lovely hair, remember. If they say nasty things, just—just take no notice."

She lunged forward and hugged me, binding my arms to my body, her head hard against the join of my ribs.

"Bye-bye, darling," I heard myself say. She had pinned my arms so tightly to my sides, I couldn't hug her back. "Come back and see me again."

"Bye, Mrs. Parr." Her voice was muffled against my belly. Then she tore herself away, leaving me without words, able only to stand and watch her dragging her suitcase toward the throng of children.

The Olivetti was on the table in my bedroom, where it had been since I'd given up the mill. In the drawer beneath it, a stack of folded messages tied together with darning wool, navy ink on sky-blue Basildon Bond. The envelopes bore cobalt Irish stamps depicting a young man casting grain. I hadn't read them for years. There was no need. Occasionally I simply held the small parcel in my hands.

I pulled the drawer wider and extracted another set of letters, these typewritten on foolscap. Phrases jumped out as I shuffled through them. *Bareheaded under the Lion Gate. Glittering, drooping under dewdrops. A pencil stub at the back of a desk drawer, the end chewed by milk teeth. Years of babble and persiflage.* I could toss the lot onto the fire and it would flare and char in twenty seconds and I would have lost nothing. I brought the stool close, sat down, inserted a fresh sheet of paper into the roller of the typewriter, and let the words rattle off the keys.

```
    Pamela, there's been a flood. Did it
wash you back here, little girl? I
thought I saw you in the mirror my
darling

    Once, twice

    But when I looked again it was only
Penny
```

"Stupid." I tore the paper out of the machine and crumpled it up. "Stupid, stupid fool." I threw the ball of paper across the room, and it hit the skirting board and flew under the bed.

27

THE WATERS RECEDED, and Pipehouse Wood turned to blue and gold under clear windy sky, with torrents of crisp beech leaves tumbling from the trees. Althea and I walked there with Stuart, Stuart mostly traveling underground with a fine disregard for the difference between rabbit warrens and badger setts, an attitude that would one day earn him a calamitous bite on the nose. Althea was equally and even more alarmingly scornful of the holes in the ground.

"Wouldn't you prefer a flatter route?" I pleaded. "I can't carry you if you fall, you know."

"Oh," she said, pointing at one of the larger badger hollows. "Just bury me here. It's better than those Druids. They're always burying each other in farmers' fields, aren't they? So inconsiderate. Just what you want to dig up when plowing. A blasted Druid."

"I think they prefer groves, Althea. Clearings. Places like Pipehouse Wood, in fact. I'm quite certain they wouldn't choose a cornfield."

Time passed, the weather turned again. Iron ragbags of clouds marauded us, discharging heavy drops and hail, but they traveled in small convoys separated by wide tracts of rough blue sky. Nothing like the dank low cover of the flood. That was a month ago now and I was so glad it had all gone, the submerged fields and fences, the tugging, knee-high brown waters. The feeling of time out of joint.

"Are you taking Lady Brock to the vicar's party, Ell?"

Lucy and I were sitting side by side at a table in the village hall.

George Horne had lost his plaster cast and regained his feet, liberating Lucy from the kennels for her time-honored Thursday morning off to attend the Women's Institute market. I'd been minding her stall for her in the meantime, presiding on her behalf over the pastel rainbows of knitted baby clothes, the bright primaries of embroidered birds and flowers. I had nothing but my humdrum preserves and eggs. I could never compete with this glory.

"You know," I said, "I think you might have surpassed your nan, in skill."

"No one could surpass my nan." But a small smile expressed her inner delight. "The vicar's party, my dear. Are you taking Lady B?"

"Oh! Yes, I am. I'd forgotten it was so soon."

Lucy cleared her throat, performed an experimental wheeze. "You ain't got one of them Fisherman's sweets, dear?"

"No, I'm so sorry, Lucy."

Her wheeze turned into a hectic, rattling cough. I reached over and slapped her gently on the back, which she said she needed and which never, in the decades that I'd been doing it, made the slightest difference. "Lucy, there's a boy with asthma at the village school, you know. He breathes in some kind of spray from a little pump. It works an absolute treat. I wonder if you—"

"I ain't got asthma."

"Really, I think you might have."

The cough quietened. She picked up her needlepoint frame and stabbed out a row of brown stitches, the outline of the tail of a wren.

"It's the dentures all over again," she murmured, after a long pause.

"Aren't you glad of your dentures?"

"Gladder not to be told what to bloomin do all the time."

Sometime after the war, I'd asked William if he could persuade George Horne tactfully to apprise Lucy of the fact that the dentist was now free of charge. That was the sum of my involvement. I gave her a saintly, forbearing smile.

She snorted, abandoned her irritation, grinned at me. Even now there was still a kink in her smile, a tweaking down of her top lip to conceal the long-gone gaps.

"Oh! I nearly forgot." Her hand dived into the front of her jerkin, a padded affair faded to salmon pink except for a shiny brick-red square testifying to a pocket recently ripped away. From the surviving pocket she produced a small white envelope, creased and grimed. "I've got a letter for you, Ell."

"Who from?"

Her eyes glinted. "Open it up."

Mrs. Parr, the envelope said. The back, spotted by some nameless brown liquid, was blank. "Really, Lucy, look at the state of it."

"I ain't a postman."

I slid my thumb under the seal. A child's handwriting, looped and regular, and on the fold of the paper the words *kind to me and gave me a warm bed.*

"How did you get this, Lucy?"

"She came up the kennels roundabout Sunday teatime." Lucy selected a new needle and a yarn of a slightly darker brown. "She was on the lam. Couldn't reach the mill in time, she said, so she popped over to me."

"That's extremely silly of her! I don't want to be party to any trouble she gets herself into. Why on earth is she writing to *me?*"

Lucy squinted at the eye of her needle. "It might be a thank-you, for having her. Better late than never."

"What did she say, when you saw her?"

"Not a lot."

"Well, how did she seem?"

"What d'you mean, how did she seem?"

"Yes! Did she *seem* upset, for example? Or anxious? Or cheerful, come to that?"

Lucy pondered, threaded needle poised.

"She read me my *Bunty* comic," she said at last.

Was it possible actually to die from exasperation? "Lucy!"

"Ellen, my dear, why don't you read your letter and find out how she is for yourself?"

"I will." On the other side of the hall the kitchen hatch rattled up, releasing a cloud of steam. "I'll fetch you a hot drink. It might help your chest."

"I've got rock cakes." Deirdre Harper folded her arms. It was a challenge.

"Two rock cakes, then, Deirdre, please, and a pot of tea for two. I'll take them over to Lucy, if that's all right."

Deirdre narrowed her eyes. She didn't like her cups to travel, even if only across the hall to the stallholders. Tea was to be taken here, at the tables set out by the kitchen. Her son's death all that time ago, in the cold sea of Norway, right at the beginning of the war—this death had turned her into a vixen, and a vixen she'd remained for over thirty years, black lips bared over long narrow teeth, at bay in the bracken. I admired her for it.

"You'd better sit down while I get it ready."

Meekly I obeyed and, once seated, pulled the letter out of the envelope.

Dear Mrs. Parr,

Please may I talk to you? Every day I go down to the humps and bumps at about half-past three. It's free time and no one speaks to me so they don't notice I'm gone. Please can you meet me there? If you're too busy shopping for Lady Brock or feeding the hens I will understand. I hope you don't mind me writing to you but I'm doing it because you were kind to me and gave me a warm bed. Yours sincerely, Penny Lacey

The writing was small and smeared in places where her fingers had moved over the paper. Every letter that could be joined was joined. I pondered on "the humps and bumps." What, and where, they could be.

I folded the letter over, and over again crossways, so that I couldn't read the writing.

Deirdre plonked the tea and rock cakes down.

"Thanks, Deirdre," I said automatically. "Those look nice."

"Made this morning."

"You lent me Patricia's shoes." I thought of this every so often, but I'd never mentioned it to Deirdre before. "When I went for my job at the Town Hall, and I had nothing except my old boots."

Her mouth stayed downturned but the memory kindled in her eyes. "Patricia wasn't best pleased."

"Shoes with a heel," I said. "They changed my life. I'm sure I couldn't have got that job in my boots."

She smiled at last. "For want of a heel—"

"The job was lost."

Her lips tightened, and the moment was gone. "Don't forget those cups, mind. I want them back."

I watched her depart. She'd slipped a pair of stockings into the shoebox as well, Deirdre, knowing that I'd have none of my own.

For want of a heel. *For want of a nail.* When did I write that? I could see my typewriter in my mind's eye. It was during the war and I was in the mill office, and I'd been pleading with a Mr. . . . Mr. Gresham, of course, for some piece of equipment that could not be had anywhere. Threatening him with the defeat of the nation over a—yes, that was it—a new protective screen, to stop river debris in the headrace getting into the turbine. The darkness had been crowding in on me, darkness of the war, and of the winter. I had the desk lamp poised over the black-topped keys so that the ranks of gold letters shone. *Bang bang bang*, and then Suky Fitch had come in and told me that Selwyn had arranged for my child to be taken away. The serried gold-gleaming black keys, and Suky's inquiring face, and the knock in my heart.

Their name was Henstrow. The woman had bandaged legs. I had stood up to Selwyn: *No. My girl shall not stay there. She will come home with me.*

There was a rattle on the roof of the village hall. Rain had come again. People were raising their voices in soft coos of dismay. A huddled throng clustered by the door, unwilling to depart; they were nudged gently backward by a wetter crowd coming in, flapping umbrellas. *What a morning,* they said. Wellingtons if I'd thought. Dark figures passed in front of me, shoulders shining wet. Dr. Bell had been wearing an overcoat, that day when the busloads came, fleeing Southampton. He was the only one of us properly dressed. Deirdre had been smoking outside in an overall, her red elbows bared, and Selwyn and I had been wearing light jackets. We hadn't waited to put on top clothes. How joyous the morning had seemed, festive. The weather had been dull, in reality, but in my memory we hurried through sparkling frost to meet our girl.

The folded letter lay in front of me, a small smudged square. I picked it up and put it in my handbag.

The crowd swelled, murmured, parted. Lucy was on her feet, gesturing one hand flat for a saucer, the other tipping an imaginary cup to her lips. I got up from the table, poured her a cup of tea, carried it to her along with a rock cake on a plate. When I set the things down she was speaking to me, saying "parched" and some other words.

I sat down slowly, and Lucy's voice became clearer. "This rock cake is properly delicious. Most people don't realize, they're only meant to *look* like rocks. Where's yours? Ellen, you've gone and left your cake on the table over there. Ellen, dear?"

"Hmm?"

"Your rock cake."

"I don't want any cake . . . I think I'll go and see William when we finish here."

"Give it to him, then," Lucy said. "He deserves it. After all, he set me right. You know, on that little matter."

I stirred myself, tried to concentrate on what she was saying. "What little matter?"

"*You* know. About you not marrying Bob Coward, and the bowl of cherries, and all that. He reckons"—her eyelids fluttered—"that as neither him nor me have ever got within spittin distance of wedlock, we shouldn't *cast aspersions* on other people's marriages. It's not *within our purview*."

She copied his measured delivery exactly, which would normally amuse me.

"Cast aspersions." My voice was dull. "Yes, I suppose you did."

Lucy was looking down at her lap. There was a faint heat in her sallow face. Then she lifted her head.

"I beg your pardon, Ellen."

That was all she said. Gracefully, with her grandmother's natural courtesy, which in Lucy was as rare as the blue flash of a kingfisher.

"And I beg yours, Lucy." I gave her a bleak smile. "It doesn't matter what you said. Not now."

I pedaled up the drive of Upton Hall. The rain had left shining ruts, small pools: the skirts of my coat were soon spattered, because that was what happened, if one dared to cycle here. One got bumped, one slid, one became muddy. But I was resolute. Penny Lacey was not my concern. I'd telephone Margaret Dennis—she was *in loco parentis*, after all—and suggest a good dollop of pastoral care, perhaps from a kindly sixth-former. For some reason a clear picture of the imaginary sixth-former came unbidden to my mind, a girl with unruly walnut-colored hair and small, friendly blue eyes, complete with steaming kettle and buttered toast. Or was it all Penguin chocolate bars and Coca-Cola now?

No, not for Penny. She'd liked my tea and toast.

I'd see the child, that was all. Speak briefly and kindly to her, and then consign her to the care of her redoubtable headmistress. I couldn't afford to be waylaid again by those mirrored glimmerings. Those half-caught glimpses that, coming warning-less in the gloom of the evening and again in the bright morning light, had sliced open my heart.

Reaching the gravel sweep in front of Upton Hall, or "the main building" as it was known now, I dismounted and began to push my bicycle down a path which had once passed under arch after arch of pergola'd roses but which now led between two rows of tennis courts. At the bottom of the tennis courts, a gate pierced a high brick wall. I wheeled the bike through the gate and, once on the other side, leaned it against the wall.

I had realized, soon after leaving the Women's Institute market, what Penny had meant by the humps and bumps.

Today the low winter light threw the desecration into relief. The traces of the paths, the greenhouse footings, the ancient vegetable beds, were picked out sharp and clear, the hollowed-out pattern of the great kitchen garden of Upton Hall which, in the autumn of 1959, had been destroyed in a matter of days. It was Mrs. Dennis, in her first year as headmistress, who had committed this act of vandalism. William's gentle contractions and decommissionings over previous years, clos-ing an asparagus bed here, felling an ancient fig tree there, had noth-ing in common with this extirpation, this ingress of a boiler-suited ground-clearance team who in the space of a week had grubbed up fruit bushes, dismantled the remaining greenhouse—apparently because of the danger it posed—and turfed over everything else. "It was my great blunder," Mrs. Dennis said these days, and nobody disagreed. The wall at least remained, deeply shadowed on the western side but diagonally bisected by the sun along the southern boundary. In the sunlit part, preserved in lighter brick, the shape of a door long since removed. Above it, on the other side of the wall, the elms rose high. They remained too, in the face of the blight which had recently taken so many. Apparently the Reverend Acton led prayers in church for these trees, that they should be spared. Some villagers disapproved, but it seemed to me to be a good use for prayer.

A movement in the shadow. She was coming down the path under the wall toward me, hopscotching over the flagstones. A child in a school mackintosh and beret. She hadn't seen me yet.

I hailed her softly. "Penny."

She hurried toward me. "Oh, Mrs. Parr! I knew you'd come. Well, I hoped you would. Actually, I was afraid you wouldn't. But here you are!"

She was actually lifting off her heels, her clear little voice a burbling fountain.

"I hope you don't mind me writing," she rushed on. "I'm glad Miss Horne passed my letter to you. We had Battenberg cake at her house and I read her a comic. She can't read at all, can she. It must be such a pain. I must say," she burst out, "it's so nice to see you again!"

Her short hair stuck out in wisps, her teeth were joyfully white. I remembered her parting embrace, as hard as the butting of a young lamb. It would be so easy to grin back, to surrender to this delight. But I forced myself to speak levelly, to keep my smile firm and reasonable.

"It was a bit naughty of you to go to Miss Horne's house. You could have got her into trouble as well as yourself. Let's walk, shall we? I'm so cold, and I bet you are too. Now, what did you want to tell me?"

We made our way up the sunlit side of the ruin. She bobbed along by my shoulder. "What it is, it's the Exeat coming up, you see, Mrs. Parr."

"The what?"

"*Exeat. That he, she, it may go out.* It's Latin. We get two a term and they're long weekends. One in October, one in November."

Of course. They'd been returning to school when one such flood came.

"Anyway," she went on, "Mummy's in the Laurels. I never know when she's going in, or when she's coming out. Daddy says I'm not to worry, and so does Mrs. Dennis. I'm not worried because it always does her good. Anyway, Mummy's in the Laurels and Dad's in Ulster, you see."

We came to a stop. She was looking up at me, waiting, her hand shielding her eyes from the weak yellow sunlight. I searched for a way to go on.

"I'm sure that's right, Penny. There's absolutely no cause to worry." We turned round and began to walk back up toward the gate. "Can't you go away with a friend?"

"I haven't got any friends. Do you know what the girls do at the weekends? When everyone gets bored? They take turns imitating me coming into the house sitting room. They open the door really slowly, and then they put their nose round, then their eyes, then their whole head, and shoulders and so on, and by that time everyone's screaming with laughter. I know I'm a bit shy, but I do *not* come into the sitting room like that."

How shamelessly vile they were. How valiant she was, with her mackintosh belt so correctly fastened. Some girls loosened their belts, let them fall behind in nonchalant dangling. But hers was buckled neatly and tightly round her waist. They probably teased her for that too. I stepped forward so that I didn't have to look at her, and found myself on the verge of stepping into a shallow rectilinear trough, now filled with rainwater that reflected the sky. It was the floor of William's shed. I stood motionless as the brick walls rose again, along with the stacks of clay flowerpots, greened and lichened and teetering. Pain flared in my lower back, as brief as summer lightning.

"I'm so sorry about Mummy. But I can't have you, Penny." I pushed out the words with enormous difficulty, as if I were trying to speak in a dream. "I'm afraid I'm busy."

I turned to look at her. Her eyes were caught in the low sun. I watched, horrified, as they filled with tears.

"Oh," she said. "Oh, well. It was worth asking." She sniffed. "I don't suppose it'll be that bad. Mrs. Dennis looks after us. On Saturday afternoon she takes us to the cinema." She wiped her nose. "Somebody said we go for a Chinese takeaway afterward. But I don't know if that bit's true."

"I hope it is." I forced my hands into my pockets. "I expect you like Chinese food."

"Yes." She shifted her feet on the path. "Okay. Well. Thanks for coming."

Unable to bear anymore I struggled into motion, covered the short distance to the gate. "Bye, Mrs. Parr!" she called as I grasped the handlebars of my bicycle, her voice high and trembling, and spurred by this final agony I struggled through the gate and broke into a lumbering trot. The back wheel of the bicycle bounced and the pedal struck my leg hard. I went faster, left the tennis courts behind, plowed on over the gravel sweep in front of the Hall. There were no footsteps hurrying behind me.

I parked the bike by the door of William's room in the old stableyard. The sun had gone down behind the roof and a lamp shone weakly on the cobbles. I knocked, and William opened up without a word. The light in his room was deep and dim, a 60-watt bulb under a flared metal shade that cast the light wide but downward, leaving the ceiling and the upper walls in shadow.

My hand was in my pocket; it closed on the rock cake, and mindlessly I took it out and handed it to him.

"Come in, my dear. Did Deirdre make this? Good. I'm partial to them, on account of their not being too sweet. Esther gave me a doughnut last week with my tea." He pushed the kettle onto the hot plate of his little stove so that it burbled to a boil. "Sickly stuff, I couldn't stomach it."

"You liked that egg custard." I tried to master my breathing. "It had a little bit of sugar and no more."

"Exactly." He nodded gravely. "I would call myself an egg custard man. Come. You're flustered. Sit down in the armchair."

I did as he said, smoothing my hand over my calf, the coming bruise where the pedal had struck it. My fingers shook. I lifted my eyes upward, over some copper pans of his own making that Althea gave him, which used to hang in the scullery of Upton Hall. Photographs at the top, women of the last century, high-necked in black, almost invisible above the shadowline. His medals, a paraffin lamp. A wooden box in the shape of a chest, with a barrel lid and a tiny key. "Do you still have your *Art of Prowling*, William?"

"Beg pardon?"

"Your Home Guard pamphlet."

"Oh. Not anymore." He spooned tea leaves into a battered metal pot, smiling. "I gave it to the school, along with all the others. So the children can do the war. What do you want with it?"

In my mind's eye Pamela took the *Art of Prowling* from the box and dropped to the floor of William's shed. Crept out though the doorway onto the stones of the path, there to be lost in sunlight.

"God!" I cried. "Why didn't that woman bulldoze that kitchen garden to pieces! Leaving the remains there, in a sort of—half-life—it's ghastly!"

"Ah!" He turned to look at me, gravely concerned. "What took you down there? It's not a place you like to go. Do you know what the pupils call it? The humps—"

"And bumps. Yes." Hot tears brimmed behind my eyelids. "I had to go to the kitchen garden. I didn't have a choice." My voice echoed in the room, harsh and unsteady. "Penny wanted to meet me there. She asked me if she could stay with me and I said no, even though I'd promised her she could come back, after last time—"

"No, no, Ellen. Listen. There are plenty of others to help her. All paid to deal with troublesome young people. It's not your place—"

"But I was so cruel!"

Silently he poured the tea into two deep mugs and set them down, seating himself on a wooden chair. "I doubt it," he said. "Cruelty isn't in your nature."

Oh, yes it was. Look at what I had done. I'd pulled a child off me as if she were a wretched scrap of a thing, as if she disgusted me. I'd shoved her into a car and shut the door. I'd pushed her legs in and shut the door and told my husband to drive on. The mirror swung, a pale moon gleamed in the glass.

"Penny's not troublesome, anyway," I whispered. "It was lovely having her."

William leaned forward, put his good hand over mine. "You're not her shepherd, my dear."

I looked down at his hand. How beautiful it was, strong and square, the fingers lithe and unknotted by work or age. I thought of the gamut of creation he could have fashioned, the life he could have had. I gazed again at the shelves. What loss there was in the grain of all those things, their lights and gleams and shadows. It welled up in the gaps between them and also in their very fabric: the patina of the copper, the tin, the dull black of the ebony frames. I met his gaze, shook my head in wonderment.

"Oh, William . You've always been so kind. Ever since you gave me your pie. And mended my bucket. You looked after us, me and Lucy and Daniel."

He squeezed my hand and released it, sank his face in his mug.

"That was an easy job," he said after a moment.

"Not to speak of my typing lessons. I've never given you anything!

Or done anything for you! You've just stayed here, William. Looking after Lady Brock all those years. Never saying one word about that bloody ruin of a garden. How can you be so contented?"

"So I should be contented!" He gave a sudden, mighty laugh. "I've got everything I want! Thank you very much."

What was it, the reddening of the inner eye, or the lack of blinking in the old, that made their eyes blaze so? Suddenly I laughed too, unable to help myself.

"I missed my old life sorely after the Great War," he went on. "Laid up at my aunt's house, my hand in a bandage. Sir Michael saved me. He made me gardener at Upton Hall under Mr. Binfield. The work was hard, you see, and Mr. Binfield didn't care that I had only the seven fingers to help me get to grips with all the new tools. But I didn't have enough time for mourning."

I tilted my head. "Are you saying I need a job, William?"

He grinned. "I'm saying idleness doesn't suit you, and since that Barney Bowyer and his Colin took over the mill, you haven't had near enough to do. Why don't you follow my example and have a little holiday of your own? There's nothing like a change of air."

I remembered him sitting in my kitchen in the warm late summer, talking of the craters of St. Eloi while the apples stewed on the stove. How many weeks had passed since then? Six, seven? It was a different era.

I got up from the armchair, and he also rose to his feet. He was my height now that he was stooped a little. I glanced up at the high shelf. "We're beneath your ancestors."

He reached up and grasped the rim of the lampshade, tilting it so the light was thrown upward to the top of the shelf. A woman framed in black looked out, her jaw and nose and chin rendered in clean bare lines, and the shadows gentle. Her gaze, from the great height, was directed at her son. My eyes roamed freely along the lines, into the soft hollows, and it was only slowly that I became aware of his silence and mine.

"Gosh, William," I said when I'd gazed my fill. "Don't you look like your mother."

"Yes, Ellen. I take after her, for certain."

He let the lampshade go and the shadow fell, and rose and fell again, but less each time until it was still. We moved together toward the door.

"Are you going to the vicar's housewarming, Ellen? I think it would give you a filip." He touched my arm. "You don't want to be roaming around this old place."

I gazed out where the lamplight fell on the cobbles, unable to look at William for what he might see in my eyes. From a distant shadow, Nipper barked. Oh, Nipper, you naughty, naughty boy.

"I'm taking Lady Brock to the party," I said after a moment. "I didn't realize it was a housewarming. Isn't it a little late? Reverend Acton's been here a good few months."

William spoke solemnly. "A housewarming, you can hold at any point in the first year."

"I didn't know that." I found myself smiling. "I'd better go home and look for a present."

He opened the door. "You do that, my dear."

28

"LORD, ELLEN, I wish you'd sell this Land Rover. It's like traveling in a meat safe."

Althea and I were driving to the vicarage on a cold cloudy midday, blasts of chill air sweeping our feet and knees.

"The heater's broken," I told her.

"I'm aware. Do you really need this great beast? You aren't hauling tree trunks out of the mill channel anymore. You could have a nice little car. One with a heater that works."

"It's useful in floods."

"And how often do we have a flood, for heaven's sake?"

I didn't reply.

"I know what I was going to tell you," Althea went on. "Our reverend was in one of those Oflags during the war. A POW camp in Germany."

"Hmm?"

"James Acton."

"What about him?"

"You're rather *distraite* these days, Ellen, if you don't mind me saying."

Distraite. Distracted. Distraught. I let it pass.

"Tell me again."

"He was a prisoner of war in Germany, dear. Tried to escape and got caught in the woods, sent back, then he tried again—oh, I can't remember how many times."

"Gosh." My attention was caught now. "Extraordinary. Why didn't he give up?"

"You'll have to ask him," Althea said. "Now here we are, and it's party time. Do try to snap out of it, darling, and enjoy yourself."

The vicarage drawing room was a vast drafty space with a ceiling high enough for stalactites, or more likely columnar icicles, to form without inconveniencing us. Luckily, today it was filled with most of the parish of Upton and Barrow End, who were keeping warm by talking as loudly as possible and fueling themselves from the buffet, where a wide range of colorful bottles stood next to a huge hot heap of home-made sausage rolls.

"God, it's an absolute scrum," said Althea happily as she was borne away by friends to a large battered leather sofa. I caught sight of Lucy, touchingly dainty and trim in a navy two-piece, merrily raising a plas-tic cup in a toast before the crowd obscured her.

Gradually the gaiety and the chatter diverted me, and half an hour later I was being propelled pleasantly through this cheerful throng when I came face-to-face with the Reverend James Acton.

"What a nice party, Reverend." I handed him a small parcel. "I hoped these might come in handy."

He unwrapped it there and then. Laughed as he drew out a pair of oven gloves. "Thank you very much. I haven't got any. Keep burning my fingers."

Traditional porridge-colored yarn woven thick, a long strip with two slip pockets, one at each end. I swore by them. "They're the best kind. I buy them from the Women's Institute market."

What an old maid I sounded.

"You don't come to church," he said.

I shook my head. "I'm afraid it would be lip service only for me, Reverend Acton."

"Please call me James."

"James. I don't mean to offend. I'm getting to be rather a pagan these days."

He raked me over with the same bold, dark blue, rather disconcerting stare I had noticed when we met at Church Walk during the flood. "Happens to a lot of women your age."

I laughed in astonishment. "Kindly explain!"

He looked somewhat, but only somewhat, abashed. "Sorry. I meant that people can get to a point where the received wisdoms don't satisfy them anymore. And women see more of life than men, often they see too much, and so it happens more to them."

"Do you think so?"

"Oh yes. Men have this great capacity for busyness, minutiae. The behavior of machines, and so forth. They don't look up, and so they miss things."

I didn't think the reverend fell into this category. He hadn't taken his eyes from my face. If he were a pirate, it was a very civilized one, comfortably taller than me. I was glad of my new suede boots with a heel. I didn't have to crane my neck as we talked.

"What an intriguing idea." I found myself smiling. "Reverend, I'm assuming this story about Germans chasing you through the woods isn't a fantasy of Althea's?"

"They actually trod on me one time. And I felt insufficiently like a pine log."

I had a sudden image of him prone in undergrowth, wide-eyed as a lizard as the guard's boot landed between his shoulders. "What on earth made you keep trying?"

"It was my duty. Let me get you another drink."

I accepted. My first had been a punch made by the Sunday School children, consisting of blue lemonade and a waterlogged cherry. "And a sausage roll, please."

He moved away toward the buffet. Over the other side of the room a pair of spectacles glinted: Margaret Dennis was sending me a friendly lighthouse-like beam, as if, were there not fifty pink-cheeked chattering people between us, she would be moving in to buttonhole me. A glass of light dry sherry materialized in front of me, along with James Acton.

"I was also lucky." He handed me the glass, and a sausage roll in a paper napkin. "To escape with my life, I mean."

I smiled. "Like my brother." Hampered only slightly by spiced pork and delicious pastry I recounted my story of Edward's hair-raising journey from Singapore to Sumatra and thence to Ceylon. "Edward told me once that he was a wharf rat of long standing, and that I should trust him. So I did."

The French windows were being opened to admit fresh air and allow guests to drift out onto a scruffy lawn, which in weak sunlight looked inviting. Without discussing it we moved toward the glass doors and crossed the threshold into the early afternoon, strolling until we were upwind of a band of determined cigar smokers.

"So what's your creed, then, Mrs. Parr?"

"Ellen, please."

"Ellen. Does your paganism include a hereafter?"

His tone was very light. It didn't feel like an interrogation. I smiled.

"I believe in the beeches in Pipehouse Wood. I can't think of anything more sensible than to worship them. And the downland flora on Beacon Hill. I believe we go down into the earth and disintegrate." I thought for a moment. "And then—how do I put this—bits of us turn into bits of other living things. A piece of moss, or a beech leaf, or an orchid. Or a raindrop. Which is as it should be, because we only came together in the first place, via a few links in the chain, from pieces of moss and beech leaves and rain. And it never stops, all through time."

"I see." He sipped his drink. His eyes over the rim of the glass were keen, amused, serious. "Well. That's the Resurrection demolished!"

"Yes, unfortunately." I was smiling. "But not the Life."

A robust figure emerged through the French windows. Margaret

Dennis, striding toward us in tartan skirt and frilly blouse. She greeted the vicar affectionately. "Lovely party. Couldn't get near you to say hello, good-bye, or how d'you do."

He grinned. "Is that what makes for a lovely party, Margaret? Hazardous overcrowding?"

"Yes, dear. One of the things, anyway. Now, may I borrow Ellen?"

The reverend made a polite ushering gesture. "By all means. I've just spotted Mr. Kennet. I've been meaning to ask him about my fruit trees."

Margaret Dennis took my arm. "Good to see you two having a chin-wag," she said, once he was out of earshot. "Haven't met properly before, have you. *Awfully* nice man, widower, in case you were wondering. Ten years now, she got cancer, very sad."

"I wasn't wondering, actually."

"What? Oh—ha-ha-ha." The syllables of her laughter were separate, like the puffs of a steam engine. "Listen, I need a favor. It's about Penny Lacey." I fixed my eyes on the Reverend Acton, his retreating back as he joined William and Althea under the trees. Althea was braced forward on her two sticks, a pair of red flared trousers hanging from her bony hips. I thought about running to them like a hunted hind, drawing the three of them round me.

"What about her?"

"Oh dear, Mrs. Parr. Your face." Mrs. Dennis shook her head. "I'm sorry. You've done so much already. And I never even thanked you properly for the hair. You saved her housemistress a dreadful ordeal at Upper Cuts. Anyway the thing is, it's the Exeat next weekend. And Mrs. Lacey's been carted off to some sort of drying-out bin. Terrible, I know. But hardly unexpected. But what with Dad in Ireland, Penny's got nowhere to go. I've made inquiries among the girls but none of them want her, poor little baggage." She sighed. "I've cracked down on the bullying but they haven't warmed to her. She's too forthright. Too enthusiastic. I try and instill precisely those qualities, honesty and keenness, in the girls, but it doesn't work. Nowadays, you see, the prevailing tone is world-weary sarcasm and indolence. So they intimidate and mock her."

Mrs. Dennis was giving me an expectant smile. Her upper teeth, I noticed, were almost as small as the lower ones. They sat, little square bricks, one row on top of the other. There was a long pause, during which laughter rose from the drawing room. The wind changed, and a noxious tide of cigar smoke began to envelop us.

"I only came to you, Mrs. Parr, because she asked for you. Bless her. Are you all right, my dear? You look a bit wan."

I watched Althea raise one stick and prod the bole of the nearest tree with it, for all the world like an elderly insect.

"It's the cigars. I can't bear them. Actually, I think I might go. If Lady Brock's ready. I brought her with me."

I moved across the grass toward Althea, leaving Margaret Dennis standing.

"Well, you've made an impression on James Acton," Althea said as I helped her into the Land Rover.

"I'm not surprised. I told him we turn into pieces of moss." I climbed in and we set off for the Lodge. "Mother certainly has. There's moss all over her grave. It's gorgeous, like a coverlet. I'd like to think there was something of her in it."

I spoke absently, took the bend faster than I should. We both leaned sideways in our seats.

"That wasn't the sort of impression I had in mind, Ellen."

I was used to Althea's voice, with its ironic drawls and hollows, the coarse gravel of its lower reaches. But the emphases seemed even heavier than usual. I gave her a quick glance. Her eyes were trained on me, deep and knowing.

"Oh, for heaven's sake, Althea. Oh, honestly."

"Why is it so impossible that a man would find you attractive, Ellen?"

I swung round another corner. "Ha! I've put paid to that. I've just learned he's a widower. Not only did I deny the Resurrection, I did it to a man whose one solace must be the hope of meeting his wife in the hereafter—"

"We're nearly at the turn, Ellen. Slow down. Slow *down*."

At her bidding I slowed, lurched onto the drive, and came to a halt by the Lodge. I applied the hand brake, took my hands from the wheel, and heaved in several deep breaths.

"Ellen, what's the matter?"

"*Bloody* Margaret Dennis—"

The mirror swung, the light flashed, a small pale child looked heavenward. I clamped my hands over my mouth.

"Margaret? What's she done, the animal? I won't have her upsetting my friends."

Althea put a hand on my arm but it did not help me. She and I were once more in the sunroom at Upton Hall with the cactus tall against the black-rimmed window. And Selwyn was upstairs playing the piano to Sir Michael, and I was feeling that delicious wash of gold over my body as Althea told me that Selwyn was in love with me. And even at that moment she was warning me that he would try, the moment he came downstairs, try his hardest to release me, that this was about to happen . . .

"*Mariage blanc,* you told me it was going to be. Do you remember, Althea? Well, it wasn't a white marriage, it was golden. *Un mariage doré—*"

"Darling girl—"

"Lucy was right, actually. I didn't get the full bowl of cherries. What life was meant to be. She just didn't understand what it was. What I didn't have—"

"Ellen, dearest friend." Althea's eyes were such a kindly brown. Just now a little aglimmer with party booze. "Whatever Lucy might say, a marriage without children—you and I know this—is a matter for nobody, *nobody* but you and your husband. Now, much as I'm enjoying the comfort of your Land Rover, I'm going to suggest we head indoors. We can sit down over a nice cup of coffee. Just set me free from this death trap." She began to struggle with the seat-belt buckle.

"Children." I laughed. "Of course, that's what you and Lucy think."

Her hands went still. "Ellen . . ."

"You think I wanted children." I unfastened her seat belt and mine, got out of the vehicle, and went round to her side. "It's not about *children*."

She clambered down holding on to my shoulder, her grasp at once unsteady and strong. "Ellen, do come in and talk to me—"

"No, I won't, if you don't mind." I walked with her to her door, a gentle hand on her arm. "Have you got your key? Good. There we are."

"Darling girl, please stay."

The door opened, Stuart began his intemperate greeting. "I'll come on Tuesday for your shopping list. But now I must go—"

"Never mind the bloody shopping!" she burst out. "Ellen, for the love of Christ!"

I turned away toward the Land Rover.

I drove without thought or destination, found myself traveling back down the main road, into the village and out the other side, sweeping along under Beacon Hill and up again onto the high roads. Just over the brow of the hill I stopped on a verge and sat listening to nothing but the tick of the engine. In the corner of my eye lay the humped shadow of an ancient yew wood, the trunks and boughs stunted and crooked as befitted trees growing all their lives in the face of the south-westerly gales. I got out and leaned on a field gate and gazed at the thin line of the hills beyond, happy for the wind to catch me about the ears and whip away the sheep bleating, whip it away and bring it back again as the light dulled. No lambs crying here in this season and I was glad of that.

"*Hey, ho, nobody at home . . .*"

I sang softly into the wind, my voice thirty years older now, husky, hollowed out by the salt water in my throat. "*Meat nor drink nor money have I none. Yet will I be merry, merry, merry* "

There had been a dislodgment. A crack somewhere, and a falling. Lucy had said my husband's name on a hot still day in very late summer. She had spoken about another fate, and she had censured my husband. The barometer started falling at that moment: it had fallen all the way to Penny. William's weathercock had whipped round on the clock tower in Waltham and I'd traveled to Althea Brock's house through the gale, and she had brushed past me, a pale child in the wind. And it wasn't finished. Those years when I was young, they were welling up as in a flooded meadow where the grass became greener under rills of clear water. The waters had long been dammed but now they were moving unchecked across the fields, reflecting the sky. They could not be held back.

I reached the mill, went out to the hens. They were shawled in feathers and disgruntled: it was fully half an hour since sunset, and they were still waiting to be shut in. *Would you like that dog fox to decimate us? Hm?* "Honestly, I wouldn't care," I told them, and they remonstrated. *Well, really.* I bolted the door on them. Pamela used to place small scraps of cabbage or sprinkles of grains on the toes of her rubberized boots and let them come and peck. "*Dink dink dink,*" she used to say. That was when she was very small. By the time she left she was more offhand with the hens—weary of their stupidity, rolling her eyes. Running out and upturning the bucket, running in again to brush her hair for school. But it was skin-deep. She still knew them all by name. On the last day she screamed for them.

Nothing warned me, not the straightening curve of her nose, the first wobbling of her milk teeth, the smoothing-out of the creases in her wrists. *Beware. Somebody will come for her.*

I went upstairs without turning the light on. I was cold, I needed a hot bath. I ran the water, peeled my woolen tights from my legs. The kneebone and anklebone jutted now, unweathered knobs, the veins a mineral seam, something precious perhaps—cobalt, lapis. "Do you know," I would have called to Selwyn, "there's something geological about my legs." Listened for his answering laugh, a phrase along the lines of "—absolute rubbish, sweetheart," or "Ellen, you're quite—." Words and laughter muffled by steam, steam cut through by his sharp cologne. Every month or so we'd dress up, drive to Southampton, and see a play or film, eat a late supper somewhere. Catch sight of a re-flected couple in the plate glass of some large emporium long risen from the smoking rubble of the war: he very dapper, she with her hair piled elegantly, tall in a high-collared coat. A couple enjoying their lengthy prime, their troubles behind them.

The geological feature sank below a rising, steaming inlet. The end of an ice age. I turned off the hot tap.

I was floating now, I had slipped my anchors. If only Selwyn were here to take me out, to tell me what nonsense I talked. I told him he was a coward, once. He was going to walk away and I called him a coward and he turned back for me, took me on. He took Pamela into his heart.

I looked at myself naked in the wardrobe mirror, thinner than when twenty-one and my hair in the dim light no longer pale blond or cream. Nothing but white would give off that glow at dusk. My face sharper, eyes more hollowed. I appeared to be more myself, truth to be told. More than at any time since the Absaloms. At fourteen, pared to the bone, I had surely been myself.

In the dusk the effect was of a monochrome photograph.

I don't want children—

You want Pamela.

Selwyn had said that, at the beginning of the war. So unwittingly prescient and precise. William could offer counsel, consolation even, but he had no idea. Althea, Lucy, they hadn't a notion. I didn't want children, I wanted Pamela. She and I were not two separate people. We were two loaves put too close together in the oven. Our loaves kissed, fused together, and when her father tore Pamela from me he created an open rip, soft, spongy, of the inner bread, lying not across my face or belly but across the years.

I put on pajamas, a dressing gown. Went downstairs into the hall, lifted the telephone receiver, and dialed.

"Althea, could you give me Margaret Dennis's number? I need to talk to her."

"No need. She's right here." I heard a surge of Brahms, the chink of a glass. Althea and Margaret appeared to be sharing a nightcap. "Are you all right, Ellen? I'm rather concerned." Like many of her generation, her telephone voice was loud and declamatory, as if radioing from the bridge of a warship in heavy seas.

"No need to be."

"Very well. I'll hand you over to Margaret."

A fumbling, clinking murmur.

"Oh, Mrs. Parr. I can't apologize enough. Althea's given me a proper ticking off—"

"It's all right. I'll have Penny."

"Oh! Are you sure?"

"Yes."

I could only do this with the utmost terseness. Small talk and blandishments were beyond me.

"Well! That's super. She'll be thrilled to be shot of us for a while—"

"When shall I collect her?"

"Midday Friday? I'll tell you what—I'll bring her to you. Save you the trouble."

· · · · ·

I got ready for bed but could not sleep. Hours passed. Orion rose, he hung in the south with his feet in Southampton Water, his body dimmed by the city's glow. I crept out of bed and went downstairs in my dressing gown and sat a while in the study, lighting a stub of a candle to keep me company. Selwyn used to read like this until the peering and squinting got too ridiculous, but I wasn't reading. I was just staring.

Under the window was a chest full of old curtains, tablecloths, things we hardly used but never wanted to throw away. I had buried the thing I craved deep inside, allowing it to get caught up, as if I no longer cared about it, in a pile of cushion covers and napkins, and crammed down deep. I'd never moved it, drawn attention to it. Just let it lie. I went to the window and lifted the lid of the chest, delved with strong fingers between heavy strata. I remembered how far down to go. Among so many other fabrics my fingers easily lit upon the thin, slightly polished cotton.

It was the dress she wore before she changed for the journey to London. Pressed into creases thirty years old. White check on sky blue, the blue reduced to a dusty iron by the candlelight, the trim of daisies on the hem similarly grayed. I held it up and it was quite shockingly small. If it smelled of nothing, so be it. I bunched the fabric in my hands and put it to my face and breathed in.

New-baked bread, sharp, slightly salty, warm. Bread—what else? Nectar, almost. Heated cotton, nearly. All of these facets of a single thing. Her body on that hot spring day. Part of her, those atoms of her that lay between the threads of this fabric, was here and had never gone. She'd been small, and here in this room she still was. I had breathed in on that day and it was my life's breath. I'd lived off it, fed from it, ever since.

She had loomed into my life like a lightening sky, illuminating what went before as well as what came after. Selwyn, my wedding day,

the first year of the war: I moved through them as through astronom-
ical, nautical, and civil twilight to the stinking bus, the grimy white
blanket woven with holes the size of a small child's finger. The gossamer hair stuck to her forehead. The tick of her tongue against her pal
ate as she sucked on nothing. Because her thumb had fallen from her
mouth. Just fallen: it was still wet. There came a change in the room,
an increasing solidity to the walls, a dulling of the interior glow as
another greater colder light swelled outside, grew and grew in brightness until it filled the room. The birds shrieked, the light passed from
air-force blue to yellow through a split-second of blinding white, and
there she was. Pamela dawned.

29

ONE MORNING AFTER a heavy fall of snow I looked out of the kitchen window to see my child pushing a huge creaking snowball around the garden. Crumbs of packed snow clinging to the soaked wool of her gloves, and her little fingers inside surely burning with cold but she would not stop. And a green track behind the ball, winding under the apple trees, and the snow reducing to white polygons clipped smaller and more irregular with each passage. Until she couldn't roll the snowball up the bank, it rolled back each time she tried, and I took her in for some hot rose-hip syrup. But she escaped again into the garden so that I saw her through the now driving snow, pushing again at the snowball, her face red, her mouth square with effort and rage, and I let out a mother's bellow of joy and love.

I remembered the days after she left, how they tripped past one after the other. Now there was a similar skipping quality to the sunrise and sunset. Time had turned on its heel, it was running back to me, and the years were reeled in.

Skip, slip, a handful of days. Then I was standing once more at my kitchen window in expectation, at a minute to midday on Friday.

The clock drew breath and struck. Ten, eleven, twelve. Outside an engine stopped. Doors slammed. Footsteps sounded on the path. I opened the front door to admit the light.

"Why, child. Here you are!"

She stood holding her suitcase, the autumn sun shining in her hair. A glorious wicked white smile. "Yes. Here I am again! Isn't it terrific?"

The words bubbled out. I closed my eyes and felt her arms come round me. In the midst of the joy I found some words for her guardian, "Thank you, Margaret. Thank you so much," as she departed with a wave. I closed the door. My child was still speaking. "Oh, Mrs. Parr, it's lovely to see you. Look at this old chair. Is it extremely ancient? It must have been made for someone with tiny legs and a huge tall back."

She ensconced herself on the low seat, legs crossed tailor-fashion. She was so neat and small.

I laughed. "It is ancient. But it's for kneeling on and praying."

She wriggled round and kneeled upright, palms together. "Please God, let me stay here with Mrs. Parr. Thank you, God. Amen."

"You can call me Ellen, dear." I was smiling. "You wouldn't want to stay forever. You'd be bored and spreading your wings in the end. Take your suitcase upstairs. We've got work to do."

My pans clattered in the cupboard as I searched for the bread tins. Here they were, blackened and dented. What a sorry sight. I poured warm water onto yeast, made a well in my bowl of flour. When I looked up, she was there in the doorway, my heart's delight, with patches on the knees of her trousers. She looked down at them. "I did these patches in my sewing lesson."

I nodded. "I'm glad you're good with your needle and thread."

"What are you doing?"

"What am I doing, indeed." I chuckled. "Can't you see? Do you want to help?"

"I don't know what to do."

Her eyes met mine, suddenly rounded and wondering. I took her hands, so soft and warm, knuckles snuggling into my palms. I stroked my thumbs across the backs of her hands.

"I'll show you."

. . . . .

The bread rose, I knocked it back, it rose again and we baked it. We peeled apples and stewed them with lemon rind. She was full of news. She had to play a fearsome game these days, she told me, called lacrosse, with a hideous tackling stick like a torture instrument and a foul rubber ball that whacked her on the kneecap. "I vow—look, Ellen. I'm making the vow right now. With this special sign." She held up her palm, thumb outstretched, fingers quiveringly fanning out. "Oh, that's not quite it."

"What is that sign?"

"The Vulcan salute."

"I didn't realize he had a salute. Only a blacksmith's hammer."

"Vulcans don't have hammers. Oh, naughty fingers. They're meant to make a sort of V." She tried once again to prize apart her middle and ring finger but they were too soft and pliant to hold the pose. "I vow—don't laugh please, Ellen—today, in this kitchen at the mill house, that I will never ever play lacrosse again . . ."

I drank in the chirruping of her chatter. I could close my eyes and listen. Just as high as before, that clear peeled piping.

We ate fresh bread and cheese. In the afternoon we walked along the mill channel, out into the fields, and into Pipehouse Wood. How the trees had grown since we were here last. A knight's hall of handsome limber beech columns. Elderly trunks, silvery, dewlapped. Something elephantine about them, their age and their burdens. And the summits roaring in the wind. She darted ahead, away down into a deep valley, up the other side, distant in the hollows. Edward and I had walked here too, before Mother died, and he'd had that bright sea-light in his eyes, and he'd seemed so young.

She came scrambling back. "Don't let's go home yet, Ellen. We're always indoors, at school."

"Except when you're playing lacrosse."

She twisted her mouth. "I'd prefer to fight a battle than play lacrosse."

We walked the lanes. The winter day was short. In the distance Beacon Hill was lying in shadow, massive and especially still this afternoon, the sun going down behind it. The hedge thinned into single blackthorns, straggling along the edge of a field of yearling ponies who clustered whickering at the gate as we approached. She held out her hand to a round-bellied chestnut who mumbled in her palm and gazed at her with moody liquid eyes. Then he gave a deep sigh, and danced away with dainty hooves over the turf. How innocent he and his fellows were.

There was a moon in the sky, a ghostly white sliver against the dulling blue.

"I'm so lonely," she said. "No one at school thinks like me. They're a pack of sneering wolves. Instead of howling at the moon they sneer at me. And Daddy's so far away. And Mummy doesn't love me at all."

"I'm quite sure she does."

"She's bored with me and doesn't care anymore. She said so."

"Listen," I told her. "Your mother isn't well. Her words come out wrong. She loves you, but she simply can't show her love."

"I don't see what love is, then." She sniffed. "If you can't show it. I wish Daddy was here." She began to cry. "And then you told me I had to stay at school. I thought I wouldn't see you again."

I kneeled in the wet grass and folded my arms around her. "My darling. I thought it was for the best, but I was wrong. I will look after you. I promise you."

She sat by the fire while I heated a casserole for supper. On the floor with her knees up, her arms folded on top of them, her chin on her arms. Her socks were half pulled off her feet, the toes empty. As I watched she put out a hand to trace the dimples in the coal scuttle with her fingertip. "It's a bullfrog," she said. "A red-gold gaping bullfrog." The flames crackled and spat in the grate. "Look at those gleams, Ellen. Isn't he beautiful."

"Would you like peas or cabbage with your stew, darling?"

"Neither, please."

The impudence of the child. I shook my head in exasperated love.

"What about pudding? Stewed apple, or egg custard?"

"Both."

"I think you know what I'm going to say next."

A long, long silence.

"Peas, please."

"That's better. Now, do you know how to play rummy?"

"Yes."

"Let's have a game. Then supper."

We sat cross-legged in front of the fire. She was lively even when sitting. Blowing her cheeks out like a goldfish when her cards were bad, chuckling when they pleased her.

Later she had a bath and went to bed in the old dressing room. I turned on my bedside light and extinguished hers so that the darkness was not absolute. As before, I didn't want her to wake and be alarmed.

"Goodnight, sweetheart."

She was already asleep. Lying on her side with her lips parted as if blowing or making the sound "O."

When she was younger I would stroke the hair back while her eyes were still shut, and the net of hair would have left an impression on the dense fine grain of her skin. And she would breathe in through her nose, a stertorous sniff, fling out a fist, an arm, and her eyelids would part to show a sliver of white, but she was still claimed by sleep. Sometimes I had to do as Mrs. Berrow had done, when I needed to wake her: stand her on her feet and blow into her face, blow so her eyelashes were ruffled by my breath, and she fell forward, sacklike, into my arms. It almost swayed me off my feet, the desire to kneel by the bed and gather her to me and kiss her sleeping face.

≈

I woke to a shaft of light falling on the bed from a chink in the curtains. I was on one side of the light, lying there with my eyes barely open, and she was on the other, kneeling on the floor in her pajamas at the edge of the bed. She seemed far away from me in a dim colorless world, her face as grave as a stone angel, utterly precious. Was it any wonder that I had grieved? Look at what I had lost, and I *had* lost her. She had been taken from me as abruptly as if by death. Was it any wonder that I was in bliss?

She sighed, and tiny motes in the light spun and scurried.

"What is it, darling?"

"My solitaire. It's not coming out."

I propped my head on my hand and considered the columns of playing cards laid out in front of her on the counterpane. "That black six, dear. Put it on your red seven."

"Ooh!" Her fingers flew over the cards. "Look, now it's coming. Nearly there!" More fluttering of cards, and then she clapped her hands. "Ta-daa! I've done it!"

"Didn't I help you, at all?"

"You might have speeded it up," she said airily.

I burst out laughing. "You're incorrigible. Draw the curtains please."

She did what I said. The angel was banished to another world. She kneeled on the deep windowsill. "I can't see a single cloud. The spiders have been busy. The hedge is covered in webs. Look how rich we are, Ellen."

"Rich?"

"All those diamonds."

I yawned and sat up. "We'd better not try and put them in our pockets."

"I read a story about a woman who cried diamonds that turned back into tears after a year and a day." She wriggled round on the windowsill, the better to tell me. "But this lady had a heart of stone and the saddest stories had no effect on her whatsoever. In the end a young knight came and told her a hilarious joke instead, and she got completely beside herself guffawing and the diamonds came popping out of her eyes. So he put them in a bag and used them to pay a cruel king so he could marry the king's daughter and take her away." She lifted an emphatic finger. "Obviously, the cruel king didn't know what kind of diamonds they were."

"Obviously."

Her hair was haloed by the sun, and I could hardly see her face.

"And so the knight and the princess galloped off on a horse, and by the time the diamonds melted they were far, far away. Isn't that brilliant?"

"Yes, it is. It's a terrific story." I got out of bed. "Now, I thought we'd pop into Waltham and get some supplies. I didn't go before, because I didn't know what you'd like. You don't have to come, of course."

She shook her head. "Can I stay here? It's so lovely and cozy. I want to do another solitaire and finish Prince Caspian. Please can you get some Frosties and Cup-a-Soups? And a Curly Wurly?"

"Anything," I said, "as long as I don't have to eat it."

She stood in the hen run in her Wellingtons, casting grain in wide sweeps like before, as if sowing a field. I watched her, holding my shopping bag and list.

"That's the way," I said. "And they can have these peelings too."

"You know when I prayed that I could stay here?" She spoke matter-of-factly, her eyes on the hens as they stalked and grumbled. "When I was kneeling on that chair in the hall? Well, I wasn't the least bit joking. I could stay here forever. I'd feed the hens. I could do the washing, too. I'm good at washing socks and things. And isn't there another school in the village? I could go to that one instead of bloody Upton Hall. And Mummy could lie on the sofa all she wanted, and Daddy could come and visit me from Ireland."

I looked out to the east, to the smaller hills and the valley. A tractor plowed a distant field, a flock of seagulls in its wake. Somewhere a church bell rang, and the whole flock rose into the air. I felt as light as the gulls, as if my feet too were lifting off the ground.

"Ellen?" I heard her say. "Isn't that a terrific plan?"

Yes. The bell sounded through the crystal air. Yes. The gulls pealed as they settled once more on the plow. "Yes." An easy little word. I whispered it. Any louder and I might break the hope that nestled inside an eggshell so thin it was almost transparent in this strong light.

"Sweetheart," I said. "I'll go shopping and come back. Straight back. I won't stay away a minute longer than I have to. I'll see you very soon."

I kissed the top of her head and left.

The town was beautiful today in this clear light, every brick clean and shining in the low sun. The air itself was brimming with something that I tried to call joy, but joy was a pale paltry little word for this sustained bright silent force. I went into the supermarket, busied myself among the aisles, locating the desired foods. I caught sight of myself in the plate glass of a cabinet containing frozen fish. A tall, presentable person in her fifties. Perhaps rather severe. I put my hands to my bun. I'd worn my hair in the same style since I was eighteen. Selwyn had liked it, the way it tumbled down when I unclipped it. But maybe it was time for a change.

"Good morning, Ellen."

Behind me in the reflection stood the Reverend James Acton, smiling, holding a wire basket.

I whirled round. "Good morning!" I felt the blush rising. "I was just thinking about my hair . . ."

How foolish I sounded. Not that I minded my own foolishness today. It was nothing compared to what was inside me.

"You're permitted." The smile grew wider. "I was thinking only about supper. I was after some fish."

"And I'm standing in your way." I shifted smartly. "I'm getting a few things for a young girl I'm looking after." I glanced down at my own basket. "She likes things in packets."

"So do I. My son gives me frequent tellings-off."

"You have a son!"

What an imbecile I was. I could have laughed out loud.

He nodded, unperturbed. "He's studying Environmental Sciences at the University of East Anglia. He's against packets, on the whole. He's staying with me just now, so I'm going to feed him a large piece of haddock."

"Excellent."

"Perhaps you'd join me one evening next week for a glass of sherry. Tuesday, say? Parishioners permitting."

My smile could not be quashed. "That would be lovely." I rummaged in my bag for paper and pen. "I haven't got your phone number . . ."

"Ask Althea."

"Do you know, I'd rather not. Sometimes I'm glad that my friends are so attentive and caring. But not all the time!"

He gave me his telephone number and I folded the piece of paper into my purse. We paid for our goods and left the shop together, stepping out into Waltham Square. The sky was the most extraordinary blue. I'd never seen anything like it. I expected a portent of some kind, a comet so bright it could be seen in daylight. The nearest thing to a comet was the weathercock. Motionless today in the still, mild air, its tail caught a sunbeam and slung it down to me, a flare of rosy gold that closed my eyes.

I heard him say, "So who is the youngster you're looking after?"

The cobbles in the square pressed against my shoes. The plastic shopping bag pinched my fingers. I felt uncommonly solid. Surrounded by another solidity, the town of Waltham, whose every brick and stone I knew.

"Ellen? You said you had a child at home."

I opened my eyes. The cobbles of the square lay shining, the buildings high and beautiful in the bold, searching morning light.

"I love this town," I said. "It's been everything to me, you know. It saved me from despair. Gave me a job. Taught me how to be happy. Brought me my husband." I glanced up again at the flash on the Town Hall's pitched roof. "William Kennet made that weathercock. Has anyone told you?"

"I only knew that he was a gardener at Upton Hall."

"Before that he beat copper. As a very young man. But the Great War put paid to that. He lost so much. Many of us here have lost so much. I think you should know that, James. Now that you've come among us, to be our shepherd."

He nodded. "I do know it. Ellen . . ." He came a little closer. "Would you like to sit down for a moment? The bus shelter's just over there."

"Why would I want to sit down?" I laughed. "I'm not the least bit tired. Actually, I haven't felt so full of vim for a long time."

He fingered his chin, gave me his lidless, intelligent stare. "Yes," he said gently. "You do seem . . . uncommonly full of vim."

We both laughed at the old-fashioned word.

"Anyway," I said. "I need to get back."

"And I . . . I think I need to make a couple of phone calls. Take care of yourself, Ellen. I hope I'll see you on Tuesday."

I watched him hurry away, vanish into the shadow of the side street. Then I began to walk back across the square. As I did so, my happiness caused my soul to rise high in the air, level with the weathercock, its burnished plumage and its proud fierce eye. Far below a young girl trudged over the cobbles to the Infirmary, her head bowed, the burden too great. Then the girl ran across the cobbles to the Town Hall, careful not to make creases in the toes of her shoes. And she stepped off the pavement, her dress flying in the warm breeze, and bumped into a man and dropped her books, and they embraced on the stones, and they married on the steps. Two small figures in the sunshine. Two small figures, and then a child, tagging along, skipping ahead.

I drove home through the glorious crisp air. The day was as perfect as a pearl in a shell.

I knew the house was empty before I even called hello. Something about the stillness and shadow in the hall told me so. I hurried into the kitchen, put our shopping down on the table, went out of the back door to find the hens shut up securely, the last grains scattered in the mud, and her Wellingtons leaning against each other by the back step. I came back inside, strode through the empty sitting room where the husks of burned logs lay cold in the grate, and ran upstairs.

There were no clothes on the floor, no rumpled sheets. The coverlet was tucked tight on the narrow bed in the dressing room and her suitcase had disappeared.

The only sound the ticking of Selwyn's little clock.

I went back into the big bedroom. The playing cards were still on the counterpane, some scattered on the floor. A few had been pushed under the bed. I bent to pick them up and came upon a crumpled, torn scrap of paper. I scanned the typewritten words.

```
    Pamela, there's been a flood. Did it
wash you back

    my darling

    looked again it was only Penny
```

I ran downstairs and out into the lane. There was no sign of her. I turned back to the house and looked in the garage. The bicycle was nowhere to be seen.

Althea answered her telephone at the fifth ring.

"Althea, it's Ellen—"

"Dear girl. James Acton has rung. We were wondering if you're quite—"

"Never mind about all that. Pamela's gone. She's disappeared."

A second or two of silence.

"Ellen, I'm going to ring up Margaret Dennis—"

"Yes, you should do that. Get William too. I'm going out to search for her. She took the bike, you see."

30

SHEETS OF WATER stood at the bottom of the farm track, reflecting the sky. Beacon Hill rose up above me, a quiet line marred by humans, their dips and hollows mined out before the coming of Christ. Huddled in the heights with their dew ponds and defenses. The ramparts worn down now by the wind, by sheep.

The bicycle lay at the foot of the track. Flung down insolently. I half expected to see a wheel still spinning.

The track was white, the fields a light white-speckled brown. The chalk skimmed just under the turf here. It was nibbling ground, not planting, but ever since the war the farmers had plowed all up the slopes, the furrows a regular weave swerving over the shoulder of the hill and on again. Thin soil and dry, the hedges at the field boundary stunted and made sparse by the soil and the wind.

"Ellen. Ellen."

The voice came from behind me. I turned to see him halfway up the track, farther away than I had imagined. The wind must have carried his voice. He labored on, a dogged old man. Even now, coming for me. Who told him? Althea? James? It had to be James. He wouldn't have reached the hill yet, if it had been Althea.

Always, all these people. Selwyn, Aubrey, Althea, William. William, as the blur resolved into barbed wire and we fell and skidded over the road. I should have fought him off, grabbed Pamela, run, in spite of my ankle, into the field. With the bicycle. And then onward, down the hill to the sea.

"Ellen. Stop."

Here he was now, his eyes in shadow under the brim of his hat, his mouth a line. He wasn't panting, even at that pace. I turned away but he took hold of my hand, clasped it in his, a firm crablike pincer.

The anger uncoiled inside me. "Let go of me."

He did not. With my free hand I buffeted him on his chest, on the lapel of his ancient tweed jacket. My fist rounded. I shook my head, shook the hair out of my eyes. "You could have helped me push the bike through the field. Torn your shirt up, to bandage my ankle—do you remember, I twisted it?" I pummeled him again. "A true friend would have done that. Sent us on our way, God speed. But you caught us instead, and took us back, and here you are again! And I'm losing her—losing her—"

I gave him another blow, and another. A yelp came from my throat. He trapped my hitting hand in his.

"Come now, woman!" He gave me a shaking, his voice a gentle roar. "Come to your senses!"

I stood in front of him weeping. My grief was packed deep like rock salt, the tears concentrated and stinging, hard to shed. I wrenched them out all the same with high, keening sobs. When I began to sway on my feet, his hands closed firmly round my upper arms. He continued to hold me in this way, though the crying took a long time.

Finally I fell silent, and he released me. "Put up your hair now, Ellen," he said.

"What?"

"Skirling around like a banshee, and your hair all tumbling down. You're a proper disgrace."

Stunned, I wordlessly obeyed, fumbling around my neck, the back of my head. My clip was gone. That brought me near to weeping again. "I can't."

He tutted gently. "Make it neat, then."

I fashioned a rough plait and tucked it into the back of my coat collar, and walked away from him. I could not look at him.

Below me the fields stretched out beneath the hill. I searched the land for cattle, dogs, people, but there was no one. Only a barren plain that would darken as the sun went down until it was lit only by a small light in the west, and then that too would be gone. Behind me William said my name, murmured, but I hardly heard him. I wanted only to walk away, far away. Yes. Later tonight I would take the seaward road on the other side of the hill, the same road that I'd taken with Pamela. And on I would go until I outstripped this pain, this desolation, left it behind in the fields and hills of Upton.

I heard his tread, soft, on the turf. He was following me.

"Leave me alone," I said, without turning my head.

"Oh, my dear," I heard him say. "If I could have kept her, stopped her going, I would have done it, to make you happy."

I could have laughed in despair. As if my happiness counted for anything. She was the only one who mattered. If she'd gone running to her father with open arms, my heart would have broken, but I'd have lost her fairly. I'd have known that *she* was happy.

"It wasn't your job to keep her," I told William. "It was mine."

Dusk was beginning to fall in the east. I thought about the road to the sea. Perhaps I'd see a bonfire, a brazier glowing in the woods, and go to warm my hands with other travelers, tramps, or trappers, folk who were abroad in the night. It would be a relief, perhaps, to speak to people who didn't know me or what I'd lost. "I must go and get that child down," I said at last. "I need to take her back to Upton Hall. There's no need for you to stay."

"I'll wait here, all the same," William said.

"I don't need you to. I don't need you."

"Well, I need *you*."

I laughed in despair. "I can't think why."

Penny was sitting beside me at the edge of the dry sheltered bowl of a dew pond, her suitcase by her knees, looking out toward the sea. She had her back to me. She hadn't turned round when I sat down next to her on the springy scented turf. I wondered if the wind had snatched away the tramp of my feet across the ground and she didn't know I was there.

But then she said, "Go away please."

Such a high, sweet little voice.

I ran my eyes over Southampton Water, along the cranes and warehouses that crouched blotted at the waterline, hatched out in bleeding ink under a bank of heavy iron-gray clouds that were massing on the sea. Below them there was a line of yellow light.

"Where were you going with your suitcase, Penny? Ireland?"

She nodded. "I knew I had to go south. But I didn't have a map. So I came up here to look. Then I saw how awfully far away it was." She hunched her shoulders, turned her face more adamantly toward Southampton. "Why are you here, anyway, Mrs. Parr? I shan't call you Ellen anymore. Since you don't care about me."

"I do care about you, Penny."

"That's not true. You only care about this Pamela girl. Even though she broke your bird."

"Yes, I did care about her." How easily the words came when looking at the sea, at that bright stripe of water fifteen miles away. "Her mother died during the war. I looked after her for a while, and then her father came and took her away to live with her cousins. She didn't want to leave, but her father and I, we made her go."

There it was. My sad little story of wartime. Viewed as through the wrong end of a telescope, distant, gem-clear.

"I loved her, you see," I said. "And you reminded me of her. And I was a bit silly about it."

Out of the corner of my eye, I saw her squint at me.

"Hm. That wasn't very fair, was it. Making her go."

The iron clouds parted, the yellow light mounted over the refinery.

"We thought it was for the best." Somewhere high above us a long sweet song of adulation began. Penny stared upward. "A lark, Mrs. Parr. Can you hear him? Where is he?"

"He'll be a little dot in the sky somewhere." I watched her as she searched. "When I came here with Pamela, we heard a lark. We were having a picnic. I had some seedcake—it was a bit stale, but never mind. We were running away, you see. Trying to escape, so that she wouldn't have to go away with her father. So we didn't care too much about cake. It was a warm day and she dozed off." I pointed. "We were lying down there, at the bottom of this bowl."

Penny didn't see. She was looking up at the sky.

I closed my eyes. Pamela lay on the warm springy turf, in that pale-blue summer dress with the trim of white daisies round the hem, her head pillowed on her arm. The grass making little prints on her forearm as she dozed. I told her about the lark and she moved her head and looked up at the sky through her eyelashes. A lock of hair blew across her forehead. In her drowsiness she seemed once again like a small child.

"If you were running away," Penny said, "why did you stop for a picnic? You'd have been better off biking as fast as you could, till you got clean away. Instead of hanging about eating cake."

Pamela's cheeks were rosy from the sunshine. All I wanted was to hold her and kiss her again.

"Maybe you knew it was useless, really. Like me. I knew you'd find me in the end." Penny sighed. "Did she like it up here?"

"She did."

"So that was good, wasn't it?"

I opened my eyes. Penny was looking at me. A small child, narrow-shouldered, with shiny light brown hair and light brown eyes. A few glints in them but they were greenish. None of that deep pebble gray of a peat brook. Eager, she was, quick and seeking life.

"Yes, it was."

"I should think Pamela had fun with you. That's why she didn't want to go." She picked at a loose thread on her knee patch, her head down. "*I've* had fun. But I don't suppose you'll want me to come back now I've torn up your letter and run away." Her voice wobbled. "I expect you'll tell the Dennis and she'll gate me."

"The Dennis." I couldn't help chuckling. "Penny, that's awfully rude. And what on earth's gating?"

"They don't let you out."

"Penny," I said, "I will make sure that doesn't happen. And I don't care about the letter. I'd already crumpled it up, remember."

She sniffed, glanced up at the sky again. "Oh! I can see the lark." She pointed. "Look, Ellen. There he is!"

I gazed upward. His soliloquy ran on and on, but I couldn't spot him. Nevertheless, he was up there somewhere. The trick was to let the gaze wander, to wait for the vision to clear. And I was starting to see very clearly now. Yes. There he was, a small brown dot in the blue, buoyed up by his own singing.

We left the dew pond and walked down the ridge. Upton Hall lay below us, a winged building of gray stone and brick. My eye was caught by movement on the path. Two figures were approaching, one wiry, holding on to his hat brim, the other tweed-skirted with a stalwart tread.

"Mr. Kennet's coming up now, Penny. He's got Mrs. Dennis with him."

They stopped short of the brow of the hill, like strangers unsure of their welcome, come to parley. Penny clung to my hand.

"Please stick up for me, Ellen."

"Always."

I let go of her hand and strode down the hill.

"Dear Mrs. Parr," Mrs. Dennis began, as I approached. "We were a little anxious. Althea—"

"Lady Brock may not have heard me quite correctly," I said. "Her hearing's not to be relied on, especially on the telephone, as I'm sure you're aware. Now, Penny needs to see her father. I'm sure you can do something about that, Mrs. Dennis. You're very persuasive."

Mrs. Dennis nodded. "As it happens, Mrs. Parr, I've arranged for him to come and visit. He's arriving in a few days."

"I'm so glad."

"Sometimes they need a bit of a wigging, these chaps." She permitted herself a broad grin. "I know the type, you see."

I turned toward the child, waiting alone above us on the ridge, and beckoned her down the hill. "You can take her back to school in my vehicle if you wish," I told Mrs. Dennis. "William and I are used to walking all the roads around here, in Upton and Barrow End."

I handed her the Land Rover keys. Then I embraced the child. "I will always be delighted to see you, Penny Lacey."

"Can I come to tea soon?" Her eyebrows were raised in excitement at the possibility. "I could bring my David Bowie record!"

If I were the parent of a child who was so easily pleased, I reflected, I would not want to spend a day out of her company.

"I shall look forward to that," I said. "Very much indeed."

William stood by me, holding his hat in front of him like a soldier in mourning, the wind buffeting the corn stubble of his hair.

"This light," I said to him. "It reminds me of the Absaloms. That spring, when we had the broken tap."

He nodded. "The sun would be the same. A yellow old thing, low in the south."

We turned and made our way down from the summit. The narrow path was in deep shadow and I held out my arm for him so that he wouldn't stumble. When we reached the top of the track I said, "I'm going on round the hill."

"Ellen, it's getting dark."

"On this side of the hill it is. But the sun's not set. I'm going round to the southern road. There'll be light for a good while yet."

"You'll catch your death."

"I'm a grown-up woman."

"A stubborn one."

I spoke softly. "Go home, William."

I could see his grin in the lowering light, his shake of the head. "Just like Ma. She wouldn't be told, either."

The road in front of me was dull, the sun going down behind the refinery.

I remembered the time I had walked this road the other way, back from Southampton and the offices of Raymond & Rose. My mother was with me: the man with the ledger had called us Calthrop. We had left in the heat, caught the bus from Southampton to Waltham. But we had no money for the journey from Waltham to Upton, so we rested at the bus shelter in Waltham and gathered our strength for the walk home. It was so pleasant and cool in the shade of the tiled roof. I remembered looking at Mother's shoe, the toe in the sunshine, the rest of the foot in the shade, and the shoe and stocking dusty.

We didn't want to be seen dragging ourselves along the main street so we climbed the stiles over the fields to the graveyard where honeysuckle grew abundant in the hedgerow. We spent some time picking the flowers, biting off the small button at the base and sipping the nectar. Each sip a minim of sweetness, and the flesh of the trumpet tube sweet as well. Then we went on to the Absaloms and dipped our cups into the bucket and drank and drank, water streaming from the cups over our hands and down our arms as we lifted them to our lips.

No hunger or thirst of my youth was as strong as my love for my child. We'd never be apart, not completely. Even after death we'd find each other. Our atoms would be released into the earth, air, water, and they'd find each other, even if it took a hundred years. One atom of her and one of me would mingle in a sun-shot blade of grass, and so we'd embrace again. And a millennium later we'd kiss in a raindrop seeding in a cloud, and after an eon we'd be hugging tightly in the scale of a fish in the sea. It would be so forever.

Down on the coast the yellow light dwindled. My steps slowed. I wished suddenly that William was here. How lionlike he had been, calling me to my senses. How steadfast, standing by me, the light catching the side of his face, his temple and cheek. But if I felt lonely now, I only had myself to blame. I could be down at Upton Hall with him, sharing a pot of tea.

His ma was the same, was she? Stubborn, like me? I remembered her portrait, hanging high on the wall in his room. That softly shadowed, but nonetheless firm, jawline. Men, in their pride, were wont to call women stubborn, when in fact we were no such thing. When the truth was that we simply knew our own minds. I could imagine sharing a few hearty words with her on the subject. I should take William to task. But she would have done that already. I could already see him smiling as I began to chide him, saying, *Yes. My mother used to tell me that.*

I came to a halt in the road, my mouth open. My breath misting in the air.

Then I turned back toward Upton.

The following morning the air was still and mild. The kitchen garden at Upton Hall lay in low relief under the weak sunshine. A giant hand could measure it out, the fingers spanning the beds, stroking the smooth worn lineaments of the paths. William was bent over one tomb of a bed, stripping away turf. The sod lifted up cleanly over the turfing iron and the soil was rich beneath. "It's all in there, still," he said between breaths. "Generations of beautiful compost. Just needs turning."

"Surely the girls can help you," I said.

I was happy to look at the soil, to talk to him about it. I had spent a night sleepless, wide-eyed at the enormity of it, of the realization that waited, like a breath held, just beyond my grasping. For I hadn't come to it yet. I couldn't, not on my own.

William pushed his hat back and wiped his brow. "Oh, those girls are going to learn double-digging, weeding, the lot. Gardening school, you see. Potatoes, cabbage, carrot, onion. A few flowers. Mrs. Dennis likes dahlias."

"So did Sir Michael."

"That he did."

"William . . ."

"How about a cuppa?" he said, avoiding my gaze.

There was no shed. Just the trunk of a fallen beech, broad and high to sit on. And a sawn-up limb of the same tree smoking on an open fire patch, the ash white in the weak winter sunlight. And a thermos flask.

"It was the day of the thunderstorm, wasn't it," I said. "When you took me into the barn and we waited out the rain. You were standing by the barn door and I was sitting on a hay bale. Crop-haired, of course. No tresses falling around my cheeks."

He poured tea from the flask, handed me the tin mug in a pincered grip. Every minute, every second I sat beside him made me more certain.

"Am I right, William? Was it then?"

With the tip of the turfing iron he nudged a branch further into the fire. "This iron is forty-five years old. Sir Michael bought it from Skelton in Southsea. I should not be putting it in the fire."

"William, *please*—!"

"Yes!" He laughed loudly. "It was that day."

"Why didn't you ever tell me? Why did you wait for it to dawn on me?"

"You might not have wanted to see it. Not want it to be true."

I watched the small flames lick at the tree bark, pale in the sunlight. The smell of wood smoke filled me, sharp and wholesome. Mother had come here. It was not so bad, to think of her in this crisp aromatic air.

"So my mother came here and sat with you, and looked at your hand and didn't flinch," I said. "Was that when it began?"

"No. She first set eyes on me in 1915. Before I went to war." For the first time he met my eyes. "I wasn't always this rum old cove, you know, Ellen Parr. All string and bones. I was something to look at."

"You are no such rum cove. And she was something to look at too."

"So she was."

"She watched me beat out the plumage of the weathercock. Her hands over her ears—she was laughing. She'd come to my workshop, to ask me if I wanted cider jars. Your cellars were full of them, you see. Godfrey Stour had left them—Godfrey and his father and grandfather no doubt. So I came to your house with a handcart. She welcomed me in. We went to fetch the jars from the apple press. So I stood with her in there and I . . ."

"You kissed her."

"She was so beautiful with that mass of hair. So fine."

I frowned. "I don't remember that."

"She cut it off. At that early time she wore her hair in the old style. All gathered up behind, but low on the neck."

I sipped the strong tea. "I only have my memory, you see. Not a single photograph or drawing of her."

"The War came and stole away all my youth and talent, all my gusto. I thought I'd never see her again. But she found me at Upton

Hall. She sat there by my charcoal stove and took hold of my hand. I lied to you, Ellen, it wasn't the work that stopped me mourning my hand. It was love for her."

"How did it end, then, William?"

He gave a long sigh, cleared his throat.

"You were born. I came through the snow with a sheepskin for your cradle. I knew I'd done wrong when your Connie admitted me to the nursery and there they were, your mother and the Captain, and Edward, and you tucked in your mother's arm. And she'd cut her hair, all that beautiful hair had gone. I bellowed out in surprise, *What have you done to your hair? It was beautiful!* It was as good as a confession. The next night the Captain came to my aunt and uncle's house where I lived, and he knocked me clean across the parlor floor. And she wrote to me in such terms. I tell you, Ellen, it hurt me worse than the wound to my hand. I was not to address her or look at her anywhere in Upton on pain of losing my job. I learned it very hard, that lesson. That her reputation trumped my love without a second's thought. I never suspected about you, back then. She told me she took pains to prevent a baby and I believed her. I think she did indeed take such pains, but nature foiled us."

I thought about that sheepskin. It had warmed my feet at the Absaloms, shoved into the bottom drawer of the chest. At the Town Hall hostel it had remained folded in my suitcase—too warm, there, to need it. And at the mill it lay on the floor by my dressing table. Selwyn had put it there, not me. Thinking it would be a soft carpet for my bare feet.

"My God," I said aloud. "Do you think she knew?"

He thrust his chin into his collar, pursed his lips. "I've got no way of knowing."

I thought of her that day when William mended the bucket. Her eyes hollowed, wandering over the damp-patched wall and the empty range. *Oh, William Kennet,* she'd said, in a voice equally hollow and wandering. *Yes. We used to know him.* And there was nothing, not a flicker of warmth, or conscience, or memory, or anything.

"All I know . . ." I spoke slowly. "All I know is that she kept that sheepskin."

"Yes."

I sighed. "I'm sorry for hitting you, William."

"You did it right softly."

"And for railing at you. You won't have to save me again, I promise."

His mouth stretched in a grin of silent laughter. "You've been an errant daughter, that's for sure," he said at last. "Not that it matters, since I'll love you forever, whatever you do."

I was starting to know it now, securely in my heart, but it came again with the word "daughter." It came and came, this knowledge, the petals opening and opening again like a blown rose. Daughter. It broke over my head, making my hair stand on end, rinsing the world.

"All that you did. It was for our sake, all the kindness."

"In particular for your sake." He smiled. "Ellen, take this the right way. You're a better woman than she. You did not buckle."

He lifted his good hand and pushed a strand of hair back from my forehead. His fingers were rough but it was like a kiss.

We grew cold. William picked up his turfing spade and resumed his work on the bed. I helped him, piling and barrowing the loose sod away to a heap under the wall. I was to lay it grass side down, so that it would rot down and compost, and neatly too. He was an exacting master.

I roamed over my landscape of long years' shame. "I wish you'd been more forthright," I said, as I filled another barrow. "I'd have been proud to be known as your daughter."

"Would you?" He unbent, frowning. "To grow up here, in those days, born the wrong side of the blanket?"

"It would have been better than the shame of being *his*."

He shook his head. "You'd have had both, my dear, and so would your mother. And you loved him, Ellen. The Captain."

"Not after he ruined us, I didn't."

We worked on until sunset. In the deeper dusk of my memory he turned up his gas lamp with half a hand while I wrote out grammar and arithmetic with a dipping pen, my wooden stool scraping on the brick floor, a bare sixteen years after the Great War. So long ago, and so hard it had been.

"Oh, William," I said. "You and I, we've earned this happiness. But I would have liked to look after you as a daughter should. You could have lived in my house, with Selwyn and me."

"I would not have cared . . ." He spoke with genteel consideration ". . . to live under a roof with you and Mr. Parr, respect him greatly though I did."

"You could live with me now. If you wanted. Shall I call you 'Father'?"

"No. Not 'Dad,' either. Not from a lady like you."

"God forbid."

Laughter bubbled up.

"We shall stay as we are, Ellen," he said.

I found myself straightaway trapped in a rough embrace, held against a thin shoulder. A somewhat bristly chin scraped my forehead. Then I was released, to gasp and breathe out and gasp again.

Pamela

2010

31

"YOU HAVE A NEW COMMENT on your blog," Joe says. "Somebody called . . ." He screws up his eyes, he's not wearing his glasses. "Somebody called Sparks, who's ninety years old."

Not long ago I had a student called Sparks, a lovely man with rings and studs in his eyebrows, nose, lips, tongue. He had to take them all out before he started work. My glass furnace is heated to near eleven hundred degrees Celsius, and it's impossible to wear metal next to the skin. It can't be that Sparks, since he's twenty-two.

"Honey, give it here."

Joe passes me the tablet and I take a look. I don't normally do technology while breakfasting in my bathrobe. We're great bathrobe people, Joe and I, fond of coziness, massages, hot tubs, neck pillows. It's a geriatric thing. You can't do physical work in your seventies without creaking in the mornings. This blog's called *Little Ruins*: I'm posting my failed works online, all my droopy vessels, the unmentionables with lop-eared handles and rubbery lips. They're normally destined for the trash bucket but now they've got a new life, nicely lit with a title and a text saying what I learned from each disaster. The comments—especially those from other glassworkers—are often hilarious.

Not this one.

> I'm just wondering if you're the Pamela Lovell who knew Ellen Parr during the war in Upton, Hampshire UK. I'm a friend of hers. You might like to know she's 90 and still

going strong! BTW I love the emerald mug with its shark
fins. How did you do that? Penny Lacey Sparks

"What's up, Pamela?" Joe's eyes, sharper now, quiz me over the rim
of his cup.

I shut the web page. "Nothing. Why?"

"You just said, 'Oh good God.'"

I try to laugh. "It's not Sparks who's ninety. It's someone else, who
I thought was dead, but she's not."

Joe grins. "I'm very happy to hear it."

His phone beeps. He gets to his feet and leaves the room, running
a hand along my shoulders as he passes.

I've been living in the desert light for thirty-five years. There's nothing
on earth like the light of the American Southwest. It shines off the
mountains, stands tall in the streets. Blazes into our house through
half-open windows and doors left ajar. Into our heads too, I'm convinced, through the chinks of our eyes and ears. It brought me Joe
Landry, solar engineer, optimist, and gorgeous man, who came
down here in the late seventies to the desert villages, small places way
off the grid, and helped them to harvest this glut of photo-energy. He
soon convinced me that he and I, Landry and Lovell, could rub along
nicely, and so it has proved. We're two unrepentant workaholics, dis-
gustingly elderly now, it's true, outrageously undomestic, extremely
contented.

The other thing I thank the light for? The way it eclipses things.
Anything that has no place under this light, anything that isn't nailed
down in the here and now, is lost in the dazzle. If I happen to say,
"When I was twenty and living in London," all I have in my mind's eye
is a puff of smog. When someone asks me where I spent my teenage
years, I see a lifting curtain of Irish rain. Plymouth and my distant
mother only reappear—I have no idea why—in the talky trill of an

English blackbird, a sound I only get to hear very rarely, on *Master-piece Theatre* shows.

Upton. I smell Upton, equally seldom, in unburned coal.

And Ellen?

I was wrong to say I thought she'd be dead. I don't think of her as dead. But I haven't pictured her alive, either. She's just been another symbol, a sort of brightness glimpsed when I look up into the blue, a watermark printed in the air.

She hardly hurts at all now.

I get showered and dressed and drive though this elemental light to my studio. I'm having a glorious time making pitchers and tumblers in the actual hues of molten glass—Fanta orange, tangerine crush, incandescent lemon cream. Succulent citrus vessels lolling and stretching and quivering their tips, tonguelike and potent. I gather hot glass, shape it and blow, heat it, shape it, and blow. I'm going to call this group *Lingual*. Joe prefers *Cunnilingual* but I can't help his filthy mind. I was nearly forty when I started this—a woman, English, and short: the blowing iron comes up to my chin. People waited for me to fail. But I couldn't afford to. I'd been a good pupil in Ireland, eager, but the only thing I liked was art. Tone, heft, bump, shine. My husband got fed up waiting for me to abandon my dabbling, my pots and my pigments, and turn to procreation. My employers, an educational publishing house, decided they would prefer an editor whose mind was actually on the job.

Sacked, divorced, and almost middle-aged. It wasn't pretty. Poor Daddy. Never a more guilty man walked the earth. It was written in his worried weary eyes and eyebags and crow's-feet and wrinkled lids. "Can you please keep calm," I told him, when everything went wrong. "Try and imagine there's still a chance for me. That one day I might do something great. That you might be proud of me."

"Sweetheart, I will always be proud of you," he said. "It's just that if . . . Oh, everything was so difficult. We had to, you see . . ."

"No, Daddy, please don't. You can't lay my mistakes at your door. If you do, you're just turning me back into that . . ."

"That what?"

"That wretched little girl. The one you posted over the Irish Sea. I have to be more than that. It's too cruel, otherwise. Do you understand?"

He did, in the end, and he had years of pride in me, and visited a lot, especially in his old age. But I don't suppose—no, I *know*. I know that since I've been in America I haven't spoken Ellen's name.

Toward noon I go to the office, take a liter of water from the fridge. Then I turn to my blog. Penny Sparks's comment is still there. *How did you do that?* she wrote, about the mug with shark fins. All she has to do is look at the explanation under the photo and she'd find out. But people never read anything these days.

I begin to type rapidly.

> Penny, that mug with fins was accidentally made by blowing glass into a cup mold. This particular mold is made of two halves which my assistant was supposed to hold together. I failed to remind her to tighten her grip as I blew, so she allowed the pressure of the inflating glass to push the two mold halves apart. The glass expanded through the resulting gaps and made those fins.

Then I sit staring at the screen. I eat a peach. The message winks at me, unsent.

My students are arriving. One of them pokes his head round the door. "Pamela, we can't find the copper cane. Sorry."

I get up off my chair, go to the door. I pause there for a second, dart back to the computer and press Send. Then I scuttle after my student into the hot shop.

. . . . .

That night I dream about an early summer morning.

The low sun's already blazing, the sky a heated blue pearl over the fields. The trees and hedgerows gorgeously pelted in racing green. A thousand tiny birds shout, and I know instantly that I'm in England.

The dream makes a jump cut to a house, the wall of a house and some windows, black paint blistering on the frames, bricks baked by the sun. I go from window to window, peering inside. The house seems to be empty. I try the kitchen window, which is in the deep shade of a pear tree. Someone's in there, standing by a stove, a big bull of a coal range. Her hair is a golden pile of strawy coils. She jerks her head toward me.

I wake up, my heart going like a kettledrum. It's not yet dawn.

Ellen had a button on the pocket of her dress, and a thread trailed from the buttonhole. Soon it would unravel, *zag-zig, zag-z*ig, all the way round, unless she sewed it up. Sewn or unraveled, I wouldn't get to see it because I was leaving.

We were standing in the doorway of my home. The car was ready outside.

So I fixed my eyes on this last piece of her, the buttonhole and the dress, which was light gray with an ink stain on the pocket that had leached with many washings into a pale-blue tide with a bright indigo margin.

Then I clung to her. My father embraced her.

She said, "You must both let go of me."

Then I remembered the hens. But it was too late and she pushed me into the car. So our last touch was her great strong hands grabbing me. Grabbing me by the legs and pushing.

Hester came and sat on my bed. She told me why Ellen would never visit, why she wouldn't be writing anymore. She said it was because

Ellen loved me. I didn't understand that, so Hester gave me bread and milk, which I did understand. And other things you might give to a very young child—paper windmills, a knitted lamb to hold. As if they were starting again with me. Painting over the years.

Hester said, *It's nice to have a hazel girl here. My own brood, they take after their father. Gangly redheads, the lot of them.*

She said, *It's nice to have a girl the same as me.*

The light leaches into the bedroom. Stealthily, so as not to wake Joe, I reach for my phone. No reply on the blog page, but that, I soon discover, is because Penny Lacey Sparks has used the studio e-mail this time.

> Oh, that is fascinating about the mug Pamela! I'd like to buy it if it's for sale. I'd love to tell Ellen about you. But only if you want me to?

That little fishhook of a question mark. My fingers hover over the keys.

Penny, I write, *may I ask who you are?*

A pause. I close my eyes and try to doze off again.

I'm in the hall of my home, in the gray light and the sudden hush as the front door closes behind me. I run up the stairs and onto the landing where there are pictures of Mr. Parr and his cousins. A row of very young men, the uniforms making their faces even more tender, grave, expectant. Photographs taken nearly a hundred years ago now, and I glimpsed them as a child in that gray light. I didn't think I'd ever looked properly, but I must have. Only one of those men survived, and I pulled his tie and teased him, that man who'd waded through the mud. And he had a young wife, and she found me on a bus.

To think of it.

And this woman, this Penny, wants to tell Ellen about me? Tell *Ellen,* about *me?* What does she imagine she has the right to say?

· · · · ·

I surface again. The sun is beginning to glow against the bottom of the shutters, making stripes over the opposite wall. I sit up in bed and open my e-mail.

> Dear Pamela, I apologize. I've been rather rude. I'm a friend of Ellen's—I've known her since 1974. I wondered if you were the Pamela she told me about, who was also called Lovell.

Joe rolls over beside me. "What's going on?"

"Sorry," I whisper. "It's nearly getting-up time anyway."

"Getting-up time." He chuckles and rolls back again.

So . . . I try to think how to put this. So Ellen doesn't even know you've contacted me?

No, she doesn't. I didn't want to upset her.

I stare at the wall and breathe in.

As if she senses the impact, she writes again.

> Pamela,
>
> I'm so sorry. I've upset you instead, haven't I. I'm an idiot.
>
> I've known about you for a long time, that's all. And she's been talking about you lately. And I know she'd never ask you to come. Because of what happened.
>
> She says you began a new life when you were small, and that she would only hurt you more by bringing it all back again.
>
> Look, I'd better just bog off. Sorry. Penny.
>
> P.S. I really do love your glass.

The alarm emits a soft silvery ping.

"Bog off," I say to it.

· · · · ·

The sun comes up a shocking dirty bubblegum, a color that would normally excite me. But today I'm underslept, shaken. So I give the sunrise a dull stare, and gulp coffee. Joe's watching me patiently.

"I can't talk about it now," I say to him.

"Okay." He returns to his slice of Small Planet six-grain toast. He never presses me, just waits. I'm the same with him. It's easy for us. We can always simply go back to thinking about our work.

"Joe, you know I told you my mother died in the war?"

"Mm-hm?"

I wrap my hands around my mug. The gesture's strange, belonging to my childhood, to the cold of Upton.

"Sorry." My laugh is unsteady. "I really can't talk about it now."

"Okay."

The sun hauls itself higher. Now a respectable grandmotherly rose. "I love you, Joe."

"I know."

I drop Joe off at work, get to the studio. Every five minutes I think of Penny's message. I try to hold it in my head. Get the import of it. Even seeing Ellen's name, reading that she talked about me: I can't compute that. I shake my head to clear it, but the words flood back in.

I've hardly been working an hour when I burn my hand. I let a blowing iron overheat in the mouth of the furnace, and I grab it without thinking. I have a huge sign above the door saying TREAT ALL METAL AS HOT and I never, ever do anything this stupid. I run ice water over the cushions of my palm and lower fingers, put a light dressing on, and leave the studio to my assistant.

My hand is agony but I must do something useful. So I go food shopping. I push the cart down the fruit aisle and try and fail to jumble a watermelon out of a deep plastic crate with one hand. Each time I get the melon to the top of the crate, it falls back in again. People glance at me as they go by but no one does a damn thing.

I start to cry.

In the end I'm rescued by an African-American lady in a red hairnet, a woman as old as me. She lifts out the melon and puts it in my cart.

"Oh, ma'am, that's very kind."

I don't hide my tears, I don't care.

She starts singing to me. *"The tide is high but I'm holdin on,"* she sings. Then she looks me in the eye.

"Yes, my sister!" she says. "We got to hold on!" And she goes on her way.

I check out my groceries and go to the car. I sit in the parking bay, blubbering. Then I open up my phone and write a message. It's short, but I can't get any further, not right now.

Penny. Please don't bog off.

That afternoon I teach a beginner's blowing class. I let everyone have a salutary look at my burn, and we run over our first-aid techniques. By the end of the class I'm disintegrating again, but nobody notices. As my beginners leave, the studio phone rings.

"Pamela?" A young voice, chirpy. "It's Penny."

It's impossible for me to speak. But it seems she knows that.

"I'm sorry," she goes on. "This is probably too much. But I had to say hello. So you know me, a bit, anyway."

Some moments pass, and I find my voice.

"Penny, are you in Upton?"

"Yes."

I squeeze my eyes shut and lean against the wall.

"It's all right," she says. "There's no rush. You can both take your time."

· · · · ·

At the end of the day I collect Joe from his office. His mouth falls
open when he sees the bandage. I explain about the burn and he looks
at my face.

"Honey," he says, and takes the wheel.

I watch him adjusting the seat and the mirror. "It's not just the
burn," I tell him.

"Oh. Right." He backs out, joins the traffic.

"It's to do with England, and the war."

"Let me drive, sweet girl." He rubs my knee. "Let me drive, and tell
me at home."

The road unrolls in the light, shining blacktop under a dome of
blue. In the distance a violet frieze of mountains hangs in the air. I
could blow it away with one breath.

32

I'm sitting by a coal fire in the living room of a B&B in Hampshire, England, a safe five miles from Upton.

The coals are fake, glittering and glowing from ruby to cherry and back again. You aren't meant to like these fires but I adore them. I'm eating a bowl of leek and potato soup, made by my landlady, and it's delicious. I've got a rug over my knees, and the TV is tuned to a program about a couple who are deciding whether to stay in England, where it pours with rain, or relocate to a country where it doesn't. An entirely nonexistent dilemma, in my view. Would I like a homemade cheese scone and a cuppa? asks my landlady. I should think I would.

She's asked me why I'm here, and I've found that my reply, "Looking up an old friend," works very well. It's easy to say and it doesn't cause adrenaline to pour into my bloodstream. That's because it's not true, of course. Whatever Ellen was, it was not a friend.

Penny and I have had several conversations by now. Each one longer, each one building on what went before. We've pieced together a bridge, or maybe a series of stepping stones, so that I can edge out into the torrent. Agreeing to consider, tentatively suggesting, firmly committing: stone by stone. Somewhere along the way Penny asked Ellen if she would like me to visit. Ellen, apparently, kneeled down on the floor. And then refused point-blank to entertain the notion.

"I know how she feels," I remember saying on the phone.

"She'll get there," Penny told me.

I've learned a bit about Penny, as well. Found the answer to a question that bobbed benignly to the surface of my mind as we conversed: why, or rather how, a woman forty years her junior—not a neighbor, mind, and not even distantly related—came to befriend Ellen in the first place. She was rescued, too—from a flood, as it happened, and an alcoholic mother, and a pack of bullying schoolgirls, denizens of Upton Hall under its new dispensation. Penny did not fit in. So Ellen took pity on her.

Other questions will arise from this, I know. But I can't ponder them now. The main thing is, it's safe to cross the river.

The landlady brings me the scone and cuppa, and in comes a muddy terrier and suddenly the room is rank with strong tea and wet dog and rain. Ellen never had a dog but Lady Brock did. He was called Nipper. Nipper had one blue eye, he enjoyed porridge, he dug holes where he shouldn't. I was naughty too—I failed to take my shoes off and covered the sitting room carpet with mud. Elizabeth was furious, so to make up for it I picked her some pretty flaming flowers I found on the runner-bean poles in the vegetable plot. That was the only time I made Elizabeth cry. I cried louder, to outdo her and to demonstrate my essential innocence, and Ellen came into the kitchen. *What is this hullabaloo?* She saw the bean flowers on the floor, where Elizabeth had thrown them. And she bent down and held me tight and tight, and I buried my face in the crook of her arm. How old would she have been? Twenty-three, four? *She never had any other children,* Penny told me on the phone. Any *other* children. Penny actually said that. Suddenly the room's too hot. Ellen's woolen arm presses against my cheek warm and prickly and quite hard too, because she was thin as well as young. She was thin and young and mine.

"Oh dear," says the landlady. "Look at your face. Is it the dog? I shall shoo him out."

"The dog's fine," I say. "I'm just tired."

The dog's fine. I'm just falling to pieces.

Later that evening Penny rings. "I'm driving down tomorrow," she tells me. "I'll be in Upton about midday. Would you like to meet me at the churchyard? I said I'd plant some bulbs for her, you see. Might be a chance for you to . . . I don't know. Gear up to it."

I'm lying on the bed with a valerian tea. Never so wakeful in my life.

"That's a great idea," I say, with as much vigor as I can muster.

"Courage, Pamela." She chuckles. "See you tomorrow."

≈

The cab has just driven away. I'm on the verge of the lane outside the church. A bulky berry-spattering yew tree throws the gate—the *lych*-gate, was it called?—into shadow. I'm a little early, and Penny's nowhere to be seen.

I don't want to go in without her, so I walk down the lane and look up at the church tower.

We came here on the last day. No, the day before. Of course we did. A spring day it was, so warm, and I still thought Ellen was coming to Ireland too. I had no idea what she'd do there. Would she stay with me and the cousins and my aunt and uncle? Or would she have a separate house? Or maybe she and I would live together in one house, with the cousins next door, and Daddy would come and visit me. But what would Mr. Parr do? I didn't have time to work that out because church ended. And then after lunch they told me, Daddy and Ellen, that Ellen wasn't coming.

I gaze up at the tower. Six hundred years of prayer in these stones, and somewhere in the cracks and crevices, my own innocent wonderings of those last hours before the blow fell.

A small woman in jeans and a hoodie is hurrying down the lane toward me.

"Oh, Pamela." She tries to catch her breath. "I'm so sorry. I was early, you see, so I took the boys up to the cottage, and then I decided to walk down."

She's slight, a bit pixielike, with short hair and twinkly light brown eyes. I hesitate for a moment, taking in the first sight of her. "So you're Penny!" I blurt.

She laughs, and we hold our arms out to each other and embrace.

"Thank you," I say. "For everything you've done, and are doing. I know she . . ."

I can't claim to know anything about Ellen, I realize. About how she feels.

Penny releases me, smiling. "Don't worry about that now."

Feeling infinitely stronger, I hand her a bubble-wrapped package. "The shark fin mug."

"That is so kind!" She nestles the mug into a pocket of her little rucksack. "I'm honored! A work by Pam Lovell!"

"Oh, yes. It's unique." I smile. "Mistakes often are."

"Really?"

"Yes. The skill is getting things to turn out the same, time after time."

"Like happy families," she muses. "They're all meant to be the same, aren't they. But unhappy ones, they're each miserable in their own special way."

"Now there's an interesting connection!"

I take her arm and we go through the lych-gate—it *is* the lych-gate, I'm sure now—into the churchyard.

Yew, leaf mold, and damp stone. I breathe it in deep, this scented air as cold as the dawn. The low sun is disorienting: at this high latitude in winter, early morning seems to fade straight into late afternoon. Penny's kneeling down by a grave almost covered in moss, taking a trowel and a paper bag from her rucksack. "Ellen thought her mum might like some crocuses."

SUSAN CALVERT

1890–1935

A LOVING MOTHER

"This is Ellen's mother?" I'm gaping. "I had no idea."

Penny looks up. "Yes," she says after a moment. "She died when Ellen was fourteen."

"My God."

"I know. Awful."

"And she's been here all this time. Ellen never mentioned her, not once. It never crossed my mind that Ellen even *had* a mother."

Penny's digging little holes, gently pushing a bulb into each one. "It wasn't a story for a young child. Especially not you, back then . . ."

My eyes wander over the grave. It's pretty, with its moss, and the headstone is scrubbed clean. "How did she die?"

"Cancer."

"And Ellen's father? Where is he?"

She kneels upright and smiles at me. "Let Ellen tell you about it all. I think she'd want to, now." She points with her trowel. "Would you like to see Lady Brock? She and Sir Michael are just over there."

MICHAEL HUGH BROCK, Bart. DSO

1885–1939

Well Done, Thou Good and Faithful Servant

HIS DEVOTED WIFE ALTHEA MARY

1892–1979

Enter Thou into the Joy of Thy Lord

A silvery glimmer enters my mind's eye, a helmet against oak paneling. "Lady Brock had a suit of armor," I call to Penny. "I used to lift up the visor and go peep-bo. I expect he'd gone, the knight, by the time you got to Upton Hall."

"He went to the Lodge with Lady Brock." Penny laughs as she works. "We used to polish him. Me and Ellen, with Mr. Kennet. Mr. Kennet's at the end of the row."

WILLIAM ERNEST KENNET
1898–1980
And he was filled with wisdom and understanding
and cunning to work all works in brass

I can see the shed right now, the brick floor where I used to sit filling little flowerpots with compost that went into beautiful dark loamy crumbs. Our mouths watered for chocolate cake just looking at it, and there wasn't a hope of getting any. The light came in through the cloudy window and the door that was always ajar for the air, and it was never cold. There was a stove with charcoal embers that always glowed, bright in the dull weather and dim in the sunshine, a stove fed by Mr. Kennet's nimble capable pincer of a hand.

Lady Brock, the dog Nipper, Mr. Kennet. The past seeps out over the gravestones and grass and trees like water over a magic coloring book, making everything vivid.

Penny comes near, her planting done, and stands beside me.

It's says, *works in brass*," I say to her after a while. "The headstone."

"If you want the King James version, it has to be brass. It was most likely bronze, in fact."

"I still don't understand. He was a gardener."

"That was after he was wounded. Before the First World War, he was a copper beater, an apprentice, very young and talented. Ellen didn't want anyone to forget that. He made the weathercock in Waltham, you know. The one on top of the Town Hall . . ."

A fiery glint as we got off the bus, far up in the sky. Ellen pointing, saying, *Mr. Kennet made that,* and we watched the bird turn in the changing wind.

"I knew that, of course! How did I think he made it? Maybe with his fork and trowel."

We both laugh but the tears are seeding in my eyes.

Penny puts a hand on my arm. "I'll leave you for a moment. My kids have come down after all. I thought you might like to see Selwyn on your own." She indicates the grave carefully. "Fourth from the end, up by the hedge."

I never in my life called him Selwyn.

She goes off down toward the bottom of the graveyard where three stripling boys have appeared in an avenue of poplars. They canter about, whooping: she gives a soft remonstrating call and they cluster round her. Even the youngest tops her by a couple of inches. I turn away from the path and pace through the damp grass along the aisles of graves to the place she pointed out, and there he is, a neat granite slab.

SELWYN EDGAR PARR

1899–1971

And that's all. A silence underneath his name and dates: space for a spouse, as yet unfilled.

Mr. Parr had a little clock, one I wasn't allowed to play with. A folding leather travel clock that clicked shut with a clasp. Maybe that was how he died, clicking neatly closed. Such a tall dry mild bending person, swabbing at my tears with a handkerchief. Sometimes, when the boys were at their worst, the only person I could bear. I'd sit in his study and try the crossword with him. I'd go to the mill early on Saturday mornings and he'd let me swing down on the pulley, all the way from the top story to the ground. Kind, he was, always, right up to the last day. And then he put his hat on and drove me away, me and my father, and he didn't even turn his head when I screamed.

The breeze picks up, chills me. I have a hole in my tights. Ellen used to call this a potato, the way the white roundel of flesh bulged out. In Ireland when it happened, Aunt Hester told me, "You've got a spud," and I remembered Ellen and my smaller stockinged leg. And I told Hester, "It's called a potato, not a spud," and I was small and very angry still, so Hester said I was quite right.

The moon hangs white, low in the powder-blue sky, just shy of the graveyard wall. The damp air slides into the damp air of Ireland where the moon was torn across with cloud and I gazed at it, that tattered moon, imagining it riding also over England in the same dark night, over Upton, and wondering if Ellen was outside shutting up the hens. If she was looking up and seeing it too. Suddenly I'm young again and my heart is bursting. The Irish Sea, the one Ellen can't cross, lies between us, and my tears are saltier than the whole of it.

Penny's coming back. Her kids lollop ahead of her up the path toward me. They look me shyly in the eye, say "Hello, Pamela," in voices at various degrees of breaking, shake hands. I'm so glad they're here. They've pulled me back from the brink. I let them bear me along, and we all troop out of the graveyard and back up the walled lane. There are rock daisies between the stones, pink and white. I hear a creaking laugh in my inner ear.

"I forgot Lucy!" I say in sudden panic. "How could I? Where's Lucy's grave?"

"Don't worry!" Penny's laughing. "Lucy's not in the graveyard.

She's up at the cottage. We're going there for lunch. That's where you'll see Ellen, Pamela. It's all arranged."

We begin to walk up the long road from the graveyard into the village. The children have pulled ahead, skylarking, vanishing into the shadow of the trees.

The questions I have so far refused to ponder lie in front of me now, along the straight road ahead. I can't go on without raising them.

"What was it like, Penny? For you, I mean. Being with Ellen."

She walks beside me, hands in her hoodie pockets, half on and half off the narrow pavement. She has a jaunty way of walking, as if at any moment she might break into a frolic.

"Heaven." She gives a sigh. "She was so kind to me. The other girls called me Pigpen because I wouldn't brush my hair, so she cut out all the tangles and made it look nice. She listened to David Bowie with me. At least, tolerated me listening to David Bowie. And on the long weekends we used to watch *Dad's Army* on Mr. Horne's TV with Lucy and Mr. Kennet. She laid in a stock of Curly Wurlys for those TV nights."

"Of *whats*?"

"It's a sweet." She's giggling. "Bendy toffee . . . I don't know what I'd have done without her."

I picture her sitting on the floor with my knight dismembered around her. Sitting there grinning, with my Lady Brock, and my Ellen.

"Did you play with the hawk?" I can't help asking. "The one Edward made out of wood?"

"Oh. Yes. There were lots of those birds. He made all different kinds. A new one every time he visited, apparently. He had a very adventurous war, you know. He—"

"Yes. We used to push pins into a map, Ellen and me." I come to a halt. "I was there, you see. In the war."

A small flock of starlings wheels above the trees. I watch them set-tle in the upper branches.

"Of course you were." Her voice is so soft. "Pamela, I know I had everything you—that you couldn't ever—"

I brush the air with my hand, a pleading motion, and she falls silent.

When I was still a young child I used to imagine what it would be like if they'd let me visit her. We'd cling to each other but all the time the hours would be passing, and all the time we'd be thinking that I had to go. Looking at the clock: just time for a walk. Just time to have a slice of lardy cake. The tears coming even as I ate. I knew, as I saw us saying good-bye again and again, as I saw myself leave again and again for Ireland—I knew it would have killed us. And if I'd come later, as an adult? It would have been worse. What would we have done then, except sit together and stare at the ruins of all we'd lost, and hold each other's hands, and cry?

This was going to happen now. This was why I should never have come.

"You made a snowball," Penny suddenly says. "You went round and round the garden, and it got bigger and bigger. Ellen brought you in-side because you were cold, but you found your way outside again and carried on rolling, and she saw you out of the window, crying because you couldn't get it up the bank. It had got too big for you to push, it kept rolling back . . ."

"What made you think of that?"

She looks bewildered. "I don't know."

"I can't remember any snowball."

Slowly I pick up my feet. I know I have no choice. A few moments longer, step by step, and here we are, rounding the corner at last, well into the shadow of the trees now, and this turn in the road has an angle that mimics exactly the curve of some internal chamber of my heart, because I know it so well. Ellen and I went back and forth, back and forth like a shuttle through a loom, in and out from the mill to the village and back again, and here I come now, on the last pass, and this time there's no stopping.

"Oh, my goodness." I clutch Penny's arm. "What on earth have they done?"

"I know."

The main street of Upton is clogged with sleek cars. Skirts of creamy gravel lap the spotless tarmac. Every window gleams, every stone is repointed. Cleansed also of people, it seems—there's no one on the road, in the front gardens, at the windows. Penny pats my hand, gently persuading me to loosen my grip. "The houses go for a fortune. Lucy and Ellen are about the only originals left . . ."

"This is where they picked up the milk churns." I point as we pass a low wall. "There was a big wooden platform. The milk lorry stopped and loaded them up." I glimpse a gleaming cottage called *the old bakery,* literally, in lowercase wrought iron. "Do you remember a bakery, Penny?"

"No, just the village shop."

"There was a butcher as well. And a saddler . . ."

My heart is too full for more talking. And although I can't see it I can smell it, somehow, the street of my childhood, dark and dirty with long ruts of mud from tractors, dung from droves of cattle that ambled by, udders jostling their back legs. The smell of that long-past street keener now as the grassy bank on the left starts to rise, and we approach Lucy's house. The boys are already bounding up the steps. Which are scrubbed russet red, I see, and equipped with an iron rail on each side, to help aged knees.

I hold on tight too. I have to, because as I climb I have the sensation that I'm falling forward.

We reach the top, and the back door opens and Lucy comes out.

"Hello, Penny. Hello, Danny, William, Josh. Oh, and here's young Pam." As if I'm just another child. "Hello, Pam."

She's smaller than me. Hair a matte dark brown with half an inch of white at the roots. Beaming with a magnificent set of dentures. Cozy in a bottle-green body-warmer with half the quilting unpicked, a pair of what look like ancient black ski pants, a yellow scarf high underneath her chin.

"Look at you, all flabbergasted that I'm still here!" She searches my face beadily, wags a finger. "Oh no. You can't kill *me* off that easily!" A brisk, stiff little embrace, her head coming up to my chin and bringing a sweet breath of lavender, and then she takes my free hand in hers.

"You're looking well, dear." She laughs in her creaking way. "I've heard all about you. You make vases and suchlike. Well, I never."

I look around. "The apple tree's gone!" I blurt.

"Yes, and those are getting on too." She jerks her head toward a pair of trees by the hedge. "Bill Kennet gave us those. Do you remember Bill, little girl that you were?"

I nod my head. Suddenly I think of Maurice, the stubborn refuser of proffered juicy stems, warm in his nest of dry grass. I was trying to feed him when a man called Aubrey came, and I said *Yes, but who is that?* A vision comes, so bright I have to shut my eyes. The tortoise, the grass, the sunshine. A father in shadow. I press my hand against my lips, to stop them trembling.

"There, there," I hear Lucy say.

"Be okay in a minute."

"I know you will."

I recover myself, open my eyes. "You're looking well too, Lucy!"

"Yup." She nods without conceit. "I've had me inhalers for years now. Never bin better. Aging better than herself, anyhow. Go on in, dear, you know the way. She's waitin."

I enter the house. I go into the small parlor, step up into the kitchen, and there, sitting at the table, is an old lady.

I can't get her properly into my sight. Not the whole of her. My eyes keep scuttling about. The collar of her blouse, cream with a dark blue print. A staring blue-veined collarbone. One blue eye and one slightly milky. Short, white hair, cloudy to go with the eye. Her hands spread out on the kitchen table. Her fingertips, broad and calloused.

I sit down, because standing is beyond me. It's as much as I can do to keep breathing.

After a moment she reaches across and takes my hand. Her fingers cling to mine.

Then her other hand reaches out for my other hand. Hers are veined and spotted, the knuckles large. Now we are fully held. Her fingers as warm and strong as they used to be. Mine, adult now, still smaller than hers. She still encloses me.

She says, "So here you are, child."

There is a pulse in her voice, as if a giant hand is gently shaking her. Her eyes look heavenward.

The house is so quiet.

"Where has everyone gone?" she says.

"I have no idea."

I glimpse her good eye, blazing blue. Any more than that, the tears will come and blind me.

"Potatoes," she says.

"What?"

"We should be peeling potatoes."

"I don't want to let go of your hands."

She laughs a little. "Sweetheart. Let's do the potatoes. We can hold hands again afterward."

The potatoes are earthy, in a straw basket in the larder. The memory hits me in the nose, because the smell of Lucy's larder is exactly the same, of cold good food. Peas sit in there, and custard, and a butter dish, along with empty milk bottles, and tins of prunes.

"How many shall I bring?"

"The lot. There are three boys."

"Those boys," I say. "How hungry they were."

"You were all hungry."

I wouldn't mind the hunger, if I could have been back here, staying with her forever. I scrub the potatoes at the sink, feeling her eyes on me.

"I'm just looking at you," she says. "Thinking how strong you must be. Penny showed me a video. It looks so graceful."

It's a relief to dwell for a moment on work. "They used to liken it to a dance. Glassblowing."

I put the wet potatoes on the chopping board. She takes one, pares it expertly with a knife. I start work with the peeler. A quiet falls over us. I let my gaze wander round the walls, linger for a moment on the only picture in the room, one I don't remember, showing a young man in army uniform with flattened light hair and small trustable eyes. Then I see the railway clock.

"Ellen! You've given Lucy our clock!"

"I live here, with Lucy now." She laughs at my astonishment. "I moved out of the mill house a long time ago."

I listen to its steady, rocking tick, so familiar that I only now hear it. "So we won't be going to the house?"

She shakes her head. "Well. We can. But it's an artisan mill now, grinding organic flour. The mill house is a tearoom, with a museum of old tools upstairs. Full of pictures of Selwyn in his overalls, and our lorry, and all the ancient Victorian Parrs." She sighs. "I got rid of the house about three years after Selwyn died. I went to Singapore with William Kennet. We visited Edward, and when I came back I sold up."

"Penny and I were talking about Edward's birds."

"The first one was the most treasured. You broke some of the wing feathers. I only found out a long time later."

"Well, I'm ever so sorry. I was probably five years old."

She chuckles.

We finish the potatoes, set them to boil. I put the peelings in a dish for the hens. I look out of the window at the patch of garden, the hills beyond. It was here, in Lucy's cottage on its high bank, that I learned how hills become bluer as they recede.

"You said there'd be hens in Ireland."

There it is. Said. There was no thought that preceded these words. It was just the blue hills, and then the hens.

"Did I? When?"

"The day I left. I wanted to feed the hens one last time but you said there'd be hens enough in Ireland." I turn round to face her. "Those were your exact words before you pushed me into the car."

She swings her head as if from a lash.

"And then there weren't any hens. Aunt Hester didn't have any."

In the silence her fingers poke, push my back, I hear my own screams. It is a hot day and I cannot stop.

I'm dumbstruck now, the tears dripping from my chin.

I stand for a while longer at the window. The lid rattles on the pan. I turn down the electric. She sits, also without moving, staring ahead of her. Her shoulders are all caved in, as if there's nothing in the middle.

I think of all the times she hugged me in bed, that hard hot fusion, those whispered endearments in the half-light. When I added my pounds, shillings, and pence correctly she would kneel on the floor to embrace me and say, *My clever little creature.* But that family of mine? It was jumping aboard a milk wagon, easy to do but nothing there to speak of. My cousins just tramped up the stairs saying "G'night, Ma," and that was it. I thought I'd die, sometimes, from lack of kissing.

"You know," I say to her, "I tried to tell myself, at least I've felt love. At least I had it once. But sometimes I wished I'd never known you."

She nods her head, somber. Looks at her hands. When she speaks, her voice is rich with grief.

"You were so heavy to pick up." She shakes her head at the memory.

"Of course you were heavy. You were precious. I remember I dropped the blanket. That was the day you came, the day of the bus. Oh yes. I know exactly what you're talking about, Pamela. There have been times since when I wished I'd never found you."

I sit down again. A pair of oven gloves is lying on the table, two pockets, one at each end of a long strip. I slide my hand into one of the pockets, feel the coarse stuff, woven wool maybe, in a tight crisscross knotting that has gone brown like burned porridge, only fit for toting blackened pans and trays and bread tins.

"I had no idea I was going to say that." My fingertips seek out the holes in the glove, the sparse thready patches inside. "It isn't why I came. I must have been possessed . . ."

"It's nothing." Her voice is blank, exhausted. "Not compared to what I did to you."

Now we're in the wilderness. For the first time I can look properly at her face as she stares at the window. *A kind wolf,* I used to think sometimes. A white defending wolf, strict with boys who put my shoes out in the rain and dribbled tea all over my schoolwork, a picture showing the proper way to eat a herring. Fiercely loving.

I take my hand out of the warm, threadbare little pocket and fold the oven gloves together. "I wrapped these up for you. All I could find was newspaper, old yellow newspaper from before the war. I got some twine and Mr. Parr put his finger on the knot."

Her lips tweak. "Those mitts are long gone, I'm afraid."

"Of course. How silly of me." I'm incredibly cast down by this. "They'd be, what, over sixty years old."

"These are the same lineage, darling. Their descendants."

I laugh unsteadily, even as my eyes fill.

"I remember yours." She starts to smile. "You saved up your pocket money and bought them at the Women's Institute. It was a lovely present. Pamela, Pamela. You must know. You were my joy, my treasure, my heart's life."

Her hands are spread on the table and I see again her old knuckles, her spread fingertips. *My joy, my treasure, my heart's life.* I cannot absorb these words. I leave them far away, shining, a fleet of freighted ships standing off in the sea roads, waiting to come in.

"Would you like to feed them now?"

"What?"

"The hens."

I shake my head and the tears fall again.

"Well. Maybe later. Sit, then. Talk to me. Tell me about your father."

I wipe my face. "I saw your mother in the churchyard. I'd rather hear about *you*."

"That's for later." Ellen straightens up, and the caved-in look is gone. She is wise again, strong, her smiling eyes roving over a rich past, acquainted with the world. "Tell me about Aubrey. His life."

The hens make short work of the grain and the peelings. They dot their beaks on the toes of my shoes, a sensation printed into my body when I was five years old. I've told Ellen about my father, how he married late in life, and happily. She remembers every detail of their meeting. "We got out Selwyn's best Venetian glasses. Your father showed us photographs of your mother, and then of your aunt Hester. And the dog called Winnie, a Labrador."

"It must have been a dreadful day."

"Not as bad as the ones that followed."

She's keeping a firm grip on the doorpost of the hen run. She's stooped now, and places her feet very carefully when she walks.

"I'm ashamed to say we put a smock on Winnie and dragged her round in a trolley that used to contain wooden bricks."

She smiles. "I'm glad that you were happy sometimes."

Maybe I was. Maybe happiness is no more than that, a smocked, long-suffering dog on a wheeled cart. It begins to prick with rain from a small cloudmass above, surprising us, since there's enough clear sky for hazy sun. "Oh, the sheets," says Ellen, and I go to pull them down into my arms. Lucy still grows black currants, I see; a little row of three bushes. I ate a black currant once, raw, and Lucy patted my head as I cried from the sourness, which, although I had been warned and warned again, I had to taste to understand. She was taking down the sheets herself at the time, and the whiteness and sourness together were blinding.

"My darling," Ellen's saying. "If I could have done anything. Anything."

My eyes close in the imagined brightness.

I bundle the sheets in my arms and we walk toward the house. "You were so young, Ellen. Only, what, twenty?"

"I was grown up. I'd been grown up for years." Her voice is mild. "Do you know, I felt younger the second time I married. Almost skittish—"

"You married *again*?"

"Yes. The vicar, would you believe." She's smiling broadly. "James Acton. He's dead now, of course. Lucy and I have outlived everyone. But James and I had twenty years together. It was absolutely super. In some ways I was rather . . . uneducated. He saw to that. Pamela, your jaw is hanging in a most unattractive way."

I laugh as the blush rises.

"You have to seize love," she says. "I did that with you. I seized you. I loved you so much, and I never stopped. So it's all piled up, I'm afraid."

Her hand lies heavy on my shoulder. The light rain continues to fall.

"I can't take it all at once," I find myself saying. "It's too much. It'll kill me."

"I was like that when I was hungry." She smiles. "I knew I needed the food but I couldn't fit it in. I had to take it away in a paper bag."

"Maybe I can do that," I say. "Put your love into a paper bag."

She holds out her arms. Along with the sheets, I am folded into her embrace. Her arms bind me fast around my shoulders. My head used to rest against her belly, just beneath her bust. Now I fit neatly under her chin, my cheek against the collar of her blouse, squashed against a brooch pinned to her lapel.

"You pair! The spuds are boiling themselves dry. We could see the steam out the kitchen window . . ."

Lucy's making her way toward us from the steps. "Oh, thank you, Pam dear. Hang those sheets in the lavvy, we'll pop 'em out again later . . . Ho, ho, you was thinking about that heart toilet, wasn't you. I can see by your face. There it used to be, and good riddance. What do you think of Upton now we're all spick and span? In't it lovely. All that cow muck and nuisance gone, and everyone so clean and respectable. I don't mind saying it now. Them Suttons and Rails, sometimes their kitchen floors weren't much better than a stall . . ."

Penny and her children fill the kitchen. Ellen, resolutely unaided, removes a heavy cast-iron casserole dish from the oven. A smell of great riches seeps from under the lid. "Where did you all go?" she asks Penny as she unbends.

"Down to see Mrs. Corey in the Absaloms. "

The Absaloms. The name comes first, and then four damp walls that were open to the sky. "Aren't they all tumbled down?"

Lucy laughs. "It's a care home now. Tickles Ellen. How after all this, she'll end up back in the Absaloms. So will I, too."

Penny puts a hand on Lucy's arm. "You don't know that."

Lucy shrugs. "*I* don't mind. It's comfy enough."

We serve the boys first. They eat their main course at the little table and then stand up to wash and dry their plates. We take them and lay the table again. The adults sit. I lift my fork to my mouth eagerly. Crying brings appetite, I find. It's a lamb stew from heaven, scraggy, knotty, and reeking with flavor. Bright lumps of root veg: carrot and rutabaga and sweet melting onion. And then a pie, one with black edges and an egg cup to keep the pastry up. Inside it, chunks of Bramley apple that I can't taste at first because my mouth is full of steam, and then taste the sharpness that stays through sugar.

"Now that's a real apple pie, if I say so myself," says Ellen.

"Made with proper tart cookers." Lucy guffaws. "Look at them kids pushing it round their plates."

The children are eating their pudding standing up, leaning against the kitchen cupboards.

"It's a bit sour," ventures the middle boy, William.

"They don't know they're born, these kids."

Penny laughs. "Lucy, you spoke the truth."

"Pass him the custard," I say. "There's no need to suffer."

In the quiet, the freighted ships put into port. Flags snap in the bright breeze. Gulls peal silently overhead. *My joy, my treasure, my heart's life.* The sea sparkles with a million tiny lights. We eat without talking. The only sound is our spoons tinkling on our plates.

Acknowledgments

I would like to thank:

My agents. In the U.S., heartfelt thanks to Deborah Schneider. In the U.K., Jo Unwin, who uttered those thrilling words, "Send me more!" and whose hard work and wise counsel led to so many good things.

My editors Helen Garnons Williams of 4th Estate and Tara Singh Carlson of G. P. Putnam's Sons. Perceptive, ingenious, patient guides on this exhilarating journey.

Sarah-Jane Forder, for copyediting. You and I know what you did. Thank you.

My friends Alison Clink, Nikki Lloyd, Crysse Morrison, and Rosie Jackson. Talented writers all, sensitive critics, and generous companions in craft.

Robert, my husband. Attentive reader, tolerant of deadlines, caring parent. Love and gratitude.

Juliet my daughter, four years old when I began this book, nine when I finished it. Beloved.

Juliet's godmother, Kate Teale, for our forty years of friendship. An inspiration to me as a woman and as an artist.

My grandparents Betty and Brendan O'Hagan, and Bill and Joan Liardet. For being brave.